TRAPPER'S BLOOD

Locked together, Nate and the half-breed exerted their sinews to the utmost. Nate blocked a knee to the groin and countered with a head butt to the jaw, which rocked Santiago backward. But instead of weakening, Santiago roared like a berserk grizzly, opened his mouth wide, and swooped his gleaming teeth at Nate's throat.

In the nick of time Nate jerked his head to one side. The breed's short teeth sheared into the fleshy part of his shoulder instead of the soft tissue of his neck. Excruciating anguish rippled down his body. Blood splattered his skin. Nate threw himself backward to break Santiago's grip and nearly cried out when his shoulder was torn open.

Santiago reared up, a patch of buckskin and a flap of skin hanging from his bloody lips. He spat them out, bent back his head, and howled like a demented coyote.

Nate drove his forehead into the breed's gut. It was like slamming into a wall. His blow had no effect on Santiago, but it did make Nate's senses spin.

Venting a howl of savage glee, Santiago stabbed downward. . . .

DEATH GRIP

Suddenly Nate had a 50-pound bundle of raw ferocity in his arms. He flung his free hand in front of his face and nearly cried out when the wolverine's iron jaws clamped down. Tottering under an onslaught of claws and teeth, he tripped over his own feet and wound up on his back.

Nate had to drop the tomahawk so he could grab hold of the animal's throat as it hurled itself at his face. Muscles straining, he held the _____ while he deflected its rapie_____ ogether, they rolled to the ri____

The _____ tcher knife, but to reach it _____ king a gamble, he swooped _____ osed on the beaded sheath— _____ of combat it had fallen out.

Before Nate could lift his arm again, the wolverine gave a terrific wrench of its whole body and broke free of his grasp. Its mouth opened wide and swept to his exposed throat. He felt its teeth on his skin.

He was going to die!

Other *Wilderness* Double Editions:

WILDERNESS

BLACK POWDER/
TRAIL'S END

DAVID THOMPSON

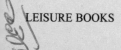LEISURE BOOKS NEW YORK CITY

45155

To Judy, Joshua, and Shane.

A LEISURE BOOK®

September 2000

Published by

Dorchester Publishing Co., Inc.
276 Fifth Avenue
New York, NY 10001

ISBN 0-8439-4775-6

The name "Leisure Books" and the stylized "L" with design are trademarks of Dorchester Publishing Co., Inc.

Printed in the United States of America.

BLACK POWDER.

Chapter One

Simon Ward smiled as he set eyes on the dark green foothills of the majestic Rocky Mountains for the very first time in his life. "At last!" he exclaimed, rising in the stirrups to survey the broad sweep of stark peaks to the west. "At long, long last."

The petite young woman beside him smiled too, but her smile was not as wide, not as heartfelt. She hid that fact from her husband of only eighteen months by declaring, "They are beautiful, aren't they?"

"They're everything I told you they would be," Simon boasted. His saddle creaked as he sat back down and turned to put a hand on her slender shoulder. "Now do you see why I wanted us to come? Take a good look, Felicity. Anything we want is ours for the taking."

Felicity Ward placed her own hand on his. "I wouldn't go that far, dearest," she chided. "Other set-

5

tlers live in the mountains. And there are always the Indians." As she said that last word, she gazed rather fearfully off across the great expanse of prairie they had spent many weeks crossing.

"Sure there are settlers," Simon said, not noticing her timid glance in all his excitement, "but they're few and far between. As for the Indians—" He dismissed them with a gesture. "We didn't see hide nor hair of one red devil the whole trip, did we? If you ask me, all those awful stories we heard were tall tales meant to frighten children."

Felicity patted his hand. "I suppose." But what she really wanted to say was that the thought of running into Indians scared her half witless. She had spent their whole journey in a constant state of dread. Her nerves, which had never been very strong, were about worn to a frazzle.

Truth to tell, Felicity would much rather have been back in Boston than in the middle of the godforsaken wilderness. She'd never realized how good she'd had it until after her husband talked her into their bold venture.

Simon lifted his reins and clucked to his bay. "Come on, my love. Let's go find us a nice cool spot under some trees to take our midday rest." He tugged on the lead rope to their two pack animals and headed out.

Trying not to be obvious about it, Simon looked over a shoulder. For most of the morning he had been bothered by an uneasy feeling that they were being watched. Yet not once had he glimpsed anyone lurking on their back trail. He figured that he was simply being childish, letting his imagination get the better of him.

With a shrug, Simon cast the troublesome notion aside. He was not going to let anything spoil his good mood. His dream was coming true and he wanted to savor every moment.

The seed had been planted in his mind over a year ago. He had stopped at his favorite tavern on the way home from his job on the docks of Boston Harbor. He had planned to down a single cold ale and then head on home to his beloved.

But there had been a newcomer at the tavern, a cousin of the owner. And lo and behold, the man had been a genuine mountain man. He had sat there in his buckskin shirt and leggings and beaver hat, and he'd regaled them for hours with stories of his wild and woolly escapades in the Rockies.

It had fired up Simon's soul as nothing else in his life ever had. Except for Felicity, of course. He had taken to spending every spare moment daydreaming about the wonderful life they could build for themselves. Acres and acres of land, a fine cabin and whatever else they wanted were theirs for the taking.

By asking around, Simon had learned more about the vast frontier which stretched between the Mississippi River and the Pacific Ocean. He'd heard that a few hardy pioneers were already there. For the most part, though, the only whites within hundreds of miles were trappers, or mountain men, as the folks back in the States liked to call them.

It was wide open country, where a man could dig in roots, grow, and prosper. Where a family could be raised as a man saw fit. Where a man was accountable to no one other than himself and his Maker. It was where he yearned to live.

Simon had figured his wife would balk when he mentioned his brainstorm. She had been taken aback, but she had agreed after only a few talks. And so the chain of events had been set in motion.

As they made their way toward the slopes of the

low foothills, Simon again had that eerie feeling of being spied on. He shifted and scoured the rippling sea of high grass. Far to the northeast a small herd of shaggy buffalo grazed. To the southeast antelope were bounding off in long, graceful leaps. It was the same sort of tranquil scene he had seen many times. He did wonder why the antelope were fleeing, and then decided they had probably been spooked by a snake or some such.

"Is something wrong, Simon?"

Simon snapped around and plastered a grin on his face. "Heck, no. What makes you say that? I was just watching those antelope. They must be about the fastest creatures on four legs."

"Too bad that you couldn't get a shot at one. People say they make good eating."

It annoyed Simon to be reminded of his sole failure. He looked down at the trusty new Hawken, which rested across his thighs. Before leaving St. Louis, he had purchased it at the shop of two brothers by the same name, and he'd also bought a pair of flintlock pistols and a big butcher knife. When he'd strolled out of that place, he'd felt practically invincible.

On the long trek west, Simon had honed his skills with all three guns. At one time or another their supper pot had seen buffalo meat, black bear, deer, fox, prairie dog, grouse, quail, and once, elk. But he had never been able to sneak close enough to antelope to bring one down.

"I'll get one of them yet, you wait and see," Simon vowed. "And when I do, you can make a rug of its hide."

Felicity averted her face and scrunched up her nose. The idea of peeling off the skin of a bleeding animal with her own two hands, and then going to all the hard work of curing it, about made her ill. She would not let on, however. She knew that Simon was counting on her to do her fair share of the work. He had even bought a butcher knife just for her, which she kept rolled up in her bedroll.

A red hawk took wing above them and soared high into the crystal blue sky with a strident shriek.

"Look at that," Simon marveled. "These mountains are so full of game, all a man has to do is walk out his door and take his pick."

"There must be a lot of mountain lions and grizzly bears up there."

"A few," Simon admitted. "But none that we can't handle." He tried to sound more confident than he felt, for he had been told that grizzlies were to be avoided at all costs. They were described as ravenous monsters, bigger even than horses and as mean as sin, able to tear a man in half with a flick of a massive paw. The last thing he wanted was to tangle with one.

Simon bore to the right to skirt the base of the first hill, his eyes on the slope for a likely spot to rest. Suddenly the bay pricked its ears and snorted. Fearing a grizzly, Simon raised the Hawken and pressed his thumb to the hammer. Then he heard the unmistakable light tinkle of running water.

"A stream!" Simon exclaimed. He slapped his legs and urged the pack horses on. In under twenty yards he came upon the bank of a narrow ribbon of rushing water which had been hidden by the tall grass. It wound out from between a pair of hills and made off across the plain.

"Will you look at this!" Simon said. "We must have been close enough to hit it with a rock for the past ten miles, and we didn't even know it was there."

"Let's follow it. Maybe we'll find a pool." Felicity

took the lead. "It's been ages since I had a bath."

The mental picture of his wife stark naked brought a lump of raw passion to Simon's throat. While it was improper to admit as much, he lusted after her with an inhuman hunger. The minister of their church back in Massachusetts would never approve. But Simon couldn't help himself. From the moment their lips first touched, he had loved Felicity Morganstern more than life itself.

They climbed as the stream did and presently came to a wide bench lined by spruce trees to the west, boulders to the north, and a small but deep pool to the south.

Felicity squealed in delight and trotted to the water's edge. Sliding down, she cupped the cold water and took a thirsty sip. "Oh, Simon. It's simply delicious. Come and drink."

Dismounting, Simon had the presence of mind to walk to the nearest trees and loop his reins and the lead rope to a limb. All the way west, he had made it a point to always picket their horses when they stopped, no matter how briefly. He had been warned by men who knew that the loss of their animals could cost them their lives.

The pool had to be five feet deep, yet it was as clear as glass. For that matter, the air itself was invigorating. It had a crispness about it that Simon had not noticed before. He stooped down and drank his fill. Sitting back, he wiped his mouth with the back of his hand and glanced at his wife, who was grinning at him. "What?"

"You just look so darned adorable sometimes."

Simon didn't see how he could. His hair was a matted mess and hung down to his shoulders. His chin had sprouted stubble which might grow into a real beard in five or six weeks. He'd not bathed regularly in more days than he cared to count. And his wool shirt and pants were about worn at the seams. He needed a bath every bit as much as she did.

No, that was not quite true, Simon mused. Somehow, Felicity always managed to look as fresh as a daisy. She always smelled like one, too. Even when they had been in the saddle from dawn to dusk, riding under a blistering sun and beset by dust and insects, by some miracle she had been able to make herself presentable in no time at all once they made camp. It was a unique knack women had, he figured, one of those mysteries of the opposite sex that men were never privileged to know.

At the moment his wonderful wife was staring at the pool as if she had stumbled on a gold mine. "Do you really think it's all right for me to take a bath?"

"Why not? There isn't another living soul within two hundred miles of us. And the stream will flush the pool clean in no time." Simon rose. "Let me fill the water skins and the coffeepot and you can have at it."

Felicity clasped her hands together like a little girl given the present of her heart's desire. "Oh, my! To be clean again! To be able to comb my hair without wrestling it to death."

Chuckling, Simon took her horse over to the others. He stripped off their saddles and the packs and arranged them close to the pool so he could watch her bathe.

Just about then the bay lifted its head again, stared toward the rim of the bench, and nickered.

Simon paused in the act of dipping the cooking pot into the pool. He had learned to trust the bay's instincts, so he knew there had to be something out there, maybe the same thing that had been shadowing them the better part of the day. An animal, more than likely, he told himself. Several times on their long trip they had been followed by curious coyotes and wolves.

Still, Simon wanted to be sure. "The pool is yours," he announced. "I'll be right back." Grabbing the Hawken, he cradled it in his left arm and headed for the rim.

"Are you sure everything is all right?" Felicity asked.

"I give you my word," Simon said without thinking.

Grass swished about Simon's boots as he walked. A large butterfly fluttered past him. He pivoted to watch its aerial antics and saw his wife shedding her dress. His mouth went dry at the sight of her underclothes and the swell of her bosom. With an effort he tore his eyes away from her and went on.

The immense plain shimmered in the brilliant sunshine. Simon could see more buffalo than before. To the north, at the tree line, he spied several large forms moving among the pines. At first he thought they were deer, but on closer look he realized they were elk. His mouth watered at the prospect of a thick steak.

Nothing else stirred within the range of the young man's vision. He grinned at his foolish worries, hefted the Hawken, and ambled back toward their camp. It occurred to him that his wife might want to bathe in private. She was touchy about things like that.

Simon respected her for her modesty. She was every inch a lady, and he would not hesitate to slug anyone who implied otherwise. Felicity knew how he felt. She laughed at him sometimes, saying that it was silly of him to put her on some kind of pedestal. Women just didn't understand men, Simon reasoned. When a man loved a woman, really and truly loved her, then that woman became the focus of his whole life. He would do anything for her, give her whatever she wanted if he had the means. More than that, he showed his devotion by always treating her with the utmost respect. If that was putting someone on a pedestal, then so be it.

Simon spotted his wife's dress lying beside the pool. There was no sign of her in the water, so he figured she had gone off into the spruce trees. Halting near their saddles, he waited for her to reappear. A minute went by. Then several more. He fidgeted and called out, "Darling, what's the matter? Did you snag your petticoat on a bush?"

There was no answer.

Becoming mildly alarmed, Simon cupped a hand to his mouth and bellowed, "Felicity! Where are you?"

Once more there was no reply.

A sensation of pure terror came over Simon as he abruptly dashed to the forest and called his wife's name several more times. When she did not respond, he darted madly among the trunks, seeking some sign of her. Ten minutes later, too bewildered to think straight, he returned to the pool.

In a daze, Simon picked up her dress and ran his fingers over the fabric. The horrible truth hit him then with the force of a physical blow and his knees buckled. His wife was gone! Somehow, something or someone had snatched her right out from under his nose!

Simon Ward tossed back his head and howled the name of the woman he loved.

Black Powder

Chapter Two

Nathaniel King was on the trail of five elk he had been tracking for the better part of two days when he heard a strange wail. Instantly he reined up his black stallion and sat listening for the sound to be repeated. It had been a human cry, yet one filled with more misery than any human voice should have to convey.

A free trapper by trade, Nate wore beaded buckskins and moccasins made for him by his Shoshone wife. A mane of black hair framed a rugged face bronzed by the sun and hardened by the elements. He carried a Hawken and had a brace of pistols around his waist. Slanted across his chest were a powder horn, ammo pouch and possibles bag. Eyes the color of emeralds studied the foothills to the south as he waited for the cry to be repeated so he could pinpoint where it came from.

Whoever had made it was plainly in some sort of

trouble. Whether white or Indian didn't matter to him. While some trappers ranked Indians as filthy savages, Nate knew better. They were people, plain and simple.

The strapping mountaineer had lived among them for a third of his life; the Shoshones had even formally adopted him into the tribe. In many ways he was more Indian than white, and he felt no shame admitting that fact.

Now, on hearing another cry, Nate jabbed his heels into the stallion's flanks and veered southward. He picked his way with care through the forest, his senses primed. It just might be that he had stumbled on a war party of Blackfeet or Piegans or some other hostile tribe.

Nate had been over this particular stretch of country before. He remembered the lay of the land well. On cresting a rocky spine, he spied a small stream below. It brought to mind the night many months ago when he had camped beside a pool on a wide bench just a little ways to the east. That was where the wail arose. He was sure.

Swinging to the west, Nate approached the bench in a wide loop. He slowed when he glimpsed four horses standing near the trees. All four were staring toward the pool. He looked, but did not notice anything out of the ordinary at first.

Then Nate heard an odd noise. It took him a few moments to identify it. Someone was crying, bawling like a baby. Even more surprising, he could tell it was a man. He moved closer and saw a figure on his knees close to the water.

The bawler had his arms clasped to his belly as if his innards were on fire. In front of him lay a garment of some kind.

Wary of a trick, Nate slowly walked the stallion to

15

the end of the pines and regarded the man closely. Right away he recognized a greenhorn. The store-bought clothes were a dead giveaway, as were the uncomfortable high-heeled city boots no trapper in his right mind would wear.

Squaring his broad shoulders, Nate nudged the stallion forward. The man was making so much noise, he never heard. A few yards shy of the camp, Nate drew rein and said quietly so as not to startle him, "Are you in pain, mister?"

Simon Ward had been so overcome by despair at being unable to find his wife that he had started crying before he could stop himself.

The young man from Boston had lived in secret horror of this very thing happening ever since they had left the last settlement way back in Missouri. Despite all his bluster to the contrary, Simon had not had much confidence in his ability to protect his wife. For one thing, he was not much of a woodsman. He had managed to keep the supper pot full every night only because game on the prairie had been so plentiful.

For another thing, Simon had never killed a human being and had no idea whether he could. The old-timers he had talked to in St. Louis and elsewhere had impressed on him that sooner or later he would have to do so. Any man who made his home in the mountains, they had claimed, was bound to run up against hostiles eventually. It was as inevitable as the rising of the sun. And where hostiles were concerned there was only one rule; kill or be killed.

Simon had not let Felicity know of his worry. He had not wanted her to think that he could not protect her if the need arose.

Now, to have the love of his life vanish without a

trace, virtually paralyzed him. Racked by intense guilt, Simon cried and cried even though he knew that he should get to his feet and go search for her. He just couldn't seem to stop himself.

But that had always been the case. Ever since he was a small boy, Simon had reacted to every undue hardship by bawling his brains out. His own brothers and sisters had branded him a bawl-baby. And while he did not do it as often as he once did, and certainly never where others, especially Felicity, could see him, he still had his moments.

Then someone spoke. Shocked to his core, Simon glanced up. His tears were choked off by his amazement at beholding a huge man who looked to be part Indian mounted on the biggest, blackest horse he had ever set eyes on. They almost seemed unreal to him, phantasms of his tormented mind.

"Are you in pain?" Nate King repeated, not knowing what to make of the greenhorn's expression. He looked at the garment, realized what it was, and scanned the area, alarmed. "Is there a woman with you?"

The reminder jolted Simon like a bolt out of the blue. Surging to his feet, he trained his rifle on the stranger and demanded, "Where is she, damn you? What have you done with her, you miserable heathen?"

The greenhorn was close to snapping. Any man could tell. Nate mustered a friendly smile and said, "Sheathe your claws, pilgrim. I'm a white-eye, like you. I haven't done anything to anyone. I heard you cry out and figured I could be of help, is all."

"You're white?" Simon said suspiciously. He had never seen a white man so dark of skin before, not even the mountain men he'd met in St. Louis. And he noticed that this one wore an eagle feather in his hair, jutting downward at the back.

Nate ignored the implication and pointed at the dress. "Listen, greener. If you don't need me, that's fine by this hos. But if your woman is in trouble, it wouldn't pay to be too proud. Savvy?"

Simon glanced down at his feet where Felicity's garment had fallen. "Oh, God! My wife," he said, fighting back a rising wave of more tears. His mind in a whirl, he swayed.

Thinking that the younger man was about to pass out on him, Nate dismounted. "Where is she?"

"I don't know," Simon said forlornly. "One minute she was right here, about to take a bath. The next she was gone." He motioned helplessly at the woods. "A grizzly must have dragged her off when I had my back turned."

"You would have heard it if one did," Nate said, turning his attention to the ground bordering the pool. "A griz likes to roar when it charges. Half scares most critters to death and makes them easy prey."

"Really?" Simon said, running his sleeve under his nose. He was still leery, but it appeared to him as if the newcomer was sincere about lending a hand, and he could use all the help he could get.

"Your wife never cried out?"

"No, sir. Not a peep." Simon indicated the rim. "I was over there, you see. My horse had acted up and I thought an animal might be nearby—" He stopped short when the stranger abruptly squatted to examine a strip of bare earth.

"It was no animal."

"What? How do you know?"

"Look here," Nate said, pointing. It had been his experience that most pilgrims could not track a bull buffalo through fresh mud, and he wanted the younger man to see for himself.

18

Simon stared but saw nothing except the earth. There were a few smudge and scratch marks with no rhyme or reason to them that he could discern. "Look at what, mister?"

Sighing, Nate responded, "Step around behind me and take a gander over my shoulder. I'll outline it with my finger."

Complying, Simon watched intently as the mountain man ran a fingernail along the outer edge of what appeared to be a half-moon scrape. "So?"

"It's the heel print of a man wearing moccasins," Nate revealed. "And this here"—he touched a shallow furrow that to the young Bostonian looked as if it had been made by a stick—"is where your wife dragged her foot trying to keep them from carrying her off."

"Them?" Simon repeated, his stomach churning as the full import of what the man was telling him sank home.

"There were two men, both wearing moccasins," Nate said as he moved along the edge of the pool to where the rushing water entered it. "One was a white man, the other a breed. They came out of those weeds on the other side of the stream, jumped it, and were on your wife before she knew they were there. One must have put a hand over her mouth and grabbed her around the shoulders while the other took hold of her around the legs. She struggled some, but it did her no good. They carried her back across and were long gone before you returned."

Flabbergasted, Simon gawked at this brawny wild man with the uncanny ability to read marks on the ground as if they were letters in a book. With this man's help, he just might be able to save Felicity.

Then it occurred to Simon Ward that maybe he was being too trusting. After all, he knew nothing about the stranger. And it was odd that the man should show up just minutes after his wife had been taken. For all he knew, the Good Samaritan might be in league with her abductors. Why, it might be, he mused, that this was no mountain man at all, but a common cutthroat.

Nate was bending to inspect prints near the stream when he noticed the greenhorn give him a mighty peculiar look, the same kind of look a person might give a ravenous wolf that had wandered into camp. Hoping to show the young man that there was no cause to distrust him, Nate straightened and offered his hand. "My manners aren't what they used to be. I'm Nate King. My family and I live in a cabin southwest of here a fair piece."

Simon automatically shook hands and marveled at the strength in King's grip. He suspected that the man could crush his fingers without hardly trying. "You have a family?"

"Sure do. My wife, Winona, is a Shoshone. We have a son named Zach and a little girl, Evelyn."

Simon believed the man was telling the truth. King's affection for his loved ones made his face light up like a candle. Simon relaxed a little, since in his estimation it was unlikely a genuine cutthroat would be a family man. "I'm Simon Ward. My wife's name is Felicity." That was all Simon intended to say, but he went on, unable to stop himself, the words rushing out of their own accord. "We came west to make a better life for ourselves, to live free as the birds, just as you and your family must do. It was my idea, you see. I talked Felicity into it. I told her everything would be fine, that no harm would come to her. I told her I'd protect her no matter what. And then she disappeared and I didn't know what had happened to her and I was at my wit's end so I—"

"Cried?" Nate finished when the younger man hesitated. The emotional outpouring had told him a lot, and none of it raised his opinion of the greenhorn.

Cut to the quick by the tone that the mountain man used, Simon blurted, "I couldn't help myself. If something really bad happens, I go all to pieces. My mother says I have a sensitive nature."

"What does your pa say?"

"That I'm an idiot."

Nate was inclined to agree with the father. He shook his head and moved on. All this was well and good, but they had a woman to find, and quickly, or the young fool might never see his wife again. "Saddle up. I'll scout around and be back in a few minutes."

Simon opened his mouth to voice a question, but King suddenly leaped across the stream and plunged into the vegetation on the other side. He had wanted to explain further, to let the mountain man know that he wasn't a whiner by nature, that he simply had the soul of a poet, as one of his teachers had put it. But it would have to wait, he reflected. King had a point. Felicity came first. He hastened to obey.

Nate glanced back once, then concentrated on the spoor. The men who had taken the woman were skilled. They had left few tracks, and probably would have left none at all had they not been burdened by their captive. Once over the rim of the bench and out of earshot, they had broken into a run. At one point the man in the lead, the white man, had slipped and gouged his knees into the soil. There was evidence of a brief scuffle. When the kidnappers went on, they ran side by side and the footprints of the white were much deeper than those of the breed.

It was not hard for Nate to determine what had happened. Felicity Ward had been fighting hard to break free every step of the way, and she had caused the white man in front to fall. The man had lost his grip. Felicity had then turned on her second captor, but before she could tear loose, the breed had knocked her out. The white man had then draped her over a shoulder and the pair had gone on.

At the bottom of the bench were hoofprints. Two horses had been ground-hitched there for quite some time. Both had urinated, one between its legs, the other behind them. That told Nate that one had been a stallion, the other a mare.

Having learned all he needed, Nate raced to the top of the bench. Ward had saddled a bay and another animal and was hard at work loading the packs.

"You have a decision to make," Nate announced.

Simon had been so engrossed in his chore that he had not heard the trapper approach. He started, and clutched at one of his pistols. "King! Damn! Don't creep up on me like that."

Nate did not waste a moment. "If we hurry, we might be able to catch them before they get very far. One of them is riding double." He nodded at the pack animals. "But we won't have a prayer if we're dragging them along. It would slow us down too much."

"You want me to leave the packhorses?" Simon said, aghast. All the worldly goods he and Felicity owned were on those two animals.

"And your wife's horse," Nate said. "She can ride back with you."

Simon was reluctant to do it. He feared that a wild beast might come along and kill the horses or spook them. Or a band of Indians might ride by and steal them. Without those animals, Felicity and he would not last long. But which was more important? he asked himself. His wife, or their personal effects?

"Give me a minute," he said, and led the three horses over to the pines.

Nate swung onto his stallion and waited by the stream. When the young man joined him, he forded and broke into a gallop. At the bottom he showed Ward the hoof tracks, then circled to pick up the trail.

"There's something I've been meaning to ask you," Simon mentioned as the mountain man rode bent low to the ground. "How do you know that one of these men is white and the other is a half-breed?"

Nate answered without looking up. "Most white men walk with their toes pointed out and take long strides. Indians, by and large, walk with their toes bent in and take smaller steps."

"So you're saying that it's plain one of them is white. That I can understand. But how can you tell the other is a breed? I mean, if the toes are bent in, maybe it's a full-blooded Indian."

"No," Nate said, rising. He had found where the tracks led away from the bench, bearing due south. "The second man's toes are only partly bent in, and he takes long steps."

"Oh."

They sped on, Nate in the lead, winding among the pines at a reckless pace. Simon Ward was awed by the mountain man's riding ability. It was as if the man and the black stallion were one. He was hard pressed to keep up but resolved not to fall behind. Not when his wife's life was at stake. Or worse.

The idea jarred Simon. Until that moment he had not given much thought to what Felicity's abductors planned to do with her. Yet it was doubtful they had taken her just to kill her. A burning rage flared in him as he pictured her being abused.

"Watch out!" Nate King cried.

Simon blinked and looked up to see a low limb sweeping toward him. At the very last instant he ducked under it and was spared. He saw King shake his head and wished he would quit making a jackass of himself. He wanted to earn the mountain man's respect, not his contempt.

If the young Bostonian had been able to read Nate's mind, he would have been even more upset. Nate was convinced that Ward had no business whatsoever being in the Rockies. The wilderness was no place for amateurs. Time and again he had run into people like Ward, folks whose daydreams eclipsed their common sense, whose hankering for living on the frontier flew in the face of their inability to fend for themselves.

Nature was a hard taskmaster. There was one unwritten law, and one only, by which the many wild creatures lived; survival of the fittest. Humans were not accorded any special treatment. When they were out of their element, they had to deal with Nature on its own terms. Which meant they were fair game for any prowling grizzly, painter or hostile.

People like the Wards did not last long. They needed plenty of time to learn how to live off the land, and time was one luxury few ever had. There were simply too many dangers.

Nate's reflection ended when the pines thinned. The next several hills were virtually barren. He scanned them for a glimpse of the kidnappers, but they were nowhere to be seen. Slowing, he leaned to the right to better study the tracks. A dozen yards further on the trail changed direction. The two men had angled to the southwest into dense woodland.

"Why have you slowed down?" Simon asked, drawing abreast of the stallion.

"Either these vermin know that we're after them

or they're just being canny," Nate said. He was about to pick up the pace when his keen eyes spotted a small object lying near the trail. Drawing rein, he slid down and picked it up.

"What do you have there, Mister King?"

"Call me Nate." Nate sniffed it, then held it up for Ward to examine.

"Why, that's part of a cigarette, isn't it?"

Nate had thought so too, at first glance. But it wasn't the hand-rolled variety of smoke favored by some of the trapping fraternity. "This is a *cigarrillo*. A Spanish brand. I saw a lot of folks using them when I took my family to New Mexico some time ago."

"But what would a Spanish cigarette be doing here? Do you think the men we're after are Mexicans?"

"No," Nate said, and let it go at that. The *cigarrillo* was a disturbing clue, one he would rather not share until he was certain. He prayed that he was wrong as he stepped into the stirrups and pressed on.

The spacing and depth of the tracks showed that the kidnappers were moving at a faster clip. The trail climbed to the top of a ridge, stuck to the crest for half a mile, and went down the other side. Either by luck or design the kidnappers had come on a game trail and taken it south to make better time.

For the next hour Nate and Simon pushed their mounts to the limit. A few miles to the west reared the regal Rockies, while to the east rippled the endless ocean of grass.

The trail crossed yet another hill, and as they reached the boulder-strewn crest, Nate abruptly reined up.

"What is it this time?" Simon inquired as the trapper slid to the ground.

"They stopped at this spot for a short while."

"To rest their horses?"

Hunkering, Nate probed for telltale signs. Blades of grass had been pressed flat, as if by the weight of a body. Broken stems testified to a brief scuffle. "They tied up your wife. She must have come around and tried to get away. See these footprints? The breed held her while the white man did the tying."

"May their souls rot in hell!" Simon said.

"Count your blessings," Nate responded, stepping to his mount.

"How do you mean?"

"She's still alive, isn't she? And they haven't tried to force themselves on her. Yet." Nate saw the young man blanche, but he did not regret being so blunt. Someone should have been equally blunt long before the Wards left Boston. It would have spared them both a heap of misery.

For the better part of two hours the free trapper and the Bostonian forged southward. At length they came to a wide clearing where there was evidence that many men had encamped for many days. There were so many tracks, all in a jumble, that it took Nate a while to sort them out. When he had, he frowned and gazed to the southeast, the direction their quarry had taken.

"Why so glum?" Simon wondered. "They're not that far ahead of us now, are they?"

"About an hour."

"Then we have the bastards!" Simon exclaimed. As an afterthought, he added, "How many of them are there, by the way?"

"I counted fourteen, but that's not the worst of it." Nate faced him.

The news was disheartening to Simon. Two against fourteen were bad odds. "What can possibly be worse?" he snorted.

"Your wife is in the clutches of slavers."

Chapter Three

Slavers! The very word was enough to bring goose-bumps to the flesh of every woman living in the mountains, red or white. They knew that if they were to fall into the hands of the coldhearted rogues, they would never see those they most cared for again.

No one knew exactly how many women had been stolen over the past decade or so. The total bandied about by the trapping community stood at seventy, or better.

It was widely known that the slavers had taken women from eight or nine different tribes as well as white settlers. There was an unconfirmed rumor that a few blacks, females *and* males, had also fallen prey. Some of the hapless victims were sold to Comanches, who paid extremely well for white wives. Others were sold south of the border to wealthy Mexicans. The blacks, according to the rumor, were carted to the deep South and handed over to certain unscrupulous plantation owners.

Only once had the slavers been caught in the act, and that by a tribe of Sioux who had harried them for scores of miles before the slavers finally released the four maidens they had kidnapped.

All the other times the slavers got clean away.

Nate had thought that merely mentioning them by name would give Ward some notion of what they were up against. But he had overlooked the younger man's profound ignorance of frontier life.

"Slavers? Who are they? Are you telling me that they make slaves of the women they abduct?"

Motioning at a log that lay beside the charred remains of a camp fire, Nate straddled it and sat. "Have a seat, pilgrim. We need to palaver a spell and set you straight on a few things. It won't do to get into a racket with this bunch with you not knowing the facts."

Simon stayed right where he was, next to his bay. "We don't have time for this nonsense, King! Every second we dawdle is another second my precious wife is in peril! I say that we ride out this very moment."

Unfazed by the outburst, Nate tapped the log. "Sit, pronto. Unless you want me to fetch you over and plunk you down." If the situation had not been so deadly serious for Mrs. Ward, he would have laughed at the comical pout her husband wore as Simon did as he wanted. Emotionally, the man was about as mature as his son, which was downright pitiful.

"Now, first things first," Nate said after Simon was settled. "I don't take it kindly of you to keep giving me a hard time. I don't have to do this, you know. There's nothing to keep me from turning right around and heading for the Shoshone village."

"I thought that you claimed you live in a cabin,"

Simon said sullenly. He did not like being treated as if he were next to worthless, and he still did not trust the mountain man completely.

"We do about ten months of the year," Nate disclosed. "But in the summer my wife likes to spend a couple of moons with her kin. My wife and children are with them now. I was off elk hunting when I bumped into you."

"Oh."

"Now listen, and listen good." Nate leaned forward. "Slavers are the foulest, meanest sons of bitches on two legs. They'll kill anyone who gets in their way without a second thought. Do you understand? If you were to charge into their camp and demand to have your wife handed over, you'd be dead the moment after you got the words out of your mouth." He paused. "Unless, of course, the slavers were in a frolicsome mood. Then they'd likely carve you up a bit to hear you scream before they rubbed you out."

Simon figured that the frontiersman was exaggerating a little. He'd heard that mountain men were fond of spinning tall tales. "You make them sound as bad as heathen savages."

"Indians aren't savages," Nate said stiffly. "But in one sense, you're right. Slavers are worse than any Indian alive. I know, because at one time or another I've tangled with practically every kind of Indian there is, from Blackfeet to Bloods to Apaches."

"If they're so evil, why haven't they been arrested and put in prison?"

Nate could not stifle a guffaw. "Who is going to arrest them, pilgrim? In case it hasn't sunk in yet, there's no law out here. None at all. Once a man leaves the States, he's on his own."

Simon realized that he had made a stupid remark,

but he was so flustered by the nightmare that had beset his wife that his mind was clouded by anxiety. "So what do we do when we catch up with these cutthroats?"

"I'll get to that in a moment." Nate stared off across the plain. He, too, was impatient to get under way, but he had to make Ward see the light. "First you have to learn who these slavers are. Some are renegade whites who are wanted back in the States, others are Mexicans wanted in their country, while still others are outcast Indians and breeds. They're no account any way you lay your sights. And each and every one of them has a string of kills to his credit."

Simon shuddered. To think that his Felicity was in the clutches of such fiends! He wished now that he had never talked her into making the journey. He wished that he had left well enough alone and stayed in Boston where they belonged. What in the world had gotten into him?

"As for how we'll handle it," Nate went on, "it depends on what we find when we overtake them. If all goes well, we'll be able to rescue your missus without much of a fuss. If not—" He shrugged.

"What then?"

"Then we do what we have to. Now let's light a shuck while we still have some daylight left. And hope to high heaven that the slavers make camp and don't elect to keep on going through the night as they sometimes do when they suspect someone is dogging their heels."

It did not dawn on Simon until they had been in the saddle fifteen minutes that the trapper had a point about being treated unkindly. It was wrong of him to still be suspicious. King was putting his life in jeopardy for two complete strangers. If the slavers were everything the trapper claimed, then King had to know that he might wind up dead before too long. It gave Simon considerable food for thought.

The tracks led them down out of the foothills and onto the prairie. Simon tried not to dwell on the fact that each passing minute took them farther from the packhorses and Felicity's animal.

Presently twilight shrouded the landscape. Simon thought that maybe the mountain man would slow down, but King held to a steady trot.

The sunset was spectacular. Framed by the pristine peaks, the sky blazed red and orange and pink. Golden rays shot over the Rockies like shafts from heaven. Any other time, Simon would have been mesmerized. As it was, he looked, then looked away.

With nightfall rose a cool breeze. Simon would have given anything to be by a warm fire. To have his wife snuggled in his arms. He fantasized of doing just that, and so vivid was his fantasy that he didn't notice Nate King had stopped. Suddenly the black stallion was right there in front of him.

"Dear God!" Simon cried. He wrenched on the reins so hard, he snapped the bay's head around. It caused the horse to veer just enough to one side to miss the black stallion by a hand's width. Simon let out the breath he had not known he was holding. He pretended not to notice that Nate King was glaring at him.

"Yell again a little louder, why don't you, pilgrim? I don't reckon the slavers heard you the first time."

"We've caught up with them?" Simon asked, elation coursing through him at the prospect of soon being reunited with his wife.

"They're yonder a little ways," Nate said, nodding to the southeast. "We'll leave the horses here and go on foot. Try not to make much noise if you can help it."

The young Bostonian stared hard into the night but saw no sign of those they were after, not even the faint glow of a distant camp fire. Figuring that the slavers had made a cold camp, he slipped from the saddle, waited for the trapper to lead off, and dogged the frontiersman's footsteps.

On all sides, chest-high grass enclosed them. Nate King hunched low and glided forward, parting the stems with the barrel of his Hawken, his ears straining to hear more of the sounds he had heard a minute before. Other than a faint rustling of the grass, he made no noise at all.

Simon tried to do the same, but try as he might, he kept stepping on clumps that crackled underfoot. Or he would push against the grass in front of him a bit too hard and it would snap off. Once King glanced around. "Sorry," Simon whispered. "I'm doing the best I can."

Nate knew that. Which was why he did not find fault with the greenhorn, but went on, moving slowly in the belief that the slower they went, the less noise Ward was likely to make. It worked to some extent.

Simon was impatient to catch sight of his wife again. He expected to come on the slavers at any second. So when a minute went by, then two, then five, and more, he began to think that maybe the mountain man was wrong, that maybe they were chasing shadows. It angered him so much that he tapped King on the back and whispered testily, "Are you sure the slavers are camped nearby? If you ask me, we're wasting our damn time."

Nate stopped and turned. It galled him to have his judgment questioned by someone whose claim to sound judgment was almost laughable. Grabbing Ward by the front of his woolen shirt, Nate hoisted him erect and pointed. "Any more questions, mister?" he growled.

Fifty yards away were the dancing flames of a camp fire. Figures were seated around it. Others moved about in its vicinity.

Simon could hardly credit his own eyes. It stupefied him that the frontiersman had spotted the camp from so far off. And he was deeply ashamed for having doubted him. He nodded, and King let go. "What now?" he whispered.

"You stay put while I go have a look-see," Nate said. He expected an argument and was pleased when Ward merely bobbed his chin. Bending low, Nate padded forward on cat's feet. When he glimpsed the fire through the thick grass, he slowed to a snail's pace.

That the slavers had seen fit to make a fire was encouraging. It meant they had no notion that someone was after them. They were bound to post guards, but not until most of the band had turned in.

Nate strained to hear snatches of conversation. A pair of men were talking in Spanish. While he had learned a little of the language down in New Mexico, he did not know it well enough to be able to understand what they were saying. Others were chatting in English, but he was not quite close enough to eavesdrop.

A dozen yards from the camp, Nate shifted his pistols. Usually he wore them wedged under his belt on either side of his big metal buckle. Now he slid them around to his hips so they would not drag on the ground.

Easing onto his belly, Nate snaked nearer. He would crawl a foot or so, then pause to look and listen. In this cautious manner he drew within six feet of the flattened area in which the slavers had made their camp.

The grass had not only been bent flat, but wide areas had been grazed to the ground. In some spots the soil had been torn up, as if by a pick and shovel.

Nate recognized the handiwork of buffalo when he saw it. The slavers had gathered a pile of dry chips and were using the dung as fuel. Its dusky scent hung heavy in the air, mixed with the aroma of tobacco and the smell of horses.

As Nate had determined earlier in the day, there were fourteen cutthroats in the band. Eight were clustered at the fire, swapping stories. A few others played cards. One man was cleaning his rifle, another honed a butcher knife. Saddles and packs were lined up near the horse string for a quick getaway if need be.

It worried Nate that there was no trace of Felicity Ward. Given the vicious temperament of slavers, he would not put it past them to have slit her throat and dumped her body on the plain if she had given them too much trouble. Simon and he might have passed within a few yards of her cold corpse and never known it.

Then a lean slaver who wore a black *sombrero* and Mexican-style clothes rose from near the fire with a tin plate in his left hand and walked over to the saddles. The toe of his boot nudged what appeared to be a large bundle wrapped in a brown blanket, and the 'bundle' uncoiled and stiffly sat up.

It was a young woman. Felicity Ward. She was slight of frame and had sandy, disheveled hair. Her face was streaked with dirt, as were her underclothes, the only garments she had on.

"I brought you some food, senora," the slaver declared. "It is not much. Beans and dried beef. But it is all we have."

"I'm not hungry, Julio," Felicity said.

"*Por favor*, you must do as I say. You have no choice. Gregor says you are to eat if I have to force it down your throat."

"Tell that brute—" Felicity began, and froze when another slaver stood and came toward them.

This one was a huge man with the torso of a bear and a face scarred by many fights. Greasy brown hair hung down past his sloped shoulders, held in place by a coonskin cap. He wore grimy buckskins and carried four pistols in his belt. "Tell me what, woman?" he demanded in a gravelly voice.

Felicity was not given a chance to answer. The man called Gregor struck with lightning speed, lunging and slapping her across the cheek with a resounding crack. She crumpled, dazed, and Gregor seized her and shook her as a terrier might shake a rabbit.

"You still haven't gotten it through your thick skull, bitch! When we tell you to do something, you do it, no questions asked. You don't say no. You don't gripe. You don't insult us. You just do it!"

Gregor flung her down and jabbed a thick finger under her nose. "The next time you rile me, I'll strip you buck naked and drag you behind my horse for a mile or two. That ought to teach you to hold your tongue."

Spinning, Gregor shook a fist the size of a ham at the Mexican. "What the hell is the matter with you, Trijillo? I thought you're supposed to be one mean hombre? When a woman won't do what you want, slap her around some until she does. Don't ever let me hear you say 'please' again."

Julio's contempt was thick enough to be cut with

a knife. "My apologies, senor. But I am not used to treating women the way you do. Where I come from, a man does not go around beating on those who are weaker than him."

Gregor motioned in disgust. "Is that a fact? Well, you'll never make a good slaver then. A good beating is the only thing that keeps most of these cows in line." He started back to the fire, then paused. "I never should have let you join up. When we get back below the border, go find yourself another line of work."

The other slavers had not shown much interest in the exchange. One man, though, a beefy breed who wore only a breechcloth and knee-high moccasins, had picked up his rifle and held it as if ready to shoot should Gregor and the Mexican come to blows. He did not lower the gun until Gregor had rejoined the group around the fire.

Nate was mildly puzzled. The leader's brutality was typical of slavers, but Julio Trijillo's behavior had not been. The Mexican had acted genuinely concerned for the captive's welfare. He gathered that Trijillo was new to the slaving trade, perhaps a bandit who had thrown in with them not really knowing what he was letting himself in for.

Not that it mattered much. The other thirteen would as soon beat their captive silly as look at her.

Of immediate concern to Nate was how to get the woman out of there without being killed in the process. Nate studied the layout of the camp. He saw Mrs. Ward sit back up and morosely pick at her meal. She was the perfect picture of misery.

It made Nate think of his own wife, Winona, and how he would react if she were to suffer the same fate. He thanked God that she was safe and sound, many miles away in the Shoshone village.

Black Powder

At that moment, back in the grass, Simon Ward squatted on the balls of his feet and impatiently waited for the frontiersman to return. To stay there and not do anything, knowing that his wife was so close, was one of the hardest things Simon had ever had to do. Horrid images fired his brain, images of vile acts the slavers might be inflicting on her. He wanted to jump up and go charging into their camp. It took every ounce of self-control he had not to.

The wait stretched Simon's already frayed nerves to the breaking point. He was so overwrought that when a dark shape reared up in front of him, he whipped his rifle to his shoulder and started to pull back the hammer.

"It's me," Nate whispered, ready to grab the barrel and shove it aside if he heard a click. He'd rather not, though, since the gun might go off and alert the slavers. Fortunately, Ward lowered the Hawken.

"Did you see her?" Simon asked urgently.

"Yes."

"Has she been harmed?"

Most mountain men were shrewd judges of human nature. They had to be in order to survive. So Nate knew beyond a shadow of a doubt that if he told the truth, nothing he could say or do would stop Simon Ward from barrelling to Felicity's side without a thought for his own welfare, or anyone else's.

"She's fine," Nate fibbed. "Eating supper, the last I saw."

"They're feeding her?" Simon said in surprise, having assumed the fiends would half starve his beloved to death.

Nate sank to one knee. "Keep in mind that to them, the slave trade is a business. They can't get top dollar for their goods if the merchandise is damaged."

"Do we go get her now?"

"No, we wait until they've turned in."

Simon was none too happy. "Since she's my wife, I think I should have the greater say. And I vote that we rescue her right this minute. You can distract them somehow while I go in and whisk her out of there."

"Won't work," Nate said, sitting. "Even if I lured them off, they're not about to leave her unguarded. Four or five would stay put and gun you down the moment you showed yourself."

There was no denying the trapper's logic, but Simon still simmered at yet another delay. Bowing his head, he tried to shut thoughts of poor Felicity from his mind.

Unchecked bittersweet memories flooded through Simon: the first time they had met at the market where she worked, their first, fleeting kiss in the back of a buggy, their hectic wedding day, and the bliss of their wedding night.

Felicity was the only woman Simon had ever known in the Biblical sense. He'd always been so shy in that regard that it had taken him months to muster the nerve to hold her hand. It was safe to say that their wedding night had been the single greatest night of his entire life.

"Do you love your wife, Nate?" Simon asked.

The unexpected question made the mountain man glance up sharply. Having lived on the frontier for so long, where folks tended to mind their own business, he tended to forget that Easterners liked to pry into the personal affairs of others. "Yes, I do," he answered honestly. "She's my whole life."

"That's how I feel about Felicity. So you'll have to forgive me if I push too much. If anything should happen to her, I wouldn't want to live."

It sounded to Nate as if the younger man were

about to burst into tears again. To forestall that, he said, "I don't hold it against you. I was your age once."

Simon scrutinized the mountain man's features. "Not that long ago, I daresay. You don't appear to be that much older than I am."

"It's not how long a person lives, but how much living they do," Nate commented. "You're right, though. I was too young to know any better when I gave up an accounting career in New York City to come live with my uncle up in the mountains."

"Where is he now?"

Nate plucked at a blade of grass. "He died shortly after we got here."

"And you've been fending for yourself ever since?"

"A friend of my uncle's took me under his wing and taught me how to stay alive in the wild."

"Really? I wish I had someone to teach me."

Nate King offered no reply. But it set him to thinking that maybe he had treated the greenhorn too harshly, that maybe he should give Simon the same benefit of the doubt that Shakespeare McNair, his uncle's friend, had given him. Do unto others, as the Good Book put it.

Simon peered toward the camp, anxious to be off. "How long do you think it will be before the slavers fall asleep?"

Before Nate could respond, a wavering scream rent the night, the scream of a woman in mortal terror. He made a grab for the Bostonian, but he was a hair too slow.

Simon Ward was off like a shot, plowing through the grass to go save the woman he loved.

Chapter Four

Hours earlier and many miles to the northwest, Winona King had realized that she was being stalked when her pinto mare swung its head around, ears pricked toward the top of the rise they had just crossed.

The wife of the man known as Grizzly Killer was a credit to her people. She did not panic. She did not go into a bout of hysteria as some of her sisters from east of the Mississippi might have done. No, Winona King merely firmed her grip on her rifle and guided the mare behind a thicket so that she could spy on her back trail without being seen.

Winona was a Shoshone—and proud of it. Her people were widely respected by their friends and widely feared by their enemies. Even the notorious Blackfeet, who raided at will over the northern mountains and plains, regarded the Shoshones as fierce fighters.

Black Powder

Since joining herself to Nate King as his woman, Winona had been in more than her share of tight situations. Her husband's wanderlust had taken her from the dry deserts of New Mexico to the sandy shores of the Great Water far, far to the west. In her travels she had met many who wanted to deprive her of her life, and she was still around.

Winona had no idea who was after her this time. Early that morning she had left her children in the care of her aunt and gone off to hunt. She wanted to surprise her man with a new buckskin shirt when he came back from elk hunting. To do that, she needed a fresh hide.

So for most of the morning Winona had sought fresh deer sign, and on finding it she had followed the tracks to the southeast.

Now it was late afternoon. A short while ago, while crossing a tableland, Winona had idly glanced back and thought she saw a wisp of dust possibly raised by another rider. She had reined up and waited to see if anyone appeared. When no one had, she'd gone on.

Then the pinto looked around, and Winona knew beyond a shadow of doubt that she had someone on her trail. Her guess was that it might be a war party of Blackfeet, or of any other tribe with whom the Shoshones were at perpetual war.

Quite often enemies were content to steal horses, or women. Winona had lost a number of close friends and relatives to marauding bands, and she did not care to share their fate.

She was not very worried. Her mare had superb stamina. It could hold its own against most any horse. In addition, she had the rifle her husband had bought for her and taught her to shoot, plus a pair of pistols and a knife.

41

David Thompson

Nate always insisted that she be well armed when she ventured anywhere. It amused some of the other Shoshone women to see her go around armed like a warrior, but Winona ignored them. Her husband was right. It was fitting that a woman hold her own in all aspects of married life, which included being able to protect herself and her family as well as any man.

Winona rested her rifle across her thighs and scanned the terrain she had traversed. Nothing moved, not so much as a chipmunk. That in itself was ominous.

A gust of wind stirred the raven tresses that cascaded down to the small of Winona's back. She had on a beaded buckskin dress and short moccasins. Around her slim waist was a red sash Nate had bought for her at the last rendezvous. She had protested, saying it was a waste of money. But he had seen the gleam in her eyes when she saw it. And, as always, all she had to do was show an interest in something and he did whatever it took to get it for her.

Suddenly the pinto sniffed loudly. Winona immediately leaned forward to cover its muzzle so it would not nicker if it had caught the scent of another horse.

Hundreds of yards off, something materialized among the trees.

It took Winona a while to make out the outline of a horse and rider, so skillfully did the man blend into the background. He was scouring the brush, seeking her, no doubt. As she watched, another rider appeared. This one was not so skillful. It was a man in a wide-brimmed hat such as she had seen Mexicans wear down in Apache country.

Winona knew of a half-dozen Mexicans who called

the mountains their home. All made their living as trappers or traders. This man, her intuition told her, most definitely did not.

The pair sat there for the longest while searching for her. Then the skilled one melted into the vegetation and the Mexican followed suit.

Winona was in no hurry to come out of hiding. Where there were two, there might be more. She planned on staying there until she was sure they were long gone, then she would fly to the village and warn the Shoshones there were enemies in the area. Her uncle Spotted Bull, her cousin Touch The Clouds, and prominent men like Drags The Rope and White Wolf would rouse the warriors of her tribe to hunt down the invaders and either drive them off or slay them to the last man.

Time dragged by. Winona decided that she had waited long enough. She was reaching for the reins when to her rear a twig snapped.

Shifting, Winona felt her blood run cold at the sight of a vague form on horseback moving slowly toward her. They had known where she was all along! They were closing in!

With a slap of her muscular legs, Winona urged the mare into a gallop. Racing around the thicket, she headed to the northwest, making a beeline for the village.

The next moment two more riders popped up in front of her, barring her path.

Winona slanted to the left and took a slope on the fly. She bent low to better distribute her weight. At the top she twisted and was perturbed to see four men were now after her. One was the Mexican. Two others were white. The last had the swarthy complexion of a breed.

At breakneck speed Winona went down the opposite slope. She wound among dense pines and presently came on a stand of aspens. Into these she plunged, moving into the heart of the stand where the thin trees were pressed so tightly together that the mare had difficulty squeezing through.

There was a method to her apparent madness. Winona counted on her pursuers following her in. Their bigger mounts would have more trouble than the mare getting through. It should slow them down enough for her to make her getaway.

But when Winona emerged on the far side and checked to see if her ruse had worked, she saw the riders separate. Two bore to the left, two to the right. They were too smart for her. They were going around the aspens.

A flick of the reins goaded the pinto onward. Winona held the rifle in her left hand. Her long hair streamed in her wake. A meadow unfolded ahead, so she let the mare have its head. When she was close to the next tract of trees, she looked over a shoulder.

The four men were still after her. In the lead was one of the whites, a grizzled, grinning lodgepole of a man who wore a round hat made of black bear fur.

Winona had half a mind to shoot him. Since she might need every shot she had if they overtook her, she raced on. The mare flowed smoothly over the ground and betrayed no sign of tiring.

It soon became clear, though, that the man in the bear hat had a faster animal. Slowly but surely his sorrel gained. His grin widened. He had a rifle, slung over his back by means of a wide leather strap across his scrawny chest, but he did not try to unlimber it to shoot the mare out from under her. He did, however, take what appeared to be a coil of brown rope from off his left shoulder and held it in his right hand.

Winona worked her legs, urging the pinto to exert itself even more. The mare had a heart of gold, as her husband would say, and did its best, head low, legs flying. Onward through the forest they sped, hurtling logs, barreling through patches of brush.

To Winona's delight, she held her own. The man on the sorrel did not gain on her any more than he already had. The other men were much further behind, so far back that she did not even consider them much of a threat.

Then, without warning, the forest ended at the base of a steep slope. And not just any slope. It was covered by talus from top to bottom, by broken bits of rock of all sizes. Loose, slippery rocks that offered no firm footing for man or beast.

Winona had no choice. If she tried to go around, the man on the sorrel would be on her before she got halfway around the hill. She had to go up the talus slope and hope the mare kept its footing all the way to the crest.

With the thought came action. Winona urged her mare to gallop straight up, and for 15 or 20 feet they made steady headway. Then the rocks started sliding out from under the mare's driving hooves. The horse slipped, righted itself, and went on, but slower now, because if it tried to gallop it would lose its purchase and go sliding back down to the bottom.

A mocking cackle made Winona glance back. The scrawny man was laughing at the mare's efforts. He had started up after them, his sorrel picking its way with uncanny skill. He still held the brown rope, but close to his leg where she could not see it well.

Winona smiled grimly to herself. She would give the scrawny one something to cackle about when he got a little closer! Hunching forward to better distribute her weight, she poked the mare gently with the stock of her rifle. The pinto, muscles rippling, climbed steadily.

A dozen feet higher, and they came to where the talus consisted of mainly small, flat rocks as slippery as shale. The mare lost her footing, recovered, then promptly lost it again. With every step the animal took, the talus spewed on down the slope. It was next to impossible for the horse to plant all four legs firmly.

Winona patted its neck to encourage it. The animal was slick with sweat and had to be tired, but it gamely plodded higher. More and more rocks clattered out from under it.

The next moment the mare's rear legs buckled. The pinto dug in its hooves and tried to push upright, but as it did a whole section of talus under its front legs gave way.

The next thing Winona knew, the horse was on its belly and sliding downward at a fast clip. She hauled on the reins. The mare tried its utmost to stand but there was no footing at all. Its legs churned. It nickered. It toppled onto its side.

Winona had to scramble to keep from being pinned. She clung in helpless frustration to the side of her saddle, yet another gift from her adoring husband. There was nothing else she could do until they came to a stop.

Twenty feet lower, they finally did. Winona carefully stood and stepped back so the mare could rise unburdened. The short hairs at the nape of her neck prickled as that mocking cackle was repeated very close behind her. She whirled.

The scrawny man sat astride his sorrel not six feet away, gazing at her in frank amusement. "I'll say this for you, squaw, you gave us a hell of a chase. But now you're ours."

A cold fury seized Winona. She gave him a taste of his own medicine, mocking him with a laugh of her own, and said, "You have it all wrong, white dog. Now you are mine." With that, she brought up the Hawken.

Fleeting surprise registered on the grizzled man's face. Then his right arm flicked up and out. The brown rope flashed toward her. Only it wasn't a rope at all. Too late, she saw it was a whip such as she had seen white men use who drove big wagons pulled by many oxen or mules. A bullwhip, it was called. And this man was a master at using his.

The tip of the whip wrapped itself around the muzzle of the Hawken. Before Winona could prevent it, the rifle was torn from her grasp and jerked out of her reach. Undaunted, she grabbed for a pistol. Her right hand closed on the smooth wooden grip and she started to swing the flintlock up even as her thumb curled back the hammer.

The whip cracked a second time, its rawhide coils looping around Winona's ankles. Just as she aimed and squeezed the trigger, she was wrenched off her feet.

Winona's right elbow smashed onto the hard rocks. Involuntarily, her finger tightened on the trigger and the flintlock went off. She did not mean to shoot. It just happened. A strident whinny greeted the booming retort of the .55-caliber smoothbore. Lusty curses exploded from the scrawny man.

The coils around Winona's ankles slackened. Kicking and wriggling her legs, she cast them off her and pushed to her feet.

The sorrel was down. A large hole in the center of its forehead oozed blood and brains. Its tongue lolled out, and its body quivered as if it were cold.

Partially pinned under the dead animal was the

man with the whip. He struggled mightily but could not free himself. Glaring at Winona, he snarled, "You bitch! You killed Buck! The best damn horse I've ever owned, and you killed him!"

Winona reached for her other pistol. "Just as I am going to do to you."

The scrawny man recoiled. He extended a hand, palm out. "Now you hold on there, squaw! You don't want to be doing that! I wasn't tryin' to hurt you. Just capture you, is all."

"I am Shoshone. You are my enemy. There is nothing more to be said." Winona began to level the flintlock.

Then a rifle blasted at the bottom of the talus slope. A lead ball whined off nearby rocks. The other three men had arrived. Another was taking aim as Winona ducked down so that they could not see her over the dead horse.

The man in the bear hide hat continued to grunt and push against his saddle, to no avail. He muttered to himself, a string of oaths such as her husband would never use.

Winona saw the three men below dismount and climb. One was reloading. His companions had their rifles trained, ready to shoot her when she reappeared. Or would they? Winona wondered. The scrawny one had just told her that they wanted to take her alive. Maybe they would hold their fire long enough for her to escape.

Using the pinto was out of the question. The mare had kept on trying to rise and had slid another fifteen feet lower. With it had gone Winona's ammo pouch and powder horn, which she had placed in a parfleche tied to the back of the saddle. She had no way to reload. And her rifle lay well past the sorrel, out in the open.

Black Powder

The way Winona saw it, her only hope lay in reaching the summit and losing herself in the forest. It would take her pursuers time to pry their friend from under the horse and scale the slope. She regretted having to leave the mare and her effects behind, but it could not be helped.

Besides, Winona would get them back when she returned with dozens of warriors and tracked the quartet down.

Girding her legs, Winona wedged the spent pistol under her sash, waited until all three men were looking down at the loose rocks under their feet, and made her move. Springing up, but staying doubled at the waist, she sprinted toward the crest. She zigzagged to throw off their aim. And it was well she did, because a rifle cracked and lead ricocheted inches from her right leg.

The scrawny man let out with a bellow. "Hold your fire, Owens, you brainless bastard! Comanches don't pay for cripples!"

Comanches? Winona mused on the run. What did Comanches have to do with anything? She took five more bounding leaps and suddenly the answer burst on her like an exploding keg of black powder. It nearly threw her off stride.

The men were slavers!

Until that moment Winona had assumed they were common bandits, men who roamed the mountains preying on anyone and everyone. Nate and she had tangled with their ilk before. But now she knew the truth, and she was sorry that she had not shot the scrawny one when she had the chance.

In early childhood Shoshone girls were warned by their mothers to beware the dreaded slavers. Winona remembered her own mother telling her about the vile bands which swooped down out of nowhere and

49

made off with screaming women and young girls. She had been five or six at the time, and the tales had terrified her as nothing else ever had.

But the slavers never struck once while Winona was growing up. By the time Winona had seen twelve winters, she had come to suspect that the stories were just that. They were meant to keep little girls in line, to keep them from straying too far from the village.

The winter before Winona met Nate, events had shown her otherwise. One day a group of warriors from another Shoshone band showed up in the village. They were painted for war and wanted the help of Winona's father and others in hunting a band of slavers who had made off with eight women and four girls.

One of those girls Winona had known, a distant cousin named Falling Star, a favorite of hers. One summer they had spent fourteen whole sleeps together, playing and laughing and having a grand visit.

Her father and the other men had been gone a long time. When they came back, they hung their heads, and their shoulders were bowed. She could still remember the shock on her mother's face.

The warriors returned with just one of the captives. They had tried to save them all but the slavers had put up a bitter fight. Five of the warriors had been killed. The slavers had escaped, taking the rest of the women and girls with them.

Falling Star had been the only one rescued. Winona had dashed over to her friend to embrace her and tell her how happy she was that Falling Star was safe and well. But she had stopped short, horrified by the blank look on her cousin's face, by the dead eyes staring back at her.

Her cousin had never been the same afterward. It was the talk of the tribe for quite some time. Falling Star lived another two winters, refusing to eat or drink or tend to herself. Her parents had done the best they could, but in the end she had wasted away to mere skin and bones, and perished.

Ever after that, whenever Winona heard the slavers being mentioned, her insides would knot into a ball and she would clench her fists in impotent rage. She hated them with a passion more intense than any emotion she had ever felt except for her love for Nate and her children. If it were up to her, every slaver alive would be rounded up and thrown alive into a den of rattlesnakes.

And now four of the vilest creatures who ever lived were after her.

Winona dispelled her memories with a toss of her head as she came to the top of the slope. The three men with rifles had reached the sorrel and were in the act of freeing the scrawny man with the bull-whip. She was tempted to use her last shot to bring one of them down but she ran on, saving the ball in case she needed it later on.

Spruce trees and brush closed around her. Winona went a short distance westward, then bore to the north. She made a point of sticking to rocky ground. In the hard soil she left virtually no tracks. When she had been running for quite some time, she halted and crouched.

No sounds of pursuit fell on her ears. Winona felt some of the tension drain from her limbs. The slavers would never find her now. In two days she would reach the village if she held to a brisk pace and traveled half the night.

Winona went on. She avoided dry twigs and limbs which might snag on her dress. Repeatedly, she looked back. So focused was she on the woodland she had covered that it was a while before she woke up to the fact that the forest ahead of her was unnaturally quiet. There should have been birds chirping, squirrels chattering, chipmunks darting about here and there. But it was as if the wildlife had vanished.

Or been cowed into silence.

The thought brought Winona to an abrupt halt. Only three things that she knew of would cause all the animals to go completely quiet. One was a roving grizzly. Another was a cougar, or painter, as the whites called them. The third occasion was when humans clashed in noisy battle.

Winona had seen no sign of a bear or a big cat. And the talus slope was so far behind her that the two shots and the shouting should not have had any effect on the wildlife.

Why, then, were the woods as still as a burial ground?

The flintlock clasped in her left hand, Winona warily advanced. She went around a wide pine, passed a cluster of boulders, and entered a clearing. About to cross, she glanced down and beheld a single footprint lightly etched in the dirt.

Winona would be the first to admit that she was not a seasoned tracker. She did know a fresh track when she saw one, though, and the print in front of her was new. It had been made by a heavy man wearing moccasins unlike any she had ever seen.

Few white men knew that no two Indian tribes made their moccasins the same way. Designs varied widely. Soles were shaped differently. Stitching patterns were also unique.

The Pawnees, for instance, preferred moccasins that were wider in the middle, while the Arapahos liked their moccasins to have wider toes. The Crows sewed their footwear in the shape of a half-moon. The Shoshones made theirs straight.

Winona did not know what to make of the strange footprint. She went to step over it and go on when an odd creaking noise drew her gaze up and to the right. In the time it took her to register the fact that a warrior in a breechcloth had been perched on a low limb and had just sprung, he was on her. She did not see the war club he held until a fraction of an instant before it slammed into the side of her head.

Then the world faded to black.

Chapter Five

Nate King leaped to his feet and ran after the young Bostonian to keep the man from getting them both killed. By all rights he should have caught hold of Simon Ward in just a few seconds. But fate conspired against him, for on his second step his left foot became entangled in grass that Ward had bent down, and before he could help himself, he pitched onto his face. "Wait!" he called out quietly enough not to be heard in the slaver camp. But he might as well have been addressing the wind.

Simon Ward heard. He just had no intention of stopping. His wife was in jeopardy. That was all that mattered. He did not care how many cutthroats he was up against. He was going to save her if it was the last thing he ever did.

The flickering flames of the fire served as a beacon. Simon cocked his new Hawken as he ran and held it close to his chest so it would not become caught in

Black Powder

the grass. He spotted Felicity in the grip of a huge slaver in a coonskin cap who held the tip of a knife to her throat. A red veil seemed to shroud his vision. His blood raged in his veins. He hardly heard the words the man growled.

"If I tell you to eat, you'll eat! Don't pick at your stinking food like a damn bird! We want you healthy, woman. Not half starved."

Simon was almost to the edge of the trampled area. Some of the slavers had heard him and swung toward the grass, but he paid them no heed. Bellowing at the top of his lungs, "Let go of her, you scum!", he hurtled into the open and raised the Hawken to shoot the man in the coonskin cap.

Simultaneously, a breed near the fire stroked the trigger of his own rifle.

Everything happened so fast after that, Simon could not keep track. He heard the boom of the gun at the very same moment he felt a stunning blow to the ribs that knocked all the breath from his lungs. As if he were a feather, he was lifted into the air and hurled back into the grass. He came down head first and was too stunned to do more than feebly lift an arm. Then an iron clamp closed on the scruff of his neck and he was hoisted aloft again. Dimly, he was aware of grass parting in front of his face. It was a shock to realize that he was being carried, and he guessed by whom.

"Let go of me!"

"Shut up!" Nate King hissed. "They're after us, you fool."

"I've got to save her!" Simon protested. "They were going to stab her!" He fought to break loose, flailing his arms and legs.

"Idiot!"

That was the last Simon heard. An anvil smashed

55

into his chin, snapping his head backward. He saw the stars cavort in a dazzling display of pinwheeling lights which lasted only a few seconds. Then something seemed to swallow him whole.

Nate had no choice but to knock the greenhorn out. The slavers were closing on them like a pack of wolves on stricken prey. So far, they had not seen him, only Ward, and he wanted to keep it that way. He had a ten-yard lead, but it taxed his muscles to run at full speed while lugging a grown man under one arm who weighed in excess of 160 pounds.

Risking a glance back, Nate could see eight or nine bobbing heads. They were spread out in an uneven line, some closer to him than others. The rest of the band had stayed behind to safeguard their captive, as he had predicted.

Cutting to the right, Nate bent as low as he could and still go on running, burdened as he was by Ward. It would have been easier on him if he used both hands to hold the unconscious hothead, but he was not about to let go of his rifle.

Abruptly, Nate stopped and squatted. He sucked in a breath and held it. Motionless, silent, he listened to the crash of bodies all around him. A slaver passed within a few yards to his rear. Another went by directly ahead, so close that Nate could have swung his rifle and clipped the man on the head. But he did not budge.

Nate's plan was to lose himself in the high grass. In order to succeed, he had to do the unexpected, the very last thing the slavers would ever expect. So, when the onrushing line had gone on by, he turned *toward* their camp. Picking his way like a stalking painter, it was not long before he glimpsed the camp fire again. Immediately he changed course to the east to circle the trampled tract. Prudently he kept his eyes on those who had stayed behind.

The man called Gregor paced back and forth and glared at everyone and everything. In each huge hand he held a cocked pistol.

Felicity Ward was being held by two of the slavers. Tears drenched her cheeks. Nate figured that she had tried to go to her husband's aid. A rivulet of blood trickled from the right corner of her mouth, but otherwise she appeared unharmed.

Three other slavers stood near their leader, rifles tucked to their shoulders.

When Nate was almost all the way around the camp, he halted and lowered Ward. Simon groaned softly, not loud enough to be overheard, thankfully. With the rifle at his waist, Nate crept closer. If he could, he would like to spirit the woman out of there, but to attempt it now, with the slavers up in arms, would be certain suicide. Her fool of a husband had spoiled whatever hope they had of freeing her anytime soon; the slavers were bound to be on their guard for days.

Shouts broke out to the north. The slavers realized that he had given them the slip, and they were spreading out further in an attempt to run him down.

Nate was not worried. No one could track him in the dark, and it would take an army of men to probe among every blade of grass within 100 yards of the camp. All he had to do was sit tight until they tired and gave up. Then he could slip off unnoticed.

The big question was what to do afterward. Nate felt sorry for the Wards and wanted to help them, but by the same token he did not like the thought of being away from his family for a long time. And it was bound to take days, if not weeks, to rescue Felicity.

Simon sure as blazes couldn't do the job by himself, Nate reflected. The Bostonian would be as helpless as a newborn if left on his own. Just as helpless as Nate had once been, before his uncle and his mentor taught him how to meet the wilderness on its own terms and live to tell of it.

Nate glanced at Simon's prone form. As much as being separated from his family upset him, he couldn't bring himself to go off and leave the Wards. Not when they had no one else to depend on. He would have to do as McNair had done for him and teach Simon enough to get by. And in the bargain he had to come up with a brainstorm to save Mrs. Ward.

Commotion in the camp brought Nate's pondering to an end. Several of the slavers had returned. One was the beefy breed who had been so protective of Gregor. Nate had a hunch it was the same breed who had helped whisk Felicity Ward right out from under her husband's nose.

"We have lost him," the stocky one announced.

"How the hell could that happen, Santiago? You're supposed to be one of the best. What would your pa say?"

Nate knew that it was common practice among some of the Indian tribes living along the border of Mexico for the men to take Spanish names. In fact, the breed did look to be half Mexican. As for the other half, Nate could have sworn there were traces of Apache in the man's face and build. But that could not be. No self-respecting Apache, even one who was not full-blooded, would stoop to ride with slavers.

"I think maybe so there another," Santiago declared in broken, thickly accented English. "He help first get away."

"Two men?" Gregor said. "I only saw the one." He jabbed a pistol at Felicity Ward. "It was her jackass of a husband. And he couldn't give a five-year-old brat the slip in broad daylight. You know that. We dogged him for half a day before we swiped his woman."

"There maybe so two," Santiago insisted. "I not get good look at this other. But him big. Him very fast. Not stupid like husband."

Gregor tucked one of his pistols under his belt and scratched his chin, his brow knit. "I've never known you or your pa to be wrong before. And it is kind of peculiar that a fool like Ward was able to track us all this way. Maybe he had some help."

More slavers had returned. A short white man picked up Simon Ward's rifle, which had fallen at the edge of the grass. The stock of the new Hawken had been shattered. "Hey, lookee here," the man said. "This is why Santiago's shot didn't drop that yak dead."

"Ward is one lucky bastard," Gregor commented. He glanced at the string of horses, then at his captive. "Listen up. I'm not taking chances. Where there are two men, there might be more. So we're pushing on right this minute. I want half of you to saddle the animals and load up the packs while the rest fan out into the grass and stand lookout. Move it."

Whatever else might be said about the slavers, they were a well-knit group who obeyed their leader with military precision.

Nate suddenly saw several head in his general direction. Quickly moving to Ward, he knelt and draped the Bostonian over his left shoulder. Holding his rifle in his right hand, he moved deeper into the grass.

It should have been easy for Nate to keep from being discovered. Had he been by himself, he could have slipped away with the slavers being none the wiser. But Simon Ward chose that very moment to lift his head and give out with a groan loud enough to be heard in Canada.

Reaching back, Nate put a hand over the greenhorn's mouth to stifle another cry. He need not have bothered. The damage had already been done.

"This way!" a slaver shouted. "I just heard them over here!"

"I want their heads!" Gregor roared. "A bigger share to the man who brings them down!"

Nate fled to the southeast, keeping low as before. He had to let go of Ward and when he did, Simon groaned again and tried to slide off him. Halting, Nate slid Ward off his shoulder.

The younger man plopped onto his knees and swayed like one drunk. "What the hell did you do to me, King? My jaw feels broken!"

"You'll be dead if you don't shut up," Nate whispered, once more covering Ward's mouth. "They're after us again."

Simon didn't care. He knew that the trapper had slugged him and he was outraged. The way he saw it, King had prevented him from saving his wife. He was befuddled. He was in pain. So he acted automatically and cocked a fist to pay the mountain man back.

Nate had about run out of patience with the man. Every time he tried to help, Ward gave him a hard time. Rather than try to explain, he punched Simon in the pit of the stomach. Not hard, just enough to cause the man to double over. As Ward did, Nate leaned down and said urgently into his ear, "If you ever want to see Felicity alive again, you had better come to your senses. We have to move, and move fast."

The mention of his wife's name cleared Simon's

head. He was still mad, but he decided to suspend their dispute for the time being and try to stay alive, for her sake. Gulping in air, his gut in agony, he pushed away the arm King extended and snapped, "All right. But don't think I'll forget that twice you've laid a hand on me."

"Come on," Nate said, moving silently off. He winced when Ward stumbled erect and followed, making as much noise as a small herd of buffalo. "Quiet!" he warned.

Off to the left a harsh voice rent the night. "Over this way! I just heard them!"

Whirling, Nate gave Simon a shove to hurry him along just as a shadowy figure bounded through the grass with a Kentucky rifle elevated to fire. Nate had his Hawken leveled at his waist. In a twinkling he cocked it and fired. The rifle belched smoke and lead and the charging slaver keeled over, discharging the Kentucky into the ground as he fell.

All hell broke loose. Shouts erupted. The flash of the two rifles had given the slavers something to shoot at, and they did. Guns cracked in all different directions. Lead balls whizzed every which way.

Nate dropped flat a heartbeat before the gunfire broke out and hoped his greenhorn companion had the presence of mind to do the same. Lethal hornets buzzed overhead and cleaved the grass to his right and his left. In the lull that followed the first volley, he jumped to his feet, scooped up the dead man's Kentucky, and turned.

Simon Ward stood a few feet away. The man had not bothered to duck down. Yet by some miracle he had been spared. "What is the matter with you?" he demanded. "One second you're pushing me, the next you're on the ground. What's it to be? Are we running or fighting?"

"Running," Nate said and gave him another shove just for the hell of it. The crackle of grass alerted him to oncoming slavers who would be on them in less than thirty seconds unless they made themselves scarce.

Simon heard the crash of heavy bodies, too. He realized there were far too many for the frontiersman and him to battle, so for once he did exactly as the trapper wanted and ran as fast as his legs could carry him. He had always considered himself fleet of foot and was confident he could outdistance their pursuers. But he soon found that racing through the grass was much harder than walking through it. The long stems clutched at his legs, seeking to ensnare him. Ruts kept cropping up, nearly tripping him again and again. To compound the situation, he had no idea if he was going in the right direction. In a very short time he worried that he might be running in circles, so he looked back to ask the mountain man. Only King wasn't there.

It had become apparent to Nate in the first few moments of the chase that Ward would not be able to outrun the slavers. Already the killers were much too close. Something had to be done to slow them down, and he was the only one who could do it.

Stopping, Nate squatted, set down his Hawken, and grasped the Kentucky by the barrel. Presently a burly shape loomed in the darkness, streaking after Simon Ward. The man never suspected that Nate was there.

Swinging with all the power in his broad shoulders, Nate clubbed the slaver on the side of the head. The man dropped like a poled ox. Nate threw down the busted Kentucky and picked up the man's rifle instead. Cocking the piece, he spied another slaver and fixed a hasty bead. At his shot, the man screeched, threw up his arms, and toppled.

Another ragged volley blistered the prairie. Nate was on the move before it rang out, taking the extra rifle along to give to Ward. He had not gone far when a man yelled.

"Hank is down! He's bleeding bad!"

"Forget him!" That sounded like Gregor, and he was awfully close. "I want the son of a bitch who shot him! No one is to turn back until then!"

Nate peered through the grass, trying to find the leader. Dropping Gregor was bound to distract the others long enough for Simon and him to make their escape. But the wily giant did not show himself.

Hastening on, Nate soon suspected that Simon must have changed course. He straightened to his full height to see above the tops of the grass, but he could not spot Ward anywhere ahead of him. With a start, he guessed that Simon had gotten all turned around and even then might be heading straight into the arms of the slavers. Pivoting, Nate headed back to save the greenhorn from his own incompetence.

Unknown to the frontiersman, not a dozen feet away Simon Ward huddled low in the grass. He had glimpsed a large figure to his rear, taken it for a slaver, and gone to ground. Now, as he heard the man move off, he smiled at his cleverness. It proved that he wasn't as helpless as Nate King liked to think.

Simon waited until he was sure the man had gone beyond earshot, then he rose and went on. He moved slowly. His right elbow brushed an object at his waist and he almost laughed out loud when he realized he still had both pistols and his butcher knife. In all the excitement, he had forgotten about them.

It reassured Simon to fill each hand with a heavy flintlock. Now he could defend himself. Using one of the pistols to part the grass as he had seen King do earlier, he hiked for several minutes. No more shouts broke out behind him. Nor did he hear anyone moving nearby.

Simon chuckled to himself. The high and mighty Nate King would be shocked to learn that he had given the slavers the slip all by his lonesome. Maybe, at last, King would regard him with a smidgen of respect. Simon didn't know exactly why that should matter to him, but it did. He had never wanted to impress any man as much as he wanted to impress the frontiersman. Maybe it was because, deep down, he liked King, and it would be nice if King liked him, too.

The object of Simon Ward's train of thought was at that very moment crouched within spitting distance of several slavers. He had discarded the extra rifle and held a cocked pistol. The slavers were talking in hushed tones, but he heard every word clearly.

"Two men dead, Gregor. Don't get riled at me, but I think we should give it up and get the blazes out of here before we lose any more. It's a mighty long ride between here and Texas. What with all the hostiles hereabouts, we need every man we've got."

The slaver leader growled like an irate bear. "Damn that greenhorn and his partner all to hell! It galls me to let them get away. But you've got a point, Jenks."

"What about Hank, Pedor and Vin?" asked the third man. "Can we tote them back now?"

"Do it," Gregor said.

Nate lowered onto his stomach as more slavers joined the trio. Orders were issued. The two men he had shot and the one he had knocked out were carted off. Nate did not move until the tramp of feet dwindled. Then he rose and cat-footed in their wake, seeking Simon Ward.

It would be totally in keeping with the Bostonian's character for Simon to be working his way back to the slaver camp to make another attempt to free Felicity. Ward wouldn't care that he didn't have a snowball's chance in Hades of whisking her away by himself. He would get himself rubbed out and leave her worse off than she had been before.

Nate hoped to keep that from happening. Every few yards he would rise and risk being spotted so he could scan the prairie on all sides. If Ward was out there, for once the man was using his head and not showing himself.

In the distance the fire twinkled. The chase had covered close to 500 yards, more than Nate had figured. He dropped down when one of the slavers turned, the man's pale face like a tiny moon against the black backdrop of the plain.

Suddenly the grass to Nate's right quivered. Since all the slavers were in front of him, he thought it was Simon Ward and shifted with a smile of greeting on his face. Almost too late he saw the near naked figure of the half-breed and the dull glint of steel in the warrior's right hand.

Santiago was like greased lightning. He lunged and stabbed and would have buried his blade in the frontiersman's chest had Nate not been holding his rifle in front of him. As it was, in the dark Santiago misjudged the position of the barrel and his knife glanced off it.

Nate felt the blade tear into his shirt close to the ribs even as he threw himself backward. He tried to level the Hawken, but Santiago was on him before he could. The butcher knife cleaved the air. Nate had to let go of the rifle to grab the breed's stout wrist. The next moment they were on the ground, grappling, rolling back and forth as Santiago strained to thrust his blade into Nate and Nate strained to keep the knife at bay.

The breed was tremendously strong, one of the strongest men Nate had ever fought. Their faces were inches apart, and he could see the feral gleam of bloodlust in Santiago's dark eyes. Flipping to the right, he heaved, trying to keep the warrior off balance long enough for him to draw his own knife. As his hand closed on the hilt, the breed's hand closed on his wrist.

Locked together, they exerted their sinews to the utmost. Nate blocked a knee to the groin and countered with a head butt to the jaw, which rocked Santiago backward. But instead of weakening, Santiago roared like a berserk grizzly, opened his mouth wide, and swooped his gleaming teeth toward Nate's throat.

In the nick of time, Nate jerked his head to one side. The breed's teeth sheared into the fleshy part of his shoulder instead of the soft tissue in his neck. Excruciating anguish rippled down his body. Blood splattered his skin. Nate threw himself backward to break Santiago's grip and nearly cried out when his shoulder was torn open.

Santiago reared up, a patch of buckskin and a flap of skin hanging from his bloody lips. He spat them out, bent back his head, and howled like a demented coyote.

Nate drove his forehead into the breed's gut. It was like slamming into a wall. His blow had no effect on Santiago, but it did make Nate's senses spin.

Another second, and everything went from bad to worse.

Santiago wrenched his knife arm loose and arced it on high to deliver a final blow, while from the vicinity of the camp raced other slavers. One killer shouted "Hold on, Santiago! We're on our way!"

But the breed was not about to wait. Venting a howl of savage glee, he stabbed downward.

Chapter Six

It was night when Winona King revived. She didn't open her eyes right away, but she knew it was dark by the cool air and the brisk northwesterly breeze. That, and the small fire crackling a few feet away.

Winona listened to what was going on around her. Two men were talking in Spanish while a third hummed softly to himself. They had to be slavers, she deduced. But that meant the Indian who had taken her by surprise was one of the band.

As if to confirm her hunch, a low, clipped voice spoke in the tongue of her husband. "Woman awake, Ricket. She pretend not be."

"Is that a fact, Chipota?" answered the voice of the grizzled lodgepole in the bearskin hat. "Well, let's test her and see."

Winona heard someone chuckle. Since they

knew she had come around, she was about to open her eyes when searing agony lanced her left arm. Sitting bolt upright, she bit her lip to keep from crying out and glared at the source of her pain.

Ricket had taken a burning brand from the fire and pressed it against her wrist. Casting it down, he cackled and slapped his thigh. "You were right, Chipota, just like always. How in the world did you know?"

The Indian in the breechcloth squatted on the other side of the fire from Winona. In its glow she could note details she had missed earlier. He was an older warrior, in his fifties or early sixties, with wide grey streaks in his long hair. "Her breathing not same," he explained.

"Sharp ears you've got there," Ricket said. "Too bad your sprout ain't along. He'd be right proud of you."

Chipota shifted his cold gaze from the fire to the grizzled slaver. "Santiago not sprout," he said flatly.

Ricket laughed. "Don't get your dander up, Injun. It's not an insult to call someone a sprout. All I meant is that he's a heap younger than you. And you can't fault me there."

The warrior grunted.

Winona rubbed the charred circle of skin where the brand had burned her and surveyed the camp. Five horses, including her mare, were off to the right, tied in a string. Two other slavers were playing cards to her left, while the fifth man kept busy cleaning a pistol. She was surprised that they had not had the foresight to bind her. It was a mistake they would rue.

"So how are you feelin', squaw?" Ricket addressed her. "That wallop on the head rattle your brains any?"

"I am fine," Winona said, when in truth her temples throbbed and she felt a little queasy.

"Good. We don't want the merchandise damaged, if you get my drift. We've got special plans for a woman of your caliber. Yessiree."

"You are slavers," Winona bluntly declared.

The grizzled scourge of the mountains and plains snickered. "Nothin' gets past you, does it, squaw? Yes, we are. And you know what that means. So just behave yourself and we'll get along right fine. Act up, and you'll sure as hell regret it. I can guarantee."

Winona lifted her chin in defiance. "My name is Winona King, slaver. And it is you who will regret it when my husband learns of what you have done. Grizzly Killer will not rest until he has tracked you down and made you pay."

"Grizzly Killer, is it?" Ricket said. "I'll admit that's some handle. Maybe around these parts it puts the fear of the Almighty into those who might raise a hand against you, but it doesn't mean diddly to us, squaw."

"It will."

Ricket squinted at her and gnawed on his lower lip. "You speak the white tongue better than most whites I know. Which means this Grizzly Killer of yours has to be white himself. What's his Christian name, woman?"

"Nate King," Winona said. She was proud of the fact that tales of her man's exploits had spread far beyond the Rocky Mountains, just like those of men like Jim Bridger, Kit Carson and Shakespeare McNair. She half hoped the slavers had heard of him, too. It might dispose them toward letting her go rather than face Nate's wrath.

"Can't say as the name is familiar," Ricket said, dashing fleeting hope on the hard rocks of reality. "I'll take it he's a trapper. Company man or free?"

"Free."

"How long has he been livin' in the wild? A short while?"

"As many winters as you have fingers and thumbs."

"Damn."

A slaver sporting a belly the size of a cooking pot raised his head from the five cards in his hand. "What's with all the questions, Ricket? Who cares about her husband? It wouldn't matter if he was Andrew Jackson himself. She's ours now, and that's all that counts."

The older man shook his head in mild reproach. "Owens, I swear that you don't have the brains God gave a turnip. If you did, you'd have guessed that I was askin' questions to find out if her man is as tough as she claims. And it sounds like he is."

"Oh?"

"Do I have to spell it out for you? King has lived in the mountains, among the Indians, for over *ten years*. Think about that. There aren't many men who can make the same claim. Most die within a year or two up in the high country." Ricket paused to spit. "That makes this Nate King the real McCoy, a livin', breathin' fire-in-his-innards mountain man. And they can be meaner than hell when they get riled."

Owens yawned to show how impressed he was.

"Poke fun at me all you want to," Ricket said, "But I know what I'm talkin' about. Remember what Hugh Glass done."

"Who?"

Ricket rolled his eyes skyward. "Lord, spare me from peckerwoods who think with their hind ends." He folded his arms. "Hugh Glass is a mountain man. One time he got himself mauled something terrible by a big old she-bear. He was so torn up, his partners left him for dead. They took his rifle, his knife, everything. And off they went."

"And people say we're rotten to the core," another slaver joked.

"Pay attention," Ricket snapped. "You see, Glass didn't die. He crawled for days until he came on a dead buffalo swarming with buzzards and coyotes. Using nothin' but a stick, he chased them off and ate the meat himself. That gave him the strength to keep on going. Hundreds of miles he traveled, until he caught up with the men who had done him wrong."

Owens laid down a card. "So what's the point, old man?"

"If you don't know, it's hopeless."

Suddenly Chipota rose. "I keep watch. This night. All nights. Grizzly Killer come, I kill." So saying, he wagged his war club a few times, then moved off into the trees without making a sound.

Winona wished now that she had not told them about Nate. The gray-haired warrior would prove a formidable adversary, even for him. Her worry must have shown, because Ricket grinned at her and nodded at the spot where the warrior had disappeared.

"Chipota is the best there is at what he does, squaw. I bet you've never seen his like before."

"He reminds me of the Apaches," Winona said.

Ricket blinked. "You've been down in their neck of the woods? That's mighty interestin'. And you're danged near right. Chipota is a Lipan. His people live in the west part of Texas, mostly. The way he tells it, a long time ago the Lipans broke off from the rest of the Apaches and took to livin' by themselves. Why, nobody rightly knows."

"A true Apache would never ride with the likes of you."

"In most cases, no. But old Chipota got himself tossed out of the tribe for killin' another Lipan. He had nowhere else to go." The slaver snickered. "Him and that breed son of his were wanderin' across the Staked Plain when we came on them. Our boss could have had us shoot them down like dogs, but Gregor is a savvy cuss. He offered to let them throw in with our outfit, and Chipota agreed."

The revelation surprised Winona. "You are not the leader of the slavers? Another is?"

The man called Owens and another one chuckled. "Do you really reckon we'd be dumb enough to have an old coot like him tell us what to do?" the former declared. "Hell, squaw. We wouldn't follow him to the outhouse."

Ricket frowned. "Pay him no mind, missy. Gregor, our boss, thinks right highly of me. That's why he put me in charge of this bunch here when we separated to go woman huntin'. Now that we've got you, we'll head for the rendezvous spot. Should take us about two days, maybe three, to get there."

The news that there were more slavers was disheartening, but Winona did not show it. She could only keep her fingers crossed, as Nate would say, that he did not come alone to find her. Her uncle and Touch The Clouds would probably join him, as might several of his close friends. There should be more than enough to deal with the slavers. Then she remembered what had happened to her cousin, and she had to suppress a surge of panic.

"The rules are simple, squaw," Ricket continued. "You do what we say when we say it. You don't sass us. You don't ever try to escape. Behave yourself, and we'll get along right fine. The choice is yours."

Winona had figured as much. They needed to understand one thing, though. "I have my own rules, as you call them. If any of you lay a hand on me, I will scratch your eyes out. If you try to hold me down, I will tear your face open with my teeth. And if you tie me and then have your way, the very first time I am freed, I will do all in my power to kill you."

"Feisty wench, ain't you?" Ricket quipped. "Well, don't fret yourself on that score, squaw. Gregor is the one who decides if we get to or not. He'd shoot any of us stupid enough to take a taste without his say-so. You're safe enough until we hook up with him."

Winona did not like the lustful smirk the scrawny man wore. It hinted that she was in for a rude lesson when they rendezvoued with the leader. But what she had told him applied to this Gregor as well. If they thought she was bluffing, they would learn the hard way that she was not.

It was despicable that any woman should ever be forced to give herself to a man she did not want to be with. Or to do it for money, as Nate said some white women did. It was the very worst of violations. It degraded women to their core. It made them out to be like dogs, to be abused as their masters saw fit.

Winona had only ever shared her body with one

man. Long ago she had decided that he was the only one for her. She would never share herself with anyone else. And if the slavers thought differently, she would show them that she would rather die than let them dishonor her.

Simon Ward did not move until he was certain none of the slavers were anywhere near him. Then he rose and stood on the tips of his toes, trying to catch sight of the mountain man. He had no luck.

When a few more minutes went by and still Nate King failed to appear, Simon worried that something terrible had happened. As hard as it was for Simon to believe, it was possible that one of the slavers had taken the trapper by surprise and slit his throat before he could cry out.

Simon no longer deluded himself about his chances of saving Felicity without the frontiersman's help. He had nearly gotten himself killed by rushing into the slaver camp the way he had done. As it was, he had a nasty pain in the ribs on his left side where something, perhaps a bullet, had creased him. He'd felt under his shirt, but there was no blood or furrow.

His sore jaw only compounded Simon's misery. He rubbed it while mulling what to do and finally opted to slink back toward the camp to see if he could find Nate King. Holding the pistol out in front of him, Simon slowly moved forward.

In a short while Simon thought he heard low voices. Halting, he tried to make sense of the words but they were too faint. A lot of rustling ensued, fading rapidly toward the camp. The slavers were heading back, apparently.

Encouraged, Simon went on. He had not gone far when a racket broke out about 50 feet to the east of his position. It sounded as if a bull buffalo were barreling across the prairie. On listening closely, he guessed that it had to be two men in a tussle. He heard their grunts, heard the thud of a fist striking home.

Daring to rise on his toes once more, Simon saw a black silhouette rear up out of the grass. He could not make out many details. That the man was immensely powerful was proven by the struggling figure he had hoisted overhead. For a few heartbeats the tableau was frozen, then the big man swept the figure downward and there was a crack so loud it resembled the retort of a pistol. But Simon knew the truth. It had been a human spine breaking.

A slew of shouts signified that the slavers had heard the ruckus and were on their way back. "There!" one yelled. "There he is! I want his hide!"

Simon dropped down, but not before seeing the big man sprint off to the southeast. He figured that it had to be Nate King, but there was nothing he could do to help the trapper out. A single shot would draw the slavers like flies to honey. It was better for him to lay low until the hubbub died down.

So that was exactly what Simon Ward did. More shots thundered. After one of them, a gruff voice cried, "I think I nailed him! Close in! We've got the bastard now!"

Despair gnawed at Simon's soul at the thought of losing the frontiersman. He was so strongly tempted to leap up and blaze away that he had to will himself to stay right where he was for the time being.

The hunt seemed to go on forever. Several times slavers passed close to where Simon lay on his stomach, but none came close enough to spot him. He was relieved when at length someone bellowed that the search was over and the slavers hurried toward their camp.

A lot of noise wafted on the breeze. The clink of a tin pot, the rasp of a knife blade on a whetstone, the whinny of horses and the barked orders of the slaver leader.

Simon was shocked. By the sound of things, the cutthroats were preparing to head on out. Felicity would be toted along whether she wanted to be or not. And it would take him quite some time to catch up since his bay was close to a mile away.

Desperate measures were called for. Simon stalked toward the trampled area. There might be some means of freeing her if he stayed alert and seized the moment.

The camp swarmed with activity. Most of the animals had either been saddled or had packs thrown on them. Some slavers were mounted. Others were busy tying on more supplies. A huge man who had to be the leader stood near Felicity, along with a portly man in buckskins and a Mexican in a *sombrero*.

Simon's heart ached at the sight of his wife. She hung her head low, despondent, her arms limp at her sides. No one was holding her, but she made no attempt to flee. It was as if all the life had been drained from her except for that needed to draw breath. Simon did not comprehend why until he drew closer.

The leader was talking. "—-pout all you want to, woman, it won't change a thing. Your husband is dead. The sooner you face that fact, the better. As for the big guy who was with him, that jasper took a ball and has crawled off somewhere to die."

Simon was devastated on two counts. First, the vile slaver lied through his teeth about Simon being killed. The only reason Simon could think of for the slaver to do it was to break Felicity's spirit so she would go along meekly with whatever the man wanted.

Second, the news that Nate King had been shot shook him to his core. He needed the mountain man more than ever.

Then the notion came over Simon that maybe the bearish leader was lying about Nate, too. The frontiersman was as tough as twopenny nails. More than likely he had given the band the slip. Or so Simon prayed.

Soon the remaining horses were saddled and the remaining packs were tied on. One of the slavers extinguished the fire while the rest filed out of the camp, bearing due south.

Simon had blundered. In his eagerness to see Felicity, he had snuck within a few steps of the end of the grass. Now, with the riders passing by within a dozen paces of his hiding place, he stood in peril of being seen.

Hunkering, Simon tensed, awaiting the outcry that would bring the band swooping down on him like buzzards to a fresh kill. It was that very moment that the fire went out, blanketing him in welcome darkness. Unless the wind shifted, he just might avoid being noticed.

The slavers rode off in single file, some in pairs. In the forefront trotted the huge leader. In his left hand was the lead rope to the gelding Felicity had been thrown onto. Her ankles had been lashed together under the animal's belly to keep her from jumping down and running off.

It tore Simon in half to have to squat there

78

while the love of his life was led away by men every bit as vicious as the grizzlies he had heard so much about. Tears formed in the corners of his eyes as he waged an inner tug of war with his emotions. Part of him wanted to break down and blubber as he invariably did in times of stress. The other part of him wanted to be strong, to demonstrate the gumption that a grown man should have.

Gradually the creak of leather and the clop of hooves faded. Simon forlornly stood and sighed. "Felicity," he said softly. "My darling."

The only answer was the whisper of wind and the rustle of grass.

Simon let down the hammer on the pistol and shoved it under his belt. He was about to go look for Nate King when he spied a trio of black forms in the middle of the trampled circle.

Slavers! Simon's mind screamed. They had tricked him and left three men behind to fill him with lead when he showed himself. But they were not going to get him without a fight! Drawing both pistols, Simon burst into the open and took aim at the closest form. He was scared witless, but he was determined to resist. Felicity would know that he had gone down fighting on her behalf, which might lessen the sting of his failure to protect her.

The Bostonian had his fingers on the triggers and was beginning to squeeze when something about the three forms struck him as being extremely peculiar.

They were on their backs, one right next to the other. Not one had moved, even when he dashed out of the grass.

Holding his fire, Simon edged nearer. Inky puddles that were spreading under two of the men explained why they were so lifeless. He stopped next to the first and lowered his pistols.

One was white, another Mexican, the third either an Indian or a half-breed.

The white man had been shot in the sternum. The ball had cored his chest and exited high on the right shoulder, leaving a hole the size of Simon's fist.

The Mexican had also been shot, but in the face. The bullet had entered low on the left cheek, passed completely through the skull, and blown out a ragged cavity above the right ear. Of the two men, this one bled the most, bits and pieces of brain mixed with his blood.

Strangely enough, the Indian's body bore no evidence of a bullet or knife wound. Simon did note that the man's arms were bent at an unnatural angle, as if each were busted at the shoulders. It took him a few moments to conclude that it wasn't the arms, but the *spine* that had been broken, and he remembered the fight he had observed. This, then, was the man Nate King had snapped over a knee as other men might snap broomsticks.

But where was King now?

Fueled by that burning question, Simon hastened back into the sea of grass. It upset him that the trapper had not appeared after the slavers departed, and he began to dread that the leader had not been lying, that the slavers really had shot the mountain man.

Simon cupped a hand to his mouth and called out softly, "Mr. King? Nate? Where are you?"

To the west a wolf wailed its lonesome lament and received the same reply Simon did: silence.

He nervously tapped his foot, unable to decide whether he should search for the trapper or go retrieve their horses. It troubled him, the animals being left unguarded. Nighttime, he had been told, was when most big predators, like bears and cats, were abroad.

Suddenly, as if to show how right he was, a rumbling growl pierced the plain. It was much too close for comfort. Simon's breath quickened. He could not tell where the sound came from, so he turned in a complete circle, trying to spy the source. If a hungry grizzly had caught his scent, he was as good as dead. The old-timers in St. Louis had stressed that trying to drop a griz using a pistol was an exercise in futility unless the bear was close enough to touch. Of course, if one of the mighty behemoths was that close, it would be on a man before he could get off a shot.

A loud crunch brought goosebumps to Simon's flesh. Something was coming toward him. He saw its bulky shape, saw stems bending to its great weight. Overcome by terror, he back-pedaled and tried to aim the flintlocks. To his dismay, his hands shook so badly that he could not hold the barrels steady.

In another moment the shape lurched into full view. Indescribable relief flooded through Simon as he recognized Nate King. But his joy was short-lived, for the mountain man uttered a groan and fell with a thud at his very feet.

Chapter Seven

Felicity Ward had never know true sorrow until now.

Her life had been enough of an ordeal making the arduous trek west to satisfy her husband's craving for adventure. It had turned into a nightmare when the pair of smelly, greasy slavers had pounced on her just as she was about to remove her underclothes. The nightmare had become a living hell as the pair hustled her southward, the man called Gregor cuffing her whenever she opened her mouth and cursing her in the most horrid language imaginable.

Still, Felicity had entertained hope. She knew her husband would not abandon her to her fate. She looked for him to show up sooner or later and save her from the loathsome clutches of the despicable crew of perverts.

Then Felicity's fondest desire had come true.

Simon had appeared—only to be shot the instant he did. And now, according to her tormentors, her husband was dead, lying back on the prairie, riddled by bullets.

It was more than Felicity could endure.

For the first time since she was ten years old, Felicity cried. She had never been one of those women who wept over every little setback life had to offer, but this proved too much.

Despite her small size and seeming frailty, inwardly Felicity had strength few of her peers could match. It was this strength that had given her the courage to forsake all that she knew. It was this strength that had sustained her during the ungodly long journey from Boston to the Rockies. It was this strength she had relied on to see her through the many long years ahead of living high up in the remote recesses of the mountains, cut off from the civilization she so liked, deprived of the comfort of family and friends.

And why had Felicity been so willing to give up all that was safe and secure and familiar? For the same reason women had been making similar sacrifices since the dawn of time, for the love of her man.

Oh, Felicity knew that Simon was more bluster than he would ever admit. She knew that he let his imagination run rampant over his common sense. In short, she knew all his flaws, but she loved him anyway.

In that regard Felicity was like many of her sisters. Secretly, she had never considered herself truly attractive or witty or charming, or any of the other things Simon constantly told her she was. Secretly, she had doubted that she would ever marry, that any man would think her worthy of being a lifelong mate.

So when Simon Ward had shown an interest in her, Felicity had been surprised. When he had courted her, she had been amazed. And when he had proposed, she had been so grateful for his ardent love that his flaws paled in comparison.

Oh, Simon! Felicity mentally shrieked. Squeezing her eyes tight, she shut off the flow of tears. Reaching deep down into the heart of her being, she found her flickering strength and clung to it as a drowning person would cling to a floating log.

Then hooves pounded beside the gelding, and Felicity looked up to discover that Gregor had dropped back to ride next to her. She dabbed at her cheeks and held her head high.

The slaver chortled. "Still have some grit left, do you? Well, we'll rid you of that soon enough, woman. By the time we reach Texas, you'll lick my feet clean every morning and love doing it."

"Never!" Felicity declared, revolted.

"Think so?" Gregor's smile was that of a man supremely sure he was right. "Others have felt the same as you. More than I could count. And each and every one of them learned the error of their ways in time. That's the key to what I do. Time. I have all the time in the world to break you." His smile widened. "Even the wildest mustang will tame down eventually."

Felicity refused to be cowed. "I pray that you rot in Hell, you devil. If anyone has ever deserved eternal punishment, it's you."

The huge man found that amusing also. "Don't tell me. I've got another Christian on my hands. Tell me, Christian, where's this almighty God of yours? Why doesn't lightning crash down out of the sky and fry me for daring to lay a finger on you?" Gregor leaned toward her. "I'll tell you why, bitch. It's because there is no God. I'm proof of that."

"You flatter yourself," Felicity said, and was rocked by a slap to the face that left her cheek burning as if from a hundred bee stings.

"I warned you before. Don't insult me or you'll regret it." Gregor clucked to his mount and pulled ahead.

Felicity Ward watched him, her fists clenched so hard that her knuckles were white. There was the one to blame for her plight. There was the brute responsible for the death of the man she loved. And he was the one she was going to kill. The others would probably tear her to pieces afterward. But so what? She would gladly give her life to avenge her husband.

All Felicity needed was for any of the slavers to lower their guard for the few moments it would take her to grab a pistol or a knife.

Then Gregor would learn the truth the hard way. There was a Hell. And he was going to burn in it forever.

At that moment, many miles to the northwest, another woman was about to defy another band of slavers.

Winona King was not about to meekly do as Ricket wanted. His threats were wasted on her. She had fought Apaches, Blackfeet and grizzlies. She had survived flash floods, fire and drought. All of which had molded her into someone able to hold her own against anyone, anywhere.

So no sooner did three of the four slavers fall

asleep than Winona cracked her eyelids and
awaited her chance. She had turned in hours ago,
pretending to be asleep all that time. With the Lipan off in the forest, no one had been the wiser.

The Lipan. He was the one Winona had to
keep her eyes skinned for, the one who could
ruin her escape. She had no way of knowing
where he was. He might be off in the trees, he
might be so close that she could throw a pebble
and hit him. Regardless, she had to try to get
away now, before she was taken even farther
from Shoshone territory.

Owens was the slaver standing guard. Or,
rather, sitting guard, because once the others had
commenced snoring he had plunked himself on a
log and pulled his deck of cards from a shirt
pocket. He had his back to the fire, and to her.

Winona glanced at each of the others in turn.
Ricket had his mouth wide enough to snare low-
flying birds. His snore was a throaty rumble worthy of a bear. It drowned out the snoring of the
remaining pair, one of whom had covered his
head with the top of his blanket.

Slowly, Winona tucked her legs to her chest,
eased onto her hands and knees, and pushed to
her feet. None of the sleepers reacted. Owens
went on playing his card game. Solitaire. Nate
had taught her how to play, but she had never
been fond of it—not like she was of checkers or
her very favorite, chess.

Winona needed a weapon. The slavers had gone
to bed fully armed, with their rifles at their sides.
Trying to slide one out from under a blanket
would be too risky.

Stacked near the fire was enough wood to last
the night. Among the broken limbs lay a short,

thick piece, which would do nicely.

Never taking her eyes off Owens, Winona stooped and carefully lifted a few branches aside to get at the one she wanted. She quietly set each down to her left. Once, she froze as Owens leaned back and stretched. His head started to twist, and for a few awful moments, it appeared that he would turn and see her. But he was only relieving a kink in his neck.

The slaver bent over his cards again. Winona picked up the limb she wanted. Her hand barely fit around it. Sliding both hands to one end, she moved toward the log.

Again Owens glanced up. Again Winona stopped. He gazed at the same point in the forest, as if he had heard or sensed something there. Could it be the Lipan? Winona wondered. If so, the warrior was bound to thwart her escape attempt. But she had to see it through. She owed it to her loved ones. She owed it to herself.

Another long stride put Winona directly behind Owens. He had picked up the deck and was shuffling his cards. Winona raised her club as high as it would go, tensed every muscle in her body, and brought the branch down on the crown of Owens's head.

The thud of the blow landing was so loud that Winona was certain the others would hear. But they slumbered blissfully on as Owens oozed to the ground and lay with his hands and feet twitching.

Winona lost no time. Placing the branch down, she snatched a pistol from under the slaver's belt and was about to do the same with his butcher knife when her intuition blared. She looked into the trees at the same spot Owens had, and her blood·chilled.

Rushing toward the camp was a stocky figure. His features were dappled by darkness, but Winona did not have to see them to know who it was.

Four long strides brought Winona to the pines along the north edge of the clearing. As the night closed around her, a series of piercing yips roused the slavers. Their jumbled voices rose into enraged bellows, and the noisiest of them all was Ricket. His next words were as clear as could be.

"After her, Chipota! Fetch her back, you hear! I want that bitch!"

Winona was going as fast as she could. She regretted that the Lipan had showed up before she could reach the horses and untie the mare. It would take her a week or more to reach the Shoshone village on foot, provided that she eluded the slavers.

The darkness worked in Winona's favor. It not only hid her, it hid her footprints. The Lipan would not be able to track her. But that did not mean that escaping would be easy. The warrior's senses were bound to be as sharp as a cougar's. Giving him the slip would tax her skill to the utmost.

Suddenly halting, Winona crouched and listened. To her rear rose the patter of moccasins, a patter that died just seconds after she stopped. She held her breath, knowing that the Lipan was no more than thirty feet away and waiting for her to make a sound, any sound.

Back in the clearing, Ricket was cursing a blue streak. He called Owens every foul name Winona had ever heard white men use, and many she did not know besides. His tantrum was to her benefit. So long as he kept ranting and raving, the Lipan would not be able to hear much. Certainly not the whisper of movement as she lowered herself to the ground and snaked through the undergrowth.

Ricket didn't seem to know when to shut up. Winona smiled at the man's stupidity. She covered a score of yards, then rose and continued on foot, confident that for the moment she had given the warrior the slip. After traveling another twenty yards, she broke into a run.

Soon the swearing faded away. All Winona heard now were typical night sounds; the rustling of trees by the wind, the cries of animals, both hunters and hunted, and the rasp of her own breath in her lungs. She came to a hill and bore to the right rather than slow herself down by going up and over.

Winona settled into a steady rhythm. Her sole hope lay in putting a lot of distance behind her before dawn. Once the sun rose, the Lipan would be on her trail like a wolf on the scent of a fleeing doe. She hoped that she would stumble on a stream long before then. Not even an Apache could track someone through running water.

As time went by and there was no evidence of pursuit, Winona felt the tension drain from her body. She also felt fingers of fatigue pluck at her mind. The blow to her head was having lingering effects. Every now and then a woozy sensation made her want to stop and rest, but she refused to give in to weakness. Not when her life hung in the balance.

All went well until Winona crossed a meadow and entered another belt of pines. Above her a roosting bird let out with raucous cries of alarm, evidently mistaking her for a predator. It was a jay, and it quieted down a minute later. But the harm had been done.

At high altitude sound carried much farther than down on the lowlands. This was true in the foothills as well, especially at night when the air was crisp and the wind usually stronger.

Winona knew that the Lipan had heard. He would suspect the cause and he would come investigate. She had to get out of there, and quickly.

Although she was winded, Winona steeled her legs and sprinted for hundreds of feet. Obstacles were hard to perceive in the dark, and she nearly collided with a log. Another time a low limb nearly ripped her face. When she could sprint no longer, she slowed to a walk.

Every so often Winona stopped and cocked her head. No alien sounds fell on her ears, but she knew better than to think the Lipan would make any. Apaches were like ghosts when they wanted to be. Their stamina, their speed, their stealth exceeded that of her own people. Which was understandable given that Apaches lived for war. For untold generations their creed had been to kill without being killed, to steal without being caught.

It was an hour or so after fleeing the clearing that Winona finally had to rest. The dizziness had returned, and with it a bout of nausea. She shuffled to a flat boulder and sank down, her arms between her legs, facing her back trail.

Nothing moved out there.

Yet.

As would any woman devoted to her family,

Black Powder

Winona turned her thoughts to her husband and her precious children. She missed them terribly and wished she was with them at that moment, snug and warm in their tepee.

Winona knew of other Shoshone women who had taken white men as mates, only to have their husbands go off and leave them once the men tired of trapping. Some of those women had given their husbands children. Seeing them always filled her heart with a secret dread that one day Nate would do the same to her, although deep down she knew that he never would.

Winona counted herself fortunate that Grizzly Killer was the exception to the rule. He was a man of firm beliefs who held to his commitments as rigidly as iron. He loved her and Zach and Evelyn and would never abandon them, come what may.

It saddened her to think that she might never see any of them again. They were the joys of her eye, her reasons for living. Without them her life would be an empty shell. If it were not for—

Winona stiffened, annoyed that she had let her attention wander when she had to stay fully alert. She anxiously scanned the forest, without result. Taking a breath, she shoved upright and went on.

Soon Winona came to a wide ravine. She stared in frustration at the opposite rim 25 feet away. There was no choice but to go around. Turning to the west, she stayed close to the edge so that when she reached the end, she would know it right away.

A sprawling thicket barred Winona's path. Rather than work her way around it, she elected to squeeze past on a narrow strip of bare earth bordering the steep drop. Wedging the pistol under her sash to free both hands, she turned so that her back was to the ravine and sidled onto the strip.

By clasping the ends of thin limbs for balance, Winona briskly skirted over half the thicket. Suddenly the ground under her buckled. She felt it start to give and tried to throw herself to the right, but gravity would not be denied.

It was a horrible feeling, plummeting into the ravine in the dark with no idea of how far it was to the bottom or what lay below. Winona pictured her body being dashed to broken ruin on jagged boulders or impaled by a tree limb.

Then Winona hit. Her shoulders slammed onto barren ground and she found herself tumbling down an incline, going faster and faster. In vain she thrust out her hands to arrest her momentum, but all she accomplished was to tear skin from her palms and break several nails.

Her hip struck a small boulder. Winona nearly cried out. She did a cartwheel and crashed down onto her back. Dust spewed over her face, getting into her eyes and nose as she shot lower.

As abruptly as the fall had begun, it ended. Winona rammed into something hard, something big, and a black fog engulfed her. Vaguely, she heard pebbles and loose dirt raining down around her. For a while after that the night was still.

With a start, Winona came to. She was on her left side. Her left leg throbbed almost unbearably. Sitting up, she bit her lower lip to keep from crying out when the agony grew much worse. Fearing that she had broken a bone, she probed the leg and located a spot exquisitely tender to the lightest touch. She was bruised and gashed but nothing had busted.

Close by was another boulder. Propping herself against it, Winona painfully rose. She stared bleakly at the ravine walls. They were much too steep for her to climb. Unless there was another way out, she was trapped as effectively as if she had placed her foot into the serrated steel jaws of a bear trap.

But Winona refused to let despair sap her will. Fighting the torment, she limped westward. The floor of the ravine was littered with boulders and dead limbs, which had fallen from above. She rounded a slab of rock, stopping short at the sight of pale bones.

It was the skeleton of a deer, a buck. Winona figured that the animal had somehow blundered over the rim and fallen to its death. The only other possibility, that the buck had survived but had been unable to climb back out and had starved to death, was too unnerving to contemplate.

A bend loomed ahead. Winona paused to catch her breath. She idly gazed upward—and her heart skipped a beat. Framed against the backdrop of stars was the outline of a stocky human figure.

It had to be the Lipan.

Winona clawed at her waist for the pistol, only to learn it was not there. It had undoubtedly slipped loose when she fell. Now she was defenseless as well as boxed in. Her plight was next to hopeless, but still she would not admit defeat. Where there was life, there was hope.

The figure disappeared. Winona hurried on as best she was able, eager to find a way out of the ravine before the Lipan found a way down. She hustled around the bend and couldn't believe her eyes.

To the left the ravine wall ran another dozen yards but to the right the ravine ended, blending seamlessly into the forest. A tangle of brush and trees offered haven from the warrior. Pivoting on a heel, she made off to the north, passing several trees. At the next one she stopped to look back.

At that exact moment the Lipan emerged from the vegetation flanking the other side of the ravine. Apparently he thought that she was still in there, because he flattened against the wall and stalked in after her.

Winona dared not linger. The warrior would realize his mistake all too soon. She noticed a long limb lying next to the trunk. It made an ideal crutch.

Half running, half hopping, Winona fled. Her battered body protested every step. Her left leg would have buckled several times if not for the limb. She broke out in a cold sweat. Sheer willpower kept her going long after others would have collapsed.

Winona was so intent on simply moving her legs that she was taken unawares when the trees thinned and a bluff barred her path. Veering to the right, she hobbled along until she came to level ground once again.

It was best to push on, but Winona needed to rest a few moments. Just a few. She leaned on the limb and worked her left leg to keep it from cramping. Suddenly, without having heard a sound, she knew that she had run out of time. She knew that she was no longer alone. Straightening, she turned.

He stood ten feet away, the war club at his side, studying her intently as if she were a mystery he was trying to make sense of. There was no anger on his face, just curiosity. "You like jaguar. You quiet. You fast."

Winona did not know what to say. Compliments were the last thing she had expected.

"You make good Lipan." Chipota gestured. "Come now. Go back. Ricket want."

"You will not take me without a fight," Winona declared, planting her feet and holding the limb in front of her as if it were a lance. It made a pitiful weapon but it was all she had. "I will not go back."

Chipota sighed. "I not want hurt you. Savvy? Come. I not touch."

"It makes no difference. I do what I must."

The Lipan was on her before Winona could lift the limb to strike. Almost casually he swatted it aside, shifted, and drove the handle of his war club into her midsection. She doubled over and gasped for breath. The limb was torn from her grasp. Fingers as hard as stone locked in her hair, and her head was jerked upward.

"You brave woman. But you much foolish."

In response, Winona tried to claw his eyes. The Lipan pulled backward. One of her nails raked his left cheek, drawing blood. She coiled for another try, but he was not about to let her. The war club caught her on the tip of the jaw this time. Her legs would no longer support her weight, and the last sight she saw as she toppled was Chipota giving her that strange look of his. Then the hard earth rushed up to meet her face.

Chapter Eight

A sharp snap brought Simon Ward out of a fitful sleep. He had dozed off seated next to the fire, his arms crossed on his knees, his forehead resting on his right wrist.

Fearing that the slavers had returned, Simon leaped to his feet and swung from side to side, seeking a target to shoot. There were none. Another snap drew his gaze to the glowing crackling embers beside him, all that remained of the roaring flames he had going at one point. He grinned in relief. There was no cause to fret. The slavers were long gone.

And so was Felicity.

That thought erased the grin. Simon sadly lowered his arms and stepped over to where Nate King lay. It had taken every ounce of strength Simon possessed to drag the mountain man out of the grass. Rekindling the camp fire had not taken long since the slavers had left a mound of buffalo chips behind.

Black Powder

To keep wild beasts at bay, Simon had built the fire as large as he dared without setting the prairie itself on fire. Then he had sat down and tried to stay awake until dawn, a hopeless task given his near total exhaustion.

The Bostonian had done all he could for the frontiersman, which was not much. Nate King had suffered a shallow stab wound on his left side and a gunshot wound to the head, a furrow dug into his scalp above the right ear. Neither were life threatening.

Simon couldn't wait for the mountain man to come around so they could go after his wife. He nudged King's shoulder. When that brought no result, he shook Nate none too gently. All the trapper did was groan.

"Nate," Simon said loudly. "Rise and shine. Every minute we waste, Felicity gets further away."

The words echoed in Nate King's head as they might inside a cave. He struggled up out of a black pit, surprised and glad to be alive. The last thing he remembered was a volley fired by the slavers and an explosion inside his skull. "Simon?" he croaked. "Is that you?"

"It sure is," Simon said, laughing out of sheer joy. "You had me worried last night, friend. The slavers claimed that they'd killed you. I was scared to death I was on my own."

Nate blinked a few times and felt a chill ripple down his spine.

"Now we can go get the horses and head out after those butchers. If we push, we can catch them before nightfall, don't you think?"

"I'm afraid it won't be that simple."

"Why not?" Simon wanted to know. He was not going to stand for any more delays. This was the day he would rescue his wife or perish in the attempt.

"I can't see."

"What?" Simon said, not sure he had heard correctly.

Nate swiveled his head to confirm it. All he saw was a gritty gray veil. "I can't see a thing. The shot I took to the head has done something to my eyes."

"No!" Simon exclaimed, more out of concern for his wife than for the man who had befriended him. To his credit, he realized he was not being considerate and placed a hand on the other man's broad shoulder. "What can I do? We don't have any water or food, but I'll go rustle up what I can if you want."

Propping both hands under him, Nate sat up. He ran his fingers along the furrow and winced. It was tender but not very deep, and it had not bled much. Bears had done more damage on occasion. Why, then, couldn't he see?

Nate recollected hearing of men stricken with head wounds who lost their powers of sight and speech. One man he'd heard tell of had reverted to being a small child and had to be waited on hand and foot or he would have died. Something similar must have happened to him. The big question was: How long would the effect last? Was it permanent, or would his eyesight return to normal sooner or later?

"Does this mean we can't go after my wife?" Simon inquired.

Every syllable was laced with raw anxiety. Nate could not blame the man. If it were his wife, he would feel the same. Closing his eyes, he pressed his fingers over the lids and rubbed lightly. It produced no change. The gray veil seemed there to stay.

Simon Ward felt the old urge to cry come over him. This new setback, coming on the heels of so many in a row, was almost more than he could bear. He resisted the urge, but only with supreme effort.

Nate did not waste time bewailing his fate. It had happened; he must make the best of it. To that end, he held out his hand and said, "Help me up. We have to get to the horses."

"And what then?" Simon asked, afraid that the mountain man intended to head for the Shoshone village.

"What else? We save your wife."

"But *how?* With you blind, we don't stand a prayer. I can't shoot or fight like you can. If the slavers spot us, we'll both wind up dead."

Nate reached in the direction of the younger man's voice. His hand fell on Ward's arm. "Listen to me, pilgrim. You can't give up. I don't think those vermin have laid a finger on Felicity yet, but they will before too long. Do you want that to happen?"

"Of course not. How can you even ask?"

Nate tucked his legs under him. "Then we leave right away. You'll have to be my eyes for the time being, until my sight returns."

Simon shook his head. The idea was too preposterous for words. Yet he had to admit that everything the trapper said was true. They were the only hope of salvation his wife had. As he assisted the frontiersman to rise, he remarked, "But what if it never does? I can't spirit her away from them all by my lonesome."

"You might have to," Nate said. Although he would never let on, deep down he was more upset than Ward. There was indeed a very good chance that he would never see again, and it frightened him as few other things could. For how could he hope to survive in the wilderness without his sight? He would be unable to trap. He would be unable to hunt. His wife would have to provide for the family. And while he knew that she would never complain, he could not bring himself to impose so heavy a burden on her.

"Which direction do I go?" Simon asked. For the life of him, he could not recall if the horses were due north, to the northwest, or to the northeast.

"Northwest," Nate said, and felt the other man take his sleeve. "That won't be necessary," he stated, refusing to be treated as if he were completely helpless. "I'll follow the sound of your footsteps."

"Suit yourself."

And so they headed out, Simon tramping along in the lead, making enough noise to scare off every snake and insect within 50 yards. It was easy for Nate to keep up. But so preoccupied was he with the calamity his family faced that they hiked for minutes before he thought of something he should have thought of sooner.

"Wait a minute. Do you have my guns?"

"No," Simon replied. "You didn't have any on you. Just your knife."

"Did you look for them? Do you have a rifle?"

Simon shook his head, then realized his error and answered, "No on both counts. But don't hold it against me. I wasn't about to go off and leave you while you were lying there helpless. Who knows what might have come along? A bear, maybe, or a cougar." He thought a moment and added as an afterthought, "Or hostile Indians, perhaps. Maybe those Blackfeet you were telling me about."

Nate doubted that was the real reason. Ward had not left his side because Ward had been afraid to. It was as simple as that. But the Bostonian was right about one thing. Nate couldn't hold it against him.

All too vividly, Nate could recollect his own anxious feelings when he first ventured to the frontier in the company of his uncle. There had been a time when every little noise had made him jump, when every shadow had been a concealed enemy. It had passed, as all things must. For a while, though, he had been just like Simon Ward.

"It couldn't be helped," Nate said. "After we fetch the horses, we'll go look for my rifle and any others we can find."

"But it will delay us even longer," Simon protested.

"We need guns," Nate insisted. "Unless you'd rather chuck rocks at the slavers if they catch us trying to free your wife."

In silence they hiked for close to ten minutes. Simon was annoyed, but he had to admit that the mountain man had a valid point. Knives and pistols were no match for Hawkens and Kentucky rifles.

So much time had gone by since they left the horses ground-hitched that Simon was dead certain the black stallion and his bay would be long gone. He figured the pair had drifted elsewhere while grazing and were now either halfway to Missouri or up in the high country somewhere. Which made him all the more surprised when he set eyes on them a few hundred feet away. They had strayed apart but were in the general vicinity of where they had been left.

"Well, I'll be damned," Simon declared, and told King what he saw.

"Horses usually won't go far when ground-hitched," Nate explained. "They keep stepping on the reins, and that stops them every time."

Simon chuckled to himself. On the trip west he had always picketed the animals securely using iron picket pins he had purchased in St. Louis. It never had occurred to him to just let the reins drag the ground.

Nate stepped forward, stuck two fingers into his

mouth, and whistled as shrilly as a marmot. The black stallion raised its head, flicked its tail, and nickered. Focusing on the sound, Nate slowly moved toward it.

The bay was not quite as glad to see Simon. It watched him approach, and when he was almost close enough to snag the reins, it snorted and shied, backing away from his hand. "Hold on, you," Simon said gruffly, which only made it retreat farther. Angry, he dashed forward and clamped hold of the reins. "Enough of this nonsense," he declared.

The bay had other ideas. Suddenly rearing, it tore the reins loose and went to flee. It only managed a few strides when a front leg stomped on the trailing reins, which brought the horse up short just as the trapper had claimed.

Changing his tactics, Simon smiled and spoke soothingly. "There, there fella. It's just me, you idiot. The man who owns you. The one who rode you for hundreds and hundreds of miles, day in and day out for weeks. It seems to me that you ought to know who I am."

The bay bobbed its head but did not attempt to run off a second time. Simon slowly took hold of the reins, then spent a while patting the animal's neck and scratching it behind the ears as he often did so it would calm down. That did the trick. Simon was able to climb on without another incident. As he forked leather, he was mildly disconcerted to see King already on the stallion and waiting for him a short way off.

"Sorry," Simon apologized. "This horse has the brains of a jackass."

"That makes him special," Nate responded. "Jackasses are smart animals. A few trappers I know own them, and they swear that jackasses can go longer without water and food than horses, and they're more sure-footed on narrow trails."

"Oh," Simon said. Not wanting to appear totally ignorant, he threw in, "Well, horses can go faster." Then he slapped his legs and trotted off. Once again he failed to keep in mind that the mountain man had been blinded, and when he realized his mistake and twisted to call out to King to follow him, he found the trapper only a few dozen feet behind the bay, riding along as if he did not have a worry in the world.

Simon didn't see how King did it. The man might have permanently lost his sight, yet he went on with his life as if nothing out of the ordinary had transpired. If it had happened to Simon, he knew that he would have blubbered like a baby and would be an utter emotional wreck for months to come, if not years.

It made Simon wish that he could take things in stride as calmly as the mountain man. He wondered how King did it, whether the man had always had a level disposition or whether the trapper had somehow learned to take what life had to offer without complaint.

Unknown to the Bostonian, his companion was plenty disturbed. Nate kept hoping that his vision would clear, and as more and more time went by and nothing happened he became more and more discouraged. He could not abide the thought of being a burden to Winona and his children. It would be better to die, he reckoned, than to inflict himself on them.

Or so Nate thought until he remembered old Otter Tail. Once a venerable warrior, Otter Tail had been wounded in a battle with raiding Bloods. An arrow had glanced off his skull. Afterward, he could no longer see.

Where others might have given in to sorrow and feelings of helplessness, Otter Tail had determined to carry on his life. He had worked hard and long to reacquire many of the skills he had before, and to improve on them. He became adept at making bows esteemed as the best in the tribe. He had his wife teach him to sew and he became an expert shield maker, as well. It was not long before warriors from many different bands were coming to him for their bows and shields. In his own way, he became a legend among the Shoshones, a shining example of what a person could do if they only put their mind to it.

Maybe, Nate mused, he should follow Otter Tail's example and make something of his life instead of throwing it away. But what could he do that others might benefit from? He certainly couldn't make bows. And his sewing was downright pathetic. He couldn't get the hang of using a sewing needle no matter how hard he tried. The last time he'd mended his own britches, he'd put more holes in his fingers and thumb than he had in the buckskin.

Nate was still mulling over his options when they reached the campsite. Simon reined up first and announced that they had arrived.

Swinging down, Nate said, "I'll stay here. It wouldn't do to have me clomping through the grass. I might ride right over a rifle and never know it."

Simon's first inclination was to insist that the trapper accompany him. Bears and buffalo roamed the high grass, and he didn't care to bump into either while alone. But as he watched Nate King grope the stallion's neck for the reins, he realized that the frontiersman would be of no help if a wild beast should appear.

"All right. I'll try not to take too long." Wheeling the bay, Simon rode into the grass, his hand on his pistol. He really thought that he was wasting his time. To his amazement, he had not gone ten yards when he came on Nate King's Hawken lying right out in the open. He knew it was the mountain man's because King had customized it with an inlaid silver plate engraved with his name.

Overjoyed, Simon went on. He was going to ride at random when it hit him that the search would be much more thorough if he adopted a regular pattern of working back and forth from east to west. Within five minutes he found another rifle and a pistol. The latter he nearly broke when the bay stepped on it. At the last moment he spotted the glint of metal and hauled back on the reins.

For quite some time after that, Simon's search was fruitless. When he looked up and saw that he had gone over 200 yards from the camp, he decided enough was enough and headed back. Partway there the polished stock of another pistol claimed his attention.

Beaming proudly, Simon rode back out into the open. Suddenly he stopped cold. Nate King was on one knee next to the three bodies, running a hand over the face of the dead Indian. It made Simon's flesh crawl. Sliding down, he walked on over.

"What are you doing?"

Nate slowly rose. "I was a mite curious. This coon nearly did me in." He absently placed a hand over the knife wound. "A few more inches to the left and I'd be worm food right now."

"How did you know the bodies were here?"

"I smelled them."

Simon took a long sniff and regretted it. There was a faint but distinctly foul odor he had not noticed before, which was bound to grow much worse before too long. "I'm surprised the coyotes and buzzards haven't treated themselves yet."

"The scent of the fire and all the slavers is still too strong," Nate said. "Once it fades, they'll feast." He raised his head. "Did you have any luck?"

"Did I!" Simon handed over the rifle and one of the pistols. He expected to be praised for a job well done, but all King said was "I'm obliged."

Not that Nate wasn't grateful, but he was more concerned over whether the Hawken had been damaged. He gingerly ran a hand over it, closely examining the stock, the barrel, the trigger and hammer.

Hawkens were next to impossible to come by on the frontier. Everyone Nate knew who owned one had bought it from the Hawken brothers in St. Louis, and there wasn't a trapper alive willing to part with his prize no matter how much he was offered.

Nate was glad to find his rifle intact. He set the stock on the ground, then uncapped his powder horn. Since he often measured how much black powder to use by pouring it into his palm until he had a pile a certain size, it was not that hard for him to do the same by touch alone. But funneling the powder into the barrel took some doing, as he simply couldn't upend his palm over the muzzle as he was wont to do. He had to cup his hand just so and let the grains trickle slowly.

Wedging the lead ball down on top of the powder proved to be no problem. All Nate had to do was take a ball from his ammo pouch, shove it partway in with his thumb, then slide the ramrod out of its housing, align it over the barrel, and push. When he had tapped the ball firmly into position, he replaced the ramrod.

"Not bad," Simon said, impressed.

"Practice makes perfect, even when you can't see what you're doing, I reckon," Nate replied. He reloaded the pistol, tucked it under his belt close to the buckle, and nodded. "I'm as ready as I'll ever be. Lead the way. You'll have to do the tracking."

Simon was about to turn. "Me?" he blurted. "You can't be serious."

"Never more so. The tracks will be as plain as day. There are eleven slavers left, plus your wife, plus extra horses." Nate mustered a wan grin. "They'll leave a trail a blind man could follow."

The frontiersman was proven right. Simon had not paid much attention to the tracks when he had hunted for the guns, but they were there and impossible to miss even though the slavers had ridden off in single file. The passage of so many horses had flattened a yard-wide path. Simon moved along at a trot.

Nate had no trouble keeping up. He was so used to riding the stallion that the two of them moved as one. Thankfully, there were no trees to dodge, no gullies to cross, just mile after mile of flat prairie.

The mountain man soon found that his other senses compensated to a degree for his eyes. He was able to gauge the passing of time by the warmth on his face. When it was warmest on his left cheek, Nate knew that the sun was to the east. When his forehead was warmest, the sun had reached its zenith. As the day waned, his right cheek warmed.

The breeze brought the strong smell of buffalo wallows to his nostrils. Nate also smelled the grass underfoot, the sweat on the stallion, and his own.

His ears told him exactly where Simon was, and enabled him to ride along without fear of colliding should the young man from Boston unexpectedly draw rein.

Toward evening the wind picked up, as it invariably did. Nate concentrated on the drum of the bay's hooves and sped up just enough to pull alongside it on the left. "We have to talk, Simon."

Ward had been thinking of all that had befallen him since his wife's abduction. On hindsight, he considered it a miracle that he was still alive. Barging into the slaver camp as he had done was without exception the most boneheaded stunt he'd ever pulled. He would not make the same mistake twice, he vowed.

While Simon's mother-in-law might be right about him having a head as dense as granite, he did know how to learn from his blunders.

On hearing his name, Simon glanced around. It took a few seconds for him to appreciate that the mountain man had actually called him by name this time, and not just 'greenhorn.' "About what, might I ask?"

"You have a decision to make."

"I do?"

"Your wife is the one in jeopardy. So you get to decide whether we push on through the night or make camp. I'll abide by whatever you choose to do."

Simon did not see where it was much of a decision. He couldn't abide the idea of Felicity spending another night in the clutches of the cutthroats. Who knew what they would do to her? But as he went to answer, he hesitated. King had been looking peaked the past few hours. Simon wondered if he should call a halt for the trapper's sake.

Before the Bostonian could speak up, however, a rumbling snort sounded just 18 feet away and an enormous shaggy bulk reared up out of the grass.

Black Powder

Simon Ward reined up and gaped in astonishment.

It was a bull buffalo. Worse, it was clearly annoyed at having its dust bath interrupted. And the next moment it lowered its massive head and pawed the ground, about to charge.

Chapter Nine

Felicity Ward did not get her chance that first day. She hoped and prayed that one of the slavers would be lax for the few seconds it would take her to snatch a pistol or knife. But they were skilled at their wicked craft and never let their guard down when close by.

It did not help matters any that the man called Gregor had evidently taken a fancy to her. The slaver leader kept her near him throughout the day. Repeatedly she found him ogling her on the sly. There was no misjudging his intent. It was the kind of look every woman knew all too well, the raw, bestial hungry look of a man in the fiery grip of lust. He wanted her. And knowing his temperament, it wouldn't be very long before he took what he wanted.

Felicity grew queasy just thinking about it. She would fight for her womanhood tooth and nail, but against a giant like Gregor the outcome was pre-ordained.

Black Powder

Toward evening the slavers called a halt. Since they had been on the go for almost 20 hours, men and animals were exhausted. They had stopped only twice, once at midday to give the animals a break and again in the middle of the afternoon when they came on a small stream.

Felicity would have given anything to be allowed to wash herself from head to toe, but she was not about to ask permission knowing that every man there would cluster around to whistle and make lewd comments. She had to tolerate being filthy, at least for a while yet.

Gregor had tossed her a blanket, told her to spread it out, and went off to arrange the camp to suit him. They were on the west bank of a narrow creek, in a clearing bordered by prairie grass and a few slender cottonwoods. Evidently the same site had been used by other travelers, because there were several charred remains of previous camp fires.

A burly slaver who was mostly Mexican but had blue eyes tended to their cooking. He was a wizard at mixing commonplace ingredients into savory meals. Throughout the day he had angled into the grass now and again, always returning with leaves or roots or tender shoots.

Now, with a stew thickened by chunks of rabbit meat boiling over the fire, Felicity sat on the blanket Gregor had spread out for her and pondered her next move. Since getting her hands on a gun or blade was out of the question, she had to make do with whatever else was handy. She scoured the ground for something, for *anything*, that would suffice as a weapon.

Gradually, the sun sank, blazing the western sky with bold strokes of red and orange. Despite it being summer, a number of distant peaks were crowned by ivory mantles of snow. It was so magnificent a scene that it moved Felicity in the depths of her soul, soothing her for the few moments she admired the heavenly spectacle.

The tramp of heavy feet brought her back to reality.

Felicity swiveled and could not help gulping at seeing Gregor leer at her as if she were a dainty morsel he was about to bite into. She held her chin high, crossed her legs, and folded her arms. Her anger flared when this provoked lecherous laughter.

"It won't do you no good to hide your charms, woman," Gregor said. "When I want them, they're mine. And there's not a damn thing you can do about it."

Locking her eyes on his, Felicity declared, "This I swear. I will kill you if you presume to lay a finger on me."

Again Gregor was merely amused. "I've heard that threat a hundred times if I've heard it once. And I'm still here. That ought to tell you something."

"It tells me that every rattlesnake has its day. But all things come to an end. Your time will come. I just pray to God that I'm there when it does."

Gregor's smirk changed to a scowl. "You have a mouth on you, woman. It will please me no end to tame you, to break you like I would a wild horse, to show you that the proper way for a woman to regard a man is as her master."

An unladylike snort burst from Felicity before she could stop herself. "You like to delude yourself, I see. But what else should I expect from a man who has to beat women into giving him what they would never offer on their own? You're worthless trash, Mr. Gregor. And nothing you say or do will ever make me change my opinion."

Felicity was looking right at him yet she never saw his leg move. The kick caught her high in the right shoulder and knocked her onto her back. Stunned, she went to rise, but suddenly he was there, astride her, his knee gouging into her abdomen while his left hand wrenched her hair.

"Have a care, bitch!" the leader snarled. "You might fetch a pretty peso where we're going, but that won't stop me from gutting you like a fish if you keep mouthing off. I can always find another woman to sell to the Comanches or the Mexicans. Whether you want to or not, you will treat me with respect."

A sharp retort was on the tip of Felicity's tongue, but it was choked off by the slab of a fist ramming into her stomach. Agony such as she had never known racked her, making her gasp and squirm.

Gregor smiled. "That's what I like to see." He caressed her cheek, then tweaked it hard until she cried out. "Pain, woman. A person will do anything to be spared from pain. Before I'm done, you'll beg me to do the kind of things I'll warrant only your husband has ever done. And you'll love every minute." Sneering, he rose and walked off.

Felicity wanted to sit up, to be strong in front of the others, but her limbs were mush, her resolve weakened. She was helpless before his brute force and he knew it. Closing her eyes, she curled into a ball.

To the onlooking slavers, it appeared as if their captive had forsaken all hope and was in abject misery.

The truth was quite different. Felicity Ward was praying, as she had many times prayed as a small child when things were going badly. She prayed for a miracle, for someone or something to save her from the ordeal she faced.

In short, for a guardian angel.

Winona King was jarred into rejoining the world of the living by the motion of her mare as it scrambled down an embankment. Pounding waves of pain lanced her head and she almost cried out. It took a while for her sluggish mind to make sense of her bouncing stomach and her sore wrists and ankles.

The slavers had thrown her over the pinto, belly down, and lashed her hands to her legs.

Winona tried to unbend but couldn't. The circulation in her limbs had been cut off for so long that her arms and legs were practically numb. Her stomach felt as if it had been stomped on by a mule. And as if all that were not enough, she felt slightly sick. Not meaning to, she groaned.

"Well, well, well," said a familiar raspy voice. "Looks as if the squaw won't die, after all. She's a tough one, ain't she, Chipota?"

"Yes," the Lipan answered.

Winona could see neither of them. By craning her neck she saw a horse behind the mare and one in front of it, but she could not glimpse either rider. Suddenly another horse darted toward the mare, coming up beside her. She learned what it meant when Ricket barked an order.

"Don't you dare, Owens! You lay a finger on her and you'll answer to Gregor!"

"I owe her, damn it! You saw the knot she put on my noggin!" Owens challenged. "I should break every bone in her stinking body."

Winona flinched as the slaver's sorrel was ridden right into her. Not hard, but hard enough to set her head to renewed ringing and her shoulders to screaming in protest.

"You heard me!" Ricket stood his ground. "Harm her and Gregor will peel your hide! And I'll help hold you down for not listenin' to me."

Something jabbed Winona between the shoulder blades. She was sure it had been a rifle barrel. For a few harrowing moments she thought that Owens would disobey and shoot her. Then another horse whipped close to her and barreled the sorrel aside.

"That be enough," the Lipan declared. "No more hurt her."

Owens did not take kindly to having the warrior tell him what to do. "Who the hell do you think you are, Injun? I may have to listen to Gregor and to this old fart when Gregor puts him in charge, but I sure as hell don't have to stand for having a red son of a bitch like you—"

Whatever else Owens was going to say was cut short by the thud of a blow landing. Winona saw Owens crash onto his back beside the sorrel. He was livid. His rifle had slipped from his grasp, but he still had two pistols and he whisked a hand to one of them. He wasn't quite fast enough. Abruptly, he froze, his expression fearful.

"You draw," the Lipan said, "and I put knife in you."

Owens licked his lips, his eyes narrowing.

For a few seconds the issue hung in the balance, and then Ricket joined them. "I tell you," he grumbled, "havin' to deal with this bunch is like havin' a passel of younguns underfoot all the time. It's a pain in the backside." He paused. "Chipota, why don't you lower your arm? I know you can fling that pigsticker into a fly at ten paces, but Gregor would have a fit if you made wolf meat of this yack."

The warrior evidently complied, because Owens relaxed and took his hand off his flintlock. Plastering a smile on his face, he slowly sat up, saying, "I reckon I wasn't thinking straight, Chipota. I didn't mean what I called you. It's just that being conked on the head made me madder than hell. No hard feelings, eh?"

The Lipan grunted.

Winona had been ignored during the dispute. Now

she twisted to see Ricket regarding her with a wry grin. "What do you find so humorous?"

"Women. The whole bunch of you are more trouble than you're worth." Ricket shook his head. "Beats me what the Good Lord was thinkin' when he created females. Seems to me the world would have been a heap better off with just men." Clucking his horse forward, he took the mare's reins in hand and headed out.

Owens had risen. He glared at Winona as she went by, but he did not say anything, perhaps because the Lipan fell into step behind her.

Winona wondered why the warrior had come to her defense. She also pondered his behavior the night before, when he had acted reluctant to bring her back. Was it because they were both Indians? That seemed unlikely, since Apaches were notorious for regarding all other tribes as enemies. No, there had to be another reason, but Winona was at a loss to know what it might be.

By bending her body away from the pinto, Winona was able to note the position of the sun. She was surprised to learn it was late in the afternoon, which meant she had been unconscious all night and most of the day.

The ropes were biting deep into her flesh. Whoever had tied her had done the job much tighter than was necessary, leading Winona to suspect that Owens was to blame. It would be just like him to take petty revenge by making her suffer. She tried rubbing her wrists and ankles together to loosen her bonds, but it only made matters worse. The skin broke. Blood trickled down over her fingers.

Finally Winona glanced at Ricket. "I would be grateful if you untied me."

The slaver laughed without looking back. "Nope. I

don't think so. As soon as you got the chance, you'd head for the hills. I won't risk havin' you give us the slip a second time."

Winona was confronted by a dilemma. She could not continue to hang there. When they finally did stop, she would be unable to move until her circulation was restored. That might take hours. And during all that time she would be completely at the mercy of her captors. "What if I give you my word?"

This got Ricket's interest. He shifted in the saddle. "How's that, squaw-woman?"

"What if I give you my word that I will not try to escape? Will you untie me then?"

"And you expect me to believe you?" Ricket crackled. "You must think I'm awful stupid."

"I would not break my word," Winona insisted. And, in truth, she wouldn't. She was a woman of honor, just like her man. It was one of the things that had attracted her to him.

Many men, even Shoshone warriors, were not always honest in their dealings with their wives. They would fool around with other women, then lie if caught. They would stay out late gambling with buffalo-bone dice, then come back to the lodge and claim they had been at a council meeting.

But not her Nate. He never lied to her. And he would rather spend his evenings in her company than with rowdy friends who had nothing better to do with their time than tell tall tales and lose their hard-earned possessions at games of chance.

Honor. It was as important to both of them as life itself. When they said they would do something, they did it. When they made a vow, that vow was never broken. So when Winona gave her word, she sincerely meant to keep it.

But Ricket shook his head, his eyes twinkling.

David Thompson

"Maybe you're not lyin'. But I'm not the one to put you to the test. We'll leave that to Gregor. You'll just have to hang there until we rendezvous with him."

"And how long will that take?"

The slaver scratched his chin. "Oh, if we ride all night, we should be at Black Squirrel Creek shortly after sunrise tomorrow. That's where we're to meet up."

Winona knew that region of the prairie well. Black Squirrel Creek fed into the Arkansas River about a two-days' ride from Bent's Fort, where Nate and she had gone many times to trade and purchase supplies. She knew some of the men who lived at the fort, including William Bent himself, and Ceran St. Vrain, both good friends of Nate's. If only there were some way of getting word to them! They would arm every man at the fort and rally to her rescue.

Trying to keep any trace of excitement from her voice, Winona casually asked, "Will you be stopping at Bent's Fort before you head south?"

Ricket snickered. "If some of us do pay the fort a visit, you can be damn sure that you won't be taggin' along. Five or six men will stay behind to keep you company."

Winona slumped, dejected. She tried telling herself that all was not lost, that eventually she would regain her freedom. But the prospects were growing bleaker. Once Ricket's band rejoined the other slavers, the odds of her being able to give them the slip would be very slim.

At that very moment, to her surprise and the surprise of every other slaver, the Lipan unexpectedly goaded his horse up next to the mare, bent down, and with a flick of his long butcher knife, he slashed the rope binding her wrists.

"What the hell!" Owens cried.

Ricket reined up and wheeled his horse. "Hold on

there, Chipota. What in the world do you think you're doing?"

The Lipan did not respond. He moved his mount around to the other side of the mare and leaned over to cut the rope around Winona's ankles.

"Damn it all!" Ricket said. "Have you gone plumb loco on me?"

Winona needed to take advantage of the situation while it lasted. She reached up to grab the mare's mane. But the blood flow had been cut off for so long that her arm did not want to cooperate. It commenced tingling, then pulsed with pain. She arched her spine to raise her body high enough to hook her elbow over the pinto's neck and hung there a few moments, waiting for the agony to subside. Her other arm and both legs also started hurting.

Chipota had slid his knife into its sheath and now advanced to take the mare's reins from a stupefied Ricket. "I watch her now," he said.

The grizzled slaver looked as if he could not make up his mind whether to be outraged or to just let the warrior have his way. Ricket sputtered, then coughed, then glanced at the other slavers and back at the Lipan. "What in tarnation has gotten into you? I've never seen you act like this before."

"I watch her," Chipota said.

"We heard you the first time." Ricket pursed his lips and stared hard at Winona as if she were to blame. "If you want the responsibility, it's yours. But mark my words. Let her escape and you'll have to answer to Gregor. He won't like it if we lose a beauty like this one."

Chipota looked at Winona. For a fleeting instant she saw something in his eyes that she had not noticed before, something which explained everything and filled her with more dread than ever. In a very real sense she had gone from the frying pan into the fire, as her mate was fond of saying. The moment passed when Chipota turned his typical stony gaze on Owens.

"She not run off. She not be hurt. Savvy, white-eye?"

Owens bristled. "Why single me out, Injun? I'm not going to lay a finger on her. But I will laugh like hell when she slips a knife into you when you're not looking. You're a fool if you think that she won't." Lashing his reins, he turned and rode off.

Ricket speared a finger at Winona. "Do you see? Do you see all the trouble women make? You're all the same. Just like my fickle ma. She used to draw men to her like honey draws bears. I lost count of all the squabbles she caused. And you're no better." He moved off in a huff.

Winona wisely made no comment. She managed to swing her legs over the mare as Chipota resumed their trek. Now that she knew what was on his mind, she had to keep her eyes on him at all times. She would not put it past him to spirit her off so he could have her all to himself. Then she recalled that he had a son named Santiago riding with Gregor. Since it was unlikely Chipota would do anything to endanger his own flesh and blood, she should be safe until the two bands reunited.

Her arms and legs ached for hours. Winona rubbed both constantly to aid the circulation. Her scraped wrists stopped bleeding but bothered her whenever she moved them.

The sun headed for the western horizon. Winona was thirsty and hungry but too proud to ask for drink or food. Several times she caught Owens giving her a look such as someone might give an insect they intended to crush underfoot. She had made a bitter enemy who would stop at nothing to pay her back. Despite what Owens had told the Lipan, she dared not turn her back on him.

As the sun faded over the distant mountains, so did Winona's flickering hope begin to fade. With each passing moment she was being led farther from her loved ones. In a few days they would be well south of Bent's Fort, in country she did not know, where there were many enemies of the Shoshones, where every hand would be raised against her, as it were.

It was enough to discourage the bravest of souls.

As night descended, Winona King felt as if she were riding into the very heart of darkness. In more ways than one.

Felicity Ward lay on her back, a blanket hiked up under her chin, and trembled. She knew it would be soon now. Gregor would return and force himself on her. And she had nothing to fight him with except her teeth and her nails.

For the past several hours the slavers had been sipping whiskey, smoking pipes and playing cards. None were anywhere near her, but she knew better than to try to flee. They would catch her before she had gone 50 yards and punish her severely.

Felicity looked toward the fire and saw Gregor upend a silver flask. She nearly jumped out of her skin when a hand touched her shoulder and someone whispered in her ear.

"Do not say a word, *senora*. Do not do anything to give me away. They can not see us here in the shadows, not when they are so close to the fire."

Bewildered, Felicity glanced around. Julio Trijillo was on his hands and knees beside her. She could not see his features. "What do you want?" she timidly asked.

"Take this. It is the best I can do."

Something long and hard was pressed into Felicity's hand. Before she could question him further, the Mexican slipped noiselessly away. Moments later she saw him circle around into the firelight and stroll over to the others.

Lifting her hand, Felicity discovered a double-edged dagger. She could not believe her eyes. It defied reason for one of the slavers to aid her. Yet Julio *was* the only one who had treated her kindly since her capture. He was not like the rest. Even Gregor had admitted as much. Why he should help her, she had no idea.

A footstep sounded close by. Frightened that Gregor was on his way over, Felicity shoved the dagger under the blanket and looked up. It was only one of the others going off into the high grass.

Felicity fingered the smooth hilt and steeled herself for what she had to do. Over an hour went by, an hour during which her every nerve was on edge. Then, at last, she saw the giant rise and shuffle toward her. She gripped the dagger and held it close to her bosom, ready to thrust when he lifted the blanket off her.

The man reeked of whiskey and sweat. Swaying slightly, he knelt on the edge of the blanket and leered at her. "The time has come, bitch," he said, slurring every word. His huge arm extended toward her. "You're about to learn that I mean what I say."

The dagger suddenly felt much heavier than it was. Felicity trembled. She feared that she would start shaking uncontrollably and not be able to carry through with what she had to do.

Just then, shots rang out.

Chapter Ten

Several hours earlier and not all that many miles to the north, Simon Ward stared in shock at the enormous shaggy brute of a buffalo blowing noisily through its flared nostrils and pawing the ground as if it were about to attack.

On the long journey west Simon had seen many buffalo, but always at a distance. The mountain men in St. Louis had warned him about the dangers of getting too close. Buffalo were as unpredictable as bears, they had told him. Where one might flee at the sight of a human, another might attack. It was best to fight shy of them at all times.

Simon had not needed encouragement to avoid the huge beasts. They sported wicked sets of hooked horns that could disembowel a man or another animal with a single toss of their massive heads. The average bull stood as high as his horse. The biggest ones weighed over a thousand pounds. They were more formidable than grizzlies—and much more numerous.

The mountaineers had told Simon tales of poor souls caught in stampedes, their bodies crushed to pulped bits of flesh and bone. He had heard of one trapper who unwittingly stumbled on a bull in a wallow; both man and mount had been torn to ribbons by the enraged buffalo.

Now, seeing one at such close range, all those stories filtered through Simon's mind, filling him with fear. He lifted the reins to flee. But as he did, he noticed Nate King. The trapper had reined up a few yards past him and was turning his head every which way to pinpoint the buffalo's exact location.

It occurred to Simon that if the bull were to charge, it would bowl over Nate first, giving him the time he needed to escape. All it would take to trigger the charge was for him to whirl and gallop off. But he couldn't bring himself to sacrifice the frontiersman just to save his skin. Not after all King had done for him. Not if he wanted to be able to look at his own reflection again without being sick to his stomach.

"Don't move, Nate," Simon whispered. "It's a bull, and it's looking right at us."

Nate could hear the thump-thump-thump of the animal's heavy hooves tearing into the soil. It gave him a fair idea of how close the monster was, of the peril they were in. "What about its head?" he whispered back.

"Its head?" Simon repeated, perplexed. "The head is on its shoulders, right where it should be."

"No. I meant, does the bull have its head up or down?" Nate asked urgently.

"Up." Simon didn't see what that had to do with anything. He sucked in a breath as the buffalo took a step toward them. If it came at them, he would shout to try and lure it away from the trapper.

"Keep your eyes on it," Nate said. "Buffalo lower their heads when they're making ready to charge. We'll have a second or two to act. Give a yell and I'll draw it off while you head for the hills."

Simon stared at the trapper in amazement, ignoring King's admonition. The man had been blinded and was virtually helpless. Yet he offered to divert the bull so Simon could get away! What manner of men were these mountaineers, as they liked to call themselves? he mused. Did they not know the meaning of fear?

Then the bull rumbled loudly deep in his barrel chest. Simon swung around and saw its head dip. "Look out!" he bellowed. "It's going to attack us!"

Nate King promptly let out a yip while cutting the black stallion to the left and raking its flanks with his heels. He bent low as the horse erupted into a gallop. It was a calculated move on his part to lure the bull after him and not after the Bostonian.

And while it might seem to be an act of rank madness, there was method to it.

The black stallion was far superior to Ward's city-bred bay. Nate had received it in trade from a Shoshone famous for the quality of his war stallions. This particular black was one of the fleetest in the entire Shoshone nation, with powers of endurance that far surpassed most others.

Of the two horses, the stallion had the better chance of eluding the buffalo.

Nate did not need to be told that his ploy had

worked, that the bull was bearing down on him and not Ward. It snorted like a steam engine, its powerful legs pumping like pistons. He whipped the reins and bent forward, flowing with the driving rhythm of the stallion, adjusting to it rather than making it adjust to him as inexperienced riders were prone to do. He could not see a thing, but he did not need to. The stallion saw for both of them.

Nate had the illusion of flying over the earth. The wind fanned his face, his hair, the whangs on his buckskins. He held the Hawken close to his left side so it would not slip loose.

Behind the trapper thundered death on four hooves. The bull was incredibly fast for its size and bulk. It had a lumbering, awkward gait, which was oddly fluid at the same time. Over short distances, it was as fast as any animal alive.

That was the key to Nate's survival. The stallion had to outlast the monster. For if the horse could maintain its lead over the first few hundred yards, the bull would tire and give up.

Simon Ward had also wheeled his mount as the buffalo surged toward them. He drew up, though, when he saw it veer after the trapper. "Try me!" he shouted without result. Thinking that he might be able to plant a ball in the creature if he could overtake it, he raced after them.

Nate had to rely on his ears to gauge the gap between the stallion and onrushing doom. He could tell that the bull slowly gained. The stallion was already galloping flat out; there was nothing he could do but await the outcome.

Suddenly Nate felt a change in the stallion's gait, just such a change as he often felt when he made it hurtle an obstacle. It had to mean there was something in front of them. But what? Another buffalo? A whole herd?

Nate almost succumbed to panic in that terrible moment of uncertainty. But he had faced worse moments before; the raging assault of a berserk grizzly, the frenzied onslaught of a hostile war party, the feral fury of a vicious painter. He composed himself and flattened close to the stallion's neck. Whatever it was, he must trust in the stallion to do what had to be done.

Anxious moments passed. Nate clamped his legs and thighs tight. The stallion launched into a series of rolling bounds, which culminated in a tremendous leap. Nate knew that whatever they were vaulting had to be big or wide or both. He tried not to think of what would happen should the stallion land off balance.

Then the big black alighted. It stumbled, whinnied, and righted itself.

Nate would have been unhorsed had he not been holding on for dear life. He heard a bellow and a crash behind him. The stallion raced on. Soon he realized that the bull was no longer after them so he slowed, puzzled.

Simon Ward knew why. He had glimpsed a wide dry wash moments before the stallion leaped. It had seemed to him to be an impossible jump. He was certain that the horse would miss the far rim, fall to the bottom, and be attacked by the bull before it could rise.

By some miracle, the stallion made it. Barely. Then the bull went over the edge in a headlong rush. It slipped and slid to the bottom in a spray of dust. There, it turned to the right instead of going up the steep side, and pounded eastward. The last Simon saw of it was as it disappeared around a sharp bend.

At a hail from Simon, Nate turned and headed back. It was only then that he noticed that the gray veil which he had been seeing since being shot had brightened to a white haze. And when he glanced down at the stallion, he thought he detected a vague hint of motion and substance where before there had been nothing at all.

"Be careful," Simon called out. "You're almost to the edge of that wash."

"So that's what it was," Nate responded. He let the stallion take it nice and slow to the bottom. The big black hesitated, then went up the opposite slope with its rear legs pumping.

"That was too close for comfort, if you ask me," Simon commented. "For a few seconds there, I thought that buffalo had you for sure."

Nate had already put the incident from his mind. It was just one of many such narrow escapes he'd had since taking up the life of a free trapper. He had reached the point where he took them in stride as a matter of course. They were normal, everyday affairs, hardly meriting a second thought.

"What did you decide about making camp?" Nate asked.

In all the excitement, Simon had forgotten about the question the mountain man had asked him earlier. "If it's all the same to you, I'd rather push on. I wouldn't be able to sleep much anyway."

"Then that's what we'll do," Nate said. "Once it's dark enough, you'll have to keep your eyes skinned to the south for the glow of a camp fire."

As before, Simon assumed the lead. He couldn't say why, but he had the feeling that their luck had changed, that it wouldn't be long before he set eyes on his wife again. And he made himself a promise. Once she was safe, he was going to let her decide whether they went on up into the mountains or headed back for civilization.

Ever since her abduction, Simon had been thinking about his decision to come live on the frontier. And the more he pondered, the more it seemed to him that he had been taking Felicity for granted. In his enthusiasm, he had failed to take her feelings into account.

Back in Boston he had gone on and on about the wonderful life they would forge for themselves in the wilderness without *once* asking her whether she wanted to or not. He had waxed eloquent about the freedom they would enjoy without giving the dangers due attention. It had never occurred to him that she might prefer to live where she did not have to worry about being set upon by a wild beast every time she went out the front door. Or that she might actually want to buy her food at a market rather than grow it in the wild. He'd just assumed that she'd want to do the same thing he wanted to do.

Well, no more, Simon reflected. In the future he would always ask her opinion and give her an equal voice in all their decisions. It was the least she deserved for giving him the greatest gift any man could ever receive: the love of a good woman.

Time passed. A myriad of stars sparkled overhead. The lingering heat of the day gave way to the brisk coolness of night. Coyotes and wolves were in full chorus, punctuated every now and then by the throaty coughs of grizzlies and the piercing caterwauling of cougars.

Simon glued his gaze to the south, vibrant with anticipation, longing to spy the firefly glimmer of the slavers' fire.

Nate King, meanwhile, kept craning his neck skyward and squinting. His longing was to detect a faint gleam of starlight against the backdrop of inky ether. But try as he might, he could not do it. Apparently his vision was going to take much longer to restore itself than he would like, if it ever did.

Much later, Simon Ward glanced to the west, toward the black sawtooth wall formed by the distant foothills and mountains. He began to stretch, idly turned to the east, and caught himself, mystified by what he saw. He reined up.

Nate heard and did the same. "What is it?" he inquired. "Why did you stop?"

"It's a camp fire," Simon reported.

"Then we've done it. We've caught up."

"But it's not to the south, as you figured it would be. It's southeast of us. I'm not much of a judge, but I'd say it's three or four miles off at the most."

Nate was picturing the lay of the land in his mind's eye. He roughly calculated how many miles they had gone that day, and announced, "Black Squirrel Creek. That's where they've stopped."

Simon lifted his reins. He couldn't wait to see Felicity again, to hold her in his arms, to apologize for placing her in jeopardy with his insane dream. "Let's go!" he exclaimed.

"Hold on," Nate said. He didn't want a repeat of their last attempt to save Mrs. Ward. "Didn't you learn anything at all last time?"

"Don't fret. I'm not about to go rushing in there and get us killed."

That was good for Nate to hear. He was about to detail his plan for saving the Bostonian's wife when the night was rent by the far off blast of gunfire. Before Nate could say or do anything, Simon Ward cried out, "My wife!", and took off like a bat out of hell toward the slaver camp.

There were two shots, followed by loud whoops. That was all. But since they came from the strip of grass near the horse string, it was enough to send the startled animals into a panic. Some reared. Some kicked and plunged in an effort to break loose.

The slavers forgot all else in their haste to safeguard their mounts. They rushed toward the animals with their rifles in hand. Someone shouted that they were under attack by Indians, and several of the cutthroats opened fire, adding to the uproar and confusion.

The slaver leader, Gregor, had spun on hearing the first shots. "What the hell!" he declared. Shaking his head to clear it, he raced toward the string, leaving Felicity Ward alone under the blanket.

She sat up, terrified of being pounced on by hostiles, and recoiled when a figure burst out of the grass toward her. She was all set to slash with the dagger. Then she saw that it was Julio Trijillo. "What—?" she blurted.

The Mexican never slowed. Grabbing her hand, he hauled her to her feet, saying, "There is no time to explain, senora. You must come with me, pronto."

Felicity was in a whirl. she did not know what was going on. But since Julio had befriended her, she figured that he intended to save her from the hostiles. Nodding, she meekly let him lead her off into the grass. As soon as the blades closed around them, he ducked low and motioned for her to do the same.

"What about the Indians?" Felicity asked while trying her utmost to stick to the swift pace the man had set.

"There are none. That was me."

A feather could have floored Felicity. "Why did you do such a thing?"

"Why else?" Julio paused to check behind them. "It was the only way I could get you away from them."

Felicity wanted to ask him a score of questions, but he motioned for her to be silent. Then he angled to the right, moving rapidly, parallel to the camp. Some of the horses had quieted, but the rest were still giving the slavers a hard time. She could hear their lusty curses. Over the din rose Gregor's roars.

"It will not be long before they notice we are gone," Julio said over a shoulder. "We must ride like the wind if we are to get you to safety."

Ride *what*? Felicity was about to inquire when a pair of horses materialized out of the gloom.

Trijillo boosted her onto a chestnut, swung onto a buttermilk, and made off at a canter. He kept his eyes on the camp and his hand on one of the fancy silver inlaid pistols he wore.

Unable to stifle her curiosity any longer, Felicity rode abreast of him and asked, "Why are you doing this? Why risk your life for someone you hardly know?" Deep down she dreaded that maybe, just maybe, the man had whisked her away from the slavers because he wanted her for himself. If so, he would find that she was going to be true to her husband at all costs. She still had the dagger, and she would use it if he forced her to.

"You are a lady, senora," Julio said. "I could not let them sell you to the Comanches, or worse." He looked at her. "I must tell you in case something happens to me. We never found your husband's body. There is a very good chance he is still alive."

Felicity's hopes soared. Could it be? Could it really be?

The Mexican rose in the stirrups for a few seconds to study the plain behind them. "As to why I do this, I am not one of those renegades, Senora Ward. Oh, I know what you are thinking. That I must be one because I rode with them. But I only joined to kill Gregor and as many of the others as I could take with me when the right time came along."

"Go on."

Trijillo faced northward. He spoke so softly that at times Felicity could barely understand him. "I had a sister, senora. Her name was Rosita. She was young and beautiful and had so much to look forward to. We lived on my father's *hacienda* near Samalayuca."

Felicity leaned to the left so she would not miss a word.

"One night Rosita turned in as she always did. The next morning the servants reported that she was missing. All the *vaqueros* on the *hacienda* joined in a great search. We found tracks leading to the north-east, toward the border, toward Comanche country."

"The slavers took your sister?" Felicity guessed, appalled.

"*Si.* Boundaries mean nothing to *bastardos* like these. They raid in your country, they raid in mine, and then they flee into the wilderness so they will not be caught." Julio bowed his head. "We lost their trail at the Rio Grande. Months went by and we gave up hope of ever seeing her again. Then we received word from a man who trades with the Comanches that she had been sold to a chief. She was one of his wives."

The yelling had died down behind them. Other than the drum of hooves, the night was still.

"My *padre*, he sent word to this chief. He offered to pay a large ransom in horses and guns if the Comanches would see that she was safely returned to us. The chief agreed." Julio passed a hand across his eyes. "The trader was to bring them to a certain spot in the hills where we were waiting. My sister became hysterical, saying that she never wanted to go back—"

"Whatever for?" Felicity interjected.

"Rosita was too ashamed. She did not want to have people staring at her the rest of her life, to have them pointing and whispering behind her back. She told the trader that she would not be able to bear the humiliation." The brother took a breath. "But the chief would have none of it. He wanted the ransom. So he threw her on a horse and made her go along."

Felicity hung on every word.

"Two days out from the Comanche village, they made camp for the night. Rosita had acted cheerful all day, as if she had accepted what was to happen." Julio swallowed. "But she only did so to trick them, so they would not suspect what she really had in mind."

"Oh, God."

"*Si.* She slit her wrists and bled to death." A bitter sound, half laugh, half snarl, issued from the man's throat. "The chief felt he still deserved the ransom, so he brought the body to us. We killed him and the seven warriors with him."

There was nothing more to be said, so Felicity merely listened.

"My parents were satisfied that justice had been served. But I was not. The Comanches were not the ones to blame for my sister's death. It was the slavers who should pay. So for two years I roamed over northern Mexico and parts of Texas trying to find the band responsible. I changed my name. I made friends with anyone and everyone suspected of dealing with slavers. In time I learned who had taken my sister, and I spread the word that I wanted to join them." Julio looked up. "Now here I am."

Profound sorrow welled up in Felicity. The man had spoiled his chance of getting revenge by saving her. "If you ask me, you were in the right place at the right time. If not for you, I'd soon share your sister's fate."

Julio did not say a thing for over a minute. "Perhaps you are right, senora. Perhaps it was meant for me to be with the slavers at just this time. Perhaps it was meant for me to balance the scales. They took an innocent life, and I save one." He glanced at her, the upper half of his face hidden by the black *sombrero*. "Just do me a favor, senora."

"Anything."

"Make it count for something. Make something special of your life. Do not be one of those who wastes the gift they are given."

Abruptly, to the south, the collective thunder of many hooves rolled across the benighted prairie.

"They are after us," Julio announced.

"But how did they know which way we went?" Felicity wondered. "They can't track us in the dark."

"They do not need to," the Mexican said. "Gregor is not stupid. He has never trusted me, that one. I think he has suspected all along and was just waiting for me to show my true colors." He rode faster and she kept pace. "Gregor knows that I will take you to your husband."

Onward they galloped, Felicity a few yards behind her savior. Repeatedly she glanced back, seeking some sign of their pursuers. Not that she was very worried. It was so dark that she believed it would be child's play to elude the slavers.

Then a horse and rider appeared as if out of nowhere. Only he was in front of them, not behind them. He pointed a pistol at Julio Trijillo and called out, "For what you did to my wife, you're going to die!"

Chapter Eleven

Winona King was not one to let circumstances dictate the course of her life. When they ran contrary to the best interests of her welfare and those of her family, she opposed them with every ounce of strength in her body. And when her physical prowess was not equal to the task, she relied on her wits.

Circumstances had forced Winona to try to persuade Ricket that she wouldn't escape. She had even offered to give her solemn word as proof of her certainty—and been turned down.

Chipota had then interfered and claimed possession of her. For the past few hours she had ridden along docilely enough, but she had no intention of doing so forever. She hadn't given her word to the Lipan. There was nothing keeping her there, except herself.

As the small band wound down out of the foothills with darkness all around them, Winona was constantly on the alert for a means of gaining her freedom. She hoped that they'd pass close to extensive thickets, or else possibly a dense tract of woodland. Anywhere the brush would serve to slow the slavers down while she made good her escape.

Ricket was too wily for her. He avoided exactly the areas she looked for, as if he knew what was on her mind and he was determined to foil her. When they stopped briefly to rest their mounts, he made it a point to hover nearby, his rifle in the crook of his left elbow. She was not going to give them the slip if he could help it.

If the Lipan observed Ricket's behavior, he did not let on. He also did not appear to pay much attention to Winona, although several times she felt his eyes on her when he thought that she would not notice.

The hothead, Owens, gave Chipota a wide berth. But he was not above glaring at Winona every chance he got.

As for the others, they generally ignored her.

Which was just as well. Twice Winona had been on the verge of making a break for it even though the vegetation was too thin to screen her. In each instance, just as she went to make her move, she realized that either Ricket or Owens or Chipota was watching her on the sly.

Then they came to the top of a high ridge and Winona saw the prairie just over the next hill. The high grass offered her a ready haven if she could reach it well ahead of the slavers.

To that end, Winona shifted slightly forward on the mare without being obvious. Pretending to be more tired than she was, she yawned and stretched. As she lowered her arms, she placed both hands on the pinto's neck.

Chipota stared straight ahead. Ricket was guiding

his animal down a short incline. Owens glanced her way, then went to follow Ricket.

This was the moment. There might not be another. Winona knew that they would punish her if they caught her, that she would be beaten, or worse, and trussed up whether the Lipan liked it or not.

The stakes justified the risk.

Whipping forward, Winona snatched the reins and yanked with all her might, tearing them out of the warrior's grasp even as she slapped her legs against the mare's sides and let out with a Shoshone war whoop.

The pinto took off as if its tail were on fire. Its first bound brought it alongside the Lipan. Chipota twisted and grabbed at her, but she was ready and ducked under his arms. Her left leg flicked out, catching the warrior in the side. The blow sent him flying. He tried to clutch the back of his horse as he fell, but his fingers found no purchase on its sweaty hide.

In a flash Winona bore down on Owens. He had already jerked around and brought his rifle up. By all rights he should have put a ball into her. But in the fraction of a second it took him to fix a hasty bead, Winona did the last thing he would ever expect her to do. She deliberately rode her mare right into his horse.

Shoulder against shoulder, the two animals collided. The mare was smaller but it had more momentum and was going downhill.

Owens cried out as his animal went over the edge of the incline. He let go of his rifle to seize his reins, but it was too late. His horse whinnied as it lost its footing and toppled.

Ricket was only six feet lower down. He yelled something, but the words were lost in the frantic

David Thompson

squeals of the two horses as the hothead's mount rammed into his. Both slavers and their horses crashed to the ground, then slid toward the bottom in a jumbled heap.

It was just as Winona had planned. She came to the top of the incline but did not slow down. Leaning as far back as she could, she took the slope on the fly. She heard Owens curse as she whisked on by.

The mare came to a level stretch, and Winona cut to the right to a switchback, which would take her to the base of the ridge. A shot rang out above her. The slaver missed.

"Don't shoot, damn you!" Ricket yelled. "We want her alive!"

Winona had other ideas. The only way they would lay their hands on her again was if she were dead. Staying in the middle of the switchback where the footing was firmest, she swept around the first bend and made for the next lower down. She thought that she glimpsed a pinpoint of light off to the southeast. It was most likely a camp fire, but she was not about to slow down to confirm the fact.

One of the slavers was hard on her heels. Winona enjoyed a lead, but it was not big enough to suit her. She flicked the reins, urging the dependable mare to go even faster. It was a grave gamble on her part, since a single misstep would send them both tumbling down the ridge.

"Stop her!" Ricket was bellowing. "Damn it, somebody stop that squaw bitch!"

The switchback leveled off at the bottom, and Winona streaked around the low hill. Ahead rippled the sea of grass. She looked back and saw only one slaver. He was a beefy, bearded man whose buckskins were as greasy as the bottom of a cooking pot. Simpson was his name, and he had hardly spoken two words to her since her capture.

Winona smiled on reaching the edge of the prairie. The mare plunged in. The grass closed around them. Winona hugged the pinto so she would be harder to spot, but it did no good. The slaver had excellent eyesight. He didn't lose track of her.

It soon became apparent to Winona that she was not going to shake him. Simpson would chase her until his horse played out, or hers did.

The mare had superb stamina, but was it enough? Winona dared not fall into their clutches again. They would guard her every minute of every day until they sold her or did whatever else pleasured their vile minds. She would never have another chance to escape.

Desperate straits called for desperate measures. Once Winona took care of Simpson, she would be in the clear. How to go about it was the big question. An idea blossomed but she balked at carrying it out. It just might get her killed. Or, even worse, put her right back where she started.

Winona raced on. It quickly became evident that the mare was tiring sooner than she had counted on. She could hold off no longer. Either she put her plan into effect, or she might as well rein up and wait for Simpson. The thought hardened her features.

The wife of Grizzly Killer would never surrender her life or her dignity without doing all in her power to preserve both.

Hooking an arm over the pinto's neck and her foot over its back, Winona swung onto its right side. It was a feat Shoshone warriors often relied on in the heat of battle. So adept were some, that they could shoot a rifle or lose an arrow while at a full gallop.

Shoshone women, as a general rule, seldom practiced the trick. They had no reason to, since they rarely engaged in warfare from horseback. When enemies raided their villages, their duty was to protect their offspring and safeguard their lodges. Both were best done on foot.

When Shoshone warriors went on raids of their own, though, there were times when women went along. Mainly they were there to hold the horses while the men crept off into an enemy camp. Sometimes the raids would go all wrong. Their enemies would rally and chase after them. It was then that a woman had to be as good a rider as any man or suffer the fate of never seeing her people again.

Winona had gone on a few raids with her father and cousins when she was much younger. Beforehand, she had insisted that Touch The Clouds teach her the tricks of horsemanship at which he was so skilled. Consequently, she was one of the better women riders in her tribe.

She proved it now by traveling scores of yards while clinging to the side of the pounding mare as if she were a human fly. She counted on it being too dark for the slaver to notice that she had changed position.

The smooth tops of the grasses brushed her back, her legs. A constant loud swishing sounded in her ears.

Winona willed her tense muscles to relax. She needed her body limp or she might break a bone. A quick check showed Simpson well over 50 feet away. She stared eastward, waited a few more seconds, then pushed off from the mare.

The grass cushioned the brunt of the fall. Winona landed on her left shoulder and rolled a half-dozen feet. The instant she stopped, she rose up into a crouch and glided back to where she had landed.

Timing now became critical. Winona coiled her

legs, her every nerve stretched taut. The grass hid Simpson and his mount. She had to rely on her hearing alone to gauge his approach. Louder and louder grew the drumming of his animal's hooves. Suddenly it reared up out of the night just a few feet away to her left.

Winona was in motion the moment it appeared. A pair of lithe bounds brought her to the steed's side. Simpson was so intent on keeping track of the mare that he didn't realize she was there until her hands closed on his leg. She heaved upward.

The slaver uttered a startled squawk as he was sent flying. He attempted to grab hold of his saddle, but it all happened so fast that he was in midair before he knew it. His rifle went sailing. His horse kept on running.

Winona saw where he crashed down and bounded forward. She had but moments before he recovered and confronted her. Clasping her hands together, she balled them into a knot and raised her arms to strike the slaver before he could stand. Everything depended on her being able to knock him senseless quickly.

It wasn't meant to be.

A heavy foot speared out of the stems and caught Winona on the shins. The blow knocked her legs right out from under her. She came down on her hands and knees and immediately scrambled to her feet again.

Simpson stood, too, but much more slowly. A mocking grin curled his thick lips. He made no attempt to draw either of the pistols at his waist, nor the knife on his right hip. Brushing at a sleeve, he regarded her closely and said, "Damn, but you're a sly one. I never would have figured you to pull a trick like that in a million years."

Winona did not respond. Shoshone warriors believed it was the height of folly to talk while in the heat of battle. And she was in a battle for her very life, whether the slaver appreciated the fact or not.

"Well, you've had your fun," Simpson said. "Now we'll just wait here for my horse to come back. And it will, in a little bit. I trained it myself in case I was ever clipped by a tree limb or some such."

The man was too sure of himself for his own good. He stood there talking down to her when he should have been acting. Winona was close enough that all she had to do was lunge and fling her hands at his waist. She wanted either pistol. She got neither.

Simpson pivoted and slammed the flat of his right hand into her shoulder even as he whipped a leg in front of her.

Unable to stop in time, Winona was upended into the grass. Pain lanced her thigh as she hit the ground, but she suppressed it and leaped to her feet before the slaver could close in. To her surprise, Simpson merely stood there, smirking.

"You're a feisty squaw, ain't you? I admire that. I truly do. But you'd better behave yourself now. I don't cotton to red devils actin' up around their betters."

At last Winona understood. His scorn did not stem from the fact that she was a woman. No, it stemmed from his disdain for anyone who happened to be Indian. In a word, he was prejudiced, as were many of his kind who believed that the only good Indian was a dead Indian. He rated her as beneath contempt. He was about to learn differently.

Winona bowed her head as if he had her cowed. She let her shoulders droop and took a step backward.

"That's more like it," Simpson said, placing his

hands on his wide hips. "I knew you'd get it through your thick red head sooner or later that it wasn't worth your while to try anything." He started to glance over his shoulder. "Now where in tarnation is that blamed horse of mine?"

The slaver played right into Winona's hands. She launched herself at him, low down this time, and heard his fiery oath as her arms looped around his legs. Although Simpson was far too heavy for her to lift, she could and did get enough leverage to jerk his legs right out from under him. The man cursed again as he tottered and fell.

Winona rolled once to the right to avoid being pinned. Reversing herself, she snatched one of the flintlocks as Simpson struggled to stand. The barrel was not quite clear of the slaver's belt when he caught hold of the pistol and tried to wrest it from her grasp. For a few tense moments they struggled. There was a loud click. Winona looked down just as the flintlock went off.

It was only by accident that neither of them was struck. The ball smacked into the ground within a finger's width of the slaver's foot and made him madder than ever. Calling her every vile name Winona had ever heard white men use and some she had not, Simpson resorted to sheer brute force, tore the pistol from her grasp, and snapped it overhead to bash her in the head.

Winona could not possibly evade the blow. Trying to block it would only result in her being battered to her knees. So instead of doing either, she went on the offensive. She kicked Simpson in the right knee.

The roar of mixed torment and rage that the slaver vented would have done justice to a rampaging grizzly. Simpson staggered backward, sputtering and snarling. "You bitch! You filthy red bitch! You broke my damn knee!" He swung the pistol in a vicious backhand.

The swing was ill-timed and awkward. Winona skipped aside, closed in before he could regain his balance, and kicked him in the other knee. Simpson went down, tripping over his own feet and landing on his backside. His features screwed in agony, he hissed at her as might a furious serpent. Then he did something she did not expect. He flung the spent flintlock at her face.

Winona easily dodged it. The gesture seemed futile until she felt his calloused palms close on her ankles. He had hurled the pistol to distract her. His real intent had been to get his hands on her, to yank her down beside him as he now did.

"You're going to regret hurting me, squaw!" Simpson growled while in the act of throwing himself on top of her. His left hand held her right wrist in a vise. His legs pinned hers. His free hand touched her waist, then slid higher. "Guess how?"

Winona fought with a savagery born of desperation. She bucked. She kicked. She thrashed and pushed. But it was as if he weighed tons. All her effort, and she could hardly budge him. His hot, foul breath fanned her face. His sweaty skin was so close to hers that she could feel its warmth. He leered and raised his free hand to touch her breasts.

Never! Winona mentally shrieked.

Her plight seemed hopeless. Other women might have given up then and there and submitted to what they deemed inevitable. But Winona King refused to give in.

Long ago Nate had taught her a valuable lesson. It had been on a sunny summer afternoon when he was teaching her how to shoot a rifle. Their talk had gotten around to personal combat, and what she should do if she were ever beset by a stronger foe when no gun or knife was handy.

"Do whatever it takes," Nate had told her. "When your life is at stake, there are no rules. There's no right way and wrong way to defend yourself. Bite, scratch, claw, kick, do whatever it takes to come out on top."

Winona had grinned at the image of her biting someone.

"I'm serious," Nate insisted. "Anything goes. Tear a nose off, or an ear. Gouge an eye out. Do whatever it takes to preserve your life. Nothing else matters." He had taken her into his arms and gently kissed her. "Not where I'm concerned. Without you, my life would be empty."

Whatever it takes, her husband had said. Winona applied that philosophy now by bending her neck and sinking her teeth into the soft flesh on the left side of the slaver's neck. The ease with which her teeth sheared through the skin was amazing. Crinkly hairs got into her mouth. So did a bitter taste, then the salty tang of blood.

A feral howl was torn from Simpson's throat. In a reflex action he lunged backward, and in doing so caused more flesh to be torn wide. Her teeth lost their grip.

"Damn your bones!"

The slaver glared down at her, raw hatred seeming to crackle around him like a physical force. He let go of her wrist and streaked both hands to her throat.

"You're going to die, bitch! Do you hear me? I don't care what Gregor wants. You're mine!"

His spittle dripped onto Winona's cheek. She hardly noticed as she clawed impotently at his locked fingers. She did notice, however, the berserk gleam animating his features. In a very few moments he would make good on his threat unless she could think of a way to stop him. In vain she punched his face and neck.

Simpson was bleeding profusely but he didn't care. All that mattered to him was strangling the life from the captive who had brought him so much suffering. "Die, squaw! Die!" he cried, and squeezed even harder.

Felicity Ward was so shocked by the unexpected appearance of the rider that she did not think to rein up, as Julio Trijillo automatically did. It was just as well, because she rode directly between the pair just as her husband was about to fire. "Simon!" she exclaimed, and halted. Intense joy vied with amazed disbelief. "Don't shoot! He's a friend!"

Simon Ward came so close to accidentally shooting his beloved that forever after when he recalled this night, he would shudder and grow as cold as ice. His trigger finger was applying pressure when she filled his sights. For the life of him, he would never know how he managed to keep from firing. But he did, and with a jab of his heels he was beside her horse and holding her in his arms.

For a few precious seconds the husband and wife embraced, each overwhelmed by happiness so profound that their hearts felt near to bursting. There were so many things they wanted to say to one another. Fate did not give them the chance.

"Senora Ward," Julio said urgently. "We must ride on. Gregor and the rest will catch us if we do not."

Simon glanced at the Mexican. He wanted to learn who the man was, to discover why a slaver had befriended Felicity. But the rumble of approaching horses alerted him to the new danger they faced.

"Lead the way, friend," he said. "We'll be right behind you."

Now that Simon had been reunited with the woman who meant more to him than life itself, he was not going to let her out of his sight. Had speed not been essential, he would have insisted that she ride double with him just so he could relish the feel of her body being close to his and know that he wasn't dreaming, that they really and truly were together again.

Julio took the lead as requested. His *sombrero* slipped off his tousled hair and hung by a chin strap. He headed to the northeast instead of due north in the hope that it would throw the slavers off their scent.

Felicity galloped beside her husband. Again and again she glanced at him to reassure herself that he was actually there. Ever since Julio had told her that Simon might be alive, she had hoped against hope that he would find her. But she had been racked by troubling doubts. The prairie was vast, after all, and Simon was no Daniel Boone.

Yet there he was, grinning at her as he used to do when they were courting and they would go for long rides in the countryside surrounding Boston, his teeth a pale half-moon in the darkness.

Felicity smiled to show her own happiness, then knuckled down to the task of keeping up with Julio. He was going faster than ever, as if it were crucial that they put a lot of ground behind them in a very short time. She would have thought it more important for them to pace their mounts so the horses would last longer. But he knew best, she reasoned.

The bay Simon Ward was riding had been pushed so hard for the past two days that it gave signs of flagging. Simon spurred it on anyway. He was not about to slow the others down and have his wife fall into the clutches of the vile slavers a second time.

So overjoyed was Simon at finding Felicity that several more minutes went by before he awakened to the terrible mistake he had made. In his haste to save his wife, he had gone off and left the man who had been willing to risk all on their behalf. He had abandoned the one person he had met since leaving Boston whom he would rate as a true friend.

But the worst part, the thought that made Simon feel sick inside, was not that Nate King was all alone, nor that the trapper was as blind as the proverbial bat. No, what upset Simon the most was that it appeared the slavers were heading right for him.

Chapter Twelve

"Simon, wait!" Nate King called out as the Bostonian sped off into the night. It was useless. The younger man was not to be denied. Nate might as well try to stop a twister or a raging hailstorm. Love was as powerful a force as Nature itself; some would say it was more powerful.

The frontiersman poked the black stallion and set out to follow Ward. He wanted to keep Simon out of trouble, to be there in case he was needed. But he had not gone more than ten yards when the stallion suddenly dug in its front hooves and slid to a stop. A distinct rattling told him why. He cut to the right to keep the horse from being bitten just as the snake's rattles sounded again.

To Nate's consternation, the stallion reared. He made a grab for its neck, but he had been taken un-awares. The next thing he knew, he was on his back on the ground and the big black was racing to the southwest. Nate went to rise but changed his mind on hearing the rattlesnake. It was so close that he could have reached out and picked it up.

Few city-bred folks were aware that rattlers liked to do most of their hunting at night. Fewer still knew that the deadly reptiles thrived on the plains. Small wonder, since the prairie was where prairie dog towns were found, and prairie dogs were a rattlesnake staple.

Nate King knew, of course. The knowledge afforded scant comfort as he lay there in the sweet-smelling grass listening to the brittle harbinger of impending death.

Nate did not twitch a muscle. He did not even blink. Any movement, however slight, might provoke the snake into striking. Rigid as a log, he prayed the reptile would wander elsewhere, and do it soon. But a minute went by. Two.

Then, to compound Nate's predicament, the black stallion's familiar whinny carried to him across the prairie. The stallion had recovered from its fright and was heading back.

Most other horses would have fled until exhaustion brought them to a stop. Not the big black. It was made of firmer stuff, yet another reason the trapper valued it so highly.

The rattling ceased. The grass close to Nate's arm rustled. The scrape of scales was loud enough for him to tell that the rattler was leaving. Moments later the stallion trotted up. Rising, he stepped toward it, one arm outstretched. As soon as he touched its sweaty side, he swung up.

The delay had proven costly. Simon was long gone. Nate listened and thought he heard hoofbeats. Taking it for granted that Simon's bay was the source, he headed out, riding slowly, a sitting duck if ever there had been one.

It troubled Nate to think that he might be wrong, that maybe he had gotten turned around when he fell and he was now going in the wrong direction. But it was a chance he had to take, for the Wards' sake.

The fall seemed to have had an unforeseen effect. Nate was gratified to note that he could now make out the motion of the stallion's head, although the horse was no more than a great fuzzy blur. To test himself, he held the Hawken within six inches of his face and moved the barrel back and forth. Again he could distinguish the motion, although the barrel itself was a dark smudge against the backdrop of night sky.

Encouraged, Nate ventured on. Given the time that had elapsed, he figured that Simon couldn't be more than half a mile ahead of him at the very most.

Then a shot rang out. Nate drew rein, puzzled. The retort came from off to the west, not the southeast, and it was much closer than he had assumed Simon would be. Had the younger man strayed off course? he wondered. That seemed highly unlikely, since Simon had the slaver camp fire to serve as a beacon. The only possible explanation was that he was the one who had strayed.

Nate promptly worked the reins and rode westward. He held the stallion to a brisk walk and bent at the waist with an ear cocked to the breeze. There might not be much warning when he ran into the slavers. He hung on every noise, no matter how faint.

So it was that Nate detected the sounds of a scuffle long before he might have done so otherwise. The loud grunt of a man was mixed with the rustling of grass. Dreading that Simon had been jumped by slavers, he hastened closer. A lusty bellow helped him pinpoint the exact spot.

"You're going to die, bitch! Do you hear me? I don't care what Gregor wants. You're mine!"

Nate stiffened. It had to be Mrs. Ward in the clutches of one of the cutthroats! He fingered the Hawken, his thumb on the hammer. The struggle grew louder. Again the man bellowed.

"Die, squaw! Die!"

So it wasn't Felicity Ward, Nate realized, relieved. He had no time to ponder the mystery, for moments later he heard the crackle of grass and a bestial growl only a few yards ahead. Instantly he reined up. By narrowing his eyes he could make out a vague pair of clenched figures. But he could not tell which was the woman and which was her assailant.

A choking sob prompted Nate to act before the woman was slain. Since he couldn't determine which one to shoot, he decided to try a bluff. Leveling the Hawken, he declared in a flinty tone, "That's enough! Get up with your hands in the air, mister! And be quick about it!"

Winona King had seen a rider appear out of the gloom. At first, she did not recognize him. Her lungs were close to bursting from lack of air; her vision danced in circles. Then, for a few heartbeats, it cleared. Winona was so astounded at seeing her mate that she went limp with shock, certain that she must be seeing things, that her eyes were deceiving her.

It was fitting, she mused, that in her final fevered moments of life she should imagine the man who had claimed her love was right there in front of her.

The vision spoke. The voice was her husband's, but he did not say the things she wanted to hear. He did not tell her that he cared and would go on caring forever. He did not say how much he would miss her, or how wrong it was that she had been snatched from him when they both were in the prime of their lives. Instead, her vision barked an order. And to her bewilderment, the slaver heard, too, because he let go of her as if her neck were a red hot ember and leaped to his feet.

But that could only mean one thing! Winona told herself. She propped her hands on the ground and attempted to sit up, but she was too weak, her mind too sluggish. She saw Simpson elevate his arms and her Nate cover him.

Something was wrong, though. Winona sensed it in the core of her being. And she was sure that whatever it was had to do with Nate.

In a rush, clarity returned. Winona started to rise. She noticed that Nate was holding the Hawken at the wrong angle, that the barrel pointed at her instead of the slaver. Simpson had noticed, also, because his left hand was slowly dipping toward his other flintlock. Strangely, Nate seemed not to realize it.

Winona could not call out a warning. Her throat was too raw. She could barely croak, let alone speak. Yet if she did not do something—and swiftly—she would lose her man. Planting both moccasins, she marshaled all the strength she had left and launched herself upward. Her right hand closed on the hilt of Simpson's long butcher knife as the slaver drew the pistol. He was extending the flintlock when the blade sank into his side below the ribs.

Simpson arched his spine, threw back his head, and opened his mouth as if to scream. No sound came out. He staggered a few steps. Winona kept pace, holding the knife in place. The slaver twisted his head to glare at her. "You lousy squaw! You've done kilt me!" So saying, his arm sagged and his whole body deflated as might a punctured water skin. He twitched for a bit once he curled onto the grass, then stopped breathing.

Nate had seen the blur of movement but had no idea what was going on until the man spoke. Filled with anxiety, he dismounted to help the woman. "Ma'am? Are you all right? I—"

The trapper never got to finish his statement. A warm form flew into his arms and suddenly words of ardent love and tender endearments were being whispered in his ear. The shock of recognition made his legs go weak. "Winona?" Her lips confirmed it and smothered his with tiny hot kisses. For the longest while after that they stood there in a quiet embrace.

Winona was the first to break the spell. Looking up, she said, "My heart sings with joy at seeing you again, husband. But how did you know the slavers had taken me captive?"

Briefly, Nate sketched his encounter with the Bostonian and the events since. Even as he talked, his vision cleared a little more. By the time he was done, he could make out her eyes, nose and mouth although they were not crystal-clear as yet. She reached up and brushed her fingertips over the skin below his eyes.

"You take too many risks, husband. Take no more until you can see again."

"I don't have much choice in the matter," Nate responded. "We have to help those greenhorns if we can." He stepped into the stirrups, lowered his arm to give her a boost, and wheeled the stallion. "Can you see any sign of a camp fire?"

"Yes," Winona said. "I will guide you."

Nate smiled as one of her arms looped around his

waist. It flabbergasted him that they were together again. By the same token, inwardly he quaked to think of the grisly fate that would have been her lot had he not stumbled on her at just the right moment. It was almost as if a higher power had a hand in her salvation.

Presently Nate could see the fire too. No voices came from the camp, which disturbed him. It was much too early for all the slavers to have turned in.

The night itself was much too tranquil, reminding Nate of the lull before a storm. He slowed to be on the safe side. Since he had given the Hawken to his wife, he drew a pistol.

"The camp is deserted except for four horses," Winona whispered. "We can go right on in."

"Unless it's a trap," Nate said. It made no sense for the slavers to have gone off and left their camp unattended. He stayed where he was for several minutes until convinced that it would be safe.

The tethered horses displayed no alarm. Nate rode to where packs, parfleches and a few saddles were piled near the crackling flames.

"It looks as if they left in a hurry," Winona commented, reading the tracks by the firelight. "Perhaps they are after your friend."

"And they took his wife along?" Nate shook his head. "They would have left her behind, under guard. No, I reckon Simon got her away from them somehow, and the whole kit and caboodle lit a shuck after him. See if you can tell which direction they went."

Winona slid off and walked to the edge of the clearing. She made a circuit of the perimeter, stooping every so often to examine the soil. Freshly overturned clods of dirt showed her exactly where the slavers had entered the grass. "Over here," she said.

Nate had been keeping an eye out for slavers. His vision was almost back to normal. A little while more and he would be able to give the renegades a taste of their own medicine.

Holding the pistol in his left hand, Nate rode toward his wife. It seemed to him that she had never been as lovely as she was at that exact moment, with the dancing firelight playing off her smooth features and the shadows at her back.

Then one of those shadows moved. Nate went to shout a warning, but the shadow pounced before he could. A brawny Indian in a breechcloth seized Winona from behind, pinned her arms to her sides, and started to drag her toward the grass. She resisted by digging in her heels and slamming her head backward.

Nate raised the flintlock and charged to her aid. He had to get a lot closer before he dared fire. Suddenly another figure popped up out of the grass, pointed a rifle at him, and fired. In the slaver's haste, the man missed. Nate swiveled, fixed as steady a bead as he could, held it, and stroked the trigger.

The cutthroat screeched as he flung his hands up and keeled over.

The black stallion was almost to the grass. Winona heard it coming. She knew that Nate would leap down to help her, and the thought filled her with dread. With his eyesight dimmed, he would be no match for the Lipan.

Fear lent added strength to Winona's limbs. She had tried to butt the Lipan in the face, but he always turned his cheek to her. She had tried kicking his legs out from under him, but he planted himself so firmly that an avalanche would not have budged him. Now Winona took a new tack. She still had the Hawken clutched in her right hand. Glancing down, she saw the Lipan's left foot next to her leg. Without hesitation she drove the stock down onto his toes.

Something cracked. The warrior took a hopping step backward, pulling her after him. Winona swung the rifle around behind the two of them and tried to snare his legs to trip him. She succeeded, but she could not hold on. The Hawken fell.

Nate saw all this as he vaulted from the stallion. He rushed to help her when yet another slaver reared up off to the right. Nate dropped as a rifle cracked. The ball whizzed overhead like a riled hummingbird. Straightening, Nate saw the slaver barrel toward him while unlimbering a pistol.

Somewhere, a gruff voice yelled, "Owens! Don't be a jackass! Stay down until we nail him!"

The onrushing slaver paid no heed.

The Hawken was only a few yards away, but Nate could not hope to reach it before Owens reached him. He needed to slow the man down for just a second or two. To that end, Nate pointed his spent pistol as if he were going to shoot.

Owens ducked and veered a few feet to one side.

Which was just what Nate wanted him to do. Taking a single long stride, Nate dived. He released the pistol in midair so he could scoop up the Hawken as he hit the ground. In a smooth roll he rose to his knees and leveled the rifle at his waist at the selfsame moment that the slaver crashed out of the grass right in front of him.

Owens had his pistol up, but as he burst into full view his attention was drawn to the fierce struggle between Chipota and Winona. Belatedly, he spied the crouched figure in the shadows in front of him.

At a range of no more than a yard, Nate fired. The Hawken boomed and kicked. The heavy caliber slug caught the slaver in the stomach and lifted him off his feet.

Owens was hurled back into the grass. He screamed as he crashed down. Rolling into a ball, he clutched the large hole in his gut and wailed in torment.

Nate moved in quickly, eager to help Winona. He drew his butcher knife as he stood over the squalling cutthroat. Owens glanced up, foresaw his impending doom, and uttered a high-pitched scream.

"*Noooooooooooo!*"

A short thrust silenced the wavering cry. Nate turned and saw the man's pistol lying on the ground. He picked it up, then ran toward his wife. More concerned for her welfare than his own, he almost missed spotting the grizzled slaver who swooped toward him.

Nate twisted, thereby saving his life. The newcomer already had a rifle pressed to a shoulder, and fired. The lead ball creased Nate's side, digging a shallow furrow low down on his ribs. It provoked an intense spasm of raw pain and drew blood, but it did not stop Nate from extending the pistol he had just snatched off the ground, curling back the hammer, and squeezing.

The slaver called Ricket had not lived as long as he had by being reckless. He truly thought that he had the big stranger dead to rights. He'd seen the man shoot Williams with the only pistol the man had on him. Then he'd seen Owens go down. Figuring that the stranger's guns were all empty, Ricket had closed in to do the job right.

The crack of the pistol was the last sound Earl Ricket ever heard.

While all this had been going on, Winona King had drawn the knife she had taken from Simpson and turned on the Lipan. She slashed at his torso as he grabbed at her neck. The blade sliced in smoothly but was deflected by a rib. Chipota grunted, seized her knife arm, and flung her to the ground.

As she came down, Winona kicked. She clipped the Lipan on the thigh. It was not a forceful blow, but it did prevent him from pouncing on her.

Chipota skirted to the left. His war club lay nearby but he did not retrieve it. Nor did he draw the knife at his hip. Evidently he planned to take her alive, or else he was going to throttle the life from her with his bare hands.

Winona was not about to submit to either. Swiveling on her back like an overturned turtle, she held him at bay with the point of the butcher knife. His bronzed hand flicked at her wrist. She parried and nearly took off a few fingers. An odd smile lit his face as he skipped to the right, tensed, and sprang.

Winona was a hair too slow. She winced when a rock-hard fist batted her arm aside and knees as stout as tree trunks rammed into her stomach. The stars swirled. Her knife was plucked from her fingers. She blinked and looked up. Chipota was on top of her, but he did not stay there.

A human battering ram clad in buckskins hurtled out of nowhere and slammed into the Lipan's chest. Both men catapulted into the grass. Winona sat up, her heart in her throat at the sight of the muscular warrior and her husband locked in mortal combat. Chipota had the knife raised to strike, but Nate held the warrior's arm back.

They rolled first one way, then another. Nate put all he had into pinning his foe so he could finish the warrior off, but the slaver twisted and shifted like a greased snake. For some reason it reminded Nate of the time he had fought an Apache down in New Mexico. Why that should be, he didn't know.

Chipota was highly skilled at close-quarters combat. All the warriors in his tribe were. Like their Apache brethren, they lived for war, and had been doing so for so many generations that they had few equals.

Chipota, in particular, had always preferred to slay his enemies up close. It gave him pleasure to see the life fade from their eyes and feel their limbs grow weak. It was why he liked to use a war club instead of a bow or lance or gun.

The Lipan's passion for dispensing death was in part to blame for his being banished from the tribe. When another warrior had made light of him once too many times, he'd leaped on the man and strangled him right there in front of half the village.

Now Chipota intended to add to his long string of victims. Muscles rippling, he sought to bury his knife in the white-eye who had rashly attacked him. He did not expect much resistance since it had been his experience that whites, by and large, were weaklings. In his previous clashes with them, he had never so much as worked up a sweat.

This white-eye proved to be the exception. Chipota strained, but was met by equal strength. He tried to tear his arm free so he could stab but was held fast by a grip that rivaled his own. He resorted to every trick he knew in order to break the white-eye's hold but was balked at every turn.

Even as Chipota fought, in the back of his mind he wondered about the white man's identity. When he had come on the pair shortly after finding Simpson's body, he had assumed the white man to be a stray trapper. But while trailing them to the camp, the warrior had seen how the Shoshone pressed herself against the white-eye, how she held him and touched him. She would not do that to just any man. No, not her.

It had to be the woman's mate, Chipota had concluded. The Shoshone had been telling them all along that her man would come to free her. The white slavers had laughed at her, having heard many women make the same claim in the past.

For once, their captive had been telling the truth.

Now Chipota was fighting for his life against an adversary every bit as formidable as any he had ever faced. As they continued to grapple, he drove a knee at the white-eye's groin.

The Shoshone's husband blocked it by shifting so that his hip absorbed the blow. Then the white-eye pivoted, hooked a leg behind Chipota's, and flipped the Lipan onto his back.

Rather abruptly, Chipota found himself staring up at the tip of his own knife as it was forced inexorably downward toward his throat. He exerted every ounce of strength he had to keep the blade from penetrating his flesh, but it was not enough.

The wily warrior worked his legs to the right and managed to bend them at the knees. All he had to do was sweep his feet up and around and he would dislodge the white-eye. But as he coiled to do so, the unexpected occurred. Hands took hold of his ankles and yanked his legs straight. Before he quite comprehended what was going on, someone sat on his shins. In desperation he attempted to tug loose, but the weight pinned his legs in place.

Insight brought a rare smile of resignation to the Lipan's lips. It was over. He had done his best but it was not good enough, not against the both of them. As the butcher knife slowly sheared into his jugular, he regretted that he had not met the Shoshone many winters ago when they were both young. It would have been nice to make her into his woman—whether she wanted to be it or not.

Nate King gave a final wrench. The blade sank to the hilt. He stayed on top of the warrior, blood splattering him on the cheeks and chin, until a hand tapped him on the shoulder.

"It is over, husband. He is dead."

Straightening, Nate slid his damp hand off the slick hilt. He was taken aback to find his wife perched on the warrior's shins. His other hand covered her knee as he surveyed the bodies lying nearby.

"I'm afraid it's not over yet. We still have to find the Wards."

At that very moment, Simon and Felicity Ward and their Mexican ally were fleeing for their lives. Julio was in the lead. Simon and his wife rode abreast of one another. Ahead of them lay countless miles of swaying grass. Behind them, hot on their trail, were Gregor and the band of cutthroats.

It had all gone so well there for a while. Simon had been convinced that they had given the slavers the slip. Then he had remembered Nate King, alone and defenseless, and he had turned the bay while yelling for the others to go on.

What possessed him to think they'd obey, Simon would never know. Almost immediately Felicity had wheeled to follow him, so of course Julio had done the same. Simon had reined up and gestured for them to turn around but they ignored him.

"Where are you going?" Felicity had demanded.

"The man who helped me find you is in trouble. I have to go help him," Simon had quickly explained. "The two of you should go on. We'll catch up by daylight, I would imagine."

Felicity looked at him as if he were insane. "You

can't be serious. After all we've been through, do you really think I would stand for being separated again? Where you go, dearest, I go."

Simon had appealed to Julio. "Talk some sense into her. You know what will happen if the slavers get their hands on us. She has to go with you."

To the young man's annoyance, the Mexican had said, "So sorry, senor, but this is between the two of you. I will abide by whatever you two decide."

"Then it's settled. We'll search for your friend," Felicity declared, and made as if to ride back the way they had come.

"No!" Simon had objected, barring her path. "I want you out of here, now! Get to safety and don't fret about me!"

A retort had been on the tip of Felicity's tongue. But it was never voiced. For from out of the night to the west rose a cry of triumph.

"Did you hear that, boys? We're closer than we thought. After the bastards!"

It had been Gregor. The slavers had thundered toward them with yips and howls. Simon had no choice but to forget about the mountain man for the time being.

That had been half an hour ago. All three of their horses now showed signs of fatigue. Simon knew it was just a matter of time before they had to make a stand, and he was not about to delude himself over the outcome. Even with Julio's help, it was preordained.

A minor godsend of sorts in the shape of a low knoll rose before them. Julio raced to the top, hauled on his reins, and was out of the saddle before his animal stopped moving. Rushing a few yards down the slope, he knelt and aimed his rifle.

Simon was only a few steps behind. He tucked his

rifle to his shoulder as a ragged cluster of slavers materialized, bearing down on the knoll like a pack of frenzied Cossacks.

The cutthroats had not expected their quarry to turn. Gregor was the first to spot the kneeling figures and bellowed, "Scatter! We're in their sights!" Suiting action to words, he swung onto the off side of his mount, Indian fashion, and angled to the north. Some of the others did the same.

Julio and Simon fired at the same moment. Two of the slavers were knocked from their mounts, never to rise again. A third was downed by Julio, who drew one of his fancy pistols in a blur and banged off the shot just as the rider was about to shoot the Bostonian. Simon whipped out his own pistol, but by then the slavers had scattered into the high grass.

"We must ride, senor, before they think to cut us off," the Mexican urged.

Nodding, Simon started back up the knoll. Felicity had climbed down and held the reins of all three animals. He had almost reached her when several shots rang out. One struck Trijillo's mount in the neck. The horse whinnied and reared, throwing the bay and Felicity's animal into a panic. She tried to hold on, but several more shots were all it took to send the three horses racing off in different directions.

Julio made a frantic bid to catch his. He chased it partway down the far side and only stopped when another rifle cracked and a ball cored his right thigh.

Simon saw their newfound friend jerk to the impact and fall. He sprinted to Julio's side. Propping an arm under the Mexican's shoulder, Simon began to haul him to the top when to his dismay Felicity appeared on the other side of Julio to take his other arm. "Get down in the grass," Simon directed. "They can't hit what they can't see."

"He helped me when I needed it."

And that was all she would say. They regained the crown without another shot being fired. Sinking low, Simon eased Julio onto his back. The thigh was bleeding badly and Trijillo had his teeth clenched. "Hang on," Simon said. "I'll cut my shirt to make a tourniquet."

"No time, senor!" Julio said, clutching Simon's wrist. "They will come soon. They will wipe us out."

Simon did it anyway. There had been a time not all that long ago when he would have broken down in tears at the setback they had suffered. He would have been devastated. But that was the old Simon Ward. This was the new. He calmly accepted the inevitable. Sliding his knife from its leather sheath, he shrugged out of his shirt and bent to his task.

Felicity had her head turned into the wind. "They're moving around down there," she reported. "I can hear a lot of whispering. They must be up to something."

"They are surrounding us," Julio said. "There is no way out now. I am sorry, senora."

"For what? Trying to save my life?" Felicity took his hand in hers. "Be still now. You'll only make the bleeding worse."

The next 15 minutes were the worst of Simon's whole life. Not because he knew that in a very short while he would die, but because of what he had to do when the slavers overran them. He glanced at his wife and prayed he would find the courage.

Julio insisted on sitting up after he was bandaged. He reloaded his guns and gave one of his expensive pistols to Felicity.

The rustling and whispering stopped, but it was not quiet for long. To the north, Gregor bellowed,

"The jig is up, Ward. I don't know how you survived being shot, but it doesn't hardly matter. Your wife is ours whether you like it or not. So make it easy on yourself and turn her over to us, pronto."

The words seemed to rise from Simon's throat of their own accord. "Go to hell, you son of a bitch! You'll never get your hands on her again!"

"That's what you think!"

A pistol cracked. Simon ducked, thinking he was the target, but the shot was only the signal for all the slavers to rise up at once and rush the knoll. He fired his rifle and one dropped, fired his pistol and a second toppled. Beside him Julio brought down two more. Felicity's pistol banged, but Simon did not see whether she hit anyone.

The onrushing line slowed but did not break. Slavers cut loose all around the knoll. Felicity gasped as a burning sensation seared her arm. She heard a bullet thud into Julio, as did a second, and a third.

Both men reloaded frantically. Simon had his rifle primed but not the pistol when several slavers loomed in front of him. He planted a ball in the forehead of the foremost. Julio's pistol took an added toll.

Then their guns were empty and the slavers were on them. Simon streaked out his knife and pivoted to plunge it into Felicity as he had promised himself he would do. He froze.

Gregor was a few feet away. The giant slaver had the barrel of his rifle centered on Simon's head. "You should have listened, boy!"

Simon would never forget the sight of the top of Gregor's head exploding in a shower of brains and gore. He thought that Julio had fired, but when he glanced around he discovered their friend was on the ground, riddled with holes.

Black Powder

The answer came in the form of two riders who tore into the startled slavers as if they were chaff before a storm. In savage fury the pair slew cutthroats right and left. Many of the slavers had emptied their guns and had not had time to reload. They were easy prey.

Six slavers fell in twice as many seconds, and then the man sprang from his black stallion and was among them, wielding a butcher knife. Three more lay wheezing in puddles of their own blood before the few who lived fled down the knoll and vanished in the grass.

Just like that, it was over.

Felicity Ward turned from the mound of earth at the top of the knoll and walked with bowed head to her horse. She looked at the others. "He saved my life and I never even knew his real name."

Nate King patted a parfleche tied behind his saddle. "I'll take his possibles to Bent's Fort. There's a letter, written in Spanish. I think it's to his folks. William Bent will see that everything goes south on the next wagon train to Santa Fe. From there, it can be sent to his family. They'll learn what he did. I expect they'll be right proud."

"I hope so," Felicity said sincerely.

Nate faced the younger man. "What about the two of you? What have you decided?"

Simon exchanged glances with his wife. "We talked it over most of the night and all of this morning. You'll probably think we're out of our minds, but we want to stick it out. We can't let all that has happened be for nothing."

"Well, I'll be," Nate said, genuinely surprised. "Whereabouts do you want to settle?"

"We were hoping you could help us out in that regard."

Winona King laughed. "I have always wanted neighbors. How would you like to live in the next valley over from ours? There is plenty of water and game. And I would have someone to visit with when my husband is gone weeks at a time trapping."

"Oh, could we?" Felicity beamed, clapping her hands.

Simon was just as delighted. "This means that Nate can teach me all I need to know about surviving in the wilderness. Let's get going! I can hardly wait to see this valley." Prodding the bay, he took the lead, but he had only gone a few feet when the trapper called his name. "What is it?" he asked, reining up.

"Your first lesson. You're going in the wrong direction."

TRAIL'S END

Chapter One

Nate King reined up the instant the forest fell silent.

A moment before, the big free trapper had been winding up a steep switchback toward a jagged ridge. He rode easily in the saddle, as befitted a man who spent so much of his time on horseback.

Like many of his hardy breed, the mountain man favored an Indian style of dress. Buckskins covered his powerful frame. Moccasins protected his feet. On his head rested a dark beaver hat crowned by a single eagle feather.

Whenever Nate ventured from his family's cabin nestled high in the majestic Rocky Mountains, he went armed for bear, as the saying had it. In this instance a brace of flintlock pistols were wedged under his wide brown leather belt. On his right hip hung a long butcher knife in a beaded sheath. On his left side was a Shoshone tomahawk. An ammo pouch, powder horn, and possibles bag were all slanted across his broad chest. And held firmly in his left hand with the polished stock braced on his thigh was a Hawken rifle.

Moments ago the surrounding slopes had been alive with sounds: the gay chirping of sparrows, the strident squawk of jays, the chattering of squirrels, and more. Then, as abruptly as if a gigantic invisible hand had smothered every living creature, the sounds had died.

Now the air lay deathly still. Nate King cocked his ruggedly handsome head from side to side, but detected no hint of noise other than the fluttering whisper of the northwesterly breeze. Yet there had to be something—or someone—out there.

Small animals were notoriously skittish. The cough of a roving grizzly, the throaty growl of a prowling painter, or the passage of a large body of men would quiet all wildlife within earshot.

Nate, though, had not heard a thing, and years of living in the high country had heightened his senses to where they were keener than those of most men.

The big trapper shifted to scan a tract of firs above him and dense pines to his right. Not so much as a chickadee stirred, that he could see. Which in itself meant little.

Predators and hostiles were not about to advertise their presence. The first inkling there might be of an attack could well be the roar of an onrushing silver tip or the searing jolt of an arrow in the ribs. He had to stay alert.

Trappers did not last long if they were careless. In recent years, hundreds of young men had flocked to the frontier to make their living at the fur trade, and many scores of them would never see their kin back in the States ever again.

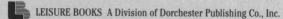

GET YOUR 4
FREE* BOOKS NOW—
A VALUE BETWEEN
$16 AND $20

Mail the Free* Book Certificate Today!

FREE* BOOKS
CERTIFICATE!

YES! I want to subscribe to the Leisure Western Book Club. Please send me my 4 FREE* BOOKS. Then, each month, I'll receive the four newest Leisure Western Selections to preview FREE* for 10 days. If I decide to keep them, I will pay the Special Member's Only discounted price of just $3.36 each, a total of $13.44 ($14.50 US in Canada). This saves me between $3 and $6 off the bookstore price. There are no shipping, handling or other charges.* There is no minimum number of books I must buy and I may cancel the program at any time. In any case, the 4 FREE* BOOKS are mine to keep—at a value of between $17 and $20!

*In Canada, add $5.00 Canadian shipping and handling per order for first shipment. For all subsequent shipments to Canada the cost of membership in the Book Club is $14.50 US, which includes $7.50 shipping and handling per month. All payments must be made in US currency.

Name _____

Address _____

City_____ State_____ Country_____

Zip_____ Telephone_____

Tear here and mail your FREE* book card today!

Get Four Books Totally F R E E* – A Value between $16 and $20

PLEASE RUSH MY FOUR FREE* BOOKS TO ME RIGHT AWAY!

LeisureWestern Book Club
P.O. Box 6613
Edison, NJ 08818-6613

AFFIX STAMP HERE

Bleached bones were all that remained of their youthful dreams, their craving for adventure.

Tense moments dragged by. Nate rested his thumb on the hammer of his rifle and lightly touched his finger to the trigger. His black stallion was gazing to the northwest with its ears pricked. He looked in the same direction but saw nothing out of the ordinary.

Ever so gradually, the woodland resumed its natural rhythm as if the gigantic hand that had been smothering everything had been lifted so the creatures could breathe again. Birds sang. Squirrels scampered about on lofty branches. Chipmunks did the same over boulders and logs.

Nate let himself relax. The danger had passed. He could go on about his business. Bending to the right, he fixed his piercing green eyes on the ground while nudging the stallion onward with a jab of both heels.

Tracks were few and far between, but there were enough for the seasoned mountaineer to keep from losing the trail. Complete prints showed five toes, although the smallest barely left an impression. Claws were also evident.

Less experienced trappers might have mistaken the tracks for those of a wolf. But Nate knew better. Wolves only had four toes, and their pads were shaped differently. The prints he followed had been made by a creature much more fierce, a creature shunned by Indians and whites alike.

Nate King was after an animal which, pound for pound, was rated the most powerful of any its size. Its reputation for savagery was unrivaled even by grizzlies. It would eat anything it could catch and kill, as well as carrion.

Early French trappers had a name for the animal, "carcajou," which was still used by some

David Thompson

mountaineers. A few of Nate's acquaintances had taken to referring to the voracious brutes as "gluttons," based on the habit the creatures had of gorging themselves to the point of stupor. The majority, however, simply used the name the creatures were known by east of the Mississippi: wolverines.

For several weeks now, a particularly vicious specimen had been plaguing Nate's family with repeated visits. At first it had only shown an interest in the many ducks and geese that routinely flocked to a small lake near the remote King homestead. His young son, Zach, had found the first clues, in the form of three ducks that had been literally ripped to shreds and a couple of clear tracks in the blood-soaked mud at the water's edge.

Nate had not been overly alarmed by the report. Wolverines, by and large, tended to fight shy of human beings. He'd assumed the beast would tire of lying in wait for water fowl and wander elsewhere. But as the days turned to weeks and the weeks became a full month, he'd grown increasingly concerned.

The wolverine had started to rove closer to the King cabin. Nate had stumbled on tracks close to the trail his wife and infant daughter took daily down to the water's edge. The animal, quite obviously, had been spying on them. He began to worry that perhaps it had designs on tiny Evelyn, as wolverines were known to be fond of fawns and other young animals.

Then the beast had developed the habit of circling the cabin late at night. Its pungent scent always spooked their horses, and the animals would prance and snort and whinny until Nate appeared to soothe them. On a half-dozen occasions he'd heard the wolverine off in the thick brush, growling and snarling as if in frustration that it could not get at the stock because of the small corral in which he kept them penned.

The final straw had been an incident the previous night.

Nate had been snuggled against the warm form of his lovely Shoshone wife, Winona, in the pine bed he had fashioned with his own two hands. Close by, stretched out on a buffalo robe in front of the stone fireplace, slept their son. Little Evelyn had been snug in her small cradle.

The cabin had been cozy and warm and tranquil.

Suddenly a tremendous uproar had erupted outside. The horses had been nickering and stomping in abject fright.

Nate had grabbed his Hawken and dashed into the darkness in his bare feet. He'd rushed to the south side of the cabin just in time to see a long, hairy form trying to force its muscular bulk between two of the rails to get at a terrified colt his wife's mare had given birth to months ago.

Out of sheer reflex, Nate had whipped the Hawken to his shoulder, fixed a hasty bead, and fired. In his sluggish state he'd missed. The ball gouged into the rail inches from the wolverine's head.

Like a streak of lightning, the scourge of the Rockies had whirled and vanished in the undergrowth.

Nate had automatically reached for his powder horn to reload and only then realized that he had left it and everything else he needed inside. Fortunately for him, his wife and son arrived, both bearing their own rifles.

"Was it the glutton, Pa?" Zach had asked.

"Sure was," Nate had confirmed.

The boy had taken a few eager steps. "Reckon we should go after it before the varmint gets away?"

Winona had glanced sharply at Nate. There had been no need for her to say a word, because they both had been thinking the same thing: It would have been foolhardy to dash into the inky forest where the wolverine was in its element. "No, son," Nate had answered. "We'd best stick close to the cabin in case it tries to get at the horses again."

Thankfully, the rest of the night had proven uneventful. At first light, Nate had thrown a blanket and his saddle on the stallion, added a parfleche laden with pemmican and jerky which his wife had thoughtfully prepared, and headed out to track the troublemaker down no matter how long it took.

To Nate's surprise, he'd located the animal's tracks with little difficulty. Now, after spending the greater part of the morning on its trail, he felt that he was drawing near his quarry.

Strangely enough, the wolverine did not appear to be in any hurry. It had traveled upward at a leisurely pace, meandering as its heart desired.

Nate had counted on finding where the creature had holed up for the day, but so far the voracious beast had given no indication that it intended to stop anytime soon. He gained the crest of the switchback and reined up to survey the ridge. The tracks led straight across.

Tightly clustered lodgepole pines covered the facing slope. The trees were so jammed together that the stallion would not be able to go faster than a brisk walk. He would fall behind his wily adversary, but it couldn't be helped. If he circled around, he risked losing the trail.

Cradling the Hawken in the crook of his left elbow, Nate trotted to the tree line. Scant sunlight penetrated the upper terrace, resulting in perpetual shadow at ground level.

Slightly uneasy, Nate warily advanced. He chided himself for letting the gloom get to him. Or was it something else? he wondered. A vague feeling came over him that he was being watched. Try as he might, though, he failed to catch sight of the glutton or any other animal that might account for it.

Men who lived in the wilderness long enough learned not to discount their intuition. Many a trapper had his gut instincts to thank for saving his hide from lurking hostiles or wild beasts.

The tall boles of the lodgepoles hemmed Nate in on all sides. He had to pick his way with care. Often the stallion squeezed through gaps where there was barely space to spare. On several occasions Nate had to lift his legs and fork them over the saddle so they wouldn't scrape against trunks.

All the while, the mountain man climbed higher. Having to constantly glance up to insure the carcajou wasn't lying in wait above him put a crick in his neck.

The tracks were harder to find thanks to a spongy layer of pine needles covering the forest floor. Even the stallion barely left prints.

Presently Nate had to dismount and bend low in order not to lose the trail. The minutes passed slowly. Off to the north, a red hawk screeched. To the southwest a coyote yipped, a rarity during daylight hours.

So engrossed did Nate become in his task that he didn't realize he had reached the end of the lodgepole growth until he almost bumped into a boulder in his path. Straightening, he discovered a twisted outcropping of solid rock dotted with many more boulders. The tracks went on into the maze.

Nate hesitated. Taking the horse in there was out of the question. He was reluctant to go on without it, yet he had no choice. Tying the reins to a pine, he hefted the Hawken, thumbed back the hammer, and cat-footed around a boulder half the size of his cabin.

Clearly imbedded in the bare earth were the wolverine's prints. The animal had been moving rapidly, as if it were suddenly in a hurry to get somewhere, leading Nate to conclude that it had a den nearby.

Before going around obstacles, Nate always took a peek first. All too vividly, he recollected the time he had tracked a black bear into some rocks and nearly been torn apart when the bear came at him from out of nowhere. He wasn't about to make the same mistake twice.

Here in the outcropping, the air was totally still. Sounds were amplified, so Nate had to be vigilant to avoid making any. He stepped over all dry twigs and patches of loose gravel.

Unexpectedly, up ahead, a bird twittered shrilly. The cry was strangled off, as if its throat had been torn asunder or its neck broken. Then a series of low rumbling growls echoed off the boulders and rock walls.

Leveling the Hawken and keeping his trigger finger tensed to fire, Nate edged around a jutting spike of stone. Before him was a narrow path, which shortly ended at an oval cleared space about five feet in diameter. In the very center lay a dozen bloody gray feathers.

Nate examined them. He nearly stepped on a tiny dark eyeball, which had been severed from the bird's head. Fresh wolverine tracks took him to a path that angled to the southwest. He went a single step and froze when a menacing snarl rose from seemingly close at hand.

Pivoting on a heel, Nate sought the source. The high boulders and rock walls had distorted the sound so badly that the was unable to pinpoint the glutton's position. But something told him the creature knew exactly where he was. Either it had somehow caught his scent, or it had heard him.

Firming his grip on the rifle, Nate inched forward. He paused after each stride. More feathers littered the ground. When he rounded a bend, he found the bird's head, partially eaten.

Nate recognized it as having been a gray jay, or Whiskey Jack, as some of the trappers called them. A little further on, he came upon a single gnawed leg and several long, black tail feathers.

The path looped this way and that, never running in a straight line for more than a dozen feet. Nate was glad when he stepped out into the open on the rim of a barren slope. He scoured the area below him, but didn't spot the carcajou. A check of the ground at his feet told him why.

The wolverine had not descended. Instead, it had slanted to the left and made off along the edge of the outcropping.

Nate gave chase. Since the beast knew he was after it, stealth was no longer essential. He poured on the speed, running flat out, and when he came to where the wolverine had skirted the southwest corner and headed due east again, a stab of anxiety speared through him.

The glutton was doubling back on itself! It was heading for the stallion!

Fairly flying, Nate flashed past boulder after boulder. He doubted the wolverine could bring down a full grown horse, but it might cripple the black so severely that he would have to put the horse out of its misery, leaving him stranded, afoot, many miles from home.

A towering boulder loomed before him. Nate started to swing around it, but stopped cold in his tracks on glimpsing a streak of motion in smaller boulders beyond. Tucking the polished rifle stock to his shoulder, he stood perfectly still and waited for the beast to show itself again.

There was a faint scraping noise, such as claws might make on stone, followed by unnerving silence.

Nate took a few short steps. He needed to lure the carcajou into the open, and to that end he extended his left arm and ran his fingernails over the rough surface of the boulder. He hoped the scratching would excite the wolverine's curiosity and it would pop into sight just long enough for him to squeeze the trigger. That was all he asked. One clear shot.

Nothing happened.

Keeping his back to the tall boulder, Nate glided along its base. His attention was turned low to the ground, where the glutton was most likely to appear.

Wolverines were not large animals. Males seldom measured more than four feet long or weighed more than 50 pounds. But every square inch of their compact frames was packed with steely sinews. And their long claws and tapered teeth made formidable weapons.

So intent was Nate on the area around the smaller boulders that he neglected to pay attention to anything above the level of his waist. Almost too late, he registered a hint of something dark brown at shoulder height and snapped his head up to see the wolverine spring from a rock shelf.

It all happened so incredibly fast.

Nate already had the Hawken raised. He spun and tried to bring the gun to bear, but the carcajou was on him in the blink of an eye. The bruising impact staggered him backward and caused his finger to curl around the trigger. His rifle belched smoke and lead.

Teeth slashed at Nate's forearm, missing by a whisker as he stumbled against the tall boulder. Automatically he lashed out, driving the stock at the wolverine's head. The beast danced aside with astounding ease, snaked in close, and bit into the fringe on Nate's leggings. He winced as those razor teeth sheared through buckskin and flesh.

Wrenching to the right, Nate swung the Hawken as he might a club. Again the hissing wolverine evaded the blow. In leaping to the right to get out of reach of its wicked teeth, Nate neglected to note a small boulder. He tripped and fell, jarring his spine when he crashed onto his back.

Snarling in feral fury, the wolverine was quick to seize the advantage. It leaped.

The only thing that saved Nate from having his throat torn wide open was the Hawken. By a sheer fluke, he brought the rifle up at the selfsame moment that the glutton's jaws lanced at his jugular. The brute's teeth crunched on the barrel rather than his vulnerable neck.

Hot, fetid breath blew over Nate's face as he heaved with all his strength. He partially dislodged the wolverine. Its claws cut into his shirt, shredding the buckskin as if it were so much wet paper. He twisted and rolled onto one knee, still holding onto the rifle.

The wolverine also held on. Digging in its oversized paws, it yanked on the barrel.

Nate let go. The predator was thrown off balance by its own momentum, giving him the fleeting chance he needed to make a grab for the flintlocks wedged under his belt. As the right one cleared the top of the belt, the carcajou released the Hawken and darted in close, its glistening teeth poised above his shin. He jerked his leg out of harm's way, then fired. His rushed shot went wide by a hand's width, plowing into the hard earth instead.

Most animals would have bolted after the first shot, let alone the second. Not the wolverine. Fear was not part of its nature. Its kind had been known to tangle with grizzlies and panthers, if they dared cross its path. Mountain men and Indians alike had witnessed wolverines drive both from prey that was rightfully theirs.

So it was no surprise that the blasts of the rifle and the smoothbore pistol had no effect. The wolverine coiled, then, apparently mistaking the smoking flintlock for an appendage of its two-legged foe, bit at the tip of the smoking barrel.

Nate drew his other pistol, pointed it at the glutton's chest, and fired at so close a range that the beast was singed by powder burns. The .55-caliber flintlock packed quite a wallop, sufficient to knock a man down at 20 yards, yet it hardly slowed the wolverine. Snarling viciously, the carcajou closed in.

Back-pedaling, Nate hurled the spent pistols at the creature's head. It dodged aside, allowing him to drop a hand to his tomahawk. Arcing the weapon overhead, he drove the keen edge at the wolverine's skull.

The carcajou's lightning reflexes came to its rescue one more time. The tomahawk swished by its cheek. Whirling, the wolverine lunged at the trapper's wrist.

A desperate yank of his arm saved Nate from losing his hand. He swung again and again, but couldn't connect.

Wiry as a cat and as elusive as a phantom, the glutton was next to impossible to hit. Nate aimed high. He aimed low. He fought with all the skill at his command, yet it wasn't enough. The wolverine kept one step ahead of him.

They continually circled one another, each seeking an opening that would end the fray. Nate thought he saw one when the wolverine snapped at his leg, missed, and slipped as it threw itself backward out of harm's way. He took a short step and drove the tomahawk at its neck. By rights, he should have separated the head from the bearish body. But the thing was too quick for him, and before the tomahawk could connect, it vaulted upward, ramming into his chest.

Suddenly Nate had a 50-pound bundle of raw ferocity in his arms. He flung his free hand in front of his face and nearly cried out when those iron jaws clamped down. Tottering under an onslaught of claws and teeth, he tripped over his own feet and wound up on his back, like before.

Nate had to drop the tomahawk so he could grab hold of the carcajou's throat as it hurled itself at his face. Muscles straining, he held the enraged predator at bay with one arm while he deflected its rapier claws with his other forearm. Locked together, they rolled to the right, then to the left.

The beast had a pungent body odor and foul breath. Nate could scarcely stand to inhale. He shoved with all his might, but the wolverine clung to him, its claws digging deep. A moist sensation crept along his arms and down over his chest.

Nate knew that he couldn't hold the glutton at bay for long. Unless he broke free, he would weaken from loss of blood and it would finish him off.

The only weapon he had left was his butcher knife, but to reach it he had to lower one of his arms. Taking a gamble, he swooped his left hand to his waist. His fingers closed on the beaded sheath—but the knife was gone! In the flurry of combat it had fallen out!

Before Nate could lift his arm again, the wolverine gave a terrific wrench of its whole body and broke free of his grasp. Its mouth opened wide and swept to his exposed throat. He felt its teeth on his skin.

He was going to die!

Chapter Two

Time stood still.

To Nate King it seemed as if an eternity went by, when in reality it was no more than five intensely horrifying seconds. Awful, harrowing moments in which he braced for the searing pain that would rack him when the creature's teeth ripped through his soft flesh.

Yet there was no pain, no agonizing spasm, nothing except the light prick of deadly teeth pressed almost gently against his skin. Gradually it dawned on Nate that the wolverine had stopped moving. It had sagged against him, then gone limp.

Gingerly, Nate reached up and pried the glutton's jaws wide enough to ease them off his neck. Shoving the animal to one side, he swiftly scrambled erect. A few feet away lay his tomahawk, which he scooped up and elevated to strike.

The battle was over. The wolverine posed no

19

further threat. Evidently the pistol shot had struck a vital organ, but the carcajou had fought on until it expired. Blood oozed from the entry hole and was forming a scarlet puddle.

Nate reclaimed his weapons, stepped over to the big boulder, and wearily sank down. Leaning back, he stared at the bestial terror and marveled at his narrow escape.

Wolverines, like grizzlies, were notoriously hard to kill. Or, as the members of the trapping fraternity liked to phrase it, they were "powerful hard to die."

No less a personage than Meriwether Lewis had first applied the saying after the men on the famed Lewis and Clark expedition encountered a few grizzlies and nearly lost their lives. One bear, in particular, had been shot eight times through its vital parts and still would not go down.

Gluttons were no less formidable. They would fight on even when mortally stricken, as the one before Nate had done. He made a mental note to fight shy of its kin in the future unless he had no other choice.

While Nate rested, he reloaded the spent flint-locks and the Hawken. It annoyed him that his hands shook a little at first, but they steadied after his blood stopped racing in his veins.

As any hunter worthy of the name knew, it was a cardinal sin to let any part of a slain animal go to waste. With that in mind, Nate drew his butcher knife and returned to the body.

Skinning the beast took less than half an hour. Nate hauled it away from the puddle, then hunkered and rolled the wolverine over. His next step was to slit the hide open down the back of each hind leg. Gripping the edge of the pelt in one hand, he slowly peeled it down over the body, cutting ligaments and muscles as it was necessary and always remembering to hold the edge angled toward the carcass.

Since Winona was much better at curing hides than he was, Nate opted to leave that chore for her. But he did take a step to insure the pelt would stay in prime shape. Using the tomahawk, he split the skull open. He had to pry a bit with his knife before he could slip his fingers into the cranial cavity and remove the brain, which he rubbed over the underside of the hide as he might a sponge. When the whole pelt had been so treated, he tossed what remained of the brain to the ground, rolled up the hide, and was ready to go.

Nate strolled back to the stallion. After the ordeal he had just been through, it felt grand to breathe in the crisp mountain air and to smell the fragrant scent of pine and the musty odor of the rich soil.

He tied the hide on the stallion, forked leather, and turned the big black eastward. At a brisk trot he descended the mountain. On reaching the level valley floor, he goaded his mount into a distance-eating canter.

Nate was eager to get home. He spent so much time away from his family during the fall and spring trapping seasons that the days spent with them were precious to him.

It was a glorious afternoon, with the sky as blue as a deep lake and the verdant valley lush with grass and flowers. Wildlife was abundant; deer grazed unafraid in the open, shaggy mountain buffalo hunted the valley's fringe, bald eagles soared high on the air currents, while everywhere frolicked birds and lesser animals.

The Rocky Mountains, Nate frequently mused, were the next best thing to paradise on earth.

Among the pristine peaks and winding valleys a man could live as he pleased, accountable to no one except his Maker. Here a man enjoyed true freedom, a state those living east of the broad Mississippi could no longer claim as their birthright.

It saddened Nate to think of how far the country had fallen in so short a time. Having lived in New York City until his eighteenth year, he had seen for himself how politicians and lawyers had taken the basic tenets outlined in the Constitution and perverted them for their own ends.

With his own eyes, Nate had read where journalists referred to the Government as if it were a holy entity with the God-given right to rule the people as those who were in Government saw fit. Such profound ignorance would one day do the country irreparable harm.

Among the half-dozen or so books lining a short shelf in the King cabin was one dealing with the works of Thomas Paine, whose sentiments Nate shared. The firebrand of liberty during the American Revolution had once written: "When extraordinary power and extraordinary pay are allotted to any individual in Government, he becomes the center round which every kind of corruption generates and forms." Paine had referred to such power mongers as "parasites," and Nate wholeheartedly agreed.

In the Rocky Mountains there were no parasites, because there was no government. Men and women, red and white, lived as they pleased. They did as they wanted, when they wanted, and woe to the fool who claimed they couldn't. Anyone who took on airs paid for his idiocy at the point of a gun, if need be.

Nate would no more give up his life in the high country than he would his arms and legs. True freedom, he had learned, was a greater treasure than gold, more desirable than diamonds. The person who had it had everything. The person who lacked it lived in an invisible prison of someone else's making.

Such were the thoughts that occupied the free trapper as he made his way toward home and hearth. Preoccupied as he was, he almost missed spotting the fresh horse tracks he came upon when still several miles from his cabin.

Drawing rein in alarm, Nate studied them closely. He counted nine riders, all tolled. None of their mounts had been shod, which indicated they were Indians. And they were heading in the same direction he was.

Nate urgently brought the black stallion to a gallop. Nine warriors were too many for a simple hunting party; it must be a war party. There was an outside chance they were Shoshones, his adopted people. But they might also be Blackfeet or Piegans or Utes, hostiles who would exterminate his family without a second thought.

Filled with fear for those he loved, Nathaniel King sped like the wind on down the valley, his ears straining to hear the war whoops he prayed would not shatter the serenity of his mountain retreat.

Once, years ago, a major by the name of Stephen Long had been commissioned by the United States Government to survey a portion of the vast unknown western stretches with an eye to finding the source of the Arkansas, Red and Platte Rivers.

Long ran into some problems. He had a hard time telling which river was which. He never found the source of the Arkansas and wrongly thought the Canadian River was the Red River.

David Thompson

The major's confusion was not limited to waterways. On reaching the Rockies, he mistook a high peak for the one previously discovered by Zebulon Pike, even though Pike's Peak was far to the south.

On his return to civilization, Long produced a map of his travels, which became the standard for many years to come. On it, he labeled the prairie as the "Great American Desert" and compared it to the immense sandy deserts of Africa. The plains were, in his opinion, "uninhabitable by a people depending on agriculture."

The peak he 'discovered' became known among the mountaineers as Long's Peak, and it was north of there, in a picturesque lateral valley ridged by lofty mountains and dominated by a beautiful lake, that Nate King had settled.

The cabin was not his originally. Nate's uncle had built it and had intended to set down roots, but a vengeful Ute had made wolf meat of Ezekiel.

Since taking it over, Nate had made many improvements. Among them were genuine glass windows. Imported from the States at great cost and brought in on a caravan from St. Louis, they were the talk of the trapping fraternity.

Most free trappers either lived with Indians or lived Indian-fashion in lodges or dugouts they abandoned at the end of each winter. Few went to all the bother Zeke had done in erecting a sturdy cabin. And none had gone to the lengths of Nate King in improving their cabin to where it resembled an ordinary home.

At the annual rendezvous, Nate's peers were not above ribbing him about his homestead. They sincerely thought it strange that he would go to so much bother. And they weren't the only ones. Nate's wife thought it strange, too.

Trail's End

Winona King had never quite become accustomed to living in a cabin. Having been reared in a succession of buffalo hide tepees, she had been absolutely flabbergasted when her new husband had proposed they move into the "wooden lodge."

She could still remember that first day, over 12 winters ago, when she had spent all of an afternoon wandering around in a daze, running her hands over the smooth logs and the stone fireplace and the floor and the furniture.

It had amazed her that her husband did not desire a lodge that could be taken down and transported to new sites as the need arose.

Her people, the Shoshones, migrated over a wide area throughout the year, and it had taken considerable adjustment on her part to accept Nate's plan to stay in one place not only for an entire winter, but for the *rest of their lives*. Secretly, she had wondered if perhaps he was in his right mind.

Now she was grateful to him.

Winona stood at the long counter Nate had built, chopping roots she planned to add to the soup she was making for their supper, and grinned as she stared out the window at her son.

It was nice having the glass. The pane kept out dust and bugs, yet let them see what was taking place outdoors.

And it was nice having solid walls instead of hides, which constantly had to be mended or replaced.

Likewise, Winona appreciated having the stone fireplace. It kept the cabin much warmer during the coldest weather than the fire in a hide lodge ever had.

Winona gazed over a shoulder at her infant daughter, who rested quietly in a cradleboard, and smiled. "I guess I am fortunate to have a husband who goes to so much trouble for us, little one," she said in impeccable English.

Evelyn cooed and gurgled.

It had taken many moons for Winona to master the white tongue, and she was rightfully proud of her accomplishment. Nate liked to brag that she spoke English better than he did. If that was true, she had him to thank, for he had spent many days and nights teaching her.

Through the window, Winona could see her son busy making arrows. He owned a rifle and pistol and he was a crack shot, but long ago Nate had decided that they should ration their ammunition as much as possible by using traditional Shoshone weapons when they hunted close to home.

Their safety was an added consideration. The sound of a shot could carry for miles in the rarified air at higher elevations, and if heard by a roving war party would draw them like a flame drew moths. By using quieter weapons, they eliminated that risk.

Winona finished chopping the last root, set down the knife, and wiped her hands on a cloth towel. Taking the cradleboard, she walked out into the bright sunlight.

"How soon do you reckon Pa will be back, Ma?" young Zachary King interrupted his work to ask.

"Before the sun sets," Winona said, remembering the promise Nate had given her. Squatting, she slid the wide straps attached to the sides of the cradleboard over her arms so that the cradleboard rested against her back. From a bench by the door she took a wooden pail "Care to join us?"

"Sure," Zach replied, glad to have an excuse to stretch his legs. He had been working on arrows since noon and needed a break. As he rose he thought of his rifle in the cabin but decided not to fetch it. They were only going to the lake, and he had his pistol.

The well-worn trail wound through pines to the water's edge. As usual, plenty of ducks, geese and brants were in evidence. Overhead, gulls wheeled and squawked.

This was the second trip Winona had made that day. Needing water for the soup, she knelt and dipped the pail in.

Runoff from the ring of adjacent peaks fed the lake. Year round the water was ice cold and so clear that a person on the shore could see the bottom a dozen yards out. Winona spied a school of small fish being shadowed by a larger one.

Zach moved a few feet off and idly regarded the forest to the west. He had something on his mind that he was reluctant to bring up, so rather than get right to the point, he approached the subject in a roundabout manner. "I've been meaning to ask you a question," he commented as casually as he could.

"Which is?" Winona responded. She looked at him and was taken aback when he averted his gaze.

"I was wondering if we'll go live with the Shoshones over the summer like we always do?"

It was a peculiar question. Each and every year since Winona's son had been born, they had made it a point to spend two or three months with Winona's people. She insisted on it, in order that Zach might learn their customs and traditions. "Of course we will, Stalking Coyote."

"Do you think Plenty Coups's band will spend time with Spotted Bull's again this year?"

Spotted Bull was Winona's uncle. He had been like a second father to her since the death of his brother at the hands of the Blackfeet. Morning

David Thompson

Dove, his wife, and Willow Woman, his daughter, were two of the best friends Winona had.

The previous Buck Moon and Heat Moon, another band had joined Spotted Bull's on the banks of the Green River. Plenty Coups was their leader. He was as highly respected as her uncle, who had recently become chief after the death of old Broken Paw, and the two had become fast friends.

None of which explained why Winona's son was so interested in whether the two bands would get together again. She slowly lifted the heavy pail, then straightened. The sight of the swirling water under the dripping pail reminded her of an incident that solved the mystery.

It had been during the waning sleeps of the Heat Moon the previous year. The two bands had been about to go their separate ways. Winona and Nate had also been about to say their good-byes and return to their cabin, so she had gone in search of Zach. She had found him on a knoll close to the river, just sitting there with his arms draped over his knees and an odd pained expression on his face. He had jumped up when she'd spoken his name and acted embarrassed that she had caught him there. Why, she hadn't known. Until this very moment.

For it was only now that Winona recalled there had been others at the river that day. Three older girls had been south of the knoll, washing garments. She had not made the connection because her son had never shown any interest in females, but suddenly she understood.

"I expect Plenty Coups will be there," Winona mentioned matter-of-factly. "Perhaps he will invite us to his lodge for a feast as he did the last time."

Zach held his tongue. He didn't want his mother

to suspect that he had grown uncommonly fond of one of the chief's daughters and had been pining for her all during the previous fall and winter. He didn't want *anyone* to know. The overwhelming feeling that had come over him when he had set eyes on her for the first time was unlike any he had ever felt before. It bothered him immensely.

Her mouth quirked, Winona started back up the trail. She would have to tell Nate and counsel with him on how best to handle their son's awakening manhood.

It was a subject they had discussed before, and Winona knew that Nate was not in favor of their son marrying early. He wanted Zach to, as he put it, "see more of the world" before settling down, a notion she regarded as silly. What difference would it make in the long run?

No matter how Nate or she felt, when Zach was ready, he would take a mate, and nothing she or Nate said would dissuade him. Love would run its own course. It always had, it always would.

A pair of ravens abruptly winged low over their heads, the steady beat of their wings bringing Winona out of her reverie. She watched the birds sail westward, in the direction her husband had taken, and hoped he was all right. Wolverines were not to be taken lightly.

She should know, since she had fought one once, many winters ago. It had been during one of Nate's frequent absences, before the children were born, and she had been lucky to survive its onslaught. Years had passed since last she thought of it.

Such encounters happened all too often in the wilderness. So often that whites and Indians alike tended to take them for granted.

In any given month, Winona might spy two or three grizzlies in the vicinity of the lake. Black bears were also regular visitors, as were panthers and wolves. Any one of them would attack her without warning if they were in the mood, but she never fretted over the likelihood. They were simply part and parcel of her everyday life, hazards to be prudently avoided. And when that wasn't possible, she was prepared to defend her life and the lives of her loved ones with her dying breath if need be.

As if on cue, to the north rose a guttural cough. Winona halted and scoured the valley without result.

"That sounded like a griz to me," Zach mentioned as he placed a hand on the smooth butt of his pistol. He wished now that he had brought his rifle. No pistol made was capable of dropping one of the lords of the wild with a single shot, and it was doubtful a charging bear would give him time to reload.

Evelyn squirmed in the cradleboard, prompting Winona to hurry on. Some of the water in the pail sloshed over the rim onto her legs, so she gripped the handle in both hands and held the pail in front of her to steady it.

Presently the cabin appeared. Winona was in such haste to get there that she was mere yards from the door when she realized it hung partway open. She stopped short so unexpectedly that her son nearly blundered into her. Puzzled, she listened but heard no sounds from inside. Yet she was certain she had closed the door behind her when she left, and she whispered as much to Zach.

Holding the pistol in front of him, the youth stepped around his mother. He looked for his father's horse in the corral, but it wasn't there. A knot formed in the pit of his stomach and his mouth went dry. He nervously licked his lips as he stalked to the front wall and ducked so he could peek into the window.

The cabin appeared empty. Zach motioned for his mother to stay put and cat-footed to the doorway. Pushing with his left foot, he swung the door wide open. No shots or shouts rang out. Bending at the waist, he darted inside and confirmed no one was there.

"All clear," Zach reported.

Winona wasted no time in placing the pail on the counter and shrugging out of the cradleboard, which she hung from a stout peg above the bed. "I must have been mistaken," she told her son, even though she was sure that she was not. To be on the safe side, she added, "But we will check around the cabin, just in case."

Zach went to the corner where his Hawken leaned. It was his pride and joy, a gift from his parents. They had bestowed it on him at the last rendezvous, and he had spent at least half an hour every night ever since, cleaning and polishing it until it shone from one end to the other.

Winona grabbed her rifle, an ammo pouch, and a powder horn. She made a point of closing the door behind Zach, then moved to the northeast corner.

In order to prevent anyone from taking them by surprise, Nate had cleared all the brush within a 50-foot radius. Winona saw no one close by or in the trees. She cautiously went on to the next corner.

Zach kept glancing to their rear. Experience had taught him that hostiles could be downright sneaky, and he was not about to lose his hair if he could help it.

David Thompson

Suddenly Winona stopped. In the dirt at the base of the north wall were a number of moccasin tracks. She pointed them out to Zach, who nodded. Sinking onto her left knee, she scrutinized them. By their shape it was plain that they had not been made by Shoshones.

A very worried Zach kept his eyes on the trees. If there were enemies about, he reflected, that was where they would be. A slight creak above them prompted him to glance up at the roof, and he learned he had been wrong. The forest wasn't the only place the hostiles might be hiding.

Over the edge of the roof plummeted four buckskin clad warriors.

Chapter Three

Nate King was worried sick by the time he paused on a grassy bench overlooking the verdant valley he had staked out as his own. The lake sparkled like a shimmering jewel in the brilliant sunshine, and to the southeast several elk were visible on a low slope. He couldn't see the cabin.

The nine warriors had descended the bench in single file and stayed in single file once they reached the valley floor. It was a tactic typically employed when a war party knew it was nearing an enemy camp.

Nate threw off all caution. His family was in mortal peril, and for all he knew they might have already been attacked. He pushed the big black stallion at a breakneck pace, vaulting logs and plowing through thickets rather than going around them.

The woods were so thick that Nate didn't catch a glimpse of the cabin until he was within a hundred yards of it. His innate caution made him slow down even though an inner voice screamed at him to rush on in there before it was too late.

In a stand of spruce, Nate drew rein and dismounted. Ground-hitching the stallion, he padded forward and cocked the Hawken. In the brush at the edge of the clearing, he squatted and parted the branches in front of him.

All appeared tranquil. The cabin was quiet and there was no sign of hostile warriors.

Nate glided to the east, to a vantage point behind an old stump situated 40 feet from the front door. It was closed. The glare on the windows prevented him from seeing inside, but he thought he detected movement. He was about to stride into the open when the latch rasped and the door opened.

Out walked a warrior painted for war.

Instantly Nate brought the Hawken up and sighted on the center of the man's chest. In his mind's eye he saw his slaughtered family lying in bloody pools on the cabin floor. His finger started to close on the trigger.

Then the warrior looked right at Nate and smiled. Holding his right hand in front of his neck with the palm outward and the index and second fingers extended skyward, the warrior raised his hand until the extended fingers were as high as the top of his head.

It was sign language. The gesture meant 'friend.'

Nate blinked, and slowly lowered the rifle as recognition set in. The style of the warrior's buckskins and the pair of long braids on either side of his head were the earmarks of a Crow. The tribe was generally friendly to whites, although there had been isolated instances where the two sides had clashed.

Looking closer, Nate was startled to find that he knew this particular warrior. Lowering the Hawken, he stepped from concealment.

The Crow's hands flew in more sign language, saying, in effect, "My heart is glad that we meet again, Grizzly Killer. It has been too many moons since last we shared a pipe."

Nate glanced at the doorway. Other warriors were inside, staring at him.

"You do remember me?" the warrior went on. "I am Two Humps. You saved my son from the renegade white who was known as the Invincible One."

Nate remembered all too well. A man by the name of Jacob Pierce had tricked the Crows into believing he could not be killed and had instigated a bloodbath that resulted in the loss of many innocent lives. During the conflict, Two Humps had befriended Nate and Nate's mentor, Shakespeare McNair. They had parted on the best of terms.

Warily, Nate set the stock of the Hawken on the ground and leaned the rifle against his leg to free his hands. "I remember you," he signed. "I remember telling you where to find my lodge, but I did not think I would see you again so soon." Nate gazed over the warrior's shoulder. "I see you have others with you. I hope they did not harm my family."

"What kind of man would I be if I repaid your kindness with treachery?" Two Humps beckoned. "Come see for yourself. Your wife and son and daughter are fine."

At that juncture the warriors inside parted, and out came Winona with Evelyn in her arms. Zach followed. Mother and son hurried over, the youth armed with his pistol and knife.

Nate finally allowed himself to relax. If the

Crows were up to no good, they would hardly have let the boy keep any weapons. He embraced each in turn. "For a while there I was mighty worried," he admitted softly so only they could hear.

"That makes two of us, husband," Winona said, giving the Crows an indignant look. She had feared for their lives when the four warriors jumped from the roof. One had torn the rifle from her grasp as three more rushed around the corner of the cabin and bore her to the earth. Only instead of slashing her throat, they had stripped her of her knife and pinned her until she quieted. The same had been done to Zach. When both of them were safely unarmed, Two Humps had appeared and explained the purpose for his visit in sign. He had apologized for their rough treatment and given back their weapons. All this Winona now told her husband, adding, "He claimed that he was afraid we might shoot him before he had a chance to explain himself, so that is why he took us by surprise."

Nate pursed his lips. The precaution made sense. It didn't do for strangers to waltz up to a camp or a cabin unannounced. Some mountaineers would shoot first and ask questions later. "I reckon we can't hold it against him," he said.

"I can," Zach groused. "I've got a goose egg on the back of my noggin. They were awful rough on me."

"You're almost an adult now, son," Nate reminded him. "So they treated you like one."

The suggestion that he was so close to manhood made Zach beam. "That's right, I am. I suppose I shouldn't hold a grudge. I might have done the same if I was in their moccasins."

Two Humps advanced. "I trust there are no bad

feelings," he signed earnestly. "Please accept my apology."

There was no denying the warrior's sincerity. Nate put his hand on the Crow's shoulder before signing, "You did what you had to do. Let us go inside. We will smoke a pipe together and you can tell me what has brought you so far from your country."

The warriors in the cabin respectfully backed out of the way and ringed themselves around the room. Most were younger than Two Humps. A notable exception was a man who appeared years older and wore a sorrowful countenance at all times. The younger ones were amazed by the wooden lodge and never tired of running their fingers over every odd object they came across. One even stuck his head into the fireplace and wound up with soot on his forehead and cheeks.

While this was going on, Nate and Two Humps sat at the table and shared a pipe. The Crow smacked the chair a few times before he would sit down and gave it a hard shake to verify it was strong enough to hold his weight.

With the amenities disposed of, Nate regarded the warrior intently. The younger warriors stopped their shenanigans to pay close attention, while the older man walked over to the table, his features as somber as a storm cloud.

"This is my brother, Bull Standing With Cow," Two Humps introduced them. "His heart is heavy because he has lost his woman and his son." The warrior motioned at the others. "All our hearts our heavy. Twenty sleeps ago our village was raided by a large band of Lakota. They struck early in the morning when the sun had not yet cleared the horizon. Many of our people were slain, and many horses were stolen."

Bull Standing With Cow grunted. "They also took three of our women," he signed. "One is my daughter, Fetches Water. She has only seen fourteen winters."

Nate sympathized. He'd be devastated if the same thing ever happened to his wife or children. It was a long harbored dread of his that one day he would come back from a trapping trip and find them gone, kidnapped by one of his many enemies.

"These Lakota have raided us before," Two Humps went on. "They are Oglalas."

"I have heard of them," Nate signed. They lived in the region of the South Platte river and had a reputation for being an extremely warlike tribe. The Lakota were more often called the 'Sioux' by most whites, the name stemming from an old French word for them, 'Nadowessioux.'

"They know no mercy, these Oglalas," Two Humps said. "They killed all they could and then escaped before we could gather our scattered horses. Many brave men died that day protecting those they loved."

Nate did not need to be reminded how bloody Indian warfare could be. He had witnessed it firsthand. "So now you are on your way to Oglala country to try and rescue the women?" he speculated.

"Yes," Two Humps confirmed. "Bull Standing With Cow is sick inside with fear for his daughter. He wanted to come by himself, but I would not let him."

A young warrior whose stocky body rippled with muscles motioned in contempt and signed sharply, "The Lakota do not scare us! We will make them regret what they have done! They will learn that the Absaroka are not timid rabbits they can attack at will!"

Two Humps frowned. "That is He Dog. He has never fought the Lakota. He was off hunting when our village was raided, or he would not be so eager to confront them again."

The stocky warrior was offended. "I fear no one!" he signed emphatically. "Let any man who claims I do tell me so to my face."

Bull Standing With Cow glowered at the younger man. "No one here questions your bravery. But courage alone does not win battles. A man must have wisdom. He must be able to think clearly at all times if he is to prevail."

"Are you saying I do not?"

"I am saying you have much to learn before you will be a warrior the equal of Two Humps. Now be still and let your elders speak. Or have you lost your manners as well as your judgment?" Bull Standing With Cow shot back.

Tension hung thick in the air. Nate knew that his friend had his work cut out for him. The Crows would have a hard enough time without petty bickering among themselves. "Just the nine of you against the whole Oglala tribe," he commented. "Those are not good odds."

"Nine were all that could be spared," Two Humps responded. "The rest had to stay to safeguard our village." His dark eyes locked on Nate. "I was hoping we could lower the odds, Grizzly Killer. We have all seen for ourselves that your medicine is very powerful. You were the one who defeated the Iron Warrior. So I have come to you for help."

Winona was in the act of making a pot of coffee. She had carried the pot to the fireplace and was about to start a small fire when she happened to glance around and saw the Crow warrior sign his last statement. Forgetting the fire for the time being, she walked to the table and stood at her husband's elbow to await his response.

Nate did not quite know what to say. He liked Two Humps and considered the man a friend, but they were not all that close. The truth was that they hardly knew one another. In his opinion it was downright presumptuous of the Crow to ask him to risk his life. He was all set to decline, but the image of a terrified 14-year-old gave him pause.

Two Humps seemed to read his thoughts. "I know I ask a lot of you, Grizzly Killer. But there is no one else to whom we can turn." He leaned forward. "We do not know the country of the Lakotas very well. You do. Or at least you told me once that you had crossed the great sea of grass when you came to these mountains to live, and another time when you visited the Mandans."

Bull Standing With Cow broke in. "We do not want you to do our fighting for us, Grizzly Killer. We only ask that you guide us to the land of Oglalas by the shortest possible route. Once you have done that, you can turn around and head home if you want." His weathered features shifted. A haunted aspect came over them. "Please, Grizzly Killer. As one father to another, I plead with you to help me rescue my daughter. I do not want her to spend the rest of her life as the unwilling wife of a Lakota who treats her worse than he does his dog." He clasped his hands together. "Please."

Winona could tell that the heartfelt appeal touched her husband deeply. Knowing him as well as she did herself, she spoke up in English before he could reply. "Think this over carefully, husband. The Sioux are formidable foes. If they learn that you helped the Crows, they will not rest until they have taken their revenge."

"A man can't turn his back on another in need," Nate noted. "My mother used to quote from the Good Book a lot. And one of the sayings always stuck in my head. 'Do unto others as you would have them do unto you.'"

"White ways are not our ways," Winona countered. "The Sioux have never heard of your Good Book. All they care about is counting coup on every white they find in their land."

Nate shifted to face her. "The girl is the main issue. How can we turn our backs on her?"

"We do not know her."

"Does that mean we just leave her to her fate? If she were ours, we wouldn't rest until she was safe and sound."

"She is *not* ours," Winona stressed. It wasn't that she had anything against the Crow girl. It was the fact that there was a definite possibility she would never set eyes on her husband again if he ventured into Lakota country that made her balk at the proposal.

"I don't see where that makes a difference. If Zach were missing and I went to Two Humps for help, you know as well as I do that he'd do all he could on our behalf."

Winona knew a losing cause when she saw one. Sighing, she tenderly touched his chin and said, "Sometimes you are too good for your own good. Very well. We will go with them."

"We?"

"Stalking Coyote is old enough to go on a raid. And I will not be left behind."

Young Zachary King had been lounging against the counter with his arms folded across his chest. He did not have much interest in the proceedings

41

since he knew his father would go the moment the Crow asked and assumed that he'd be left behind once again to watch over his mother and sister. It was the same old story every time his father went traipsing off. So he was all the more shocked when he heard his mother say he should be in on the raid. Excitement quickened his pulse as he straightened and nodded. "I think Ma's right," he declared. "Some of the Shoshone boys my age have gone on raids already. And you said just a while ago, Pa, that I'm almost a full-growed man."

Nate wanted to bite his tongue. He had made the comment to bolster his son's esteem, not to imply the boy was mature enough to go on the war path. Having nothing better to retort, he responded curtly, "You stay out of this, young 'un. You're not a man yet, and until you are, what I say goes."

"What we *both* say goes," Winona corrected him, "and I say our son should join you. He will learn much. And his rifle will come in handy if the Lakotas spot us."

"There you go with that 'us' business again," Nate griped. "A raid is no place for a woman with a baby."

"Evelyn will pose no problem. I will tend to her at all times," Winona pledged. "And you know that she will not cry and give us away while we are on the trail, so you need not worry in that regard."

Nate gazed fondly at their infant. He had never quite grown accustomed to the Shoshone custom of toting a baby out into the woods every time it bawled and hanging the cradleboard from a high limb until it quieted down, but he had to admit the tactic worked. Four or five times of such harsh treatment was enough to stop most babies from ever blubbering aloud. They learned early on to keep their emotions under control, or else.

It was a hard but essential lesson. The wail of an infant might give a village away to marauding enemies. Older children, when they played, knew to keep their voices down. It was a price they had to pay in the name of survival.

Two Humps had been watching the trapper and his wife with growing anxiety. When they fell silent, he signed, "Is your woman against your going, Grizzly Killer?"

"She does not want anything to happen to me," Nate hedged. "She thinks it best that I take my whole family along, and I agree."

Zach whooped for joy and spun in a circle.

Winona smiled and squeezed her husband's shoulder in gratitude.

He Dog sputtered and stormed toward the table. "Do my ears hear right?" he angrily signed. "This white man wants to bring a *woman* on a raid? I will not hear of it."

Two Humps turned on the younger warrior and half rose out of his chair. For the benefit of the Kings, he used sign language instead of the Crow tongue. "It is not your place to say who comes and who does not. As for a woman making war, need I remind you that there is a woman warrior living with Long Hair's band who has counted more coup than you have? If Grizzly Killer wants his wife to come, she can."

"She will slow us down," He Dog signed. "And these mixed-breed cubs of hers have—"

Nate King exploded out of his chair. He reached the stocky warrior in two bounds and slammed his fist into the Crow's chin. He Dog was knocked back against the wall. Belatedly the hothead clawed for a knife on his right hip. Nate did not let him draw it. Another right to the jaw rocked

He Dog to one side. A left jab and an uppercut stiffened him as rigid as a board. And a roundhouse right flattened the man in his tracks.

Breathing heavily from his exertion, Nate slowly drew one of his pistols and pivoted. Some of the other warriors had started to move toward him but they stopped at sight of the flintlock.

"Enough!" Two Humps urgently signed. "We came here to ask Grizzly Killer's help, not to insult his woman or to attack him."

All the Crows but one heeded their leader. A lanky warrior made as if to lift his lance but checked his movement when two loud clicks sounded.

Winona King had her rifle in hand. Zach had produced his pistol. Both guns were trained on the lanky warrior's torso. He had only to see the fires blazing in the Shoshone woman's eyes to change his mind about aiding his friend.

Moving to his family, Nate placed his pistol on the counter within ready reach and signed, "You all heard He Dog. He had no right to heap abuse on us. He had no right to say those things about my wife."

The Crows exchanged glances. Little hostility was evident.

Winona believed that most of the warriors agreed with her husband. But since it was her ability which had been called into question, she elected to demonstrate to them that she would be useful in the days ahead. "I want all of you to step outside," she signed, and exited without bothering to confirm that they complied with her request.

Stepping to the left, Winona searched the woods and spotted a large knot on a tree about as far from the cabin as an arrow could fly.

Voices murmured. The Crows were gathered in

a group, a few eyeing her skeptically. Nate and Zach were by the window.

"See that knot?" Winona asked. Without waiting for a response, she aimed, compensating for the distance by hiking the barrel a hair, held her breath as her husband had taught her to do, counted to three in her head, and lightly stroked the trigger. Smoke and lead belched from the barrel, the smoke forming a cloud which momentarily hid the tree from view. She lowered the gun and signed, "I would be grateful if one of you would go examine the tree."

Two warriors bounded off. They hollered on reaching the trunk and pointed excitedly at the knot.

Two Humps nodded and smiled. "They say you hit the knot in the center," he signed. "I am impressed. It is a feat that would challenge our best bowmen."

"So there is no one else who would speak against me?" Winona asked, deliberately staring at the lanky warrior.

No one did.

Nate walked over to Winona and looped an arm around her shoulders. He was so proud of her, he was fit to bust. For the umpteenth time since the day they became man and wife, amazement came over him that so lovely and competent a woman had chosen him to be her mate. For the life of him he did not know what he had done to deserve her.

"We will go off by ourselves and hold a council," Two Humps said. "I will ask each man to give his opinion, and those who still do not want a woman along will be told to return to our village."

He Dog had to be carted from the cabin like a sack of grain. He was still unconscious and blood dribbled from the corner of his mouth.

The Crows melted into the forest to the south. Zach waited until they were out of sight, then laughed and exclaimed, "Tarnation! You sure showed them, Ma! And Pa! You tore into that man like a riled grizzly!"

"It's no laughing matter," Nate scolded. "I shouldn't have lost my temper. He Dog doesn't strike me as the forgiving type. I'll have to keep my eyes skinned the whole time from now on."

"I'll watch him like a hawk too," Zach volunteered. "If he tries to make trouble, we'll teach him some manners."

Nate hoped it wouldn't come to that, but he had to face facts. They hadn't even left yet and already he had earned the hatred of one Crow and the ill will of a second. If he had a lick of common sense, he would back out before it was too late. But he couldn't. Not with the welfare of the 14-year-old girl at stake.

"Let us go inside," Winona said. "I must check on our daughter and begin to pack." She held her rifle at arm's length. "I must remember to bring extra ammunition. Something tells me that we are going to need it."

Chapter Four

At first light the next morning the war party of vengeful Crows and the King family departed. Not one of the Crows backed out, not even He Dog or his lanky friend, Runs Against.

Nate wasn't surprised. He Dog had a score to settle. The dour looks the pair frequently bestowed on him when they thought he wouldn't notice were ample proof they had it in for him.

The other Crows, though, were as nice as could be. Bull Standing With Cow, especially, pledged his undying friendship, and told Nate in sign language that for as long as they both lived, his lodge was Nate's lodge and anything he owned was Nate's for the taking.

Since Nate had been asked to serve as their guide, he led the way to a notch in the ring of heavily forested mountains to the east. Beyond it, they paused on a wide shelf to enjoy a sweeping panoramic vista of the many stark lower peaks and rolling green foothills below, as well as the well-nigh limitless expanse of prairie stretching eastward for as far as the eye could see. It was a breathtaking sight.

A switchback brought them to a meadow luxuriant with grass and flowers. Presently they came on a gurgling stream and paralleled its winding course lower to where it flowed into a swift but shallow river. This was the Big Thompson, as a few of the mountaineer men called it, and further on the river coursed through the spectacular Big Thompson canyon where towering rock ramparts hemmed the party in on both sides.

Some of the warriors muttered uneasily and cast distrustful glances at the remote heights. Nate didn't blame them. He had never much liked the closed-in sort of feeling that riding through the canyon always sparked. And, too, there was the ever present danger of massive boulders falling from on high. Twice in the past he had narrowly escaped being crushed to a pulp when that happened.

Which explained why Nate so seldom took the Big Thompson route. There was another way into this remote valley, a winding trail long used by Indians and animals alike. The going was much easier and more open. Unfortunately, it would have brought them out of the mountains a good 20 miles south of where the Big Thompson canyon would.

Winona rode behind her husband, their daughter nestled in the cradleboard on her back. Her mount was a favorite surefooted mare. In addition to her rifle, she had a knife and a pistol.

The Shoshone woman did not fail to note the bitter looks that He Dog and Runs Against gave her man. She didn't let on how pleased she was to see He Dog's swollen, puffy lips and cheeks. Whenever the party stopped to rest, she made it a point to keep her eyes on the two. If either lifted a finger against her husband, she would shoot them dead without hesitation.

Zach was also watching his father's back. When he thought of it. He was so thrilled at being allowed to go on the raid that his blood practically sang in his veins. He was giddy at the prospect of counting coup.

Shoshones measured manhood by the same standard as the Sioux, the Cheyenne, the Crows and Blackfeet and many other tribes; by brave deeds performed in the heat of battle. When Zach visited with his mother's people every summer, he heard countless tales of the exploits of famous warriors. War was all the boys his age liked to talk about.

In order to rise in public esteem, a Shoshone boy had to count coup on his enemies. The more coup he counted, the more esteemed he became. It was as simple as that.

Young Zach was no stranger to bloodshed. He had a number of coups to his credit already. He had even killed. But he wanted more coups, the more the better, and he prayed that the Great Mystery would grant him his heart's desire when they struck Lakota country.

In the meantime, the boy was intoxicated with excitement. He felt more alive than he ever had. The very air seemed invigorating, and his whole body tingled at times. He could barely sit still in the saddle and constantly shifted to take in all there was to see.

So it was that Zach was the first to notice movement at the rim of the towering cliff to their right just as the war party entered a shadowed stretch where the walls narrowed, affording them barely enough room for their horses to proceed in single file.

Zach looked closer. Eagles sometimes perched on the rim and he liked to watch them take flight. Occasionally, bighorn sheep appeared, prancing about the sheer cliffs as if they were on solid ground. But the thing he saw moving was huge and brown, and for a few moments he imagined it was a grizzly tumbling end over end. Then he recognized it for what it was. "Pa! One of the boulders is falling!"

Nate took one glance and hollered, "Ride! Ride!" while motioning for the Crows to do just that. He jabbed his heels into the stallion's flanks and took off at a gallop, hugging the wall to his right to avoid a misstep which might send him sliding into the river.

The pounding clatter of heavy hooves drummed in Nate's ears. He would much rather have moved aside so his wife and son could go past him, but there wasn't enough room. Above him erupted a tremendous booming crash as the cabin-sized boulder bounced off a spur of rock.

A look back showed the warriors were in full flight.

The boulder was falling faster, gaining momentum rapidly. It smashed against the cliff time and again. Deafening crashes resembled the peal of thunder.

The trail grew steeper, forcing Nate to concentrate on his riding to the exclusion of all else. A short slope brought him to a wide level area where he could give the stallion its head, but instead he cut to the right and slowed so Winona and Zach could get in front of him as he wanted. Once they were past, he fell into place beside Two Humps.

The last warrior in line was also the youngest. His name was Feather Earring and he made no attempt to conceal his rising fright. Nate saw him look upward again and again, gauging whether he would get out of the way in time.

It was close. Feather Earring was almost to the bottom of the short slope when the boulder impacted in the middle of the trail less than ten feet behind him. The ground shook as if from an earthquake and the high walls themselves seemed to shake and shimmy. A thick cloud of dust swirled skyward above the boulder as dirt and small stones and other debris rained down.

Nate smiled in relief. They were safe. Or so he believed until the clouds parted and the circular boulder rolled down the slope in their wake, going faster and faster with every foot it traveled.

"Go! Go!" Nate cried, urging the Crows on. Not that they needed to be prompted. They all saw the immense monster hard on their heels and lashed their mounts with their quirts or their reins.

Feathered Earring let out a yelp. His horse had stumbled and nearly fallen and he had lost precious ground to the stone titan. He had a bow in hand which he frantically applied to his mount.

Ahead lay a bend. If they reached it, they would be safe. But *could* they? Nate wondered as he flew across the level area with the wind in his hair and dust in his nostrils. The rumbling crunch of the boulder was growing louder by the second. He could have sworn it was right behind him.

Incongruously, little Evelyn was smiling and giggling, having great fun. Her cherubic face and tiny fingers poked from the top of the cradleboard. When the mare swept around the bend and nearly lost its footing, she squealed in delight.

Zach was so close to his mother that he had to

haul on the reins of his pinto in order not to crash into the tottering mare. The trail broadened, enabling him to veer to the right. He went a score of yards, then drew rein to see if the Crows gained cover. Two Humps, Bull Standing With Cow, and He Dog came around the bend one right after the other. So did two other warriors. To his dismay, there was no sign of his father.

Nate had slowed again to goad the warriors on. Runs Against flashed past him. So did Flying Hawk and Long Forelock. Feather Earring was yards back, flailing his flagging horse with all his strength. It was doing no good.

The boulder was almost upon them. Rolling at an incredible rate of speed, with part of it in the river and part on dry land, it was like a raging bull or a runaway steam engine. There was no stopping it. Gravel, branches and brush were smashed to bits under its incalculable weight.

Nate could delay no longer. Slapping his legs, he sped around the bend, twisting as he did. He saw the nose of the young warrior's mount appear. And then there was a horrid screech and he saw Feather Earring and the animal caught under the onrushing goliath. There was wild desperation in the Crow's eyes as the boulder rolled up over him. Man and horse were bent and flattened and reduced to a commingled reddish mass of oozing gore, pulverized flesh, and shattered bones.

The boulder plowed across the river, throwing a wide spray in its wake. It rammed into the opposite wall with an ear-blistering concussion, fracturing the craggy surface in a regular spider's web of small cracks and wider clefts.

Panic seized some of the Crows's horses. The animals pitched and plunged, whinnying in a frenzy of unbridled fear. The warriors held on for dear life. Flying Hawk was thrown onto his shoulder and lay there, dazed. He Dog was nearly unhorsed but grabbed his sorrel's mane and belabored it about the head and neck with his fists until it calmed down and stood trembling like a frightened child.

The black stallion quaked a few times but that was all. Nate rode over to Winona and Zach and placed a hand on each of them in turn. He did not say anything. Words weren't necessary.

The Crows called a halt then and there. A council was held. Since they conversed in their tongue, the Kings had no idea what was being discussed until afterward when Two Humps summarized the dispute.

Four of the warriors had been in favor of going back. Led by Long Forelock, the faction maintained that the death of Feather Earring was bad medicine, an omen of worse to come.

Bull Standing With Cow made an eloquent appeal, asking those who had children if they would be so eager to give up if it was their child and not his. He also pointed out to those who were not married that they had a sacred obligation to do all in their power to help members of their tribe whenever and wherever help was needed.

The four men changed their minds.

The Crows wanted to do right by Feather Earring but there were no trees nearby, nor was there enough left of him to scrape up and bury. They compromised. From a gravel bed in the river they gathered enough to cover the pulped remains with an inch-thick layer. A simple ceremony was performed and the journey resumed.

From there on until the end of the canyon, each and every one of them rode with his or her eyes glued to the boulder-strewn heights. They avoided making any undue loud noises.

At last the canyon widened and rolling foothills unfolded before them.

The sun hung high in the afternoon sky, but not high enough to justify stopping for the night. Nate pushed on, wending lower past earthen and sandstone cliffs.

They were shy of the prairie by just a few miles when twilight overtook them. Nate knew the region as well as he did the proverbial back of his hand. He selected a spacious clearing near the river for their camp. Enclosed by cottonwoods and willows, it offered adequate shelter from the wind and screened their fire from prying eyes.

The Crows were in a somber mood. Saddened by the loss of their companion, they were not much interested in eating or talking.

Nate made coffee and a stew from a rabbit he shot. He did the butchering while his wife went off by the river to feed their daughter.

Winona did not care to have the Crows watch her breast-feed. Shoshones as a rule were not shy about normal bodily functions, but she had learned that other people did not share the Shoshone outlook. Some whites, for instance, considered it a sin for a woman to expose her breasts in public. Some Indians, the Cheyennes foremost among them, were just as reserved about nudity. She did not know the Crow attitude, but she was taking no chances. In the interests of harmony, she sat at the water's edge with her back to the men and cradled Evelyn in her arms.

The child sucked greedily, kneading Winona's supple flesh with her small fingers. Nate had once told Winona that among his people it was not uncommon for a mother to stop breast-feeding when an infant was no older than a year and a half. The revelation had shocked her.

Among the Shoshones, a mother often breast-fed until the child was three or even four years of age. Her people were of the conviction that doing so instilled an even temperament. Cutting a child off early crimped the child's character, contributing to insolence and rebellion later in life.

Soon Evelyn had drunk her fill and was dozing in perfect bliss. Winona covered herself and gently rocked her daughter, staring down into that innocent face, her heart brimming with love.

Winona was glad that their second child had turned out to be a girl. Boys were fine—she loved Zach as dearly as she did Evelyn—but it was nice to have a girl she could rear as her mother had reared her. She looked forward to passing on the many lessons she had learned at Morning Dew's knee.

Over at the string of tethered horses, Zach King was grooming his pinto. It was a nightly ritual of his ever since his father traded for the animal.

The terrible incident in the canyon had dampened Zach's enthusiasm. Try as he might, he couldn't get the awful image of the young warrior going down under that boulder from his mind. But for the grace of the good Lord, that might have been him, or his mother, or his father. It impressed him as nothing else could that the raid should not be treated as a lark. It was a serious, grave affair which might result in the deaths of all of them if they weren't almighty careful.

Suddenly Zach became aware that he was no longer alone. Turning, he was startled to find He Dog a few yards off, regarding him with open disdain. He ignored the hothead and went back to stroking the pinto with a horsehair brush.

Footsteps came closer. The Crow uttered a mocking laugh.

Zach slowly turned again. The warrior was so close that he could smell the bear fat in He Dog's hair. Making his face as blank as a slate, he set the brush on the pinto's back and signed, "Question. You want?"

He Dog shouldered Zach aside to stand next to the mount. "You call this a horse, white dog?" he signed haughtily. "I would not give it to a girl to ride."

Anger flared in Zach and he clenched his fists. He was all set to take a swing when it occurred to him that might be exactly what the warrior wanted him to do. He Dog was goading him into a fight, probably counting on his father to rush over and get involved.

Plastering a fake smile on his face, Zach said in English, "Why, you mangy polecat. You're plumb no account any way I lay my sights. If you had any brains, you'd know that getting my pa riled is as dumb as can be." Switching to Shoshone, he added, "Your heart is as foul as buffalo droppings. If I were a warrior, I would kill you and be done with you."

He Dog glared. He did not need to understand either language to know that he had been insulted. He raised an arm as if to backhand the boy, then looked up, frowned, and walked off without another gesture.

Bull Standing With Cow strolled up. His kindly eyes conveyed regret, and something more. "I saw, Stalking Coyote," he signed. "If I did not need his help so much, I would tell him to leave. Please bear with him until my daughter is safe."

"I will try," Zach promised.

An awkward few moments went by. Bull Standing With Cow sighed and patted the mare. "My daughter is not much older than you," he signed. "She was just taking an interest in boys. In another winter she would have married, and in two or three I would have grandchildren to sit on my knee."

"It can still happen. We will save her. Watch and see."

The Crow father gazed into the darkness. "I wish I had your confidence, Stalking Coyote. But I have lived too long. I know that good intentions do not always insure events will turn out as we would like them to. Sometimes matters are taken out of our hands."

"We will do all we can to help you. You know that."

"Yes," Bull Standing With Cow signed. "Your father is an honorable man. The Shoshones think highly of him. The Utes, too, I hear. As do my people. He is like the Blanket Chief, straight and true in all he does."

The Blanket Chief, Zach knew, was a mountain man named Jim Bridger, perhaps the single most widely respected white man living west of the Mississippi. The warrior had given his father quite a compliment.

Over by the fire, Nate King rose. He saw his son signing to Bull Standing With Cow but could not make out what was being said. Picking up his Hawken, he strolled to the river.

The night was moonless. A pall of gloom hung over the camp, befitting the mood of the Crows.

Nate spied the silhouette of his wife against the lighter backdrop of the river. Her gaze was on the myriad of stars sparkling like jewels in the inky firmament. "Are you fixing to spend the whole night in this spot?" he joked.

Winona grinned. "It is so peaceful here, husband. Our daughter is sound asleep and I do not want to disturb her yet."

Sinking down and crossing his legs in front of him, Nate listened to the whisper of the current and the sigh of the wind in the cottonwoods. "I see what you mean," he commented softly. The tension drained out of him like water from a sieve and he leaned back on his hands. "I hope to high heaven we haven't bitten off more than we can chew," he voiced his uppermost concern.

"Are you worried?"

"I'd be speaking with two tongues if I claimed otherwise. But we've gone up against worse. I reckon we can handle whatever comes along."

Of the many traits her husband possessed that Winona King admired, his perseverance in the face of adversity was foremost. When up against an insurmountable obstacle, he liked to say, "Where there's a will, there's a way." And then he would go on to overcome it.

Winona tenderly placed her hand on his wrist and leaned over to peck him on the jaw. "I am sure you are right," she whispered.

Nate kissed her lightly on the lips. Two of her fingers traced the outline of his knuckles and he could feel the smooth flesh at the tips where formerly her nails had been.

Years ago, shortly after they met, Winona's parents had been slain by Blackfeet. In keeping with Shoshone custom, as a token of her grief, she had chopped the ends off of a couple of fingers on her left hand. There had been a time when the mere thought of her sacrifice would have caused Nate to break out in goosebumps. But no longer. He had grown to accept the custom, just as he had grown to accept a great many things he once had branded as plain obscene.

Life was warped in that regard. Back in the States there were plenty of whites who hated Indians simply because they were different. Savages, the whites called them. Yet if those who did the name calling could spend some time with those they hated so much, they'd learn, just as Nate had, that when all was said and done, the red man and the white man were closer kin than most would admit.

"I think tomorrow Zach and I will take turns riding behind everyone else," Winona mentioned.

"So you can keep better tabs on He Dog and his pard," Nate guessed.

"It is not wise to have an enemy riding at your back. You never know when you might sprout more arrows than a porcupine has quills."

Nate chuckled. "Goodness gracious, dearest. You're starting to sound a lot like Shakespeare McNair."

"I wish he were with us now."

"So do I." Nate missed his closest friend and mentor greatly. A few moons back Shakespeare and his Flathead wife, Blue Water Woman, had gone on a long delayed visit to her people. Shakespeare had told him it would be unlikely they'd be back at their cabin, located about 25 miles north of the King homestead, until the first leaves started to fall.

Evelyn stirred, and Winona reached down to cover the infant's face. As she straightened, she peered through the trees toward the prairie and tensed. "Husband, look."

Far out on the plain, barely visible, flickered a dancing point of light.

"Another camp fire," Nate realized. He almost jumped up and dashed to their own fire to put it out. But it was small and shielded by the vegetation. He doubted whoever was out there had spotted the pale glow. "I'd best have a talk with Two Humps. The Crows have to help take turns keeping watch tonight, whether they like the notion or not."

Winona took his hand as he rose. "No matter what happens on our journey, I want you to know you have done the right thing. You make me proud to be your woman."

"Thanks," Nate said. He didn't add that if anything happened to their children or her, knowing he had done right would be damn small consolation. Yet he was thinking it.

Chapter Five

The spot was easy to find, thanks to the acrid scent of smoke lingering in the brisk morning air and the spiraling white tendrils that wafted upward now and again from the smoldering embers of the camp fire.

Nate crouched in high grass a score of feet away and scanned the vicinity. Even at that distance he knew white men had been responsible. The charred remains formed a wide circle, indicating the fire had been a big one. And only white men made fires so large that they dared not get too close for fear of being singed. Indians invariably built small ones so they could sit close to the flames to keep warm.

Rising, Nate cautiously emerged from cover. It puzzled him that the camp had been made right out in the open in a small flattened area rather than in a gully or near a knoll where there would have been protection from the stiff night winds and hostile eyes would have been less apt to spot the blaze. No mountain man worthy of the name would have camped there. It had to have been greenhorns, Nate reasoned.

The trapper found tracks, but they only added to his puzzlement. There was one set, and one set alone. Boot prints, judging by the size and shape. And the man had been afoot. There was not a single hoof track anywhere.

Nate hunkered and scratched his chin, pondering. The boots confirmed his hunch about a greenhorn being to blame. Experienced mountaineers preferred lightweight moccasins to unwieldy store bought footwear.

It bothered Nate that the man was afoot. Being stranded without a horse was a certain death warrant for any man not able to fend for himself. The wilderness was a harsh taskmaster. Those not able to wrestle with the wild on its own terms inevitably paid for their weakness with their lives.

The tracks bore eastward. Evidently the man was on his way back to civilization. But for him to expect to cross the vast prairie on foot was akin to expecting a miracle. Grizzlies and other predators were more numerous than fleas on an old coonhound. And hostiles were everywhere.

Rising, Nate held his Hawken aloft and waved it from side to side, the signal they had agreed on if it was safe for the rest to join him. They were hidden in a wash over a hundred yards off and promptly appeared, riding abreast, with Zach leading the black stallion.

"What did you find?" Winona asked as she drew rein.

Nate explained in sign language, pointing out the tracks as he did. Then he surprised the Crows by signing, "I would like to speak to this white man. He left a short while ago, so it should not take long for us to catch up with him."

He Dog promptly objected. "What do we care about this stupid white man? Bull Standing With Cow's daughter is more important. I say we press on. This will only delay us."

Nate faced the father. "He Dog has a point. The decision should be yours. If you want, the rest of you can ride to the northeast and I will overtake you before the sun is straight overhead."

The Crow reflected a few moments. "A short delay will not matter much. And I do not want us to be separated. We will all go after this white man."

"Thank you," Nate said sincerely. Forking leather, he galloped on the greenhorn's trail. The man had not made good time. Within ten minutes Nate spied a solitary figure plodding along under the brilliant sun.

"I should go on ahead," Nate signed. "He might shoot if he mistakes us for enemies."

"Can I tag along, Pa?" Zach asked. He was burning with curiosity to learn more about the stranger. Other than the annual rendezvous and regular visits by his Uncle Shakespeare, encounters with white men were few and far between.

"No," Nate replied, deliberately looking at He Dog. "You'd best stay here with your ma." He rode off before the hothead or Runs Against could complain, holding to a trot until he was close enough for the greenhorn to hear him.

Since Nate was not partial to being shot at, he hollered in greeting, "Hold up there, friend! I'd like a few words with you!"

The man slowly stopped and turned. His movements were awkward and sluggish, as if he were drunk. His eyes narrowed and he peered uncertainly around him as if he could not see well.

Nate moved closer. He was shocked to discover the man was unarmed. No rifle, no pistol, no knife, nothing. Other than a worn set of grungy woolen clothes and a leather possibles bag, the man had no possessions whatsoever. "I mean you no harm. I'm a white man, like you."

The greenhorn's thin lips quirked upward. "White?" he croaked.

Nate came to a halt. He'd come across men on the verge of starvation before and recognized the signs. The sluggishness and confusion were typical. Plus the man was skin and bones, the clothes hanging limp on his wasted frame. "My handle is Nate King. I'm a free trapper. Who might you be, hoss?"

"Emmet Carter," the man rasped. His eyes commenced to water, but whether from the sunlight or because he was crying, Nate couldn't tell.

"Well, Emmet, it appears to me that you could use some help. What in blazes are you doing out here in the middle of nowhere all by your lonesome?"

Carter licked his lips and coughed. "I'm heading home, to Maryland."

"You fixing to walk the whole way, are you?"

"My horse was stolen by Injuns. They took practically everything. My supplies, my guns, my water skin." Carter sniffled. "It was the last straw, King. A man can only take so much."

Nate slid down. The greenhorn was swaying and his hands shook as if with palsy. "Let me guess. You came west thinking you'd make your fortune in plews, and you struck off for the Rockies on your own?"

Carter nodded. His cheeks were slick with tears. "But you found out the hard way that trapping isn't all its cracked up to be. I'll bet you hardly caught any beaver."

"Just one," the man said, "and then I couldn't cure the damn hide right. It got all stiff and hard on me."

It was the same old story Nate had heard dozens of times, with minor variations. Back in the States, certain so-called journalists and other un-scrupulous types were filling the heads of young men with all sorts of lies and half-truths about the glorious life of wealth and leisure awaiting anyone who spent just a few years trapping for a living. The fact was that free trappers never made more than enough to get by, while company trappers made a pittance.

The only ones who got rich off the fur trade were the heads of the big fur enterprises. But that was the way it had always been, in all facets of life. Those with money lorded it over those with-out, and arranged things so that more and more wealth flowed into their hands at the expense of honest hard-working souls who were trod under their financial heels. Or, to put it more succinctly, the rich stayed rich and the poor made them richer.

"You must be hungry," Nate declared, offering a piece of pemmican from his possibles bag.

Carter snatched it and bit off half in one bite. He chewed greedily, groaning all the while.

"Tell me," Nate coaxed, "when was the last time you had something to eat or drink?"

"I can't remember. I think it was three days ago."

"Then have a seat and I'll treat you to some of the best jerky this side of the Divide. My wife made it herself." Nate helped the greenhorn sit and stepped to his horse to open a parfleche.

"I don't know how to thank you, mister," Carter said, his voice quavering with emotion. "You have no idea the nightmare I've been through." He sniffled some more, louder than before. "To tell you the truth, I can't quite believe this is happening. I half think I'm dreaming this whole thing, that in a few minutes I'll wake up and find I've been chewing on grass or some such."

"Don't fret yourself. This coon is real enough." Nate gave him a half-dozen thick slices of jerky. "Your guardian angel must be watching over you, mister. Another day, and you would have keeled over and never gotten up again. You must be mighty tough to have made it this far."

The compliment had the opposite effect than Nate intended. Unexpectedly, Emmet Carter broke down and bawled like a distraught baby. He cried and cried, his face buried in his arms, blubbering and wheezing until he had cried himself dry. At length he wiped his nose with the back of a dirty sleeve and looked up. "I don't know how I'll ever be able to repay you for saving my life."

"You're not out of the woods yet, hoss. Were it up to me, I'd take you back to my cabin and fatten you up, give you a chance to regain your strength. Then in a month or so I'd escort you to Bent's Fort so you could hitch up with the next caravan back to Fort Leavenworth."

"You can't do that?" Carter asked, a forlorn note hinting at a sudden panic that salvation was about to be denied him. He glanced at the stallion, and for a moment it seemed as if he contemplated leaping erect and trying to ride off before Nate could stop him. But he stayed where he was.

Over the next several minutes Nate filled the man in about the Crows and the rescue mission to save Fetches Water.

The greenhorn listened intently, his mouth constantly crammed with jerky. "These Crows are friendly, you say?" he asked when the mountain man concluded.

"Friendly enough, although one or two of them would slit your throat as soon as look at you," Nate conceded. "But the only way out of the fix you're in is for you to throw in with us. Once we have the Crow girl safe, we can get you to William Bent, a friend of mine."

Emmet Carter never hesitated. "I don't have much choice, do I? Bring on the Crows, King."

So Nate did. Another council had to be held, conducted in sign for his benefit. The two troublemakers objected vigorously to having the greenhorn along, but Two Humps overruled them. So long as the man did not slow them down, the venerable leader had no objections. Nor did Bull Standing With Cow.

In an hour they were on their way, Carter riding double with Zach. The boy was glad to make the man's acquaintance. He had never met anyone from Maryland before and asked dozens of questions about the greenhorn's life there.

Nate and Winona overheard most of the talk. They learned that Carter was the son of a shoemaker, that he had balked at following in his father's footsteps and decided to strike off on his own. So he'd spent every last penny he had to outfit himself as a trapper and lit a shuck for parts unknown.

Winona was happy that her son and the stranger were getting along so well. She could not help but note that Carter acted ill at ease when close to any of the Crows, which she blamed on undue fear that he would be harmed.

That night the war party camped between two

knolls bordered by a ribbon of a stream. Supper consisted of antelope, a pronghorn He Dog dropped with an arrow at a range of 70 yards, a remarkable shot by any standard.

The men took turns standing guard. Nate had the last watch and got to see vivid bands of pink and yellow decorate the horizon as the sun made its advent known. He had coffee perking when the rest roused themselves from under their blankets.

Emmet Carter was like a new man that morning. The rest and the meals had done wonders for his constitution, and he chatted amiably with Zach from dawn until they fell asleep that night.

And so it went for three more otherwise uneventful days.

Nate got to know Carter better and regarded him as a decent enough young man who would make something of himself now that he knew riches never fell into one's lap like manna from heaven. He had learned the hard way that most people had to make ends meet through the sweat of their brow. Schemes to get rich quick only benefitted the schemers.

Then came the fifth day, and that evening Nate picked a site on a low bluff where scrub trees clustered thick around a small clear spring. While several Crows collected dead wood for the fire and Winona was busy preparing coffee, Nate took his son hunting. They descended the slope and bore to the east. Hardly had they rounded the end of the bluff when they spooked five does which bounded off, flashing the white undersides of their erect tails.

"Look, Pa!" Zach bellowed, giving chase. His pinto was fleet of foot, and in moments he was close enough to shoot. But drawing a bead from the back of a moving horse was hard to do. No sooner would Zach fix the sights squarely on a target than the deer would swerve or bound high into the air, spoiling the shot.

Nate stayed alongside his son. He refrained from firing to give Zach the practice. One of the does began to lag and he called out, "You have to think one step ahead of them. Aim high just as that last one starts to jump."

Zach let go of the reins and used his legs to guide the pinto, a Shoshone trick he had been taught when he was barely old enough to sit a horse. Wedging the stock tight against his shoulder, he sighted down the bobbing barrel, steadied his arms, and did exactly as his father had instructed him. He found that by aiming high, the deer bounded directly into his sights at the apex of each jump. All he had to do was adjust to its rhythm and stroke the trigger at just the right instant.

At the blast, the doe crumpled as if all four legs had been splintered. It slid to a stop and rolled onto its side, convulsing just once before it went limp with its tongue jutting out.

"I did it!" Zach cried, proud of his accomplishment. It was a first for him, a feat he could brag of when he visited the Shoshones and all the boys were bragging of special deeds they had done since last they were together.

Among most tribes, a man's prowess as a hunter was of critical importance. After all, no woman wanted to move into the lodge of a warrior famed for counting coup but who couldn't keep the supper pot supplied with a variety of game. Likewise, the quality of a warrior's clothes, the state of his lodge, and a great many other everyday items all depended on a steady supply of hides, bones, feathers and other bodily parts of various animals.

So Zach took almost as much joy in improving his hunting ability as he did in counting coup. He had learned a tactic that would serve him in good stead in the future.

Rather than butcher the doe on the spot, they threw it over the back of the stallion, then returned to camp. Bull Standing With Cow helped them skin the deer and cut the meat. Two Humps gave Winona a hand setting up a makeshift spit.

Soon everyone was gathered around the fire, waiting for their morsel. Emmet Carter sat near the Kings with his arms wrapped around his legs. He was unusually pensive, which Nate chalked up to fatigue since they had spent over ten hours on the go that day.

The venison was juicy and tasty. Nate treated himself to two helpings, and when he was done he licked his fingers clean and sat back to let the food digest.

Carter was still eating. He could never seem to get enough, gorging himself at every meal. Pausing to wipe his hands on his pants, he smiled at Nate and commented, "I want to thank you again for all you've done for me. I'll never forget it."

"Thank me when we get you to Bent's Fort, not before," Nate said.

"How long would that be, do you expect?"

"My best guess would be about a month yet," Nate said, "provided everything goes smoothly. Which it never does."

"A month," Carter said in transparent disappointment. "I hope you won't hold it against me if I think that's much too long to wait."

"Not at all. I don't blame you for wanting to get back sooner. After all you've been through, you're probably straining at the bit to head east."

"My sentiments exactly," Carter declared. "It's

nice to know we see eye to eye."

Nate didn't attach much significance to the conversation and turned to the cradleboard to spend time with his daughter. She laughed for joy as he played with her fingers and made silly faces. When she grew tired, Winona went off to feed her and Nate laid on his back with a forearm over his eyes to ward off the glare from the fire.

The trapper was more weary than he realized. He dozed off, awakening later when Winona threw a blanket over him and once more toward midnight when He Dog was giving another warrior a hard time about getting up and keeping watch. After the hothead complied, Nate drifted into dreamland, confident that Long Forelock would awaken him when it was his turn.

The yip of a coyote snapped Nate out of a sound sleep. He had the impression only an hour or so had gone by. Stretching, he observed that the fire had nearly burned itself out. That perplexed him. And his perplexity mounted when he turned his face to the heavens and realized the stars were all wrong. By their positions, it was much later than it should have been. In fact, dawn was less than an hour off.

Nate sat up. His wife and children slept soundly nearby. On the other side of the fire were seven Crows. The eighth had to be on watch.

Quietly rising, Nate sought some sign of the warrior. But there was none. He studied those who were sleeping and concluded that Long Forelock was the one missing. The obvious conclusion was that the Crow had gone off somewhere and dozed off.

Moving around the spring to the horses, Nate scoured the bluff in vain. Mystified, he walked to the end of the string. Suddenly it dawned on him that a horse was missing. He counted to be sure. It was Zach's pinto.

Now alarmed, Nate made a swift circuit of the camp. He saw no one and was going to awaken the others when he glimpsed a shadowy shape lying amid thick brush. Drawing a flintlock, he went over.

It was Long Forelock. The back of his skull had been caved in with a large rock, splitting it like an overripe melon and spilling his brains onto the ground. There was no consolation in the knowledge that the warrior had undoubtedly died instantly without being aware of what had happened.

An icy chill came over Nate as he walked back to the fire. The spot where Emmet Carter was supposed to be sleeping was bare. The greenhorn was gone, and a hasty check revealed he had swiped Winona's rifle, Zach's pistol, a blanket and a sizeable chunk of leftover deer meat with him.

Nate stood and stared eastward. He felt as if every lick of blood were draining from his body. "You damned fool," he said under his breath, and bowed his head, the enormous consequences of the greenhorn's treachery bearing down on his broad shoulders as if he were the mythical Atlas bearing the weight of the entire world.

After a while Nate stirred. He checked that his pistols were loaded before he saddled the stallion. Into a parfleche he packed enough jerky and pemmican to last him several days. As he was tying the straps, Two Humps rose on an elbow.

"Are you leaving us, Grizzly Killer?" the Crow signed.

Nate could think of no way to break the news gently. "The other white man has killed Long

Forelock and stolen the paint that belongs to my son."

In a twinkling Two Humps was on his feet. Nate led him to the body and stood back while the warrior knelt and clenched at the grass in impotent fury. When Two Humps calmed, he turned.

"I do not understand. How can he have done this? None of us mistreated him. Tell me *why*," he pleaded.

"I will know that when I catch him."

"And what will you do then?"

Nate merely looked at the body.

The others were waking up. Winona saw her husband approach and sensed right away that something was amiss. On hearing his account, she began to pack up their effects. "We will go with you," she said.

"No."

When two people have lived together day in and day out for years, they get to know one another as well as they do themselves. Nate's misery was like a physical force to Winona, a sword knifing deep into the depths of her soul. "You do not need to take this all on yourself."

"I was the one who insisted we lend him a helping hand. The blame is all mine."

Over half of the Crows agreed. He Dog and Runs Against and two others were outraged and all for pursuing Carter themselves. It took all of Two Humps's powers of persuasion to convince them to let Nate deal with the betrayer.

Young Zach was fit to be tied when the commotion woke him up and he learned about his pinto. "Why'd he take my horse?" he railed. "What did I ever do to him?"

"He took the paint because it was used to him," Nate answered. "He'd ridden it for days and knew it wouldn't act up when he threw on your saddle."

"The varmint," Zach snapped. "I'd like to get my hands on him!"

"Think again," Nate said, and stepped into the stirrups. His loved ones and the Crows were equally somber as he turned the stallion. "Head to the northeast for two days," he directed Winona. "I should rejoin you long before then, but if not, camp and wait for me."

"Take care, husband."

"Always."

Nate lifted the reins but paused when He Dog strode forward.

"Prove you are our friend, Grizzly Killer," the firebrand arrogantly signed. "Bring us the hair of your white brother and we will know that your words are not as empty as the air around us."

The stallion raised a swirl of dust as it trotted around the spring and on down the bluff. To the east a golden crown framed the plain, but there was only darkness in the heart of the man called Nate King.

Chapter Six

Winona King did not like the idea of being left alone with the Crows. But she made no protest when her husband rode off. She understood why he had to go. And she knew that Evelyn, Zach and she would slow him down. So she stoically accepted the fact and got on with the business at hand.

Nate had been out of sight but a few moments when Winona caught He Dog giving her a look that did not bode well. But it didn't worry her unduly. If trouble arose, she was confident she could count on Two Humps, Bull Standing With Cow and Flying Hawk to side with her.

Then, too, Winona was armed. Nate had given her his Hawken and she also had her pistol. She had demonstrated back at the cabin that she knew how to use a gun as well as any man, so He Dog would think twice before he tried anything.

Winona was eternally grateful to Nate for teaching her how to shoot. It permitted her to hold her own wherever she went.

Men, by virtue of their greater bulk and superior physical strength, tended to lord it over women. Even some in her own tribe liked to strut about as if they were bull elk at the height of rutting season, and in their lodges they treated their wives worse than they did their prized war horses.

At the annual rendezvous, there were always drunks to deal with. White men, Winona had learned, could be unspeakably wicked when they were under the influence of firewater. They often tried to force themselves on women who spurned their advances, causing fights to break out.

But no man, drunk or sober, white or red, would ever try to abuse a woman who could defend herself. A flintlock enabled a woman to compensate for her smaller size and put her on equal footing with any man. With a gun she could assert herself and stand up to those brutish males who would inflict suffering on anyone weaker than they were.

It was a King family custom for Nate to read to them several times a week. Once, years ago, during one such session, Nate had mentioned that certain wise men among his people had put on paper a list of all those things which were crucial to the welfare of white men and women everywhere.

Near the top of that list, Nate had told her, was the right to bear arms. It was not to be denied any citizen, as the whites called themselves. Those wise men had known that those who could not defend themselves were virtual slaves to those who had power over them. Winona had been much impressed by their wisdom.

An added factor that helped ease Winona's

mind about her husband's departure was the presence of their son. Stalking Coyote was young, true, but he had counted coup. He had slain enemies in the heat of battle, and would leap to her defense if any of the Crows acted up.

Zach was prepared to do just that. Astride Long Forelock's horse, he stayed close to his mother all morning. If He Dog or Runs Against rode anywhere near them, he was quick to heft his rifle and glare until the warriors fell back with the others.

Two Humps and Bull Standing With Cow were another story. The warriors took turns spending time with the Kings. Zach figured the Crows liked their company, but his mother was more astute. Winona knew it was their way of forestalling trouble. He Dog and Runs Against were not about to bother her when the older warriors were present.

Noon found them miles from the bluff, resting the horses at an isolated stand of trees.

The spring day was cool with a brisk breeze. Winona gave pemmican to Zach, then ambled to the opposite side of the stand and sat with her back to a tree to feed her daughter. She laid the heavy Hawken across her thighs and made herself comfortable.

It was quiet and peaceful there. The serenity, combined with the soft rustle of leaves overhead and the pleasant sensation of Evelyn's sucking, induced Winona to doze. Minutes went by.

Suddenly the feeling of pressure on Winona's legs vanished. She sat bolt upright and was stunned to discover the rifle was gone.

Standing to her right, holding the Hawken loosely in one hand with his other resting on the hilt of his long butcher knife, was He Dog. Smirking, he leaned the rifle against a sapling just out of her reach, then signed, "Did you lose something, woman?"

"Do you always play games more fit for children?" Winona retorted. She casually covered her breast without disturbing Evelyn, who slumbered on her chest. As she lowered her arm she contrived to place her hand close to the butt of her pistol without the Crow noticing.

"It seems to me, Shoshone," He Dog signed, "that you have never learned your proper place. It is not fitting for a woman to show disrespect to a warrior."

"Nor does a true warrior show disrespect to a woman," Winona said, refusing to be cowed.

He Dog ignored her comment. "You should never have taken a white man as your husband. Whites do not know how to treat their women. They are too soft on them."

"Be sure to tell that to Grizzly Killer when he returns. I want to see the look on your face when my soft husband beats you senseless as he did back at our wooden lodge."

A scarlet tinge flushed He Dog's cheeks, and he took a half step toward her. "If you were mine, I would soon teach you to hold your tongue."

Winona smiled sweetly and put as much venom in her tone as she could muster. "Crow, I would not be your woman if you were the only man left alive."

"You are Shoshone. What do you know? Any Crow woman would be proud to live in my lodge."

A thought struck Winona and she signed, "Question. Do you have a wife yet? Or are Crow women as smart as I think they are?"

He Dog bristled and bent to seize her. He rooted himself in place when her pistol blossomed as if by magic, the muzzle so close to his face that he was staring into the barrel.

Winona motioned and the warrior slowly backed off. She set the flintlock on her lap and signed, "Never, ever lay a finger on me, Crow. I will not go easy on you as my husband did for Two Humps's sake."

"Your husband is a fool. He should have rubbed me out while he had the chance," He Dog responded. "No man puts a hand on a Crow and lives to brag of it. I have held back because Bull Standing With Cow has asked me to." The stocky warrior leaned toward her, his swarthy visage aglow with fiery spite. "But know this, Shoshone. Once we have rescued Fetches Water, I will hold back no longer. Your precious white man will pay. And you will be in need of a new husband."

So signing, He Dog spun and stomped off, his spine as stiff as the trees around them.

Winona shivered. Whether from the cool breeze or the threat, she couldn't rightly say. He Dog was not to be taken lightly. For all his faults, he was a man of his word. He planned to kill Nate, and nothing would stop him short of his own death.

Brush close by shook as if to the passage of a small animal. Or a man on hands and knees. Thinking that the Crow had circled around to take her by surprise, Winona put a hand on her pistol just as the brush parted to reveal her protector.

Zach strolled into the open, his cocked pistol out. "If he'd kept it up, I aimed to put a ball into him," he stated. His father had long ago made it plain that when his father was gone, he was the man of the family. Safeguarding his mother and sister was a responsibility he took seriously.

"Were you spying on him the whole time?"

"Sure was," Zach confided. "I never let him out of my sight. Runs Against is another bad apple, but He Dog is the worst of the two."

"You heard what he said. I think we are safe until after we find Bull Standing With Cow's daughter."

"Never take anything for granted where your enemies are concerned," Zach quoted. "Isn't that what Pa is always telling us?"

It was. Winona smiled as she tucked Evelyn into the cradleboard. At moments like these her son reminded her so much of Nate that it was as if he were a smaller version of her husband. He helped hoist the cradleboard onto her back and handed her the Hawken. "Thank you," she said. In a good mood for the first time that day, she headed for the war party.

"I wonder how Pa is faring?" Zach remarked.

Just like that, Winona's fine spirits evaporated. "We'll know soon enough," was all she would say.

At that very moment the man they were both anxious about was bearing eastward at a steady trot. Since daybreak Nate King had held the stallion to a brisk pace in the hope that he would overtake Emmet Carter before the day was done. But as time passed he acknowledged that it might be wishful thinking on his part.

The greenhorn was pushing the pinto mercilessly. They had not stopped once, near as Nate could tell. If Carter kept on the way he was doing, the poor horse would play out on him in a day or two. Until then, the trapper had to content himself with sticking to the trail and trying not to worry about his loved ones.

To occupy himself, Nate tried to imagine what sort of man would betray his trust the way the greenhorn had. He'd done all in his power on the Easterner's behalf, and look at how Carter had repaid him!

The younger man's upbringing probably had something to do with it, Nate reflected. From what he had learned, Carter's folks had pampered him when he was little. They'd never made him do chores or work at odd jobs to earn money on his own. Consequently he'd come to think that anything he wanted should be his for the taking. Carter had been spoiled to the extent that he figured life owed him a living when actually it was the other way around.

But the greenhorn's lazy parents were only partly to blame. Carter had to shoulder a large measure of the fault for never growing past the selfish stage most younguns went through. There came a time when any growing boy had to accept full responsibility for his acts. Those who never learned this most important of all lessons went through life, as Nate's grandmother had once phrased it, "as brats in men's clothing."

Emmet Carter wanted to go home. So he figured that meant he had the right to do whatever he liked to achieve his goal. Killing was justified because it was in his own best interests. Stealing was acceptable because he needed what he stole. There was no ironclad right or wrong, in his eyes. He did as he pleased without regard for anyone else.

Nate had known men like Carter before, mainly during the years he'd spent growing up in New York. City life, he'd observed, tended to breed selfish individuals much as alleys and basements and tunnels bred rats. He suspected that it had something to do with the fact that in cities, men and women had all their wants met simply by handing over a few dollars or a handful of coins. They never had to hunt game for their supper or for hides to make clothes. They never had to go without so long as they earned enough to make ends meet.

In the country it was different. Rural folk not only had to earn a living, they had to butcher animals for food and cure pelts for clothes and do a hundred and one other things that city dwellers wouldn't think of doing. Country folk were more in touch with the world around them, more in harmony with the cycles of nature and basic survival.

Nate's mentor, Shakespeare McNair, claimed that one day there would be more city dwellers than country dwellers. Nate hoped he wasn't around to see that happen. The day it did, America would cease to be a country of basically honest, hard-working people who respected others as they respected themselves, and become a nation of selfish individuals who were always looking out for their own interests before all else.

Shaking his head to dispel his train of thought, Nate buckled down to tracking. For the better part of the afternoon he pressed on through the high grass. He lost count of the number of rabbits he spooked and the number of frightened prairie chickens that took wing. Deer were common. So were roving coyotes and packs of wolves, which gave him a wide berth.

About three o'clock Nate rode over a low rise and came on a fair-sized herd of buffalo. The snort of a bull was all it took to stampede the huge brutes southward. He reined up until the last of them were gone, then swung wide of the choking cloud of dust they had raised.

The herd had trampled the grass to bits and their flying hooves had torn up the ground in spots, erasing Carter's trail. Nate had to hunt for a while before he found it again, losing valuable time in the process.

Well before sunset Nate foresaw that he wouldn't catch up with the greenhorn that day. He slowed to a walk the last hour and stopped for the night in a buffalo wallow, where he got a small fire going. His meal consisted of jerky and pemmican.

Before turning in, Nate walked to a nearby hillock and scanned the prairie ahead. No telltale glow gave Carter away this time. Either the man was learning from his mistakes, he hadn't bothered with a fire, or he was farther ahead than Nate counted on.

The big trapper slept fitfully. He kept dreaming of Winona, Zach and Evelyn, and imagining them in all kinds of peril. Well before the sun brightened the sky he was in the saddle, taking up the chase again.

It was the middle of the morning when Nate located the spot where Carter had spent the night. The greenhorn had stumbled on a spring and shot a rabbit. So both the man and his mount were refreshed and raring to go. Catching them would be harder than ever.

Nate rode on. So accustomed was he to always having his Hawken at hand that it felt strange to be without it for once. He still had the pair of polished smoothbore flintlocks, but they were only reliable at short range.

Shortly before noon a brown hump appeared a few hundred feet to the northeast. At first Nate mistook it for a solitary buffalo, but as he drew nearer the creature heard the stallion and reared up onto its hind legs.

It was an enormous grizzly. The mighty carnivore rumbled an ominous warning, its gaping maw wide, its giant paws cleaving the air as if it were eager to do the same to the mountain man.

Nate never slowed but he did swing to the south. The monster watched him closely, and he feared that it might drop onto all fours and charge before he was a safe distance away. Grizzlies were as fleet as horses over short distances; he'd seen one topple a Shoshone warrior from a mount moving at a breakneck gallop.

Suddenly the bear sank back down. The hump on its broad shoulders was the only part of it that Nate could see. The grizzly moved in his direction, then inexplicably changed course, hastened westward, and was soon lost to view.

Nate stayed alert. Where there was one bear, there were sometimes more. Relaxing was out of the question until he had put two miles behind him.

He had lost more time. Not much, but enough to insure that Emmet Carter would elude him a second day.

Night caught Nate in the open. He made a cold camp, picketed the stallion, and curled up under a blanket with his arm for a pillow. It must have been two in the morning when a light sprinkle of cold raindrops fell, enough to awaken him and give him the chills. The rest of the night he tossed and turned.

Stiff and bedraggled, Nate rose at sunrise. He ate on the go, a handful of pemmican which barely sufficed to satisfy his gnawing hunger.

An hour later the trapper crossed a gully. Under an earthen overhang were the glowing embers of Carter's fire. Scattered feathers showed that the greenhorn had eaten his fill of prairie hen.

Nate was encouraged by the fact that he was only an hour behind his quarry. Apparently Carter believed that he had gotten clean away because the tracks were spaced much closer together; he was holding the pinto to a rapid walk.

Raking the stallion with his heels, Nate did the opposite. From time to time he rose in the stirrups to scan the prairie ahead. The thrill of success sent a tingle down his back when at long last he beheld an ant-sized figure almost on the horizon.

"Got you," Nate said softly to himself. He reduced his pace by half to maintain the distance between them. It would be unwise to let Carter spot him just yet. He had to sneak close enough to overhaul the greenhorn in a burst of speed.

All went well until noon. Nate kept the man in sight without giving himself away. Then a few low hills appeared, and Carter rode to the top of one and stopped. It was too far for Nate to see clearly, but it was evident the greenhorn had spotted him. The pinto wheeled and streaked on down the hill as if fleeing a prairie fire.

There was no recourse for Nate but to ride flat out. He wound through the hills rather than up and over them and saw Carter about half a mile distant.

Nate was a seasoned judge of horseflesh. He'd picked the pinto for his son because the animal had three qualities he admired most in a horse: a calm disposition, stamina, and speed. Now those same qualities were being displayed to his detriment, since the pinto was proving every bit as hardy as his own stallion. He gained ground, but not much.

Presently a long line of trees testified to the presence of a stream. Carter gained cover. Nate tried to keep him in sight but couldn't. He kept going and was well out from the cottonwoods when something tugged at the top of his beaver hat a fraction of a second before the sharp retort of the rifle wafted across the plain.

Instantly Nate slanted to the north and executed a trick taught him by a Shoshone warrior named Drags The Rope. He swung lithely onto the off-side of the stallion so that only his forearm and one foot showed. By peeking under the big black's neck, he guided it toward undergrowth less than 200 yards from the point where Carter had disappeared.

Nate thought he had thwarted the greenhorn, but he was wrong. Another shot rang out. The ball whizzed within inches of the stallion's head. Carter was trying to kill it! he realized, and swung back up. Bent low, he zigzagged for sanctuary.

Only one other shot boomed before Nate reached the undergrowth. There should have been two or three. Either Carter was as slow as molasses at reloading or he was conserving his ammo.

As tall weeds and trees closed around him, Nate straightened. To the left grew a thicket. Behind it he reined up and ground-hitched the stallion. Drawing both pistols, he edged to the east until he came to the stream, another wide but shallow waterway called different names by different tribes. The Shoshones referred to it as White Bark Creek, as Nate recollected.

Easing into the water, Nate hugged the bank and moved to the southeast. His intent was to catch Carter in the strip of vegetation between the stream and the prairie. Soon he came to a deep pool formed by a large tree that had fallen ages ago, partially blocking the flow. The water rose to his knees, then his waist. Since it wouldn't do to risk getting the pistols wet, he sought a suitable place to climb out.

That was when the brush above the bank crackled.

Nate pressed flush with the bank and crouched so that only his head and his hands were above water. He heard footsteps, then a muttered oath.

"Damn it! Where the hell did he get to?"

Emmet Carter's shadow materialized on the surface of the pool. Nate couldn't see the greenhorn, even though the man was so close he could hear Carter breathing. The shadow shifted, and Nate was positive that the man had his back to the stream. He cautiously rose to his full height and extended both pistols, sure the man had blundered right into his clutches.

But Carter was gone.

Nate scanned the pool but there was no trace of his shadow. He lifted a foot and scraped it along the bank, seeking purchase. There was none. The mud was as slick as bear fat.

Retracing his steps to a spot where the bank had crumpled leaving a wide cleft, Nate gingerly climbed a slippery incline. He paused every few seconds to scour the trees, but it was as if the earth had swallowed Carter up. Hunkering, he moved into a patch of high weeds and lowered onto his belly.

Nate had to adjust his strategy to compensate for the advantage the stolen rifle gave Carter. The man could fire at him from a long way off, while he had to wait until Carter was within 60 feet of his position, preferably less.

Not so much as a sparrow stirred anywhere. The shots had either scared the wild creatures off or silenced them, which worked in Nate's favor. He could hear faint noises better. And any movement he spied would more than likely be the greenhorn slinking along.

Soon something did move, in cottonwoods to the west. A flash of white and black hide revealed where Zach's pinto had been hidden. Nate started to crawl toward it. As he emerged from the weeds the horse let out a loud whinny, which was answered by another horse. But it wasn't Nate's stallion.

Whipping around, the trapper was startled to see five Indians nearing White Bark Creek from the east. Lured by the shots, they had come to investigate. They were well armed and had fanned out.

Even worse, they were Lakotas.

Chapter Seven

Two days of travel brought the war party to Red Willow Creek. They concealed themselves deep in a band of timber and kept a constant watch on the surrounding prairie.

As well they should. The place where they camped was less than 40 miles from the junction of the South Platte River with the Platte itself, where Nate had anticipated they would find the Oglalas encamped at that time of year.

It had been Nate's idea not to follow the South Platte all the way from the Rockies to where it merged with the larger Platte. His reasoning had been that they were more likely to encounter Sioux along the river, so he had stuck to the open plain. He'd outlined his strategy to Winona prior to leaving their cabin, and she'd agreed with it.

Now, deep in the heart of Lakota country with her young son and small daughter, Winona wished her man was at her side. She tried not to worry, but he had assured her that he would re-join them well before the end of the second day. Sunset was not far off, yet he hadn't appeared.

To complicate matters, the Crows were restless. Being in the heart of enemy territory had put them all on edge. He Dog was the worst of the bunch. He paced like a trapped animal and snapped at his companions when addressed.

Even Two Humps wasn't immune. Many times he walked to a high stump at the edge of the clearing and climbed onto it to survey the sea of grass to the south. After the fifth time, he came over to where Winona rested with her children. "Where is he?" the warrior signed. "He should have been here by now."

"Grizzly Killer advised us to wait," Winona reminded him, "so that is what we will do."

"But for how long?" Two Humps asked. "You know as well as I do that the longer we stay here, the greater the chance of our being discovered."

Bull Standing With Cow had been watching the exchange. "If the Lakotas spot us, they will rouse every warrior in the tribe. We will be chased all the way back to the Shining Mountains." His features saddened. "I will never see my daughter again."

"We must be patient," Winona stressed. "It is unlikely the Oglalas will come across us. We are too well hidden." She gestured at Red Willow Creek. "There is plenty of water and grass for the horses, and we have enough pemmican to last several more sleeps."

He Dog stomped up. "I, for one, do not intend to stay here that long. Even if we do not make a fire, the Lakotas might find us. All it would take is for one of our horses to nicker when a war party or a band of hunters is passing by, or for the wind to shift."

Runs Against grunted in agreement.

Outwardly calm but simmering inside, Winona said, "Are we so helpless that we cannot cover the muzzles of our horses when Lakotas are near? As for the wind, we are too deep in the trees for it to carry off much of our scent." She paused and gave He Dog a haughty glance. "If I, a *woman*, am not afraid of the Lakotas, why should you be?"

The stocky warrior thumped his chest and responded, "I am not afraid of the Lakotas or anyone else!"

"Prove it," Winona shot back. Then, cradling Evelyn, she gently rocked her daughter and refrained from looking at the Crows. One by one they drifted off until only Two Humps remained. She raised her head.

The leader was smiling. "You are wise beyond your years, my Shoshone friend," he said, "and as sly as a fox."

Winona grinned, balanced the cradleboard on her legs, and replied, "Women learned long ago to rely on their wits when dealing with men." Her grin broadened. "In a battle of minds, most men are unarmed."

Two Humps started to rock with laughter but caught himself and walked off chuckling.

A few feet away, Zach leaned against his saddle, his rifle propped at his side. He admired the clever manner in which his mother had handled the situation and commented as much.

"We are not out of the woods yet," Winona said, resorting to a figure of speech her husband often used. "He Dog will pout until his patience is at an end, then he will cause more trouble. The next time, I might not be able to stop him from going off to find the Oglala village where Fetches Water is being held."

"He's a damn jackass," Zach stated before he could stop himself. Flustered, he hastily blurted, "Sorry, Ma. I didn't mean to use such strong language in front of you."

"I have heard stronger, Stalking Coyote," Winona said. "My ears will not fall off." She slid her daughter from the cradleboard and playfully held her in the air while giving a little shake. The child giggled and pumped her legs as if anxious to walk.

The Crows were huddled in two groups. In one was Two Humps, Bull Standing With Cow and Flying Hawk. The other included He Dog, Runs Against, Bear Ears and Yellow Owl.

Zach stretched. He opened a parfleche and helped himself to a strip of jerky. It was the first food he had eaten all day. Although he would not let on to his mother, he was so concerned about his father that it had spoiled his appetite. "I've been thinking," he mentioned between bites. "If Pa isn't back by nightfall, do you want to go look for him?"

Winona was of half a mind to consent but she answered, "Your father can take care of himself. We will do as he asked us and stay put until he catches up."

"But what if—" Zach began, stopping when his mother raised a hand.

"When you have lived as long as I have, my son, you will learn not to worry so much. Most of the time the things we worry about never happen. As your father likes to say, take one day at a time."

"That's easier said than done."

Winona nodded. She stared off to the south, careful not to let her son see the burning anxiety that blazed like twin bonfires in her eyes. *My husband*, she thought, where are you?

Nate King froze on spying the Lakotas. He had no idea if they were Oglalas, Minniconjous, San Arcs, Brules, or Hunkpapas. It didn't much matter. All Lakotas were hostile to whites. If they saw him, they'd try to make wolf meat of him.

The Sioux were scouring the west side of White Bark Creek. A tall warrior in the middle of the group abruptly pointed to the south with his lance and spoke a few words. In the blink of an eye the five warriors dashed off, entering the water further down and splashing across into a cluster of saplings.

Rising into a crouch, Nate ran toward his son's pinto. He no longer cared about Emmet Carter; the greenhorn was on his own. Nate had to get out of there before the Lakotas returned.

The paint stood with its head hung low, close to exhaustion. Its legs and sides were flecked with dirt, its body caked with dust. It snorted when Nate grabbed the reins and untied them from a tree limb, but once it sniffed at his arm the pinto let him lead it northward.

Nate was halfway to the thicket when a piercing shriek prickled the hair at the nape of his neck. Halting behind cottonwoods, he saw the greenhorn burst from the saplings the Sioux had gone into. Carter hobbled as he ran, an arrow jutting from high on his thigh. Panic etched his countenance.

On his heels came the five warriors. They were in no particular hurry. Two of them bore to the left, two others to the right, to hem him in, while the tall warrior with several eagle feathers in his hair followed the greenhorn into the creek.

Whining in pathetic terror, Emmet Carter spun and trained the rifle on the tall warrior. The Lakota stopped and sat calmly, a bow in his right hand with an arrow notched to the sinew string.

"Leave me be!" Carter cried. "Just turn tail and go or you'll be sorry!"

The bluff didn't work. The warriors simply stared at him, waiting.

"I mean it!" Carter yelled shrilly. "So help me God, I'll drop the first one who so much as lifts a finger against me!"

None of the Indians moved a muscle. Nate dared not move, himself, or they might spot him. He had to stand there and watch the tableau unfold. Carter's plight elicited no sympathy. The man had brought it down on his own head; he would have to reap the consequences.

Several of the Lakotas were smirking. This was sport to them. Rough, grim sport, to be sure, but the kind they enjoyed the most.

A hefty specimen armed with a lance edged his war horse closer and poked the tapered tip at Carter. He was having fun, not really trying to connect.

Carter misconstrued. "I warned you!" he wailed. Elevating the rifle, he stroked the trigger.

At the blast, the hefty warrior toppled from his horse, landing on his backside in waist-deep water. The ball had caught him well up on the right shoulder, passing under his collarbone. Dazed, he reached up and touched a finger to the trickle of blood seeping from the wound.

The lighthearted mood of the Sioux was gone. Their faces cast in flinty lines, they slowly closed in on the greenhorn.

"Damn you! Stay back!" Carter howled, clawing his stolen pistol free. Slowly back-pedaling, he swung the flintlock first at one warrior, then at another, trying to cover all four of them at the same time. "I'll shoot the next one of you in the head! Just see if I don't!"

His railing had no impact on the Lakotas. They continued to move toward him, although none, as yet, lifted a weapon.

Carter was on the verge of hysterics. "I know about you filthy savages!" he screamed. "I've heard the stories! And if you think I'll let you torture me, you have another think coming!" Shifting, he scanned the woods and called out in desperation, "King! Nate King! I know you're there somewhere! If you can hear me, I'm sorry for what I did! I just wanted to get home! Please help me! Together we can fight these bastards off!"

Nate frowned. Now the warriors knew there was another white man nearby. They were scanning the trees, and one was making for the west bank. Nate would have shot the greenhorn himself, but he needed both pistols primed for when the Sioux came after him.

"Answer me, damn it!" Carter screeched. "You can't just let these butchers rub me out! I'm white, like you. You can't stand by and let them kill me!"

The warrior on the west bank was peering into every shadow, checking behind every bush.

Nate had to act. Taking a single stride, he vaulted onto the pinto and took off like a bat out of hell to the north. Wolfish yips told him the Lakotas had spotted him. He looked back just as the tall warrior, in a blur, streaked the bow up and unleashed a shaft that transfixed Carter's right arm. The greenhorn screamed and dropped the pistol into the water. Two Sioux promptly rode him down.

That was all Nate had a chance to see. The warrior on the west bank was flying toward him, a lance upraised to hurl. Nate goaded the tired pinto on and was almost to the thicket when the Sioux drew within throwing range.

Twisting, Nate extended his left flintlock. The .55-caliber bucked and boomed, and the warrior catapulted backwards over the rump of his mount. Cries of outrage issued from the Lakotas as he jammed the spent piece under his belt.

Speeding to the stallion, Nate scooped up the reins and fled. His only hope lay in outdistancing them. Body bent low, he trotted to the northwest and within moments laid eyes on the prairie. And more Lakotas. Seven or eight warriors were rapidly bearing down on the cottonwoods.

Cutting back to the right, Nate rode parallel with White Bark Creek. He stuck to dense brush and covered 50 yards without being seen. Then a bellow warned him that the Sioux were in hard pursuit. The pinto was doing its best, but it was on its last legs. He would be better off on the stallion, but there was no time to switch.

Arrows whizzed down around him. Most were wide of the mark, but a few missed him by a hand's width. He veered farther to the right and plowed through high weeds to find himself almost at the edge of the creek bank. Legs pumping, he flew northward.

Sioux were surging toward the big trapper from the rear and from the left. Their war whoops and yips formed a harsh chorus, which grew louder as they narrowed the gap.

Nate was swiftly losing ground. The pinto just was not up to a sustained chase. Hauling hard on the stallion's reins, he guided the big black up alongside the smaller paint. Girding himself, he raised his legs and tucked them up under him. It was difficult to keep his balance, but he managed.

More arrows sought his life as Nate coiled and sprang to the left. For a dizzying moment he hung suspended in the air between the two horses, and for a harrowing instant it seemed as if he would drop straight down and be trampled. Then he alighted on the stallion, clamped his legs tight, and reluctantly allowed the pinto to slow to a walk even as he brought the stallion to a pell-mell gallop.

The Lakotas erupted in baffled yells. Two of them gave up their pursuit to catch the paint, but the rest rode faster than ever.

Nate swiveled. There was no sign of Emmet Carter. He figured the man was a goner, and he was determined not to suffer the same fate. With the stallion under him, he at least had a prayer of eluding the Sioux.

White Bark Creek wound to the left, so Nate bore to the right. Cold water soaked his moccasins and the bottom of his leggings as he angled into the water and barreled for the other shore.

From out of nowhere hurtled a warrior. The man had a fusee, a trade rifle given to Indians for two to three times its value in prime plews. He pointed it and squeezed the trigger but nothing happened. The gun misfired. Undaunted, the Lakota wielded the fusee as he might a club.

Pulling his other pistol, Nate shot the warrior squarely in the forehead. The Sioux fell into the creek with a tremendous splash. The riderless horse halted. Seconds later Nate gained the top of the far bank and hurried into the trees before the bowmen could get his range.

Over ten Lakotas swarmed into the water, each eager to be the one who counted first coup.

Both Nate's flintlocks were empty. Since it was

next to impossible to reload on the fly, he shoved the second one under his belt so his hands would be free for handling the reins. Bit by bit he widened his lead.

Even if Nate got away, his problems were just beginning. Thanks to Carter, the Lakotas were alerted to the presence of enemies in their country. War parties would be sent out from every village. Soon the territory would be swarming with hostiles. The Crows and his family would be lucky if they got out alive.

The tree line appeared. Once past it Nate would rely on the stallion's superior endurance to save his bacon. A glance over a shoulder revealed the nearest warriors were not quite close enough to let their arrows fly.

In no time, glistening grass enclosed him. Nate spied a ridge to the east and made for it. The stallion's brief rest had rekindled its customary vigor, and it was flowing over the ground with a smooth, powerful gait.

When next Nate checked, the Lakotas were so far behind, their bows were useless. His confidence growing, he smiled and began to plot how best to rejoin his family. Quite clearly he would have to do most of his traveling at night, laying low in ravines and gullies during the day.

Inexplicably, the Sioux commenced hollering and howling as if they were demented wolves. This went on and on, without letup.

Unable to comprehend why and thinking it might be a ruse, Nate watched them closely. They were spreading out wider than ever, a pointless act in his estimation, since they had no hope of overtaking him. One of them had a rifle which he pointed at the clouds and fired off.

It made no sense.

Then an answering shot sounded on the ridge, and Nate faced front to discover another dozen or so warriors on the crest. Already they were fanning out, too, working in concert with the Lakotas behind him.

"Damn!" Nate exploded, wheeling the stallion to the south. He had almost made a fatal error.

The warriors to the west were trying to head him off. Several were well out ahead of the main pack and smacking their quirts against their mounts like men possessed. Those on the ridge were farther away, but the slope lent them speed as they poured down onto the flatland.

Nate checked to verify his knife was still in its sheath. If they caught him, he was not going to go down without a fight. There would be none of the useless posturing Carter had done. It would be do or die time, as the saying went.

The stallion, as always, responded superbly. Few horses were its equal, as it demonstrated to the Lakotas by racing beyond the reach of those about to close the trap.

An arrow flashed in front of Nate's face. The lean warrior responsible quickly began to notch another shaft but stopped at a shout from a fellow Sioux. Yet a third man was about to throw a lance but lowered the weapon instead.

Nate did not like that one bit. It meant they wanted to take him alive, and their only reason for doing so would be to torture him at their leisure later on.

Some tribes, like the Apaches, were known to relish inflicting torment on captives. Often it was done to test the mettle of their enemies. Those who held up well, who did not whimper or plead for mercy, were usually accorded a quick death to honor their bravery. But those who caved in were treated to even worse abuse; they could scream and beg all they wanted and all their captors would do was laugh at them.

The Blackfeet were notorious for torturing trappers. They had a long-standing grudge against white men which stemmed from a clash between members of the Lewis and Clark expedition and several warriors.

According to the stories Nate had heard, the Lakotas were not as partial to torture. At least, they were known to adopt captive women and children into their tribe and treat them as if they were full-blooded Sioux. Male captives, though, were seldom so fortunate.

The pounding of hooves resembled the din of a buffalo stampede. Swirling clouds of smoke rose in the wake of the Lakotas. Their long hair whipped in the wind, lending them the aspect of a horde of painted demons.

Suddenly the terrain itself turned against Nate. A wide gully appeared before him. He had no other option but to slow briefly as he negotiated the steep slope. Then he bore to the left and sped madly around a bend and along a straight stretch rife with dry brush and loose earth.

The Lakotas were elated. Their yells rose to the clouds as they pursued him along the rim.

Nate earnestly sought some way up out of the gully on the other side. But the slope was too sheer for the stallion to climb, perhaps too sheer for a man to scale.

Praying that there would be a break in the wall somewhere, Nate rushed around a sharp turn to the southeast and saw one. Only it was on the same side as the Lakotas. No sooner did he thunder past it than a quartet of warriors reached the gully floor.

The stallion picked that moment to stumble. Nate was nearly unhorsed as its head jerked low and its hind quarters rose in a bounding hop. He was able to stay on, but it had given the warriors an opportunity they were quick to take advantage of.

Lakotas were on both sides, so close they could reach out and touch him. One on the right did, trying to snag his arm, but Nate tore free and swung a backhand blow that missed.

The warrior on the other side instantly lunged and caught hold of Nate's leg. Nate felt himself start to spill to the right. Spinning at the waist, he slammed a fist into the Sioux's elbow and the man released him. But the very next second the warrior on the right attempted once again to seize a limb.

Constantly swinging back and forth, Nate held them at bay. He couldn't do so, however, and hold the big black to a gallop. Gradually he slowed, which turned out to be just the thing the Lakotas were waiting for.

A third Sioux pressed in close behind the stallion. In his one hand he held a coiled length of buffalo hide rope. In the other he gripped a small noose which he now swung rapidly in a tight circle.

Nate noticed the man, but most of his attention was claimed by the pair trying to pluck him from his saddle. The brave on the left swooped in closer than ever. Turning, Nate arced back his fist to land a solid punch.

With a deft flip, the third Lakota sent the small noose sailing neatly over Nate's hand. The buffalo hide settled around his wrist, constricting when the warrior gave the rope a stiff tug. Nate tensed every muscle in his arm to resist the rope's pull, but it was a lost cause. Especially when the warrior brought his mount to a sliding stop.

There was a terrible spasm in Nate's shoulder, and he became airborne. Yanked clear off the stallion, he saw the earth rushing up to meet his face. The pain was exquisite. Marshaling his wits, he struggled to sit up and tear the rope off, but before he could the sky seemed to rain Lakotas, warrior after warrior pouncing on top of him until they bore him down by the sheer weight of their numbers.

Nate's last conscious sensation was of a tremendous blow to the head. Then a black void engulfed him.

Chapter Eight

Wi-No-Na of the Shoshones woke up with a start. She had been having a terrible dream in which her husband was being slowly strangled by a dozen pair of brawny hands at once. She had not seen the faces or even the bodies of his killers, only those awful hands.

Profoundly disturbed, Winona rose onto her elbows. Beside her in the cradleboard slept little Blue Flower, as beautiful as only a sleeping child could be. Nearby lay Stalking Coyote, his rifle at his side. Across the fire dozed the Crows, except for Bull Standing With Cow, who was keeping watch. He had moved off a score of feet and sat on the stump with his back to the low fire.

Rising, Winona pulled her blanket tight around her slender shoulders and walked over to him. The aged warrior looked up at her, his features as sorrowful as any she had ever seen. There was no need to ask what he had been thinking about.

"You are up early," the Crow signed.

Winona shrugged.

Bull Standing With Cow gazed off into the darkness to the south of their camp. "I understand. I am very worried about your husband also. He should have rejoined us by now."

"He promised us he would catch up and he will."

The warrior sighed. "Is that your head talking or your heart? We both know that nothing short of death would keep him from your side. I am afraid that if he does not show by sunset today, we must fear the worst."

"I will never give up hope."

"As well you should not," Bull Standing With Cow signed. "You are a credit to your man. In many ways you remind me of my own woman when she was much younger. I trust your Grizzly Killer knows how lucky he is?"

Winona changed the subject. "One more day of delay will not make much difference. But you saw He Dog earlier. He will not want to sit around here much longer. How do you propose to control him?"

"Control He Dog?" Bull Standing With Cow said, and chuckled softly. "I might as well try to control a great brown bear or a mad bull buffalo. No one can tell him what to do. At best, we can try to convince him that it is better for everyone if we lay low for a while longer. Whether he will agree is impossible to predict."

"You should not have brought him."

"I knew it was not a smart thing to do," the Crow admitted, "but I was desperate. Of all the warriors who survived the Lakota attack, only nine agreed to go with me. I could not afford to refuse him."

He paused. "And there was another factor I had to take into account."

Winona's female intuition served her in good stead. "Your daughter?" she guessed.

Bull Standing With Cow blinked. "Yes. He Dog has shown an interest in her for some time. Soon she will be eligible, and I expect he will court her."

"How does Fetches Water feel about him?"

"She never told me. She has always been a quiet girl who keeps her innermost thoughts to herself." The devoted father smiled wanly. "But then, most women do, don't they? Long ago I learned that women are much better at keeping secrets than men are. And I think I know why that is."

"This I would like to hear."

"It is simple. Women protect their hearts with the same devotion a man will protect his loved ones or his best war horse. Women place more value on that which takes place inside of them, while men place more value on things they can see, touch, and hold."

Winona grinned. "You are very wise—for a man."

They both laughed lightly, and for a few moments the father's sadness was gone. But it returned the instant he stopped. He wearily rubbed his eyes, then stifled a yawn.

"If I do not get some rest soon, I will not be good for anything. But I am so worried about my daughter that I can hardly eat or sleep."

Sunrise was over an hour off. Winona put a hand on his shoulder and offered, "If you want to get some rest now, I will stand watch for you."

"I would like to, but what would the others think?"

"They know how hard you have been pushing yourself," Winona noted. "I will be right back."

She fetched the Hawken and Evelyn and perched on the stump with the cradleboard across her legs. The Hawken she leaned within easy reach. "There," she signed. "I am all set. Enjoy your rest."

The Crow studied her features before moving off. "I am old enough to be your father," he signed in parting, "but I tell you now that if I were twenty winters younger I would do my best to steal you away from Grizzly Killer."

Tiny fingers of flame were all that remained of the fire, casting a feeble glow. Bull Standing With Cow curled up next to it and pulled a blanket up over him.

It was the quiet time of the night, when the nocturnal predators were bedding down for the upcoming day and the daytime animals were not yet awake.

Winona rested her hands on her knees and listened to the whisper of the wind in the tall trees. Alone with her thoughts, she could not help but think of Nate. Was he still alive? Something deep within her assured her that he was, but that same something told her that he was in dire danger. She yearned to be with him.

Presently a few birds chirped, and it wasn't long afterward that the woods were filled with the avian chorus that always preceded the dawn.

Evelyn stirred but went back to sleep. Winona contented herself with holding her daughter close and shutting her mind to the apprehension gnawing at her insides.

A thin streak of pink appeared to the east. Winona turned her head to admire its brilliant hue and suddenly sensed that someone else was close by. Placing a hand on her pistol, she shifted.

He Dog had the look of an unkempt mongrel in a foul temper. He was unarmed, but his big fists were clenched as if to pound on anyone who dared antagonize him.

"Why do you stare at me?" Winona demanded. "What do you want?"

The warrior sneered at her. "What is wrong, woman? Do I make you uncomfortable? Does it fill you with fear? It should. Because before this is over with, you and that man of yours will regret treating me as you have." He nodded toward the plain. "Where is he, woman? Why is he taking so long? Is this a trick on your part to keep us from saving Fetches Water?"

The idea was so preposterous that Winona almost laughed. "Were you hit on the head by a falling tree?"

"Do not mock me," He Dog warned.

"Then do not say stupid things," Winona retorted. "Why would we want to stop you from rescuing her?"

"Your man is white, and whites are never to be trusted. They do not think like normal people, so who can say why they do what they do?"

"You talk in circles."

The warrior advanced but halted when she started to draw the flintlock. "Know this, woman. I intend to make Fetches Water my wife one day. Nothing will stop me from freeing her, not the Lakotas, not your husband, and certainly not you. If the mighty Grizzly Killer has not shown up by the time the sun is straight overhead, I am leaving to find her."

Winona watched him go off into the bushes. The day had gotten off to a wonderful start, and she feared that it would only get worse before it got better.

A lot worse.

*　　*　　*

A jostling motion revived Nathaniel King. That, and a knot of pain on the back of his head that throbbed insistently. His mouth felt as dry as a desert and his stomach was queasy. He became aware that he was lying on his stomach and that his wrists and ankles were bound.

Nate opened his eyes. He had been thrown over a sorrel being led by the Lakota warrior skilled with a rope. Other warriors rode on both sides of him, one leading his stallion and the pinto. They were talking quietly among themselves, completely ignoring him.

Dawn was at hand. Nate figured the band had been riding most of the night. They were climbing a grass-covered hill, and when they came to the top, they reined up.

Below lay a wide river glistening greenish-blue in the morning light. Shimmering cottonwoods, drooping willows and sturdy oaks fringed both banks. To the west a smaller river merged with the wider waterway, their junction dotted by gravel bars and tiny isolated islands of vegetation. To the east, the pristine main river wound off across the prairie until lost in the golden haze.

Nate knew where he was. The wide river was the Platte, the smaller river the South Platte. Which meant that the enormous village spread out between the two rivers had to be the encampment of the Oglala Lakotas.

Hundreds of lodges were arranged in traditional fashion, all with their entrances facing eastward. From many wafted tendrils of smoke. Dozens of women chatted at the rivers while filling water skins. A number of children and dogs were abroad. It was an idyllic setting, deceptively so since Nate knew the type of reception he would receive.

Two members of the returning band fired off rifles or fusees while others shouted and screeched.

Tepee flaps were thrown wide and people poured out to greet the newcomers. The women hurried from the rivers while the children ran to the edge of the camp.

Nate had witnessed the same event many times in Shoshone villages. Whenever warriors returned in triumph, they liked to make a grand entrance. It was customary if they arrived late at night to wait until the next day to ride in.

The returning Sioux formed into a long column with Nate at the center. Several had noticed he was awake, but they left him alone. He tried moving his arms and legs and soon gave it up as a lost cause.

Amid much fanfare, the warriors descended. Onlookers pressed forward for a glimpse of Nate. The men were openly hostile, the women were filled with glee, while many of the children made bold to dash up to him and tug at his hair or his clothes. Dogs sniffed and growled.

The Lakotas were much like Nate's adopted people, the Shoshones, in that they lived in buffalo hide lodges, and in the same style of dress. The men favored moccasins, breechcloths and buckskin leggings; the women were partial to leather dresses with short sleeves. Many had donned heavy buffalo robes to ward off the morning chill.

Generally speaking, the Lakotas were slightly smaller in stature than the Shoshones but much more muscular. They were a handsome people, and they carried themselves with dignity and pride.

The band headed for a particularly large lodge.

From within came a warrior who had more wrinkles than the prairie had blades of grass. His hair was streaked with gray and he walked with the aid of a long stick. Joining him were several middle-aged warriors, one sporting an elaborate headdress that hung almost down to the ground.

The warrior who had roped Nate in the gully now slid off his horse. Taking hold of Nate's arms, he pulled hard, dumping Nate at his feet. Nate instantly lashed out with both legs, striking the warrior in the shins. The man staggered but kept his footing and began to draw a knife. Only a stern word from the aged Lakota stopped him.

Two other warriors roughly hauled Nate upright. Another loosened the loops around his ankles so he could walk. He was shoved forward and tripped, landing on his knees in front of the tribal leaders.

A groan behind him was the first inkling Nate had that he wasn't the only captive. Gruff words were uttered. The next second Emmet Carter was pushed to the ground beside him.

The greenhorn was in bad shape. His entire right side was caked with dry blood from the arrow wound in his arm. The arm itself was badly swollen. His face bore bruises and welts and there was a nasty gash on his left temple. Bent at the waist, his eyes shut tight, he pressed the stiff limb against his stomach and moaned loudly.

Nate's feelings about the man had not changed one bit, but he felt compelled to nudge Emmet's elbow and say out of the corner of his mouth, "Quit bellyaching, Carter. You can't show any weakness. The Lakotas respect courage, not cowardice."

The younger man looked up. "King!" he exclaimed in amazement. "Am I glad to see you! I thought that these sons of bitches had lifted your scalp!"

"They could have at any time," Nate mentioned. "Which makes me suspect that they must have real special plans for us."

"What do we do? How do we get out of here?"

Before Nate could reply, the man in the war bonnet took two steps and kicked the greenhorn in the sternum. Carter was knocked onto his side and cried out shrilly. He made a feeble effort to stand, but cringed when the warrior drew back a leg to kick him again.

Some of the onlookers laughed.

"Don't just lie there!" Nate whispered. "Show them you have some gumption. Get up!"

"And be kicked again?" Carter said. "No thank you. I'll just stay out of their way until they lose interest in me."

"*That will never happen*," Nate stated, and was suddenly clipped on the shoulder by the warrior with the rope. He rocked with the blow but stayed on his knees.

A discussion broke out. The Lakota tongue was totally alien to Nate, so the best he could make out was that the older warriors were questioning the members of the war party about the greenhorn's capture, and his. The pair who had tried to pull him from the stallion spoke at length, as did the warrior with the rope. Finally the tall warrior who had put a shaft into Carter stepped forward and addressed the throng.

Nate didn't like the way the Sioux were staring at Emmet. Carter had doubled over with his forehead on the dirt and consequently didn't notice.

The ancient warrior was the last to speak. Whatever he said was short and to the point. He motioned once at Nate, once at Carter.

At a yell from the man in the headdress, the Lakotas converged. Iron hands gripped Nate and he was half carried, half dragged to a nearby lodge. Without ceremony he was tossed inside, smacking onto his shoulder and jarring his chin. Shrugging off the effects, Nate wriggled to the entrance and poked his head out the flap just as a terror-stricken scream wafted through the village.

A space had been cleared to the west of the big lodge and was ringed by Oglalas. A couple of warriors were dragging Emmet Carter toward a thick pole that had been hastily imbedded in the earth. He shrieked and kicked and thrashed, to no avail. Within moments he had been lashed to the pole and stripped buck naked.

Nate wanted to tear his eyes from the spectacle, but he could not. "I tried to warn him," he said softly to himself.

The warrior Carter had shot stepped through the crowd. He had been bandaged and carried his lance in his left hand. Trailing him was a chestnut which he mounted and rode to a point directly opposite Carter. Leveling the lance, he tucked it to his side.

Carter had stopped struggling and gawked at the Lakota in wide-eyed horror. When the Sioux started toward him, he turned beet-red in the face, then strained against the ropes in a frenzy, blubbering like a madman the whole while.

The Lakota picked up speed, gradually bringing the chestnut to a trot. As he neared the pole he leaned forward and extended the lance.

Emmet Carter was practically beside himself. "*Nooooo!*" he wailed. "No! No! No!"

The Sioux were holding their collective breath in tense anticipation. The only sounds other than the greenhorn's bawling cries were the rhythmic pounding of the horse's flying hooves. They grew louder and louder as the horse went faster and faster and were punctuated by an ear-splitting screech of mortal anguish.

The lance sheared into Emmet Carter at the exact spot where his lead ball had penetrated the warrior, the point bursting out his back. The warrior let go and rode on around the pole to the acclaim of the onlookers.

Carter stiffened, then fainted. He hung as limp as a wet sack.

Kneeing the chestnut in front of the captive, the Lakota bent and wrenched the lance out. Blood and gore spewed forth with it. A brief lull ensued as he rode back into the crowd and climbed down.

Nate rested his cheek on the ground. His turn would be next, he was sure. He hoped that he would bear up better than Carter was doing. If, by some fluke, his family heard of his passing, he wanted them to be proud of him.

A commotion signaled the arrival of a half-dozen bowmen, among them the tall warrior and several others who had been at White Bark Creek. A woman bearing a hollow gourd walked out to Carter and splashed water on his face to revive him.

Carter took one look at the archers and went into hysterics. Disgust was evident on the faces of many of the Lakotas.

First to notch a shaft was the tall Sioux. He took deliberate aim.

Carter struggled mightily, swinging from side to side and shaking from head to toe in a futile bid to spoil the Lakota's aim.

With an audible twang the arrow streaked from the bow. The warrior had intentionally aimed low, and the arrow imbedded itself in the pole between

Carter's legs. Carter squealed like a stuck pig while the throng expressed their admiration of the warrior's skill.

The next warrior also missed. Likewise the third and the fourth. Each shaft, though, came a little closer to the figure at the pole than the shaft before it.

Then it was the tall man's turn again. Everyone, Carter included, knew that this time the warrior wouldn't miss. Carter repeated his insanely frantic jig. He hollered and begged and cried.

The arrow impaled him in the groin.

Nate wished he could cover his ears so he would not have to hear Emmet's pathetic high-pitched blubbering and whimpering. The man went on and on, quaking and weeping until even the Lakotas seemed to tire of hearing it and a second shaft imbedded itself in his left thigh. Another ripped into his right.

Carter raised his tear-streaked face to the blue sky and beseeched, "*Save me*! Dear Lord, please don't let this happen!"

Nate would have given anything to have a rifle. He crawled back into the lodge and lay curled into a ball in the gloomy interior. The thunk-thunk-thunk of arrows striking home sounded like the steady beat of a small drum. In due course Carter's blubbering dwindled to sorrowful sobs and occasional screams.

When next Nate peered out, Emmet Carter bristled with arrows yet somehow still lived. His head had not been touched and he turned it repeatedly as if seeking someone.

Abruptly, Carter trembled violently. "Forgive me my sins!" he croaked at the heavens. "I never meant—"

The next moment, he died.

Nate King rose onto his knees. Four Lakotas cut the body down. Each and every arrow was removed before the corpse was toted off to be left out on the prairie for scavengers to feast on.

Ground-hitched near the large lodge were the black stallion and Zach's paint. Nate gauged the distance, saw that none of the Oglalas were facing in that direction, and made a bid for freedom. Scooting out under the flap, he ran for all he was worth. He heaved against his bounds, but they were too tight.

Nate was astounded when he reached the horses without an outcry being raised. He darted to the off-side of the stallion and hiked his leg to slip his foot into the stirrup. By giving a little hop, he succeeded.

Now came the hard part. Nate coiled his left leg and jumped straight up, but he couldn't rise high enough to straddle the saddle. He had to stick his foot back in the stirrup before trying it again. The result was the same.

Frustrated, Nate ducked under the stallion and straightened next to the pinto. This time he might have better luck. It was much smaller.

In another two seconds Nate was mounted. Bending low, he pumped his legs. The horse slowly turned and he guided it toward the far side of the large lodge.

That was when shouts broke out.

Nate slapped his legs harder. The pinto began to pick up speed, but not nearly quick enough to suit him. He heard onrushing footsteps and swiveled just as a couple of fleet Lakotas leaped. With his hands bound he was helpless to prevent them from yanking him off the horse and throwing him bodily to the earth. He kicked and connected, but then more men arrived. His arms were clamped tight and he was jerked to his feet.

Over a score of warriors surrounded the trapper. Angry as riled hornets, they propelled him westward, retracing their steps past the lodge and hustling him toward the center of the ring of Lakotas.

And toward the pole drenched with Emmet Carter's blood.

Chapter Nine

He Dog did not wait until the sun was straight up. The golden orb was barely an hour high in the sky when he stood up and signed, "Enough of this waiting! I am going to find Fetches Water now. Anyone who wants, come with me."

Runs Against and Yellow Owl promptly rose and indicated they would join him. Two Humps objected verbally, and the next thing, all the Crows were embroiled in a vehement dispute in their own tongue.

Winona and Zach could do nothing except sit there and wait for the Crows to finish. The Hawken lay on a blanket at the Shoshone woman's side, and she picked it up and held it in her lap.

Soon all the warriors were on their feet, some gesturing angrily. Bull Standing With Cow was making an earnest appeal to He Dog, but judging by He Dog's expression he was wasting his time.

Winona was prepared when the stocky hothead,

Yellow Owl, Runs Against and Bear Ears headed for the horse string. Springing to her feet, she leveled the Hawken and cocked it.

At the metallic rasp, the four Crows halted. He Dog glared, then signed, "Do not try to stop us, woman."

Stepping a few paces to the left so her daughter would be out of the line of fire, Winona stood tall and said to Zach, "Translate for me. I dare not take my hands off the rifle."

"Sure, Ma," the boy responded. He had leaped up when his mother did, resolved to do whatever was necessary to protect her.

"Tell them this," Winona said, and her son began to relay her words as best sign language allowed. "Say that we agreed to help them because Two Humps is Grizzly Killer's friend. Say that we knew the dangers, but that did not stop us. We have risked all on their behalf, yet now we find that they have no respect for us and no regard for our lives."

"Your tongue speaks false," He Dog replied. "I am the only one who has a grudge against you. These others are leaving with me because they know I am right."

"Are you?" Winona rejoined. "Or are you letting your affection for Fetches Water cloud your mind?" She paused. "If you ride off, all our hard work in slipping into Lakota country undetected will have been for nothing. In broad daylight you are bound to be spotted sooner or later. The Oglalas will overwhelm you, and what will happen to Fetches Water then?"

"What do you think might be happening to her *now*?" He Dog said. "I am not going to waste more time when even as we speak a Lakota bastard might be forcing himself on her."

Winona lowered the muzzle a bit. So there it was. The real reason the warrior was so passionately determined to rescue the girl.

"If you intend to shoot, shoot," He Dog went on. "It will prove that you lie when you claim to be a friend of the Absarokas." He addressed the men with him, then added, "None of us will lift a finger against you. So squeeze the trigger." Holding his arms out, he faced her. "Shoot me if you really believe it is in Fetches Water's best interests."

Winona could not bring herself to do it.

He Dog nodded. "I did not think you had it in you to kill someone who is not trying to kill you, and I was right." He lowered his arms. "You need not go with us, woman. Stay and wait for your precious white man. By the time he shows up, we will have rescued Fetches Water."

"Ma?" Zach said as the four warriors stepped to their mounts. He raised his rifle, but his mother shook her head and eased down the hammer of her own. "Why are we just letting them ride off?"

What should she say? Winona mused. That in his twisted way, He Dog had a point about the greater danger to Fetches Water? That she could not bring herself to shoot him or any of the others down in cold blood? That she could not blame the Crows for not wanting to wait there forever for Nate?

"Ma?" Zach repeated.

Bull Standing With Cow approached. "I am sorry, my friends," he signed, "but we cannot let them go off by themselves. Two Humps, Flying Hawk and I must go along."

"I understand," Winona signed.

"I wish I did," Zach muttered aloud.

Winona stepped to her blanket and knelt to fold it. "Saddle our horses quickly, Stalking Coyote," she said. "We must go with them, too."

"But Pa told us to sit tight."

"He will find us eventually." Winona noticed Zach's confusion and elaborated by saying, "Think, son. What is one of the first things the Lakotas will do if they come on a band of Crows in their own country?"

"Attack them."

"Besides that."

"I don't—" Zach began, and abruptly recollected the time the Shoshones had found evidence of a Piegan band near their village. "Some of them will go after the Crows while others will backtrack to see if the band is part of a larger war party."

"And if the Sioux backtrack, where will that lead them?"

Zachary King looked at the tall trees and the bubbling creek and the stump. "Right here."

Nate King offered no resistance as the Lakotas pushed and shoved him over to the bloody pole. Outnumbered as he was, it would have been pointless. Plus, he wasn't about to do anything that smacked of rank cowardice. He would show them that not all white men were like Emmet Carter.

Hide thongs were used to bind the big trapper's hands and feet. One of the Sioux wore his beaver hat. His pistols had been claimed by two others. A fourth sported his knife in a beaded sheath. Wearing mocking grins, the warriors completed their task and walked back to where the bowmen were notching arrows to their strings.

Nate squared his shoulders and regarded the archers with forced detachment. The onlookers had fallen silent again. Among them was the ancient warrior, who studied Nate closely.

The tall warrior slowly elevated his bow. As he had done with Carter, he sighted carefully down the shaft. He aimed high, though, not low, and held himself perfectly still.

To Nate, it seemed as if the razor sharp tip were pointed straight at his heart. An urge to close his eyes came over him but he resisted it. His mouth felt dry, his palms damp. Suddenly the shaft flashed from the bow. He could see it clearly, see the glistening tip and the revolving feathers almost as if the arrow were moving in slow motion. For a heart-stopping moment he had the impression it was going to transfix his chest. Then there was a loud thud and the quivering shaft was so close to his neck that he could feel the smooth wood brushing his skin.

Nate's breath had caught in his throat. He let it out and willed himself to relax to calm the blood racing madly in his veins. His legs tingled as if from lack of blood and grew so weak that he had to exert all his willpower in order not to sag.

Another warrior moved forward to shoot. This one did not take nearly as long aiming. His string twanged and the arrow sped across the intervening space to sink into the pole on the other side of the trapper's neck.

Again Nate betrayed no fear. Some of the bowmen exchanged glances. Three more times arrows were shot, one sticking into the pole between his legs, two others missing his ears by the width of a hair.

The ancient warrior said something that caused the bowmen to lower their weapons. The tall one handed his to another man. Drawing a knife, the tall Lakota briskly advanced. When he was within five paces of the pole he gripped the knife by the blade and held it above his shoulder, poised to throw.

Nate locked his eyes on the Oglala's. No enmity was apparent. The warrior was simply doing what had to be done. He made his face muscles go rigid to keep from flinching. The very next instant the Lakota's arm whipped down and the knife leaped from his fingers.

The blade bit into the pole above Nate's head. He nearly grimaced when it nicked him. A moist sensation spread across his scalp and down past his left ear. He was bleeding.

Murmuring broke out among the assembled Sioux. The aged chief consulted with a handful of other apparent tribal leaders. Listening in were the tall warrior and the man who had snared Nate in the gully. The latter did not act pleased by whatever decision was reached. He protested vigorously. The gray-haired Lakota responded, and the roper walked off in a huff.

Nate was perplexed. He had expected to be accorded a swift and painless death if he demonstrated he was not afraid, but the Oglalas quite clearly had something else in mind. Several of them untied him from the pole, bound his wrists, and escorted him to the same small lodge in which he had initially been tossed. This time they did not treat him roughly. They even let him stoop and enter under his own power, perhaps out of respect.

Since the smoke flap at the top of the lodge was closed, Nate had to sit in near darkness and ponder what his next move should be.

That the Sioux had spared him was amazing. By all accounts they were not fond of whites and had already slaughtered a few trappers foolhardy enough to cross their territory.

Shakespeare McNair had once told Nate that many years ago the Lakotas and the whites had been on friendly terms. In fact, it had been an Englishman who first encountered them back when they lived along the Missouri River. On seeing that they used knives made of bone and stone, he had gone east and later returned with steel knives which he had handed out for free. Among the Minniconjou, among whom McNair had stayed for a short time over 40 years ago, that winter was known as They First Saw Steel Knives.

But sometime after that a dispute had arisen between several trappers and their Hunkpapa hosts. According to Shakespeare, the trappers had been drunk and one of them had stupidly insisted on making advances at the wife of a Hunkpapa leader.

None of the trappers had left the village alive. Ever since, there had been bad blood between the Lakotas and the whites.

So Nate had no reason to count on his reprieve being permanent. He figured that in their own sweet time the Oglalas would get around to finishing him off. They probably had something special planned for him, he mused, like the time he had been captured by Blackfeet and they had made him run a gauntlet.

Nate had to escape while he could. He decided to await nightfall and try. Moving over to the side of the lodge, he leaned against the buffalo hide to rest.

It could not have been more than a minute later that the flap was thrown wide and sunlight bathed him. He squinted as into the lodge came the tall warrior and the ancient leader. Straightening, he scrutinized their features for a clue as to why they were there, but both men were inscrutable.

The older man knelt and set his staff down. At a nod from him, the tall warrior cut Nate loose. The chief's gnarled hands moved slowly as he resorted to sign language, saying, in essence, "I am called Ant. I was born Minniconjou but came to live with the Oglalas when I took an Oglala woman as my mate."

Nate signed, "I am Grizzly Killer, a Shoshone."

Ant's features crinkled in wry humor. "How strange. You do not look like any Snake I have ever known. Or do the Shoshones now dress and act like white men?"

"They took me into their tribe when I took one of their women as *my* mate."

The leader chuckled. "It does not surprise me to learn this. The Snakes know a brave man when they see one." Ant gazed at the lodge wall as if peering into his own past. "I have lived longer than any Lakota alive, so I have counted many coup, fought many enemies. And none have ever shown more courage than the Snakes." He paused. "The Absarokas are brave, too, but they do not like to do battle unless they stand a good chance of winning. The Hohe would rather flee than fight. As for the Flatheads, they resist when they are attacked, but once they start to lose, they run. Practice has made them good runners, too. I never could catch one."

Nate did not know what to make of the old warrior's friendliness, so he made no comment.

"Question. What was the name of your friend who did not die so well?" Ant inquired.

"He was not my friend," Nate signed. "I was hunting him down to kill him when the man beside you found us."

Ant and the tall warrior conversed briefly. "Were those your shots Thunder Hoop and the rest of the war party heard?"

"The white man was firing at me," Nate detailed. "He had stolen a horse and two guns from my family and he knew I wanted them back." He also remarked, "As for his name, it can only be said in the white tongue." Aloud, Nate stated, "Emmet Carter."

Ant tried to say it several times but could not accent the syllables properly. "It twists the tongue," he conceded. "So from now on we will refer to him as He Who Bawled."

Thunder Hoop had not resheathed his knife. He did place it on his leg to sign, "Tell us, Grizzly Killer, why were you in our country?"

"I was chasing He Who Bawled," Nate reiterated. "He did not know this was land the Oglala roamed."

"He did not know much at all, if you ask me," Ant said. "Who taught him how to be a man?" The warrior made a clucking noise. "Such weaklings reflect poorly on a people."

"I could not agree more."

Ant clasped his hands and was quiet for a short spell. "What are we to do with you, Grizzly Killer? Many want to kill you and be done with you, but there is a quality about you I like. There is something I see in your eyes that tells me you are a man much like myself."

"You flatter me."

"You also remind me of the first white man I knew. We called him The Knife Bringer. He gave the Minnniconjou many steel knives when I was barely old enough to walk. I can still remember my father holding his close to the fire every night to admire the fine steel."

So the story Shakespeare had told Nate was true. He made bold to sign, "Not all white men are bad. Even though your warrior captured me and brought me here against my will, I bear the Oglalas no ill will. Nothing would please me more than to be able to smoke the pipe of peace with you and call you my brother."

Ant acted pleased. "I would be just as honored. But that cannot be, for you have admitted that you are a Snake now, not a white man, and the Snakes are our enemies." His fingers hung in the air a moment. "We kill our enemies."

Nate had tried. He did not let his disappointment show.

"Or most of our enemies," Ant amended his statement. "We do not make war on women and children, as the Blackfeet and Absarokas do. I still remember the time three women went off to cut wood and the Crows rubbed them out."

Nate took a gamble. "Is it true that your people raided the Absarokas within the past couple of moons?"

"Yes," Ant signed proudly. "Our warriors slew many Crows and stole many horses. They also brought back captives who will be reared as Oglalas. In time they will forget they were ever anything else." He indicated the tall warrior. "Thunder Hoop was on that raid. He counted four coup. And he brought back a pretty girl who will soon be married off to a deserving man."

"Is her Crow name Fetches Water?"

Ant was surprised. "It is. How did you know, Grizzly Killer?"

"A friend of mine heard about the raid from a Crow who was there," Nate hedged.

Thunder Hoop wasn't satisfied. "Since when do Absarokas get along well with Snakes?" he asked suspiciously.

"I did not say my friend was a Shoshone," Nate

responded. "Remember I was born white, and the whites get along well with both tribes."

The tall warrior and the aged leader talked at length. Ant signified the parley was at an end by picking up his stick and pushing off the ground. "It has been a pleasure meeting you, Snake Who Is White. Tonight we hold a council to see what we will do with you. I, for one, will propose that we grant you a death due a true warrior."

"I thank you," Nate replied sincerely, and did not object when Thunder Hoop tied his wrists behind his back.

The moment the flap closed behind them, Nate scooted to it and peeked under the bottom edge. Ant walked off toward the big lodge while the tall warrior entered a tepee further away. Painted on its side was a lightning bolt in the shape of a circle.

The horses were back in front of the council lodge. Both had been hobbled.

Nate would have liked to note more details, but a pair of moccasins materialized before his eyes.

The Sioux had posted a guard.

"This is a mistake, Ma," Zachary King declared. "I can feel it in my bones."

Winona shared her son's sentiments, but she goaded her mare northward anyway. They had gotten ready to go as swiftly as they could, yet they were well behind the two groups of Crows.

He Dog and his three companions had ridden out first, deliberately leaving everyone else behind, and were now a quarter of a mile ahead of Two Humps, Bull Standing With Cow, and Flying Hawk, who in turn were well ahead of the Shoshone and her son.

"Doesn't He Dog have any brains at all? Doesn't

he see that being strung out like this is asking for trouble?" Zach groused.

"I doubt he cares."

"He doesn't care whether he lives or dies?"

Several dark shapes had appeared on the horizon to the west. Winona was studying them to insure they were buffalo and not Lakotas. "He Dog is in love with Fetches Water. All he cares about is saving her."

Zach rose and shielded his eyes from the glare so he could see the four warriors who were in the lead. "It's awful hard for me to imagine a man like him caring for anybody."

"Love can be a mystery at times," Winona agreed. "But never doubt its power, son. It is stronger than the muscles of the mightiest man, more lasting than the sky above and the earth below. Love is forever."

The youth mulled that over for the next five miles.

On all sides the high grass rustled in the breeze. Coyotes slunk off at their approach, and on two occasions antelope gave flight in great bounding leaps. Scattered clusters of buffalo regarded the riders with the patent belligerence of their shaggy breed.

Winona hardly noticed the wildlife. All she cared about was spotting Oglalas before any Oglalas spotted them. Blue Flower was awake and uttered soft sounds every now and then. Shortly before midday Winona slowed, shrugged out of the cradleboard, and breast-fed her daughter on horseback.

Zach was on proverbial pins and needles. It was dreadful, being exposed out in the open in the middle of hostile territory. His worry was more for his mother and sister than for himself. He couldn't abide the notion of either of them coming to harm.

He Dog and his three friends never slowed, not even at noon as had been the war party's habit. They pushed on north toward the junctions of the South Platte and the Platte.

The afternoon waxed and began to wane. Winona was thankful for the absence of Lakotas, but she was also mystified. They were so near traditional Oglala haunts that it defied belief they had not encountered any Sioux yet.

At one point Zach shifted to scan the flat ocean of prairie to their rear. He observed how the grass had a knack for springing back up after the horses went by, and it provoked a question. "Are you sure Pa will be able to track us? I know I'd have a hard time."

"Your father was taught by one of the best trackers alive, Shakespeare McNair. He will find us," Winona avowed, while inwardly she suppressed a latent fear that he might not.

Zach felt like talking to take his mind off his worries, so he mentioned, "I've always sort of liked the plains. But to be honest, Ma, I don't think I could ever live out here."

"Why not?" Winona prompted.

"Take a gander. It's too darned flat. And boring. What good does it do for a body to be able to see as far as the eye can see if there's not a blamed thing worth looking at?" Zach shook his head. "No, ma'am. Give me the high country, where there are peaks that nearly touch the clouds and snow pretty near all year long and a person never knows what is over the next ridge."

Up ahead, Two Humps had slowed. Winona saw him straighten and stare toward He Dog's bunch.

"Do you feel that way, too?" Zach asked.

Absently, Winona said, "Where I live is not so important to me. What is important is that I be with my man and my children. I could be happy anywhere if Nate were happy too."

"You do like our cabin, though, don't you? And where it is and all?"

Winona reined up. It was difficult for her to distinguish details, but there seemed to be a commotion among the foremost Crows. Her nerves jangled when she realized He Dog, Runs Against, Bear Ears and Yellow Owl were racing back toward Two Humps and company. "No!" she said softly.

"What is it?" Zach asked, following her gaze. He saw Two Humps. He saw He Dog. And he saw a large band of warriors bearing down on them. At that distance they were no more than a blur, but he didn't need to see them clearly to know who they were.

Lakotas.

Chapter Ten

Darkness seemed to take forever to descend. The afternoon dragged by as if every minute were weighted down by two-ton boulders.

Nate King did not waste a single one of them. Within moments after discovering a guard had been posted, he moved back into the deepest patch of shadow at the rear of the lodge and commenced striving his utmost to slip free of the thongs binding his wrists. He strained. He yanked and tugged. He worked his hands back and forth.

The pain became excruciating. At length Nate's muscles ached clear up to his shoulders. Worst of all was the agony in both wrists, compounded when the skin split, making them slick with blood.

Thunder Hoop had done his job well. Hours of effort hardly loosened the loops. Yet he refused to concede defeat. Teeth grit, perspiration beading his brow, blood dripping from his fingers, he rubbed and chafed and heaved without cease.

It was about an hour before sunset when low voices right outside the flap drew Nate to the entrance. A peek showed that another warrior was taking the place of the first man. They were talking and joking. In a little while the first man departed and his lean replacement stepped to the right of the flap and stood there with the butt of a slender lance propped at his feet.

Nate noted the lengths of the shadows of the nearest tepees, then crept back to the rear. He was running out of time. At the rate he was going, it would be morning before he freed himself, and his wrists would be in such bad shape it would be a miracle if he didn't bleed to death first.

Inspiration born of desperation came to him. Nate sat on his haunches and tucked his knees as tightly to his chest as he could. Then, exerting every ounce of strength his powerful frame possessed, he attempted to slide his hands down over his buttocks.

It appeared to be an impossible challenge. More precious minutes went by as Nate pushed and wriggled and hiked his backside off the ground again and again. Yet he barely moved his hands an inch and a half.

His sense of urgency mounting, Nate eased onto his left side and reapplied himself. He shimmied like a snake while hunching his posterior and extending his arms as far as he could. A fraction at a time his wrists dipped lower. He had to bow his elbows outward to get his forearms past his thighs, and even then it did not seem to be enough to do the trick.

Nate could never say what suddenly made him stop and glance at the entrance. Call it gut instinct. Call it a premonition. Whichever, as he looked up the flap parted and the head of the Oglala poked inside.

The warrior was still a few seconds as his eyes adjusted. Then he spied the trapper and nodded to himself that all was well. The flap closed behind him.

Nate took up where he had left off. He found that by repeatedly lifting his rump while simultaneously hunching his shoulders until they throbbed, he could work his wrists downward by partial degrees. Again and again and again he did it, his arms screaming at him to stop.

Then came the moment Nate had worked so hard toward, the exhilarating instant when his bloody hands worked loose and were under his legs. The strain on his arms evaporated. He took but a second to gird himself, then snaked his arms up and around his legs and feet.

Nate sat up. Wiping his hands on his pants, he bent and applied his teeth to the thongs. The salty taste of blood filled his mouth. He chewed as if he were starved and this were his last meal. The leather was tough but had been softened somewhat by the blood and all his tugging. Like an oversized beaver, he gnawed through loop after loop.

His joy was unbounded when his hands fell free. They ached abominably and he had to move his fingers a while to relieve the stiffness. When they were back to normal, he rose in a crouch and stalked to the flap.

Twilight claimed the Lakota encampment. It was a tranquil time of day, when families were gathered together to eat and few people were abroad. Even the dogs were inside, awaiting their nightly scraps. Smoke from scores of cooking fires wafted from as many lodges. Horses stood quietly or grazed on sweet grass.

The warrior standing guard had moved a few more steps to the right and was leaning on the lance. If his expression were any indication, he was bored half to death.

A few pebbles lay near the flap. Nate inched his hands out far enough to retrieve one. He checked to verify there were no Lakotas in the immediate area, then flicked the pebble high into the air, between the guard and the lodge. When it hit about ten feet away, the warrior idly gazed in that direction, seeking the cause.

Nate silently pushed the flap outward and uncoiled. Careful to stay close to the tepee, he placed each foot down silently. He was almost within arm's length of the Oglala when the man yawned and pivoted toward him.

It was hard to say which of them was more surprised. The Sioux opened his mouth to alert the camp but Nate stifled the shout with a quick jab to the chin that staggered the warrior. Stunned, the Lakota speared the lance tip at him. Nate parried the thrust with a forearm and delivered another punch, this one an uppercut that rocked the Sioux on his heels. The warrior's legs crumpled, and as he fell Nate connected a third time.

The Oglala was unconscious when he slumped prone. Swiftly Nate stooped, hooked his hands under the man's arms, and dragged the warrior inside before anyone could notice.

No outcries were raised. The village lay undisturbed under the darkening sky.

Nate hastily stripped the Lakota of his knife and lance. He cut strips from the warrior's leggings and used them to tie the man's limbs and fit a gag in place.

Time was growing short. It would not be long

before the headmen of the tribe converged on the big lodge for the council Ant had mentioned.

Nate emerged, then hesitated. The stallion and the pinto were 20 yards off. It would be child's play for him to escape. All he had to do was dash over to them, mount up, and slip into the darkness.

But he couldn't. Not yet.

Somewhere to the south a dog barked as Nate hurried toward the lodge bearing the painted emblem of the circular lightning bolt. Murmuring forewarned him that others besides the tall warrior were inside.

Crouching beside the closed flap, Nate lightly pried at the edge and parted it a crack. A fire crackled softly. Hovering over a buffalo paunch in which boiled the family's supper was a woman Thunder Hoop's age. The warrior himself sat toward the back of the lodge, facing the entrance. He was engaged in conversation with a man half his years, perhaps a son. Two younger women were over by the left wall, preparing food.

Fetches Water was also there. The different style of her long dress and her braided hair marked her as not being Lakota. Huddled next to a pile of folded robes, her pretty features downcast, the Crow avoided looking at her captors.

Nate backed off before he was spotted. How could he get her out of there without raising a ruckus? he asked himself.

To the west a flap opened and an older woman stepped out. She went off toward the Platte, a water skin in hand.

Rising, Nate strolled to his horses. It was a test of his nerves to walk along as if he didn't have a care in the world so that he would not arouse suspicion if seen from a distance. Darting behind them, he drew the butcher knife and cut the hobbles on both animals.

The flap to the council lodge was open. Within glowed a small fire, and someone chanted in a singsong voice.

Nate snuck to the opening and risked a look. Ant sat crosslegged, his arms on his knees, his wrinkled face upraised, his eyes closed. Placing the lance down, Nate slipped inside and circled to the left, staying in shadows. The old warrior droned on.

To the southeast a horse whinnied. Voices sounded. Nate halted and listened, dreading that the Lakotas had found the bound warrior. But the voices were much too distant.

Ant abruptly stopped chanting and cocked his head as if he were listening also. When he had satisfied himself that all was well, he lifted his head and resumed.

Nate cat-footed up behind the ancient warrior. At the touch of his blade to the side of Ant's neck, the Lakota stiffened and fell silent. Nate warily moved to the right without relaxing the pressure so the chief could see him.

Ant's dark eyes sparkled with mirth. He actually smiled and spoke a few words in his tongue. Slowly lifting his arms, he signed, in so many words, "It is good to see you again, Snake Who Is White. But I did not think it would be so soon."

Lowering the blade, Nate wedged it under the front of his belt so it was within ready reach, and responded, "I do not desire to harm you. I do not want to hurt any of your people. With your help, I will not have to."

"How kind. I will be sure to tell all one hundred and twenty-nine warriors in our village when they surround you."

Nate stood and motioned for the Oglala to do the same. "Even the loss of one man is one too many. Whether anyone dies will be up to you."

"How can that be? I am not the one who has a weapon."

"You are the one whom your people look up to the most, the one they will listen to if things do not go as I have planned."

"And what would you have me tell them?" Ant asked as he reached for his staff.

"That is for you to decide."

Nate helped the aged warrior rise, then steered him to the opening. He left the lance where it was, took Ant's elbow, and walked toward Thunder Hoop's lodge.

Suddenly a large dog appeared and padded toward them. He slowed to sniff noisily and studied Nate as if he could not quite make up his mind whether Nate was supposed to be there or not.

Ant spoke sharply, waving the staff. The dog veered to the north and was soon gone. "That is Crow Rising's animal," he signed. "He lets it wander as it pleases. It is always sticking its nose where it does not belong." He sighed. "In the old days, someone would have carved it up long before this to teach Crow Rising a lesson."

Nate used sign to say, "When we get there, announce yourself. I will be behind you, so do not try anything. Only take four steps inside, no more."

"If I take five will you cut off my ears? I know that is what I would do if I were in your place. Chopping off an ear is always a good way to get another man's attention. It hurts, but it does not kill him."

It was hard for Nate to tell whether the Lakota was serious or not. As they neared the lodge he slid to the rear and drew the knife.

Ant gave the hide flap a whack. Thunder Hoop called out and Ant replied. At a single word from Thunder Hoop, Ant pushed the flap aside with his long stick, then bent to go in.

All the occupants had shifted toward the entrance. Nate made it a point to keep the chief between himself and the others until Ant had taken the required four steps. Then he showed himself, the blade resting against Ant's neck.

One of the women gasped. Another dropped the parfleche she had been rummaging in. The young man barked something and started to lunge toward a lance which had been propped against the wall. Thunder Hoop stopped him with a single word.

Nate knew that every second was critical. He jabbed a thumb at Fetches Water and beckoned. She gawked, not knowing what to make of him, and made no move to comply. Again Nate beckoned, yet she sat there like a proverbial bump on a log.

During the long ride from the remote Rockies, Nate had heard the other Crows call Bull Standing With Cow by his name many times. He repeated that name now and was rewarded by having the girl leap to her feet with a hand clutched to her throat. She repeated her father's name, her lilt framing a question. Once more Nate said it, smiling to show he was on her side. He smiled and nodded at the flap.

The young Crow had to have her doubts. A white man she had never met had burst into the lodge of Lakotas who were holding her against her will and acted as if he wanted to help her. So Nate didn't hold it against her when she moved with all the speed of a turtle toward the opening.

Thunder Hoop made no move to interfere. His eyes betrayed keen resentment, but he did not go for the knife at his side nor for the bow lying nearby. His hands on his legs, he watched with the eyes of a hawk, awaiting an opening he could exploit.

The warrior's son, though, was another matter. He couldn't sit still and kept glancing at the lance. Had his father not been there, he would have grabbed it and attacked.

Nate never took his eyes off the younger one. When Fetches Water went on by and he heard the flap move, he backed up, gently pulling the chief with him as a shield. At the entrance he put his free hand on the Lakota's shoulder and pressed. Ant got the idea. Together they backed on out and Nate threw the flap shut.

The young Crow was waiting, poised like a terrified fawn to bolt at the first threat.

Pointing at the horses, Nate hustled Ant toward them. He saw Thunder Hoop and the son look out of the lodge, but neither raised an alarm. They wouldn't, not so long as they feared that he would slay Ant.

Fetches Water went to climb on the stallion, but Nate snapped his fingers to get her attention and indicated the pinto. She was on its back in a twinkling, raring to go. Nate stepped to the stallion, gripped its mane, and vaulted up.

Ant stepped close so that only Nate could see his hands move. "Your bluff worked, Snake Who Is White. It does my heart good to know that there is one white man left who is not a weakling."

The girl's impatience was growing but Nate had to ask, "If you knew I was bluffing, why did you do as I wanted?"

"I am fond of my ears," Ant said, grinning as he

moved closer to his lodge.

Wheeling the stallion to the east, Nate brought it to a gallop. Fetches Water did not leave his side, her walnut-sized eyes casting to the right and the left as if she thought the very shadows would spring out at them.

They had covered ten feet when Thunder Hoop's bellow boomed loud and clear. More shouts ensued, and soon the cries were being spread on all sides as here and there Lakotas scrambled from their dwellings.

Nate had picked eastward because there were fewer tepees to pass before reaching the prairie. They rushed on by four of them without incident. Then, from the next, a warrior holding a bow spilled out. The man spotted them and tried to notch a shaft. Without missing a beat, Nate cut the stallion and slammed into the Lakota, sending him flying.

A rifle cracked. Maybe Nate's own Hawken. But the shooter was aiming at moving objects in the dark, and missed. Before another shot rang out or any arrows could be unleashed, they sped out onto the plain and were embraced by the inky veil of night.

Nate wasn't fooled. They had escaped from the village, but they were still in mortal danger. The uproar in their wake was all the proof needed that within a span of minutes every last warrior would be on their trail.

All 129 of them.

Miles to the south lay a dry wash littered with small stones and bits of wood and grass. Ages ago it had been a robust stream fed by runoff from a majestic mountain to the west. But a landslide on a barren slope had altered the course of the runoff forever, and in practically no time at all the stream had withered and dried up and was now home to isolated pockets of weeds and an occasional snake.

At that exact moment it also sheltered a Shoshone woman and her two children.

Winona King had spotted the wash shortly after turning and fleeing southward at sight of the Lakotas. It ran from west to east but turned to the north at the spot where she glimpsed its outline. Had it not been for a break in the high grass, she would never have noticed it at all.

Without hesitation, Winona had reined sharply and trotted down to the bottom. Its banks had proven high enough to hide the horses, so she had quickly traveled a stone's throw to the first bend and on around.Drawing rein, she had slid off, then ran as fast as she could with the heavy cradleboard on her back to the point where the horses had descended.

Zach was with her every step of the way. He divined her plan the moment he saw the wash and prayed the ruse would work.

Winona started to arrange the grass they had trampled so the wash would not be visible unless someone was right next to it. But the clatter of hooves gave her pause.

"What's wrong, Ma?" Zach asked.

"Two Humps and those with him. We must signal them so they can join us."

Zach didn't like the idea one bit. Since they had been the farthest south when He Dog blundered onto the Lakotas, it was entirely possible the Oglalas hadn't seen them. But the Sioux were bound to have noticed the second group of Crows. Attracting Two Humps to the wash might give their location away. "Are you sure that's a good idea?" he wondered.

"No, but we must do it," Winona said. The safe thing to do would be to let the three Crows go on by. And the other Crows, too. Then the Lakotas would sweep on past their sanctuary without a sideways glance. But that meant denying aid to friends who needed it.

The clatter grew louder. Winona rose high enough to see Two Humps, Bull Standing With Cow, and Flying Hawk. They were 60 or 70 yards to the north and almost the same distance to the east. Well beyond them were He Dog, Runs Against, Yellow Owl and Bear Ears. The latter was bent over, clinging to his mount's mane, apparently wounded.

Even farther back were the Lakotas, 15 all told, thirsting for Crow blood. Whooping and flourishing their weapons, they rode as if they and their animals were one.

Winona exposed her head and shoulders, then waved. Two Humps and those with him were so intent on outracing their pursuers that they were looking neither to the right nor the left. She pumped both arms, hollering in Shoshone, "Two Humps! Bull Standing With Cow! Over here!"

None of the three men looked in her direction, perhaps because Flying Hawk was lashing his horse with his quirt and yelling.

"Here! Look this way!" Winona cried in English, jumping so they would see her.

Against his better judgment, Zach did likewise, screeching at the top of his lungs. "Are the three of you hard of hearing? Stop!"

The trio of Crows were abreast of the wash but 50 yards out. Bull Standing With Cow stiffened as if he heard them, yet then he looked off in the opposite direction and did not slow down.

"No!" Winona railed. "Please! We're over here!"

"Here! Here!" Zach echoed.

Unheeding, the warriors flew onward, their horses raising a thick cloud of dust.

"They'll never spot us now!" Winona declared, and took several strides. She was too late. The dust obscured the warriors, just as it would prevent them from seeing her.

Zach felt sorry for their friends, but there was nothing else that could be done; He Dog and the others were rapidly approaching. It galvanized him into springing to his mother and clasping her wrist. "come on, Ma! Those Lakotas will spot you if we stand out here much longer!"

Her son was right. Winona could see the foremost Oglalas clearly. And while she was willing to risk her life and those of her offspring to help the first three Crows, she would not endanger her loved ones for the four whose own stubbornness had brought misfortune down on their heads.

Winona and Zach dashed into the wash and crouched at the rim. They spread the grass stems to hide their passage. No sooner were they done than He Dog and those with him fled madly on by. An arrow jutted from the back of Bear Ears, who swayed precariously.

In the time Zach could have counted to ten, the Lakotas were there. In a tight knot the fierce warriors flashed past, half of them no more than vague shadows in the dust. Zach had his rifle pressed to his shoulder, but the Lakotas had eyes only for the bitter enemies in front of them.

Winona watched the Oglalas until they were out of sight. A twinge of guilt assailed her for not even trying to save He Dog's group. After all, she mused, she'd be just as impetuous and reckless if it had been Grizzly Killer or Stalking Coyote or Blue Flower who had been taken captive.

She shrugged off the self-recriminations. No one could hold it against her for doing what had to be done. Crying over spilt milk, as her man liked to say, was a waste of time and energy.

Sitting, Winona removed the cradleboard to check on her daughter. Evelyn wore the patient angelic smile of the very innocent, and giggled when Winona held her tiny fingers and blew on them.

"Well, we did it," Zach commented in amazement. "We gave those buzzards the slip. But since we're all alone in the middle of their territory, with Pa nowhere to be found, I have a question for you."

Winona looked at him.

"What do we do now, Ma?"

Chapter Eleven

The Lakotas were known far and wide as formidable warriors. In later years they would be one of the last Plains tribes to submit to the U.S. government's relentless campaign of Indian subjugation. Only when their way of life, embodied in the buffalo, had been almost exterminated, and their women and children were starving, did the last proud remnants submit to government control.

But in the early decades of the 1800s, the Lakotas were still a proud and free people, lords of all they surveyed. In battle they held their own against the powerful Blackfoot Confederacy to their north and against the Crows and Snakes to the west.

All white men had heard of their prowess as fighters and trackers. Nate King among them. So he knew that his chances of eluding the scores of riders who fanned out from the Platte River encampment in dozens of small groups were next to nil. Still, he had to try. Circumstance and experience had forged him into a man who never gave up no matter how great the odds against him.

As Nate and Fetches Water looped to the south after having ridden for two miles due east, he mulled over the situation.

The darkness worked in their favor in that it hid them from the Oglalas. But it also could work against them by concealing a band of warriors until Nate and the girl were right on them.

The Sioux also had the advantage of knowing the region well, since they spent several moons there every summer and had been doing so for many years.

Nate stopped often to listen. So far the sounds of pursuit had been faint; occasional hoofbeats to the west and north, a few shouts to the southwest.

The big trapper held to a brisk walk for the next hour to reduce the noise they made. There was no moon but enough starlight to bathe the rippling grass in a pale glow. He ascertained direction by the North Star and other celestial constellations, a knack every seasoned mountaineer developed if he wanted to last long in the wilderness.

Fetches Water did not let out a peep. She stopped when he did, listened when he listened. His smiles served to bolster her confidence, but she was still a nervous wreck. Distant sounds made her stiffen and gasp.

Nate had an added worry in the form of his family. By this time, he reasoned, they were probably wondering what had happened to him. If they had followed his instructions, they should be about 30 to 40 miles south of the Platte. But if they hadn't, if the impatient Crows had pushed on, then they might be much closer. In which case there was a very real likelihood the Sioux might stumble on them while hunting for the girl and him.

The prairie was alive with other sounds besides those made by the Lakotas. Coyotes yipped. Wolves howled their plaintive refrains. Grizzlies growled and painters screamed.

Nighttime was "the killing time," as a trapper Nate knew had once put it. The hours of darkness brought countless savage predators out of their dens to roam in search of hapless prey. Meat eaters preferred the mantle of inky gloom to the blazing brightness of the sun. At night they could prowl undetected, and pounce when least expected.

Nate tensed when a snort and a guttural cough pinpointed a bear less than a hundred feet to the northeast. He knew that it might be a harmless black bear, but he wasn't about to take anything for granted.

They angled to the southwest for a mile or so. The cough wasn't repeated, so Nate figured they had given the beast the slip.

Gradually the stars overhead changed position as the hours went by. It was the middle of the night when Nate felt safe in stopping briefly to rest the horses. Dismounting, he let the stallion graze while he walked off a few yards to survey the benighted prairie.

The Crow girl joined him. She didn't like to be left alone and it showed. Nervously rubbing her palms together, she stared bleakly toward the Platte.

"Do not worry," Nate signed. "They will not find us. Soon you will be back with your father."

The knowledge of sign language was not a skill restricted to men. So the girl was quick to respond, "Who are you, white man, that you help me this way? How do you know of my father?"

Nate signed, "I am Grizzly Killer, a friend of Two Humps. I was once brought to your village as a prisoner of the Invincible One, but I later showed your people that he was not all he claimed to be."

"I remember you now," the girl said. "My father always said that your medicine is more powerful than anyone he ever met."

Over the next few minutes Nate explained how Bull Standing With Cow had asked for his help. He did not reveal Carter's treachery, nor did he see fit to mention his scrape with He Dog, although he did tell her the names of the warriors who had accompanied her father.

"So He Dog is with you," Fetches Water said somberly. "I should have known he would come."

"You do not seem happy about it."

The girl frowned. "Soon I will be old enough to take a husband. He Dog wants me, and he has let it be known that anyone else who courts me will answer to him. I am afraid he will be my only suitor."

Nate sympathized. Coming of age was a special event in the life of an Indian girl. It was usually marked by an elaborate ceremony. Then, depending on her attractiveness and popularity, she would be courted by as many men who were interested.

The courtship was strictly chaperoned. Potential suitors would show up in front of the family's lodge with a buffalo robe over their shoulders. If the girl was so inclined, she would take turns slipping under the robes of those lucky enough to catch her eye and spend time whispering and perhaps fondling one another. She could refuse to be embraced, and she was always free to slip out from under the robe whenever she so desired.

In time one of her suitors might make bold to send a friend to her father's lodge with however many horses the suitor could spare. If the girl accepted his marriage proposal, she took the horses to water or added them to her father's herd. If she wasn't interested, she sent the horses back or paid no attention to them.

There were few hurt feelings. In most instances the young men knew if their sweethearts would accept or not. At other times, the unions were arranged in advance by the parents of both parties.

For He Dog to assert that Fetches Water was going to be his, no matter what, was a serious breach of tribal etiquette. If he were allowed to carry through with his threat, it would ruin one of the grandest phases of the young girl's life.

"Any young man who truly cares for you will not let He Dog scare him off," Nate consoled her. "I would guess that you end up having more suitors than you know what to do with."

"I hope so."

They listened but heard no riders. Nate was eager to go on, so they were under way within a short while. Their little talk, he observed, had served to ease some of the girl's anxiety; she did not ride as stiffly as before.

About four in the morning, just when Nate was beginning to think that they actually had a prayer of getting away, the wind wafted low voices to them from the west. Stopping, he put a finger to his lips to caution the girl not to speak.

The sound faded, but Nate made no move to go on. Soon the wind picked up again, and with it came the indistinct words of whoever was out there. The language being used was hard to identify, but Nate suspected it was the tongue of the Oglalas.

Slipping off the stallion, Nate gestured for the girl to stay where she was, then he drew his knife and stalked off to investigate. He could move rapidly thanks to the wind, which rustled the grass so loudly that his movements would go unnoticed.

Unexpectedly Nate came on a shallow basin he estimated to be a hundred feet across. Huddled beside a tiny fire at the bottom were five Lakotas. Their horses were lined up behind them.

It was one of the search parties. The men were tired and had elected to rest until daylight. A few were munching on pemmican, and at the sight of it Nate's rumbling stomach nearly gave him away. He backed up a few feet so they wouldn't hear and suddenly bumped into something that had not been there a minute ago.

Thinking that the Oglalas had posted sentries and he had bumped into one, Nate whirled, bringing the knife up for a thrust. He checked his swing almost too late, then grabbed Fetches Water by the arm and drew her into the grass where he signed, "I told you to stay with the horse. Do you realize that I nearly stabbed you?"

"I refuse to be by myself," the girl responded, "so I tied them and followed you."

She was young but she was resolute. Nate knew he'd be wasting his breath if he tried to convince her to go back and wait for him. So, easing onto his elbows, he snaked to the basin with her at his side.

Three of the warriors the trapper recognized. One was the man who had staked a claim to his fine beaver hat. Another had a flintlock and Nate's powder horn and ammo bag. Still another was the Sioux so adept at roping.

Nate would have given anything to get his effects back, especially the pistol. Without a gun he felt half naked. He might as well wish on a star, though, since it would be certain suicide for him to charge on down there and seek to overpower five armed warriors.

Or would it?

Grasping the girl's hand, Nate led her to their mounts. By sign, he conveyed his intentions.

Fetches Water regarded him as if he were insane. "Do not do this thing, Grizzly Killer. You will only get yourself slain. Some food and a gun are not worth your life."

"I also want my hat back," Nate reminded her as he stepped to the stallion. Winking, he swung up. "If something happens, head due south. In less than two sleeps you will come to a creek. Your father and the Crow war party should be there."

"Please," the girl signed.

Bending, Nate patted her head as he went by. He clucked to the stallion and swung wide to the north to approach the basin from a different direction. That way, if he was rubbed out and the Lakotas backtracked him at first light, the girl would have ample time to get away.

Holding the knife at his waist, Nate flattened on the big stallion's broad back. At a plodding walk he neared the west rim. With the black sky in the background, he felt confident the warriors wouldn't spot him.

When the Lakotas materialized, Nate stopped. Their five horses were directly below him. He smiled to himself as he slowly straightened, tossed back his head, and did his best imitation of the screeching cry of a mountain lion. Even as he uttered it, he attacked.

The five Sioux war horses reacted predictably.

David Thompson

Whinnying and plunging in fright, they lit out across the basin for the far side. In their headlong flight they were not about to stop for anything or anyone, including the startled warriors who leaped erect in their path.

One of the warriors crumpled under flailing hooves. Another was struck head on by a gelding and sent sailing as if he were an ungainly bird. In their panic two of the horses ran through the fire, scattering burning brands every which way and raising a cloud of smoke.

Nate was right on their tails. A stumbling Oglala appeared in front of him and he swung the knife overhand, slamming the hilt onto the top of the man's head. The Lakota dropped like a rock.

From out of the smoke popped the Sioux wearing Nate's hat. Nate promptly hauled on the reins and rode him down. Then, vaulting to the ground, he sought his last foe.

It was the roper. The Oglala hurtled out of nowhere with all the feral fury of a berserk bobcat, his own knife flashing in a blur.

Pivoting, Nate countered a flurry of swings, their blades ringing together like chimes. The onslaught drove him backward, and he tripped over an unconscious Lakota. Unable to stop himself, he toppled.

The roper yipped and swooped in for the kill.

Flat on his back, Nate managed to get his right arm high enough to ward off the blow. Sparks seemed to fly from their knives. Again the Oglala came at him and he scrambled to the rear, barely staying out of reach as the warrior slashed down at him repeatedly. He couldn't keep it up forever, though. Inevitably, the Sioux would connect.

In order to buy time to regain his feet, Nate lashed out with both legs and caught the Lakota

152

low on the shins. The man skipped to the left. Shoving into a crouch, Nate ducked under a wide strike, then leaped, the point of his knife aimed at the warrior's throat.

The roper was as agile as he was quick. Twisting and dodging, he evaded Nate and retaliated with a vicious stab below the belt.

More by accident than design, Nate parried and circled. The Lakota circled too, while around them fluttered wisps of smoke. One of the prone Sioux groaned. Nate feinted, chopped, spun and blocked. He was skilled at knife fighting, but the Oglala was his equal if not his better.

The fire had not gone out. Dancing flames cast their shadows on the surrounding slopes, resulting in a macabre shadow ballet.

Grunting, the Oglala flicked at the trapper's face, at his neck, at his midsection. Nate was hard pressed to stay one step ahead. Back-pedaling, he went on the defensive.

Then the roper did a strange thing; he reached behind him with his left hand. Darting in close, he cut at Nate's eyes. Instinctively, Nate brought his knife up to protect himself, and when he did, the Lakota's left arm reappeared. In the warrior's hand was the coiled rope, which darted out like the tongue of a serpent and looped around Nate's ankles. Before Nate could wrench loose, the rope tightened and his legs were yanked out from under him.

Instantly the Oglala pounced.

Winona King was riding toward Red Willow Creek in the dead of night when a peculiar tingle ran down her spine. It was as if an icy finger had stroked her from her head to her hips. She arched her back and looked around in consternation.

The air had not grown colder. The wind had not intensified. Winona had no explanation for the sensation.

Her people were ardent believers in omens and signs. From childhood she had been taught to look for the hand of the Great Mystery in all things. Which led her to hope that her odd feeling hadn't been a premonition of some sort.

Zachary King, attentive to his mother's every movement, immediately asked, "Are you all right, Ma?"

"Yes," Winona answered, hiding how disturbed she was.

"We should be there about the middle of the morning, don't you reckon?" Zach inquired. It had been her idea to head for Red Willow Creek, since that was where his father would expect to find them. He had wholeheartedly agreed in the hope it would see them reunited that much sooner.

There was a hitch, however. Now they were heading in the same direction the fleeing Crows and the Lakotas had gone. If the former had eluded the latter, they might encounter the returning Oglalas or stumble on their camp at any time.

So Zach rode with one hand always on his rifle and never lowered his eyes from the surrounding plain. He stayed close to his mother so if trouble did crop up, he would be right there to defend her and his sister.

Winona, on the other hand, entertained no worries about the Sioux. She was sure that she would hear them long before they spotted her. And, too, her mare was as reliable as a dog in that the animal would prick its ears at the sound of voices or other horses.

By traveling at night they reduced the risk. For

hours the prairie had been deceptively tranquil. So much so that Winona wanted to hold Blue Flower in her lap, but she needed to keep her hands free, just in case.

"Say, what's that?" Zach asked when a pinpoint of light flared in the distance. "A camp fire?"

"Yes. We must get closer," Winona said.

"It might be the Lakotas."

"It could be the Crows."

Unwillingly Zach let himself be guided in a horseshoe loop that brought them up on the site from the west. When they spied a number of figures hunched close to the fire, Winona reined up and whispered, "From here we go on foot."

"Why don't I go by myself?" Zach suggested. "One of us has to watch that the horses don't stray off, anyway."

Winona had to grin at his not so subtle tactic. "Our horses are well trained," she reminded him quietly. "We will stick together."

Neither of them were surprised to find that the warriors were Lakotas. Some were asleep, others swapping tales around the fire. Zach figured his mother would turn around once she had seen who they were, but to his astonishment she crawled closer. It seemed pointless to him until he saw the three bodies lying in a row.

Winona had spotted them from a long way off. Their identities were of no real consequence since they were beyond all help. But she had to know. Something deep within compelled her to get close enough to see their faces.

To do that, Winona had to skirt the camp to the north. Creeping along at the edge of the grass, she froze when one of the Oglala mounts raised its head and looked right at her. In her preoccupation with the corpses, she had forgotten that the wind would carry her scent toward the camp if she were not vigilant.

Zach imitated his mother. When a warrior glanced at the horses, he braced for a shout to ring out and expected to see the entire war party swarm toward them. The warrior didn't give the animals a second look, however, and turned back to his fellows. Presently the horse also lost interest.

Winona disregarded the tiny voice advising her to turn around before it was too late. Advancing, she soon saw the downturned face of one of the dead men.

It was Bear Ears. He had been stripped of all his clothes, so his wounds stood out like dark sores on his skin. In addition to the arrow that still jutted from his back, he had a large jagged hole in his side where a lance had sliced between his ribs. Where his throat had been was a gaping slit. And his scalp had been lifted.

Winona had to go farther to see the next Crow.

Runs Against had put up a terrific fight. Seven wounds marked his chest, several of them gashes left by knives or tomahawks. The fingers of his right hand were missing, as was his hair.

To go on invited discovery. Yet Winona couldn't stop herself. It was as if an invisible hand moved her along against her will.

The body nearest the fire was that of He Dog. Oddly, his clothes were still on him and there were no visible blood stains on them. Unlike the others, he was on his back, not his side, and his wrists were tied in front of him.

Winona assumed the Sioux had not yet gotten around to taking his scalp and whatever else struck their fancy, which in itself was unusual but not worth lingering over. Twisting, she signaled for her son to start back.

At that exact moment two of the Lakotas rose, walked over to He Dog, and jerked him off the ground. The Crow's eyes snapped wide. In blatant defiance he glowered at them.

"Goodness gracious! He's alive!" Zach whispered.

Winona could not believe it, either. She bore no affection for the man, but it bothered her to see him in the clutches of his merciless enemies. Far better for He Dog if he had died outright as Bear Ears and Runs Against did.

The Oglalas made the Crow kneel and then took turns heaping abuse on him. He was cuffed and kicked until he could barely hold himself up. A stocky Lakota drew a knife, seized He Dog by the hair, and jabbed the point under his skin at the hairline. The Lakota made a swift motion, as if he were slicing off the scalp, but he was only pretending. His friends laughed. He Dog endured their mirth stoically.

Winona had seen enough. It was time she got Stalking Coyote and Blue Flower out of there. Turning, she said to her son, "Lead the way. Remember not to move the grass."

"I know what to do," Zach declared, piqued that she would see fit to remind him. He wasn't a boy any longer. His parents had no call to remind him how to do things every chance they got.

Mother and son made slow progress. Many of the sleeping warriors had awakened, so now there were twice as many up as before. Some moved about, stretching their legs. As yet, none were near the west side of the camp, but that might change if one of them had to heed Nature's call.

Suddenly a roar of rage rent the night. An

Oglala had picked up a burning brand and applied it to He Dog's arm. The Crow caught them all off guard by lunging up off the ground and barreling into his tormentor. The Oglala staggered into the fire and let out a yelp. It elicited hearty laughter which changed to irate bellows when their captive spun on a heel and sprinted toward the high grass.

And toward Winona and her children.

Chapter Twelve

Nate King's legs were looped together by the Lakota's buffalo hide rope, but that did not prevent him from arching them to his chest and then ramming them outward.

The warrior was in midair, his knife arm cocked. Caught in the chest, he was catapulted onto the remains of the fire. Amid a shower of glowing embers and flaming limbs, he roared and bounded upright.

Rather than spend vital moments unwinding the rope, Nate severed it. He was almost to his knees when the Oglala came at him like a human whirlwind. The man's knife weaved a glittering web of gleaming steel which Nate barely parried.

The roper was beside himself. He took gambles no one with a shred of sense would take. Time and again he overextended himself or left himself wide open. Nate attempted to capitalize, but the man's lightning reflexes compensated for the mistakes.

The Lakota showed no signs of tiring. If anything, he appeared to be growing stronger. And wilder. Skipping out of reach of Nate's knife, he took one long step and leaped.

His blade streaked upward.

Nate was just starting to shift to the left. By a fluke, the warrior's stroke missed his torso and the man's arm came up under his own. Automatically Nate clamped his arm down, pinning the Oglala's at the wrist. The roper tugged, then clawed at Nate's neck with his other hand. It did not stop Nate from snapping his head forward and smashing his forehead onto the Sioux's nose. Warm blood spurted over them both. The Lakota jerked back but could go nowhere with his knife arm trapped.

It was the moment Nate had been waiting for. A short stab, and his blade sank to the hilt in his adversary's stomach. The Lakota stiffened and gurgled. Nate bunched his shoulder, twisted the knife, and sheared down and to the right, ripping the abdomen wide. As the Oglala sucked in a long breath, he swiftly retreated several steps.

The roper was in shock. He gaped down at himself and feebly attempted to stem the loss of his organs by placing both hands over the rupture. It was hopeless. Groaning, he sank to his knees. His knife fell to the grass. He looked up and spoke, his expression pleading.

The tongue was unfamiliar but the meaning was clear. Nate knew the warrior wanted to be put out of his misery. A belly wound like that was not always fatal right away. The Lakota might linger for hours in agony that defied belief. Nodding once, Nate moved closer. Executing an expert thrust to the heart, he did as the man wanted.

The Lakota closed his eyes and pitched over.

Suddenly something moved behind Nate. Whirling, he prepared to defend himself a second time, but the other four warriors were still unconscious.

Fetches Water had led the horses down into the basin. "I could not wait any longer, Grizzly Killer," she signed. Seeing the blood that speckled his features and clothes, she urgently added, "Are you hurt? I can tend your wound."

"I am fine," Nate wearily signed. The fight had taken a lot out of him, and he wanted nothing more than to curl into a ball and sleep for a week, but that was not meant to be. Hurrying from Lakota to Lakota, he retrieved his hat and pistol, as well as his ammo pouch and powder horn.

The girl helped herself to a knife and a bow. "I will not let them take me again," she explained.

Nate climbed onto the stallion. There was no trace of the horses he had driven off. With any luck, he mused, they either were on their way back to the village or had scattered to the four winds. It would take the better part of a day for the men he had knocked out to reach the Platte on foot.

Side by side, the pair trotted southward. Nate never relaxed his guard, and it was well he didn't. About two hours after the clash, a large knot of riders hove into sight to the west. Nate and Fetches Water reined up and held their breaths in anxious anticipation. The band was heading to the northeast. The warriors must have passed within 70 feet but failed to spot them.

The moment the hoofbeats faded, Nate went on. His companion impressed him with her composure. For one so young, she had all the qualities of a mature woman. And she was lovely. Small wonder that He Dog fancied her.

Dawn found them well over halfway to the area

where Nate expected to find his family and the Crows. He debated whether to lay low until sunset and elected to forge on. The sooner he reunited the girl with her father, the safer she would be.

Fetches Water agreed. Her fatigue showed, but she did not give in to it.

Twice before noon, bands of Lakotas appeared in the distance.

In the first instance, Nate promptly dismounted and made both horses lie down. While the girl held her hands over the pinto's muzzle, he did the same with the stallion.

The band contained nine warriors strung out in single file, bearing northward. They never came near enough to spot the trapper or Fetches Water.

The second instance was a closer call. Again Nate resorted to his trick of having their mounts lay in the grass. Pistol in hand, he watched as the band drew within 30 feet of their position. A heated discussion occupied the Lakotas, otherwise they would have seen him and the girl for certain.

Toward evening a belt of trees reared above the prairie like an island in the middle of a vast ocean. The belt widened, becoming a telltale band of lush vegetation of the sort that always flanked water-ways.

Presently the horses were slaking their thirst at a bubbling creek while Nate scoured the nearby woods. In a small clearing he discovered the remains of a fire, which he pegged as no more than three or four days old.

Plenty of tracks had been left, and Nate was bending to inspect them when he heard something that sent him flying back toward the creek with his pistol drawn and cocked.

Fetches Water had uttered a shrill cry.

* * *

Winona King was rooted in place by the unforeseen sight of He Dog sprinting for his very life toward her and her children. They dared not leap erect and flee, or the Lakotas would see them. Yet if they just laid there, the Crow was bound to trip over one or the other and give their presence away.

"What do we do?" Zach hissed in alarm. There were so many Oglalas, they would be overwhelmed in moments if they were spotted. He might be able to drop one or two—before the rest were on them like a pack of ravenous wolves.

"Roll out of his way," Winona proposed, "and hope they do not notice the grass move."

He Dog was almost there. The beating he had suffered had taken a toll and he slowed, wheezing in pain. It was a mistake. Four fleet Sioux had given chase and were almost upon him. Hearing them, the Crow turned like a bull at bay and shrieked a challenge. They laughed, believing him to be helpless with his arms bound. They were wrong.

No one who knew him would ever deny that He Dog had many faults. But cowardice was not among them. Lowering his head, he charged the foremost Lakota and bowled the man over. He Dog spun and kicked another in the knee. The crack of bone must have been music to his ears, because he howled with glee and hurled himself at a third opponent.

This Sioux was more savvy. Dropping flat, he whipped his legs into the Crow's, upending He Dog, who landed hard on his shoulders. Before the Crow could rise, two of his enemies were on him. Try as they might, they couldn't pin his shoulders or legs. He Dog kicked and butted them with his head, knocking one man over and bloodying the other's mouth.

More Lakotas streamed from the fire. The Crow didn't stand a chance. He was buried under a half-dozen flying forms. A swirling melee broke out, attended by grunts and sharp cries and yelps of pain.

Then the warrior with the broken knee lurched upright, his features contorted in rage. He glared at the tangle of flying arms and legs while slowly drawing his long knife.

Winona knew what was going to happen next, but she was powerless to stop it. If she shot the Lakota with the rifle, the rest would be on her and her children before they took two steps. Clutching the Hawken in impotent dismay, she watched the inevitable outcome.

He Dog had still not given up. He thrashed. He snapped his legs right and left. He heaved his broad shoulders.

The warrior with the broken knee was watching intently, waiting for an instant when the press of bodies parted and he could see the Crow clearly. Suddenly that instant arrived. He Dog had shaken three men off his chest and was struggling to stand. In a flash the Oglala struck, lancing his blade into the Crow just under the sternum.

He Dog never uttered a sound. His body deflated like a punctured water skin and he melted to the ground.

One of the warriors checked and confirmed that the Crow was dead. It sparked an argument between the man who had killed him and several of the others, who apparently had wanted to take He Dog on to their village.

Winona wished they would go back to the fire. The nearest ones were less than ten feet away, and she feared they would glimpse Stalking Coyote or her if they turned toward the grass. Her heartbeat quickened when a burly specimen wearing eagle feathers did just that. He shifted and peered into the dark with narrowed eyes as if he sensed that he was being watched.

Winona's whole body broke out in goosebumps. She did not move a muscle, not even to blink. The Lakota scanned the grass and took a half step forward.

Just at that juncture, Evelyn squirmed. Winona felt her back move as the child shifted in the cradleboard. Should Evelyn cry out or so much as coo, the Sioux would hear her.

The burly warrior took another pace. He might have taken more except that a companion called out to him. The burly one hesitated a few moments, then gave a toss of his shoulders and rejoined his fellows. He helped tote the body.

Winona lost no time. The second their backs were to the grass, she snaked to the rear, whispering, "Quickly, son. To the horses."

Zach needed no prompting. His heart had about leaped into his mouth when the Lakota came toward them. He had been dead certain his days on earth were over, and he had been set to sell his life dearly. His belly scraping the ground, he crawled on his mother's heels.

They moved swiftly, Winona spurred on by an inner urgency, a foreboding that unless they got out of there something terrible would happen. And it did. At the selfsame second she laid eyes on the silhouettes of their horses, her daughter did the unthinkable: Blue Flower cried out in her sleep, a short, high-pitched wail.

From the camp rose an answering shout. At least one of the Lakotas had heard.

Throwing caution aside, Winona rose and ran. Her son could have gone on ahead, but he did not leave her side and did not mount his horse until she had mounted hers.

More yells issued from the camp. Figures were moving into the grass. One was on horseback.

"Ride!" Winona said, and did so, flying southward, gouging her horse with the stock of the Hawken to get it to go faster.

Young Zach glanced back. Several of the warriors had seen them and were gesturing excitedly. Soon the entire war party would be in pursuit.

The Sioux who was already astride a horse whooped and gave chase, waving his lance overhead.

Zach looked at his mother, then at the Sioux. On purpose, he slowed, keeping his mother in sight but allowing the warrior to gain on him. The man was 60 feet off. Then 40. At 30 feet, Zach sighted down his rifle. At 20 feet, as the warrior threw back his arm, Zach King fired.

The shot flipped the Lakota from his steed as the booming retort rolled off across the plain.

Winona twisted in surprise. She slowed until her son caught up, and chided half-heartedly, "You should have told me what you were going to do."

"No time," Zach said. "I couldn't let him get close enough to hurt you or sissy."

Her chest swelling with affection, Winona buckled down to the task of outdistancing the Oglalas. Their horses were tired but flowed smoothly across the prairie. When the sounds of pursuit grew in volume, she altered course to the southwest.

Zach could no longer see the Lakotas. He laughed lightly at their narrow escape, thinking of the tale he would get to tell his Shoshone friends. It would make them green with envy.

All of a sudden the grass thinned and before them lay a long stretch dotted with low dirt mounds. Winona realized the peril first and called out, "Prairie dog dens!" She jerked on the reins and swung to the left to go around the colony.

So did Zach. But as his horse began to turn, one of its front legs stepped into a dark hole. The resulting snap resembled the breaking of a large dry branch. A wavering whinny issued from the animal's throat as it pitched into a roll. Zach saw the ground sweeping up to meet him and frantically dived to the right so he wouldn't be crushed. A flying leg hit him in the side, jarring the breath from his lungs. He barely heard the tremendous crash nor a second louder snap.

Winona reined up and sprang to the ground before her horse came to a complete stop. She dashed back to her son, kneeling as he tried to sit up. "Be still," she cautioned. "You might have broken bones."

Zach let her probe to her heart's content while his swimming senses returned to normal. His vision cleared and he saw the stricken horse on its side, wheezing as blood gushed from its open mouth. The left front leg looked as if someone had taken an iron mallet to it and pulverized the bone.

"Can you stand?" Winona asked. He appeared to be unhurt, but she had known warriors who took spills and were never the same in the head again.

"I'm fine," Zach said. His mother helped him stand, regardless. He took a few tentative steps. Other than a throbbing bruise on his arm and a pulled muscle in his calf, he felt fit. Nodding at the horse, he said, "What do we do about him?"

The humane thing to do was put the animal out of its misery. But a gunshot would give them away to the Lakotas. Winona started to draw her knife. "We must do it quietly," she said.

"Let me, Ma." Zach moved in front of her and hunkered. The horse looked up at him with wide, anguished eyes. "I'm sorry, fella," he said softly. "I tried to avoid the darn burrows." His blade could split a hair; slitting the horse's throat posed no problem.

Now they had to ride double. Zach swung up behind his mother and was face to face with Evelyn, who grinned in impish glee. He held onto the sides of the cradleboard as they bore to the south, well shy of the prairie dog colony.

Winona did not let on that she was greatly concerned. The extra weight would tire the horse quickly, calling for frequent stops to rest. And if the Sioux caught sight of them, they couldn't possibly outrun those swift war horses.

Long into the night the pair put mile after mile behind them. At dawn they halted, but only briefly. Winona fed her daughter, Zach stretched his legs, then off they rode.

"We will keep going until we reach Red Willow Creek," the Shoshone declared. "There, we can hide and decide what to do next."

Morning gave way to afternoon. The day was hot and their horse plodded wearily along. Winona stifled yawns and occasionally shook herself to stay awake. Her daughter was asleep, and Zach had his eyes closed and was propped against the cradleboard when pinwheeling black dots high in the sky drew Winona's interest.

The dots were birds. Big birds. Presently Winona discerned that they were buzzards circling above their next meal. The scavengers of the wild were as common as buffalo, and she had no interest in going to investigate until she saw a chestnut horse all by itself, grazing near where one of the birds landed.

Letting her son sleep on, Winona made for the spot. The chestnut heard them and looked up but did not run off.

Eight or nine buzzards were clustered on a body. The only part of the man not covered by the big ugly creatures was his feet. The scavengers grew restless as Winona approached. A few squawked at her in irate annoyance for interrupting their gory repast. Winona simply ignored them.

One of the birds took a few awkward steps and launched itself into the air, its great wings flapping loudly. It was the signal for the rest to do the same. Not a single buzzard remained when Winona drew rein.

Yellow Owl lay on his back, his arms outstretched. He had been dead for quite some time. From his left side protruded an arrow. The angle suggested that he had turned to look at the pursuing Lakotas and been struck under his arm. Apparently he'd been able to keep on riding and had eluded the Sioux, but eventually the wound had proven fatal.

The buzzards had been thorough. The Crow's eyes, nose and ears were gone, as were both lips and his tongue. His stomach had been sheared open, and his intestines hung in partial loops. The fleshy parts of his shoulders and thigh had also been consumed. In some places, bone gleamed through.

Winona did not care for her children to see the grisly remains, so she went on. But someone already had.

"I hope to high heaven I never end up like him," Zach commented. "I can't stand the thought of those varmints pecking away at my innards."

"They serve a purpose, like everything else," Winona reminded him.

"I reckon so, but picking bones clean of rotten flesh isn't a purpose I'd go bragging on."

Winona had to laugh.

"I suppose He Dog and those other two are buzzard bait by now, too," Zach said. Picturing them being eaten made him queasy.

"I would say so, yes."

Zach recalled the terrific fight He Dog had put up. "You know, Ma," he said, "I never did like that contrary Crow very much, but if anyone asked, I'd have to say he went out like a warrior should."

"He was a credit to his people," Winona concurred, and meant it. She had been raised to believe that a man's worth was measured by his courage, and there could be no doubt that He Dog had shown his inherent bravery at the end.

For the rest of the day and into the gathering twilight, the Shoshone woman pushed their mount. When, at long last, she beheld the trees bordering Red Willow Creek, she brought the horse to a canter.

The woods were quiet when they arrived. At first Winona did not take note of it. She sat on a log and satisfied Blue Flower's hunger while Stalking Coyote took their mount to drink. Only when she was sitting there, slumped in fatigue, and had time to think, did Winona realize it was eerily silent. Birds should have been singing. Insects should have been buzzing and flitting about.

At the edge of the water, Zach saw his mother stiffen. With a start, he divined why. He brought his rifle to bear, scouring the vegetation for hostiles or beasts.

Deep in the brush, something moved. A shadowy figure appeared, then another, and two more.

Winona leaped up and spun to confront them. Zach ran over next to her, whispering, "More Lakotas, Ma! It has to be!"

But the boy was wrong. Smiling broadly, into the open walked Nate King. His wife and son took one look and were in his arms, hugging him close, too choked with emotion to speak. "About time the three of you showed up," Nate said in mock gruffness. "We were about to set out and find you."

"We?" Winona repeated, moisture rimming her eyes.

From the cottonwoods emerged Two Humps and Flying Hawk. Behind them came Bull Standing With Cow, his arm around the shoulders of a pretty young girl.

"Fetches Water?" Winona exclaimed, and when her husband nodded, she said, "But how?"

Nate escorted his loved ones to the clearing. They talked on and on, sharing their experiences. Winona and Zach laughed when he told how he had flown to Fetches Water after hearing her shriek, only to find her in the arms of her father.

The Crows were saddened to hear of the deaths of their four friends. Bull Standing With Cow pledged to help the families of the slain men as best he could.

"As for you, Grizzly Killer," the grateful father addressed Nate, "I will never forget what you have done for me. From this day on, we are brothers. Whatever is mine is also yours, and if I can ever help you, just ask."

Earlier that day, Flying Hawk had dropped a buck. Ample meat was left over, so Winona and

Zach helped themselves, the boy wolfing large gulps.

Shy of midnight, the Crows turned in. Nate and Winona strolled to the creek bank to be by themselves. The trapper placed his hands on her hips and drew her close, then paused as her lips were about to touch his. Their son had walked up. "Something wrong?" Nate inquired.

"I was just wondering," Zach said with an air of innocence they knew only too well.

"About what?"

"This summer. I think it would be nice if we spent some time with the Crows."

Father and mother exchanged knowing looks. "any special reason?" Nate probed.

Zachary King, otherwise known as Stalking Coyote of the Shoshones, gazed with a rosy gleam in his eyes at the sleeping form of the beautiful Absaroka girl by the fire and said with a straight face, "No. Not really."

WILDERNESS DOUBLE EDITION

SAVE $$$!

Savage Rendezvous by David Thompson. In 1828, the Rocky Mountains are an immense, unsettled region through which few white men dare travel. Only courageous mountain men like Nathaniel King are willing to risk the unknown dangers for the freedom the wilderness offers. But while attending a rendezvous of trappers and fur traders, King's freedom is threatened when he is accused of murdering several men for their money. With the help of his friend Shakespeare McNair, Nate has to prove his innocence. For he has not cast off the fetters of society to spend the rest of his life behind bars.

And in the same action-packed volume...

Blood Fury by David Thompson. On a hunting trip, young Nathaniel King stumbles onto a disgraced Crow Indian. Attempting to regain his honor, Sitting Bear places himself and his family in great peril, for a war party of hostile Utes threatens to kill them all. When the savages wound Sitting Bear and kidnap his wife and daughter, Nathaniel has to rescue them or watch them perish. But despite his skill in tricking unfriendly Indians, King may have met an enemy he cannot outsmart.

_4208-8 $4.99 US/$5.99 CAN

Dorchester Publishing Co., Inc.
P.O. Box 6640
Wayne, PA 19087-8640

Please add $1.75 for shipping and handling for the first book and $.50 for each book thereafter. NY, NYC, and PA residents, please add appropriate sales tax. No cash, stamps, or C.O.D.s. All orders shipped within 6 weeks via postal service book rate. Canadian orders require $2.00 extra postage and must be paid in U.S. dollars through a U.S. banking facility.

Name_____
Address_____
City_____ State_____ Zip_____
I have enclosed $_____ in payment for the checked book(s).
Payment <u>must</u> accompany all orders. ❑ Please send a free catalog.

WILDERNESS
TRAPPER'S BLOOD/ MOUNTAIN CAT
DAVID THOMPSON

Trapper's Blood. In the wild Rockies, a man has to act as judge, jury, and executioner against his enemies. And when trappers start turning up dead, their bodies horribly mutilated, Nate King and his friends vow to hunt down the ruthless killers. But taking the law into their own hands, they soon find out that a hasty decision can make them as guilty as the murderers they want to stop.

And in the same action-packed volume...

Mountain Cat. A seasoned hunter and trapper, Nate King can fend off attacks from brutal warriors and furious grizzlies alike. But a hunt for a mountain lion twice the size of other deadly cats proves to be his greatest challenge. If Nate can't destroy the monstrous creature, it will slaughter innocent settlers—and the massacre might well begin with Nate's own family!

____4621-0 $4.99 US/$5.99 CAN

Dorchester Publishing Co., Inc.
P.O. Box 6640
Wayne, PA 19087-8640

Please add $1.75 for shipping and handling for the first book and $.50 for each book thereafter. NY, NYC, and PA residents, please add appropriate sales tax. No cash, stamps, or C.O.D.s. All orders shipped within 6 weeks via postal service book rate. Canadian orders require $2.00 extra postage and must be paid in U.S. dollars through a U.S. banking facility.

Name_____
Address_____
City_____State_____Zip_____
I have enclosed $_____ in payment for the checked book(s).
Payment <u>must</u> accompany all orders. ☐ Please send a free catalog.
        CHECK OUT OUR WEBSITE! www.dorchesterpub.com

WILDERNESS

#24

Mountain Madness

⟵————————————⟶

David Thompson

When Nate King comes upon a pair of green would-be trappers from New York, he is only too glad to risk his life to save them from a Piegan war party. It is only after he takes them into his own cabin that he realizes they will repay his kindness...with betrayal. When the backshooters reveal their true colors, Nate knows he is in for a brutal battle—with the lives of his family hanging in the balance.

___4399-8 $3.99 US/$4.99 CAN

Dorchester Publishing Co., Inc.
P.O. Box 6640
Wayne, PA 19087-8640

Please add $1.75 for shipping and handling for the first book and $.50 for each book thereafter. NY, NYC, and PA residents, please add appropriate sales tax. No cash, stamps, or C.O.D.s. All orders shipped within 6 weeks via postal service book rate. Canadian orders require $2.00 extra postage and must be paid in U.S. dollars through a U.S. banking facility.

Name_____
Address_____
City_____State_____Zip_____
I have enclosed $_____ in payment for the checked book(s).
Payment <u>must</u> accompany all orders. ❑ Please send a free catalog.
    CHECK OUT OUR WEBSITE! www.dorchesterpub.com

WILDERNESS

#25
FRONTIER MAYHEM

<--->

David Thompson

The unforgiving wilderness of the Rocky Mountains forces a boy to grow up fast, so Nate King taught his son, Zach, how to survive the constant hazards and hardships—and he taught him well. With an Indian war party on the prowl and a marauding grizzly on the loose, young Zach is about to face the test of his life, with no room for failure. But there is one danger Nate hasn't prepared Zach for—a beautiful girl with blue eyes.

___4433-1 $3.99 US/$4.99 CAN

Dorchester Publishing Co., Inc.
P.O. Box 6640
Wayne, PA 19087-8640

Please add $1.75 for shipping and handling for the first book and $.50 for each book thereafter. NY, NYC, and PA residents, please add appropriate sales tax. No cash, stamps, or C.O.D.s. All orders shipped within 6 weeks via postal service book rate. Canadian orders require $2.00 extra postage and must be paid in U.S. dollars through a U.S. banking facility.

Name_____

Address_____

City_____ State_____ Zip_____

I have enclosed $_____ in payment for the checked book(s).

Payment <u>must</u> accompany all orders. ❑ Please send a free catalog.

CHECK OUT OUR WEBSITE! www.dorchesterpub.com

WILDERNESS
BLOOD FEUD

<——————————————>

David Thompson

The brutal wilderness of the Rocky Mountains can be deadly to those unaccustomed to its dangers. So when a clan of travelers from the hill country back East arrive at Nate King's part of the mountain, Nate is more than willing to lend a hand and show them some hospitality. He has no way of knowing that this clan is used to fighting—and killing—for what they want. And they want Nate's land for their own!

___4477-3 $3.99 US/$4.99 CAN

WILDERNESS

#28
The Quest
David Thompson

Life in the brutal wilderness of the Rockies is never easy. Danger can appear from any direction. Whether it's in the form of hostile Indians, fierce animals, or the unforgiving elements, death can surprise any unwary frontiersman. That's why Nate King and his family have mastered the fine art of survival— and learned to provide help to their friends whenever necessary. So when one of Nate's neighbors shows up at his cabin more dead than alive, frantic with worry because his wife and child had been taken by Indians, Nate doesn't hesitate for a second. He knows what he has to do—he'll find his friend's family and bring them back safely. Or die trying.

___4572-9 $3.99 US/$4.99 CAN

Dorchester Publishing Co., Inc.
P.O. Box 6640
Wayne, PA 19087-8640